Also by John Argo
   Novels:
      Lantern Road: 8 by Argo (SF anthology)
      Pioneers (SF novel)
      This Shoal of Space (SF novel)
      Neon Blue (suspense)

   Website:
      http://www.johnargo.com/
      http://www.thehauntedvillage.com/
      http://www.neonbluefiction.com/

This Shoal of Space

A SF novel by
John Argo

Clocktower Books 2002

A Clocktower Book

Published by Clocktower Books
6549 Mission Gorge Road, PMB 260
San Diego, California 92120

Please contact the publisher to inquire about electronic and print on demand editions of these and other titles: editors@clocktowerfiction.com/. Alternatively, you may reach the author at johntcullen@johntcullen.com/.

Here are some websites you may wish to visit:

> http://www.clocktowerbooks.com/
> http://www.shiningbook.com/
> http://www.johnargo.com/
> http://www.sharpwriter.com/

Dedication

This book is for Carolyn and Andrew, with love—not to mention Mr. Tufts, Lucy, and all the goldfish who've ever stayed with us.

Prolog

— i —

On a tropical evening, 100 million years ago, in what would one day be called West Africa, a young T. Rex crept close to a brackish pond to drink. She was but a dark shadow as she hid among the lush ferns and cycads that glowed faintly with the day's last sunlight.

Something in the pond had gotten her attention the last time she'd been here, and she hoped to kill once more before nightfall.

In the moments before sunset, the sun was a small bead of intense light amid the orange and vermilion brushstrokes that covered the western sky above the South Atlantic Ocean. Somewhere in the world, a volcano had vented, blasting thousands of tons of material into the atmosphere, causing these colorful sunsets, but that had been seasons ago, and the world was pretty quiet just now. The sky above was a dim powdery blue, with hardly a cloud in sight. On the horizon far to the east, a line of black stretched from north to south as though drawn in charcoal: the edge of night.

She breathed in deeply of the thick, humid air that smelled of leaves and mud and rotting wood. A breeze carried the first chill of evening temper.

Before stepping onto the grassy bank, the T. Rex froze behind lush ferns and sharpened her senses to detect any danger. This in no way interfered with the unblinking intensity with which she peered at the pond.

Except for the buzz and flutter of insects, the vast swamp was still. Chromium blue and red butterflies fluttered among the flowers. Dragonflies with shining green eyes hovered over the water. In the time when predators drank, even the birds ceased their fluttering and hid in the tree canopies dotted here and there above the otherwise flat swampland. The air around the pond smelled fetid from a herd of triceratops that had finished drinking and lumbered away.

The dinosaur decided it was time to act. Detecting no immediate danger, she stretched her neck with snake-like slowness. Her head glided out of the ferns. Her tough hide, patterned in big orange, black, and white polygons, blurred in rapidly failing light. The moments of drinking were her most vulnerable. She made a slow, bird-like step forward, soundless, without disturbing ferns. She would spend two or three minute at most, crouched at the pond. Her belly and neck would be close to the ground for protection. But first, she would wait another moment or two. If the slow-swimming thing stirred, she would explode upon it with the speed of a bullet and the deadliness of a meat grinder.

1

Streaking toward Earth, from a point beyond the Milky Way in the Lesser Magellanic Cloud, was a ten mile long vessel shaped like an arrow and as black as space itself.

The ship was on a collision course with disaster, as yet undetected.

Only the absence of tiny star pricks where the ship passed might betray it as something not fashioned by nature; but there was nobody yet on Earth capable of such discernment, and there was nobody awake in the ship. The ship was a space ark containing an entire planet's living creatures suspended in deep sleep.

Nobody knew where their race had originated, and they called no planet home. They were eternal migrants, hopping from world to world, from galaxy to galaxy, appropriating worlds, destroying the natural ecology there, and, in a few centuries rendering those worlds uninhabitable by the sheer waste of their way of survival.

On shipboard, they were economical and led exactly measured lives. Everything on shipboard was about conservation. When they made planet fall, the other side of their nature demanded that they, and the life forms that traveled with them, consume everything that lived, and multiply until the very possibility of life was snuffed out. Everything was geared toward a single purpose: to build more space arks. With each planet fall, the number of these space arks multiplied severalfold. Each time in greater numbers, they would move on, targeting several worlds where they had just destroyed one. They were few in number, but in effect like locusts.

The aliens were nocturnal, shadowy beings, and their eyes glowed a deep, ember-rouge as a form of social interaction; but when they hunted, their eyes were black as buttons, sucking in light and emitted none of their own. Each had either three or five small, crooked horns atop its skull crest. All life on the ark was either three-limbed or five-limbed, binary symmetry not being in their genetic makeup. Their DNA was three-stranded, and they were an odd mix of few or many limbs.

While the 1,000 crew members lay in suspended animation in glassy tubes near the center of the ship, the ship's core brain directed all operations on board, from the slightest, like the wink of a warning light, to the biggest, like turning the ship. The core brain was a room-sized spaghetti of heavy iron alloys looped around each other with more twists than a human brain, although such metaphors meant nothing in 100,000,000 B.C.E.

From the core brain, a nervous system of conduits and cables spread through the entire ship, through the hull, the bulkheads, the control rooms, to every nook and cranny. When the live crew were awake, they moved about their business along dim corridors with dots of soft bronzy lighting along the walls. While the crew were cryogenically suspended, the core brain created a virtual copy of the corridors in its conduits, and shadowy avatars of each crew member moved along these corridors, eyes reddening in greeting as their paths crossed, and dulling back down as they passed each other.

The core's mission was simple: sustain the mission; defend the ship and its cargo; repair any damage to the ship; heal any cargo that was unwell, for they were the link to the future. The success of their race depended on every living member thriving under maximal conditions. Sometimes the ship took along samples of intelligent life, even if it had differently stranded genetic material.

Besides the 1,000 crew, the ark carried another million of their intelligent kind in suspended sleep. The latter's' usefulness would only arise when the mother ship was in orbit, and hundreds of smaller landers took them down to the surface. There, they would subdue and wipe out any native life, replacing it with pet creatures from their own ecosystem. These included millions of insect types, housed in hives that got buzzy and swarmy around planet fall; sea dwellers in various solutions of water; flying animals; and higher-evolved equivalents of Earth's buffalo and gorillas and other land mammals.

The aliens would not be awakened until the mother ship was in orbit and the first landers had scouted the surface. Then the aliens would be eager to embark on their new conquest. Leaving the mother ship in orbit, they would descend upon the Earth in small ships. Bit by bit, they would send down their companion life forms to speed up the process of cleansing the host world of any traces of its native life forms. All the alien species would multiply while the arks were being built. Bit by bit, nuclear and chemical poisons would destroy the host world. Collector specialists would assemble crews and cargo, making sure all species were represented, and the ships would move on, leaving huge numbers of its own life forms to die. Sometimes the ship was a force for killing, at other times for healing, whatever was best for the ship's survival. Having done this for eons beyond memory, they were expert at it. They had slept for a million years, and now their next fruit was ready for the picking.

From a million miles out, Earth had glowed in the solar ecliptic like a tiny bluish ball from. Now, barely 2000 ship lengths away, the planet dwarfed the ark. Earth was a luminous, swathed in rings of cloud, but continents peered through broad, cloud-free swaths. The land was many-colored, promising a lively diversity of opportunities.

Unseen by the ship, a one kilometer chunk of rock approached. It was an asteroid, a tiny planet jostled out of its orbit by a gravitational jostle between Mars and Jupiter. It spun away on its new dynamic, making a long ellipsis toward the sun. Along the way, it was attracted by the twin masses of the Luna and Earth. The asteroid veered sharply inward along its ecliptic, coming around the Earth-Moon system at over 100 miles per second, and headed directly for the intergalactic ark.

In the seconds before disaster struck, the ship functioned as it had for the past million years. The long halls of the ship were dark; they were crammed with tubes *and spheres and blocks, vents and machines of many purposes and descriptions. A dull light suffused the ship, kind of amber on the brighter end, like light shining through a beehive; and tending toward a darker brown on the darker end of its spectrum, like the fading of consciousness in the grip of a spider's web. It was starlight, filtered, and just enough for the purposes of maintenance. In long view, some corridors faded into the indecipherable beehive lighting; other corridors faded into equally unguessable darkness colored like chitin on a beetle.*

The ark was piloted by an electronic avatar of the Pilot, occupying a virtual bridge that existed in a computer peripheral in the actual command room. The analog's head glowered in the near-darkness of the cockpit. Three small crooked antlers projected from its head.

The ark was on the night side of Earth when, too late, the analog Pilot discovered the unexpected temporary moon that came careening around the Earth to make less than one complete orbit before assuming a new ellipse that would months later end with entry into the sun.

The avatar did all that it could. It tried to guide the ship and turn on force shields and at the same time waken the Pilot. With only minutes to spare, the sand-colored mountain approached at shattering speed.

The ship had a final line of defense: a nuclear weapon that could streak toward the threat, annihilating it. It was a weapon that would incinerate the Earth's surface in the bargain. But it was too late now. The damage would happen. The ship was programmed to rebuild itself. When it did, it had two priorities—the health of the creatures on board, and the reestablishment of its defenses, beginning with the nuclear capability.

The sand-colored asteroid's craters and ice sheets silently grew larger by the second. Though brightly lit by direct sunlight as well as moonlight, it cast a shadow before itself that darkened the space ark to almost pitch black inside as massive death approached. Ship's alarms sounded throughout long murky corridors and coldly steaming bays and pens.

The collision was soundless.

The asteroid never even slowed down. It broke the long arrow-shape of the ark into a hundred pieces that fit along the asteroid's front surface, melding with craters and plains and bumps. It plowed the pieces ahead of itself into space. Nothing on board remained alive.

Only a few pieces survived the collision, all from the massive computer core. With its surface on fire, and its spaghetti melting together, the core broke up into pieces that streaked down and crashed to earth in what would one day be called Africa.

The avatar did not know the ship was gone. It only knew that it was blinded. Frantically, it sent impulses out to wake the Pilot, to save the ship, to reconstruct the damage. Its frantic messages and protocols streamed out looking for paths and conduits that no longer existed. As long as it could pick up power from the planet's magnetosphere, it would continue to perform its mission as it had been programmed to do. It would be a long 100,000,000 years until the next milestone in that mission.

On Earth, the female T. Rex froze again, still staring out from between kelly green leaves. Directly ahead lay the pond where she'd gone to drink the past few sundowns. Under the murky surface, between floating lily pads and lacy white flowers, she saw the exposed belly of a young diplodocus, a long-necked, herbivorous pond lizard.

He reveled in twilit water warm from being in the sun all day.

She savored his faintly oily life-smell. Parting her jaws and two-inch teeth, she tensed every muscle in her body to strike and kill.

There was a breaking of the surface, a pleasurable snort as the pond lizard breathed.

In the final moment of dusk, fireflies winked. Nocturnal creatures began their barks and bellows.

The pond lizard, smelling his stalker, panicked and dove down in a deep gurgling arc.

Finally she exploded after him, a ferocious grin in front, a mad whirl of white and black and orange polygons behind. The water seethed with pounding fury as she followed him. Her limbs were hammers beating water into foam.

She did not notice that a long silent line appeared in the star-spattered sky. A stutter of smoke puffed at the tip of the line, glowing redder and hotter as it entered thicker atmosphere. There was a flash. Flash and smoke had disappeared, lost in the constellations, unheard, unseen.

Her teeth caught his tough tail. Tasting his blood, his oil, his death fear, she tossed her jaws and shredded his tail and his rear legs. She turned him kicking and struggling pond lizard onto his back, but kept his head under water. The water seethed white with foam, vermilion with blood.

Slowly, the pond quieted as he drowned.

She dragged him ashore, up into the leaves where she could hide with her kill. There, she raked claws through his underbelly, churning up viscera and half-digested vegetable matter. Smelling all this, she groaned hungrily and buried her battery of teeth into him.

At that moment, something struck the earth nearby.

Surrounded by fire, the T. Rex screamed and bolted from her prey. She ran zigzag with her back on fire, but to no avail. The entire forest all around was on fire.

Rolling in water, screaming, she managed to quench her burning flesh.

Then she lay in shock, leaking from her spinal column. She did not know about shock or spinal fluids, of course; she only knew by instinct that she was dying. She lay on her side, trembling. After a pause, her rib cage would expand in a single, labored heave, pulling in air. After another pause, her chest would collapse again, forcing the air out in a shuddering blast. Pause after pause, her body went through his involuntary, autonomic cycle, trying to push oxygen through her system. But her spine lay open, and blood covered the charred skin on her back. Spinal fluid glistened on her blackened vertebrae. The night was closing in, and she closed eyes. She did not yet smell her enemies, but she jerked her tiny forelimbs helplessly, anticipating their arrival. Her hind limbs and her tail felt numb and cold.

Her panic subsided, and she felt a new presence in her head. It was not an enemy, but something good, like mating. She lay still and let it probe inside her. After a while, she could sense a tingling in the wounds on her back. In what part of the ship are you? something asked, and she could neither understand nor answer the question, but its urgency made her feel submissive and cooperative.

You are hurt. I will repair you.

She felt lines of force surround her, pulsing and healing. She felt warmth returning to her hind quarters.

What part of the ship is this?

After a long silence, the voice said:

Something has happened to the ship. I must repair it.

Even as she drank, she felt that same presence in her head. She saw something... it was as if she looked behind over her shoulder, only it was not behind, it was inside her, in the back of her head: A dark shape, like something that moved in the night. It had three crooked antlers on its head, and its eyes glowed like embers. It was not like mating. It was not like devouring. It was more like danger. Too late, she raised her head with a resounding snort to blow water from her nostrils so she could smell the air, trying to figure out where this new threat came from.

You are not one of us.

She whirled, trying to defend her newly healed back. But there was nobody there. She whirled again. And again. Snarling. But the presence was always behind her, and it said more things whose tone of hate was clear to her:

I must destroy you.

Scene in a blackened Cretaceous Period swamp: A Tyrannosaurus Rex roars in fear and defiance as she whirls this way and that, slamming her tail on the wet earth, showing her teeth through the lightly drifting smoke.

Clumps of blackened grass still smolder here and there, but the dampness in the swamp has moderated the effects of a part of the computer core crashing down just a few yards away.

A rounded thing, black as onyx, shaped like a boulder, protrudes slightly from the mud. Faintly at first, and then more quickly, lines of force play over its metallic surfaces. Waves of cold bluish light crackle back and forth, building in amplitude, until several lines of light crackle through the air. Zigzag fashion, the blue lines dart from the boulder to the pond, reaching an apex of heat, turning from blue to red, then to yellow, and just for an instant, to white. During the instant when the ropes of light are white, the T. Rex explodes in gobs of gore and sticks of bone. In the next instant, the light has disappeared from the air; only smoldering tissue remain of the dinosaur; and, yards away, a few last waves of blue light lick the rounded thing's surfaces before dimming out. For a few hours, millions of fine dry flakes fall, and coat the ground like some accidental white plastic, before blowing away in the wind.

— ii —

LOMÉ, TOGO (ENS) Fall 1984—Making a surprising detour in his pilgrimage through West Africa, Pope John Paul II visited the capital of this small former French colony. The pontiff made a one-day stopover in the nation's capital, a city of 150,000, many of whom believe in Africa's Animist, or nature spirit, religion. Surprising his entourage, the pope insisted on visiting an island in the middle of Lake Togo. Amid rattles, drums, and shrill pipes, local spirit doctors welcomed him onto this forested island where the pope visited for two hours with animists in ghostly face and body paint. They are said to guard shrines containing evil spirits and devils held captive by magic since the creation of the world. The demons are imprisoned in statues, rocks, and other fetish objects. The witch doctors showed the Pope empty shrines that had been looted of their fetishes during the past century by European and American adventurers. The stolen totems, they said, were now in Europe or America. Those spirits, they told the Pope, had already begun their evil work in the world.

— iii —

San Tomas, California: Relentlessly, the mocking spirit tormented Dr. Johnathan Smith, D.D. by whispering cruel and dirty things in his head. You have one foot in hell already, it said laughing, you can't beat me and you can't get me out of your head and I'm going to take you to the pit of demons with me!

In the cheap rented room, torn plastic curtains had been drawn. Sunlight angling through made a dance of dust motes striking a tangle of clothes half in, half out of a suitcase. The cover flap of the suitcase lay open like a screaming mouth.

Tangled pants suggested disembodied men trying to run away. Rumpled shirt sleeves suggested ghosts waving for help.

In a corner stood the wooden statuette carved centuries ago in Africa. The statue's scarred face suggested maniacal amusement at Smith's pain. The statue's insides had been hollowed out centuries ago by its Togolese creators; and the core had been filled with a a strange heavy-black substance like iron, which Smith was convinced was a bit of alchemy directly from Satan's retorts. The statue, retrieved by missionaries in Africa, now brought him to San Tomas.

Courage, the aged fundamentalist thought, twining his arthritic fingers together over his ragged shirt and heaving chest.

The telephone rang.

The old man reached out, drew back his hand, then picked up.

"Smith, this is Mulcahy... ...Hello? ...Hello?"

"Thank God, it's you finally."

"Smith, what's wrong?"

"It's tormenting me terribly." Inside his head, a red-eyed demon chuckled.

"Is there some way I can help you?" Mulcahy sounded tired and dubious.

"You don't seem to believe me, but I have a piece of Satan sitting here in the room with me. It's the evidence we need, Mulcahy. We can prove the existence of Satan, therefore of God." ('...Up to your ass in dirty sex,' the devil interjected in Smith's head.)

Mulcahy said after a moment's consideration: "I could walk over and meet you by the Zoo entrance."

"Please! I need a witness."

"It's all nonsense, you know. There has to be a scientific explanation. There is, if we look for it."

"You fool," Smith said, feeling contempt mixed with anxiety to confront Satan. "We're so close. Why do you keep crapping out on me?"

An hour later, as lights winked on in office buildings silhouetted against the darkening sky, Smith shuffled toward the main entrance of the San Tomas Zoological and Botanical Gardens. Under his arm, wrapped in a dirty pillowcase, was the statuette, weighing heavily. The zoo was closed, and the last one or two of its office staff were just leaving. They avoided the old man. He barely noticed them.

A sudden cawing sound; a large bird thing threw itself between branches. Smith looked up into towering eucalyptus trees. "I know you're here," he whispered.

Someone—or something—chuckled in the darkness. A merciless sound. *I'm going to kill you! I'm going to tear out your heart! Ha ha ha...*

"For God's sake, Mulcahy, where are you? Hurry!"

Something stirred under the trees, something wrapped up in a darkness more total than the blackness of night. Smith's mouth opened, and once again his heart beat wildly. He stepped back, short of breath. He held his hands to his aching chest as though he must somehow relieve the pressure. He felt powerless to run. Where in God's name was Mulcahy?

Oh God, the stars.

The thing he had pursued and that in turn now pursued him, stepped between Smith and the sky. Loomed over Smith. The statuette fell clattering to the sidewalk. The demon pulled back its cowl to reveal its face. It looked ... the thing was... what? Ancient, inscrutable, Egyptian... part man, part jackal?... But instead of jackal ears, it had three small crooked horns. Three eyes burned like pools of hot red wax. Its carrion teeth were exposed in a predatory grin.

...Was THIS the face of Satan?

In his final moments, as the hideous demon loomed over him, he had a vision of the end of the world. He didn't understand the pieces of the puzzle, but he understood the vision as a whole for it fit with everything he'd studied in Revelations. There was something under the sea—a huge ship of some kind, long and black, its corridors pearled with strings of lights. Nearby lay a broken airplane with one light on inside, and that light was the engine of a nuclear furnace that would bring the end of the world. The demon face closed on him, and he took his last breath.

— iv —

San Tomas, California: Gilbert Burtongale, a tall scraggly man of 40 with long dirty hair and beard stubble, sole heir to the town's oldest and greatest fortune, stood in the darkness outside the zoo his family had founded in the 1800's. Gilbert wondered why the red-eyed presence in his head had made him come here. Some old fool shuffled up the walk holding something in a bag. The old man cried out in the windy darkness, and Gilbert only heard part of what he said: "...Mulcahy...are you...hurry!" Gilbert looked about uneasily. The old man cried: "...know you're there..." Gilbert fingered his switchblade knife, ready to open it. But things took care of themselves, as the Thing in his head had promised, not with words, just with feelings.

There! What flew through the air? A large bird. No. Something...furry. A bear? Yes, a flying bear. The old man looked up in horrified, frozen silence as the animal flew over the zoo wall and directly into his face. The old man fell down, and the bear blanketed him. The animal snarled once, briefly, tearing the old man's heart out in one digging motion, one rip of its claws.

Gilbert stared in fascination. But the Thing made him turn his head. Far away on a moonlit path, a figure in black strode along smoking a cigar. The cloud of silvery smoke hovered over Mulcahy's head like a crooked thought. Gilbert brought the knife out, with a snarl of his own. He'd been long wanting to— But No. The Thing did not want... It was most important to...

The bear vanished. Evaporated as Gilbert watched. The old man lay sprawled and broken in a lake of blood. His heart lay yards away where it had landed during the frenzy. Gilbert picked up the statuette, whose battered face smiled wickedly, a blurry and mysterious visage in wood. Its metal core seemed to throb with poisonous love.

Gilbert climbed into the driver's seat of his van. He stashed the statuette under his seat, slipped the door shut, and drove away on quiet cylinders before Mulcahy could probably notice. Gilbert drove up to the zoo entrance a quarter mile away and honked the car horn. As he waited for the night guard to open up, he cherishingly regarded at the old, tattered photograph taped to the roof: A beautiful young woman, smiling with sunny innocence, her hands clasped by her chin in sensuous indolence. I will possess you, Mary-Shane, he thought, and we will die together, yet live forever. Soon, my love. Soon.

Part I

Mary-Shane

Chapter 1.

"Mom, what's a faloshian?"

Mary-Shane brushed a wisp of hair from her forehead while concentrating on the road ahead. "Not now, honey." A blue van was just cutting into traffic behind her. They had just been to the doctor's office and she was fighting an inner scream of panic. Her son's cancer had been in remission for nearly five years, but now a questionable something had appeared in a leg X-ray. At the same time, life demanded that it be lived from minute to minute. She was late for everything, as usual. A basket of overdue library books bounced on the back seat.

Kippy frowned and pulled in his chin. "There's a dead one outside the zoo. They said so on the news this morning."

She held up her left hand in the slipstream to help the magenta nail polish dry. Traffic was heavy, and she needed to find a way to cut over two lanes. The blue van kept creeping up behind on her right blind spot. "Kippy please, I'm trying not to miss the exit to grandma's house. You can tell me there, okay?"

Serious tone: "Oh, okay."

A pair of young men whistled in Mary-Shane's direction. She barely turned her blonde head and raked them with her Icy Glance. She turned onto a side street. The blue van drifted away. Minutes later, as she pulled onto shaded Mulberry Street, Mary-Shane saw that, once again, her mother was displeased with her. Mary-Shane knew how to read her mother's house. If Mother was pleased, she would be waiting: watering the lawn, smiling, waving. Instead, Mother was inside. Sullen, without any sign of welcome, the house seemed to turn its face away.

Mary-Shane stopped the car and looked at her son. "Want a hand?" The old question.

"Naw." The familiar answer. Kippy pushed the door open with his right arm. With practiced speed and confidence, he swung first one leg, then the other, onto the street. Mary-Shane regarded her son through a thick layer of old love and pain. Wearing his school uniform, he was ten and looked beautiful. She was proud. "Grandma's mad about something," Kip noted with a glance up the hill. "What do you suppose it is this time?"

They had a silent walk up to the house together. He worked hard on his clicking crutches. She, wearing medium heels and businesslike skirt, but gray sweat jacket with dangling hood, matched his pace with hands clasped behind her back.

"Kippy, can you wait here a few minutes?" She indicated the lath gazebo vined with pink and white trumpet flowers. She banged on the door. No answer. She rattled the handle, but the door was locked. She fumbled in her pockets until she found the key. In contrast to her annoyance, Kippy sat patiently. He had one forearm draped over both crutch handles while his interested gaze followed the flight of a butterfly. His name was Christopher, but as a toddler he'd invented the nickname that would follow him through life. As Mary-Shane got the door open, she tried to take along some of Kippy's calmness.

"Mom!" her voice echoed through the house, "Mo-om!"

Mother's house was a dark swirl of silvered mirrors, petulant lace, sullen mahogany.

"Mary-Shane, dear, you don't have to shout and bang around."

Mary-Shane gave a jump. "I—I—you scared me."

Mother smiled ceremoniously while placing pussy willow twigs in a small vase. "I was here in the kitchen the whole time. Where's Kippy?"

"In the gazebo." Mary-Shane threw the envelope down on the table. "Here are the rent checks." She did not apologize that they were three days late.

"Why didn't he come in?" Mother searched for the perfect spot to place a twig she held like a spear.

"I just wanted to drop these off. I'm late for work. Is something wrong?"

Mother circled around the vase. "There." She stabbed the twig into place, then wiped her hands on her apron. "I wouldn't say wrong, Mary-Shane." She put the vase on a high window sill. "There. Tomorrow or the day after I'll cut some marigolds and add them in. That'll look nice, don't you think?"

Mary-Shane took nail polish from the sweat jacket's belly pocket. Sitting at the table, she worked on her right hand. Waiting.

Mother looked through the checks. "Was someone short?"

"No, just late. Davidson forgot to leave his rent money with me before he went on a weekend trip."

"If you're ever short—"

"Naw."

"How did Kippy's doctor appointment go?"

"The doctors found a blip or something on his leg." Her fingers trembled.

"Mary-Shane!"

"They want more time to evaluate the results." She wasn't sure if she could be patient with Mother just now.

"Mary-Shane, I thought..." Mother looked ready to cry. "Five years... remission..."

Mary-Shane snapped: "Doctor Boutros said he's sure Kippy is probably okay but he wants to check with another specialist."

Mother said, "Darling, I know you love him so." Mother rubbed Mary-Shane's back. "Make sure he always gets his rest, and eats right, and..."

Mary-Shane felt herself starting to lose it. "What do you think I have done every day for years, Mother?"

Mother sat down, folded her hands on the table, and looked at Mary-Shane. Mary-Shane felt her looking but did not look up. After a minute or two, Mother sighed. "It's none of my business, Mary-Shane, but Harold Berger has called several times this week."

Mary-Shane closed the nail polish bottle. "I don't believe it." A flush crawled up her cheeks.

"He is trying awfully hard to reach you, darling."

Mary-Shane pictured Howard in her mind, cocked an imaginary elbow back, and punched him into the next country.

"Kippy really likes him."

"Kippy loathes him, Mother. And by now, so do I. I have to go. I have to drop Kippy off at school, and I'm late for work."

"Mary-Shane, the boy needs a man in his life."

"I'm not going to marry Howard."

Mother reproved with a look that said, there you go again, bitch in tight jeans, make all the boys crazy.

Mary-Shane changed the subject: "I asked for a promotion."

"At that job?" Mother made 'job' sound dirty.

Mary-Shane rose. She was glad she'd asked Kippy to wait outside. "Mother, no guy is interested in a widow with a crippled son. I work damn hard and I need something better than life with Howard the nerd. I'm going to be thirty in two years. No Prince Charming is coming along to rescue me, so THAT JOB as you put it is my only hope to make it on my own!"

"He is a wealthy man. A good man. Young. Good-looking. What more could you want?"

Mary-Shane strode away through the house assaulted by dull rumblings of china behind glass. There was something she was walking away from. What was it? A black hole in her past, graying toward daylight with numb time in a women's prison, a threat to lose Kippy if she did not shape up...

Her mother's voice rose to a near hysterical pitch as she invoked Mary-Shane's failed marriage. "For God's sake, Mary-Shane, don't do it again! Remember what happened with you and Frank! Remember what he did to you and Kippy!"

Mary-Shane was glad to get back into the sunshine. "Ready, Kip?"

"Yep." Click of crutch. "How'd it go?"

Mary-Shane knelt and embraced him, remembering the enigmatic darkness in her past. His free hand stole around her neck. She smelled a hint of bath soap in the wet ends of his hair. Nobody was going to take this guy away from her.

They walked to the car. "Grandma wants me to do something I don't want to."

"Oh, is that all?" Kippy tossed the crutches in. "What else is new?"

"Kippee-e," she warned as he climbed in. Tugging her door open, she saw that he was grinning. Driving away unnecessarily fast, she tossed the nail polish bottle in the glove compartment that bulged with paperbacks. "Well, at least I got my nails finished."

"Oh yeah Mom, I almost forgot. They got a dead faloshian at the zoo. Do you think they'll have a picture of it in the paper?"

Chapter 2.

Mary-Shane breezed into the City Room of the San Tomas Herald, ignoring a dirty look from Managing Editor Mart Willow.

At the Obituary section, tucked in a nook near the newspaper's morgue (library), Mary-Shane let out a big breath and threw down jacket, hair brush, purse, and jangling keys. Terri 'Wiz' Kcikiewicz, her fellow obit writer, was just finishing a midmorning yogurt. Odd duck, Terri; kept a vase in the form of a skull on her desk. Anchored in a sea of paper, Terri looked up and her glasses slid down her nose, as they always did.

"Hi Wiz," Mary-Shane said. She sipped coffee from a foamed plastic cup and brushed her blonde curls.

"Hi kid. How's the boy?" Wiz had a gap between her upper front teeth.

"They found a blip on his right leg. The doctor is going to consult another specialist."

Wiz looked sad. "When do you find out?"

Mary-Shane sighed. "He said a day or two." Pushing aside an overwhelming cloud of dread and grief, she threw her hands up while circling around her desk looking for her stapler. "Why is Mart Willow here? I thought he was on vacation this week."

Wiz cleaned out her cardboard yogurt cup with a paper towel. "He was. They called him back in. Must be something big. He's been growling around like Father Zeus all morning."

Mary-Shane found the stapler and banged on the top drawer handle of her desk, at the same time pulling on the middle drawer. On the third try, the desk unlocked itself. "Don't suppose anyone will ever fix this thing. Everything is going to pieces, Wizzie. My car, my hair, my life."

Wiz nodded. "Well, the main thing is you and Kippy. He's going to be okay. Speaking of old bumble-butt..."

"Oh God." Mary-Shane scrambled into her chair and logged into the newspaper's microprocessor network. She sat brightly and erectly, clicking away at the keys as Mart Willow's sullen redness floated past. The morgue door slammed and Mary-Shane exhaled.

Wiz slipped the empty yogurt container into the huge handbag by her desk. Mary-Shane liked Wiz, eccentricities and all. Used the cups in her garden, Mary-Shane remembered. Sometimes she envied Wiz, even if Wiz was fifteen years older. Wiz had a guy in her life, and she carried a glow. Mary-Shane, after breaking up with Howard Berger three months ago, had zilch for romance. Mary-Shane attacked the first obit: Rocco Balsamo, 89, died in Belgrave Park after a long illness. Mr. Balsamo had been a member of Plumber's Union Local 5679 for fifty-nine years. He was also a past Grand Panjandrum of the Lodge of Oriental Potentates. What was a panjandrum, and was that the right spelling? "Hey Wiz, pass me the dictionary, will you?"

"What are you looking up?" Wiz asked as her glasses slipped down.

"Pan-jan-drum. Why?"

"I was just wondering if you were near the t's someplace."

"I could make a detour." Mary-Shane licked her finger and turned pages. Her left contact was beginning to sting.

"Theologian," said Wiz, whose spelling was legendarily bad. "One ell or two?"

Mary-Shane started to laugh. Wiz looked sheepish. Mary-Shane felt a frown replace her laughter. "Hey, you got a dead one there?"

"That's why we're in the obit department."

"No kidding," Mary-Shane said. "Kippy was saying something about a Faloshian, I thought he was saying. Couldn't figure out what he meant. One ell, Wiz."

"Thanks. Here, check this out. It's a doozy." Wiz tossed a handful of pages across.

Mary-Shane picked up the copy. As she did so, she bit loudly into a large red apple. The morgue door opened. Oh no, she thought, and looked up. There was Mart Willow, looking directly at her. As she looked at him, a dust mote flew up and her eye burned. She blinked at him several times in rapid succession. She hid the offending eye with her hand. Mart huffed off to his office.

"Winking at him now," Wiz observed.

Mary-Shane lowered her head onto the desk and hid under her hands. She shook her head and wondered why she had not called in sick.

"Cheer up," Wiz said. "I'll take you to lunch."

"Oh goody. Maybe I can eat some poisoned mushrooms and posthumously prove to my mother that I really did care about anything. Geez, this is weird." She read the beginning of Wiz's obit: Johnathan Smith, 68, died under mysterious circumstances yesterday evening on Zoo Lane. Dr. Smith, a professor at Whitbread Baptist Seminary in Oak Ridge, Tennessee, was a prominent fundamentalist theologian... "Good spelling, Wiz."

"Went through the checker three times."

"Died right near the main entrance to the zoo, sounds like. That's what Kippy was talking about," she repeated in wonderment.

"Note," Wiz said, leaning forward so that her ebony hair dangled lankly. She said in a very soft voice, "Died on Zoo Lane. Right on the Burtongales' doorstep."

Mary-Shane caught the implication. The Burtongale family had founded San Tomas and owned chunks of it, including the zoo. "Do you suppose that's why bumble-butt, instead of shooting elk in Canada, is here shooting the shit with us?"

Wiz nodded. "Afraid so. The old Burtongale mafia rides again. And here comes another one now."

Jules Loomis, City Editor and, like Mart, member of the Burtongale clan by marriage, stopped at Mary-Shane's desk. Jules was short and pudgy, given to wearing un-ironed white shirts and baggy pants with trademark suspenders. He held papers in one hand and an editorial pencil in the other. Hair uncombed, he puffed on a curved-stem pipe. Mary-Shane liked his tobacco; it wasn't aromatic; too much bite in the aromatics, Jules had once explained after coffee and Danish at Vogelmann's; it was more woodsy like a hay barn in the fall. Jules had hired Mary-Shane six years ago, and he liked her, tended to protect her, although Mart was technically Jules's boss, and might have fired her long since.

Jules, not given to formalities, nodded to Wiz while restuffing and relighting his pipe. To Mary-Shane: "See you a moment?"

She took a few moments to tidy up so Wiz could continue obits. Then Mary-Shane walked down the hall where he was already back in his office. She knocked on the door.

"C'mon in."

She let the wood window-door slide shut with a glassy rattle, and eased herself into one of the old-fashioned wood office chairs around his desk. The morning edition lay folded nearby. A sidebar read: "BEAR DEAD IN CAGE. (Special) Andy, a four year old grizzly bear, unexplainedly..."

Jules relit his balky pipe and put his feet up on a desk drawer. "Coupla things. One, just want to let you know Mart Willow was in here this morning sounding me out about why you were late again."

Mary-Shane felt a welling up of anger.

"I told him it was your son's checkup. Then he mentioned you've been out or late a bit more than usual the past week or two and I had to say I suppose that might be true, because it is true."

Mary-Shane banged her fists on her knees. "I'm sorry."

Jules calmly continued: "I also told him, hey look, I seem to remember the same thing happening every three months or so like clockwork and damned if it ain't the week before your boy's checkup. I told him I figure she maybe can't sleep for worrying and why don't he go away and worry about his own problems."

"Thanks, Jules. Honestly."

He added darkly: "There is the other thing too."

She knew what it was and felt a rushing in her ears. A dark, turbulent spot in her memory flicked on, blackwhite blackwhite, censoring, canceling...

"I don't like to bring it up, but of course Mart knows you had some difficulties with the law years back. You know I think the world of you, but from time to time that will come up again."

Blood rushed in her ears, and his voice came across like words filtered through a wall.

"Oh well," he said, that settled. Puffing on his pipe, hands in pockets, he walked around the office. "You've been after me to get on the City Room staff as a reporter. I'm going to send you along with Perry for a while. Let you play assistant police reporter. See how you do."

"Yow!"

"I've pushed it with Mart Willow and he says no. Mary-Shane doesn't have a degree. I said neither do I but I'm city editor. He didn't say anything but his look said, you'll never maker it any higher. Anyway, I was talking with Perry Stein about you. He's willing to take you in the field."

"Jules!" She gripped his arm. "Yowee!!"

"Shh-hh, don't let Mart Willow see you. Seeing you happy always ruins his day."

She clapped her hand on Jules's forearm. "What is it between me and him? Why does the sight of me put him in a rage?"

Jules puffed and gazed far away. "Oh, I don't know. It's only a guess. Chemistry, probably. It happens like that. He's an old office nazi from way back, and you're sort of a free spirit."

"Why do you stand up for me, Jules?"

"Because, frankly, my dear... You're almost the only ray of sunshine in this dismal place. Go with Perry. Take a shot at it. I want to give you your chance."

Chapter 3.

Perry Stein's car was at least a block long and smelled strongly of disinfectant. In the back seat were several mops and buckets. Perry and his wife took night cleaning jobs around town.

"I thought you gave that up," Mary-Shane said as they drove along Canoga Avenue, where flowers bloomed by the shopping mall.

Perry was a tall, curly-haired Samoan with thick-lensed glasses and one wandering eye. "Naw. Matilda and I talked about it some. On a small-town paper like this you don't make enough money. Not if you have five kids like we do."

Mary-Shane watched expensive San Tomas stores glide by in unwavering sunshine that drew the wealthy to this peninsula. "This is exciting, Perry. I love the newspaper. Do I get to do some writing? I'm looking for a real kick-start out of this ditch I've been in all these years."

"For now, you tag along. You'll get your chance."

"Sure, Mart Willow will fall all over himself to promote me."

"You always did have that little bite, like maybe a jalapeno too many. What you need to do, Mary-Shane, is look for a story. Maybe a big story. Something you can put your personal stamp on. Then you'll be on your way."

She sat back dismayed. "It's Mart Willow again, isn't it? What does he think— if they print something I write, the paper will explode in people's hands? What an asshole."

"It's not my idea of a way to break you in," Perry sympathized.

The corridors of the city morgue were shadowy and cool in contrast to the growing heat outside. "I'm trying to act nonchalant, Perry, but this is my first trip to a real morgue, so grab me if I pass out."

The body of Johnathan Smith was not, as Mary-Shane had imagined, in a cruel-looking room whose walls were covered with aluminum doors and whose concrete floors had bloody drains. Instead, it lay under a sheet in a plain, almost cozy, paneled room at one corner of the building. The blinds were drawn, but comforting sunlight peeked through. One of the live men in the room was San Tomas PD Lt. Vic Lara, the primary police investigator on the case. Mary-Shane thought he had beautiful shifting eyes. She felt attracted to him, and yet something about him gave her goose bumps. Had she known him in a dark past life or something?

Perry's wandering eye wandered. She had once, over coffee and Danish at Vogelmann's, heard someone of less sensitivity ask Perry how his eye got to be that way. He had held up one index finger and curled it into a hook. "Childhood fishing accident." That answer always left a silence. ("Actually it's Lazy Eye," Perry had later confessed).

The Medical Examiner pulled back the sheet and there lay Mr. Smith on his gurney. It reminded Mary-Shane of old Frankenstein movies, the way his body had been ripped to pieces and approximately sewn back together. "It would have been a big, quick, powerful, and very violent animal to do this," he said. "There have been no reports of animals missing from the zoo——."

"Except a bear named Andy," Mary-Shane said while Perry nudged her side.

"Well yes, so I hear, but he dropped dead in his cage. Hardly a predator." The M.E. smiled as if speaking to a not so bright child; Mary-Shane was used to that, although it irritated her; consider the source, she always told herself. He continued: "Actually, the only animal I know that fits that description is *homo sapiens.*" He waved a finger over his work. "Miss, er, Mary-Shane," the M.E. said, "the cuts and stitch marks around the neck are from the autopsy, in case you don't know. So are the big cross cuts on the chest. As to the rest of the damage— someone or something kind of tore him apart. They simply reached in and tore his heart out. It was found some distance from the body, partially eaten by a small animal."

Mary-Shane found the sight was neither viscerally horrible nor clinically neutral, but somewhere in-between. She felt sorry for Johnathan Smith. His reattached arms were crossed at the wrists, fingers lightly curved in rubbery repose, awaiting some funeral ceremony.

"...Like Ripper work," Lara said. Lara had a kind of hardboiled way, Mary-Shane thought, talked with his chin cocked sometimes back, sometimes up, hands in pockets. Lara looked lean and mean in his starchy suit.

The doctor sighed. "There's a sick one out there."

Mary-Shane looked more closely at the face. In death, Smith did not look particularly peaceful, given the odd twist of the lips and the faint shine of eyeballs between stiff eyelids.

"Miss MacLemore," Lara said, "sometimes people try to figure out the dead person's expression. There isn't any expression, just the odd way muscles and ligaments shrink and harden."

"Call me Mary-Shane. Thanks for that information, Lieutenant."

"You working with Perry, Mary-Shane?"

"On and off," she said. The way he regarded her gave her the chills. Had they been acquaintances somewhere long ago? Her mind, with a subconscious life of its own, groped: In an earlier life? Beneath the ocean floor? She reached for metaphors and found no perfect one, only a memory of terrible violence, like a private Big Bang. She shrank from the past, glad to return to the warm and sunny present.

Lara's look was penetrating but opaque. "See you around, huh?" His gaze caressed her the way one stroked a cat.

Chapter 4.

In the car, headed towards the zoo, Mary-Shane asked: "Perry, why are the Burtongales all nervous about this?"

He made a cynical face. "Afraid of the publicity? Paranoid? Who knows. I'd like to leave this town and get on a better paper. One not owned by a ninety year old woman dictator."

When Mary-Shane and Perry arrived near the zoo, they found, still piled to one side, sawhorses and tangled yellow tape marked "Police Line—Do Not Cross." There were stains on the sidewalk, puddles with long thin paint-like runnels going to the gutter. Mary-Shane knew the smell of dead animals in bushes, and these stains had in them the smell of death. The stink invaded her sinuses and hammered her brain, making her feel faint.

"Are you okay?" Perry asked.

"Excuse me," she said and walked away quickly. She made it about a half a block to a sandy area and there blew lunch like a garden hose.

Perry hollered something from a distance but wind tattered his words.

She waved and yelled: "I'll be okay in a minute."

Something gripped her mind and made her walk slowly, as if searching for something. She took small steps. She held her purse in both hands. It was very still there on the sand. A frog burruped nearby. A cricket cricketed. A bird clucked. Something violent had happened here on the sand long ago. It had been covered by blood. By deep sadness. She bent over as though programmed, and picked up the tiniest of things. At first she thought it was a seashell. Then she saw it was a tooth. A human tooth, too big to be a child's; somehow, she knew: an old person's tooth, bronzed with age underneath, bleached by years on top where it had lain on the sand, this beach not of the sea but of time. An echo welled up in her mind: Herself, long ago, drowning in tragedy, something to do with this tooth. She put the tooth in a clean tissue and hid it in the bottom of her purse. Then she gargled from a small bottle of mouthwash.

"...Taking it rather hard," he admonished. "If you want to be a police reporter..."

"Don't talk just now," she ordered.

He fell silent and touched her elbow, and thus they walked to the zoo entrance. There, the whatever that had just roiled the floor of her mind stirred the sand one last time: Her legs tingled, and her heart fluttered in clustered beats. It was as if a cloud had briefly darkened the sun. She became dizzy as she stared up into the elaborate 19th Century scroll work atop the zoo entrance. Bridging several brick and marble pylons was the legend "Wallace Burtongale Memorial Zoological and Botanical Gardens of San Tomas." As she read the legend, its letters began to writhe and wiggle in her mind. A sickness knifed her gut. A knowing of death, a shock of dying. But whose dying, hers? Something, briefly, touched her mind. An elderly man with mussy gray hair and truthful eyes stood inside of her, his lined face shining and finally free of pain. Her inner self turned away in deep guilt and shame and helplessness. Had she helped kill him? What else was there in this deep internal nightmare? But there was no accusation in the man's eyes, only an understanding she knew she did not deserve. He held out his hand as if she had something of his.

"Mary-Shane!" Perry was shaking her.

She held her head in both hands, but her mind was her own again and she let go. "I'll be okay," she said. The feeling had passed, but her legs felt weak.

"You're white as a sea shell," Perry said, looking alarmed.

"Let's go for that big story," she said, heading toward the neo-Egyptian ramparts, jackals, and sun disks, of the zoo portal.

Everywhere inside the zoo, there was evidence of construction (or reconstruction, Mary-Shane wasn't sure which). Small pickups carrying electrical or plumbing supplies crawled on the pebbly paths among the habitats of elephants, giraffes, and wildebeests. Ladders leaned against walls, canvases were thrown over benches, orange cones stood in odd places. Men and women in overalls moved purposefully. Vans were parked in odd places.

The domed hall of the main administration building rustled with footsteps and voices. A receptionist behind an oak lectern directed them down a long hallway. The walls were covered with huge panels showing prehistoric animals. Brontosaurus, ninety tons of him, yachted through a pond. Whatsasaurus shrilled fearfully as T. Rex made salad out of him. At the end of the building was another, smaller domed hall with a tiled floor. A large portal led out into a small parking lot fringed with tropical plants. The air inside the dome was pleasantly cool. There were several office doors, each with its brass name plate. One nameplate read "Dr. Wallace Burtongale VI, Ph.D., Curator." The next door was that of "Dr. Roger Chatfield, Ph.D., Assistant Curator." On this door, Perry knocked.

"Just a minute," a man's voice shouted. The door opened. Dr. Chatfield, a tallish tanned man in his thirties, wore khaki. "Please pardon the mess outside. We're doing some major remodeling." He was good-looking, but Mary-Shane did not like him. Too self-assured, with those serious eyebrows. Perry evidently knew Chatfield, for they shook hands like old friends. Perry introduced Mary-Shane.

With Chatfield was another man, tall, balding, about fifty. He wore a priest's black suit and white collar. He wore steel-rimmed glasses and an expensive gold watch. He waved a banana-sized cigar. Chatfield said: "Mr. Stein, Miss MacLemore, allow me to introduce you to a friend of the zoo and gardens. Bishop Donald Mulcahy."

Mulcahy jammed the cigar between his teeth and energetically seesawed their hands. He had to bend down to do so. "Pleased to meet you." He seemed more a hard, realistic businessman than a priest at first glance. "We're over in the cathedral basilica near the zoo." Mulcahy said, "Church and zoo are old friends."

"Mr. Stein and Miss MacLemore are from the newspaper. They've stopped by to see me about the Smith matter."

"Oh?" Mulcahy sucked thoughtfully on his cigar. A steel-wool tangle of smoke floated away from his changed face. "How interesting. Good, Roger, well, I won't keep you. Been nice visiting. Good day, Mr. Stein. Nice day, Miss MacLemore."

The bishop strode off. He left a shawl of smoke over one shoulder, and Mary-Shane was surprised that she sort of liked the smell. Probably not your nickel stogie. More than likely, from the looks of the bishop, a pampered and humidored delicacy. His smoke had a dry, rare essence that reminded her of the smell of money in bank lobbies.

Chatfield had a high-ceilinged office with book-lined walls and dark furniture. Mary-Shane and Perry sat in sturdy leather-padded chairs making a semicircle before Chatfield's desk. "Can I get you some coffee?" His gaze told her he was interested in her.

Perry nodded. "Please. Given the way the morning has gone."

"Black no sugar," Mary-Shane said, wanting to keep things straight-forward.

"Been a real bear, I take it," Chatfield said as he poured from a ceramic service. They sipped from thick souvenir cups Mary-Shane found pretty: A maroon panda climbed in green bamboo against a creamy off-white background. How nice, Mary-Shane thought, to be able to work in an office with greenish light filtering in overhead.

"It's Miss MacLemore's first day on the police beat, and already she's had to see a dead guy with his heart torn out and visit the scene of his murder."

Mary-Shane flushed, angry that he would be patronizing. If he mentioned anything about her barfing, he would get his head thumped. Chatfield hovered like a boy sitting on a fence rail. "Are you interested in police work, Mary-Shane?" Bright voice.

She nodded. "It's a killer."

Chatfield glowered a moment, then laughed. Perry said: "I tried to reach Wallace Burtongale all morning, but the secretary says he's unavailable for comment."

Chatfield said: "Maybe I can help you?"

Mary-Shane noticed photos all over his desk. A boy and a girl. Were they his? And the brunette with the mysterious smile and the sensuous eyes; his wife? Wow, Dr. Chatfield, you've done well. And now he was interested in Mary-Shane? Whoa, no lipstick of mine will find its way to this man's collar.

Perry said: "This guy just happened to get his ticker ripped out on your doorstep. Come on, Roger, why the zoo of all places to dump a body? The guy was a theologian. Was he on a religious quest? Remember, I'm giving Miss MacLemore the A-ticket tour of investigative journalism."

There was a sudden shaking, a droning that rattled windows and drowned out conversation. They looked up. Mary-Shane glimpsed the silvery fuselage of a military cargo plane modified with all sorts of antennas and listening dishes.

"Perry, we've had bodies dumped here over the years, you know that. All those transients living down in the woods behind the zoo, all the drugs... I had a call from Miss Polly"(the 90-year-old Burtongale matriarch with the world view of an Albanian dictator)"this morning. She wants to downplay speculation. There is absolutely no connection between the body and the zoo."

"Not that the zoo has anything to hide." The question tumbled from Mary-Shane's lips, laden with sarcasm that surprised her. She caught her breath and looked up into Perry's open-mouthed stare. "What about the dead bear?" she blurted.

Chatfield's brow wrinkled. "Andy," he said in wonderment. "I have no explanation," he said honestly. He shrugged. "As Miss Polly has often remarked, what this zoo is all about is the tourist dollar. What's good for the zoo is good for the town. Jobs, Miss MacLemore. I'm asking you and Mr. Stein not to overplay the zoo angle."

Before they left, Mary-Shane pulled the tissue from her pocket. "You are a biologist, right? Would you have any idea what this is? I found it near the zoo entrance." She gave him the tissue.

He unwrapped it with a puzzled face. "Why, it's a tooth." He held it up in the filtered light. "It's a human tooth. From an adult." He smelled it, ready to rumple his nose, then merely shrugged. "It's old." He handed it back to her. "It's some poor alcoholic vagrant's lost tooth." He smiled broadly. "You find all kinds of things at the zoo."

"Jeez Mary-Shane, it's not anything you did or said, but I kind of got the idea you were a bit frosty with him," Perry said when they were outside walking on the zoo grounds.

"You were just imagining things, Perr'. I was wondering, though, why you didn't pump him some more for a crisp story angle."

"Mary-Shane, there's no logical connection between the zoo and this guy's death. We're a family paper, not a tabloid."

"I'm sorry, Perry, I'm just trying to be gung ho here on my first and probably last day as temporary acting assistant police reporter."

"A little less *picante* please."

"Come on, I'll buy you a root beer at the souvenir shop."

Perry wiped his forehead in the noonday heat. Overhead, the silvery C-130 was doing slow circles over San Tomas Peninsula. "What do you suppose he's doing?" Perry said watching the plane.

She shrugged. "Probably just playing in the sunshine." They walked across the zoo grounds. "Don't you just love this?" "Let's take a short cut," Perry said. "I'll phone in a short piece to make the late afternoon edition." Perry led her along a narrow, grass-choked path hidden in the swarmy shade of ancient magnolia trees. Suddenly she felt again the numb feeling she'd felt outside the zoo. She put her hand to her forehead. Oh no, not again!

"Mary-Shane, what's the matter?"

"I- I'll be all right. It's just—the heat, maybe."

"I hope so." Perry took her elbow and gently guided her along. Her mouth felt dry and her heart beat rapidly. The trees were swarmy with insects. Shade hung in the tree limbs like molasses. They came to an odd little structure. Its roof was of mission tile, pagoda-curved at the edges. On the northward side was a three-foot relief of the sun, rendered as a dreamy dimpled face stippled with moss. The eyes seemed closed. Its smile was at once promising and ominous. Its solar rays were wiggly. The path ran in a broad circle around the Pagoda. There were several benches in the inner edge of the circle.

"Here," Perry said, "sit down."

"Thanks." She was taking quick, shallow breaths. Her skin felt cool, but was wet with perspiration.

"I'll go get you a soda. Stay here."

"No—" she grasped his sleeve.

"It's just a hundred feet away on the main drag," Perry said. "Some ice water maybe and then off to see the zoo nurse, huh?"

Before she could stop him he was gone. She clasped her hands between her knees and sat back. Startled, she leaned forward. propelled by a breeze from the shady canyons, a hot dry wind raked her eyes. There, was there someone standing in the smoky shade just past the utility house? She rubbed her eyes and stared. Frank! No, that's crazy. Frank is dead. Stop it, Mary-Shane. Maybe I need to see my shrink again. When she looked again, the figure was gone, replaced by wavering round leaves.

Something brushed by her leg and she started together, hands upraised, hair standing on edge, drawing in a breath as sharp as an inward scream.

"Sorry to disturb you, Miss." A heavyset, middle-aged black grounds keeper in overalls shifted a curved pipe from one corner of this mouth to the other. He wore leather work gloves and carried a whisk broom and dust scoop, both on long handles to prevent stooping. The pipe smelled woodsy. The *Dark Feeling* left her as abruptly as it had come over her.

"Oh, please, don't mind me," Mary-Shane said happily. "I was just staring.. at the.."

"That there's an interesting lookin' building, ain't it?" His brush whisked right and left, and the dust scoop jumped like a small dog at his feet, snapping up the flying dust and debris. *Whisk, whisk*, went the brush; *Snap, snap* went the dust scoop as if to nip at his ankles.

"That's a utility shed?"

"Yes ma'am. That there's the old central power and gas and water house. They shut it down to put in a whole new power line from the city. That shed there is going to be just a backup. Got a diesel generator in there in case the power goes down. Sorry I disturbed you."

"I'm kind of glad you did, Mr.—"

"Washington. J. W. Washington." He pulled off a dirty glove and shook her hand. His hand was dry and heavy, reassuring somehow, with thick smooth fingers and a fine little gold ring.

"Mary-Shane MacLemore," she said, rising. She couldn't resist: "Not Roger Washington?"

He grinned. "My uncle." *Whisk, whisk*, he went; *Snap, snap* went the dust scoop. "You be good now, hear?"

"Oh I will, Mr. Washington. I swear I'll try."

He seemed to hear the sass in her voice and gave a knowing little gurgle of a laugh as his broad back receded along the walk.

She took a deep breath and sat down. One part of her was tempted to run and find Perry as fast as she could. But another part of her wanted to hang on, to stay, to find out just what it was about this day and this place and about herself. She had the deep, turbulent sense that someone or something was trying to communicate with her. And she had the more disturbing feeling that somehow she had changed. Perhaps because someone or something had somehow taken up residence in a dark and little-visited rear corridor of her mind.

"Mary-Shane!" Perry came running, holding a big cup in one hand and wet paper towels in the other. The dear!

"Thanks, Perry. I'm better now." She drank ice water while he held a cool towel to her forehead. "What men don't go through."

She did look back, on the way out. The sun on the pagoda was smiling to itself, perhaps filled with the taste and the memory of her fear. The eyes were still nearly closed, but in a manner that suggested they had been staring after her, and quickly shut when she turned to look.

Chapter 5.

Gilbert Burtongale stood inside the near-dark Pagoda and watched a blue glow reaching from the hidden places, under the oil tanks and engines, from the underground water tanks.

"Thank you," he whispered out loud to the unseeable demon-force growing under the ground and in his brain. He had always had something lurking in the back of his mind; every first-born male Burtongale did. The glow strengthened in the undefined darkness among tanks and equipment. Gilbert unlocked the Pagoda and pushed the door open a crack. He held his hand up and squinted at the sunlight. His breath caught. His heart missed a beat. She!

He peered out from his hiding place. Mary-Shane sat on a bench facing the Pagoda, not twenty feet away. Had she seen him? Was that why she had that pale, shocked look? Then some old blackie came along and talked with her. Now it was old darkies where years ago it had been Frank MacLemore. He longed to take her curls in his fingers and smell them deeply. She was a bad girl, wild, to run with Frank as she had. Why? when Gilbert had wealth, good family, everything. Once Frank had seen him looking at her, and one look told him what Frank told other men: Touch her, you die. Frank had been nobody to fool around with. Reluctantly, Gilbert had put her out of his mind. After the burglary and the murders in Chicago, Gilbert and Frank had parted ways; Frank had died; and Mary-Shane had gone to prison.

Oh, look at her now. She was not like other women. She was a thing of rare beauty. Look how her face lit up like a little sun as she laughed. Look how saucy that precious mouth was, how quick and bright those eyes. How her beautiful face caught the sun. How her knees tantalized from under the jeans skirt. How her firm thighs flattened slightly on the bench. He saw a flash of the blue mound of her panties... Another man came; another one of them! and Gilbert wanted to kill him. Gilbert, a card-carrying, weapon-bearing member of the master race, hated the scum who had taken over the country. It would not be long now. Once the ship had rebuilt itself, once the something was back in its Pilot seat! Either that or it would destroy the world. Either way, Gilbert would get what he wanted, and most importantly that was Her.

She rose, and Gilbert longed to touch the firmness of her naked legs, the exquisite perfection of her rear end, the gentle and feminine curve of her back. Hungrily, Gilbert watched the cocky gracefulness of her movements. I deserve her, he told himself. His gaze followed her naked calves past hanging boughs. And soon she would be his.

Chapter 6.

"You really should get a checkup," Perry said on the way back to the newspaper office.

"I will, Perry. Now let's see if I get to stay on this story." She was going to take Perry at his word. She was going to find a story that would change her life. She was going to do it for Kippy. And for herself. For the first time, she was going to have real independence.

Jules Loomis, a while later, seemed surprised that she even asked. "Why of course." He relit his pipe, and she strained to smell the smoke. "Perry says you have a good investigative streak. He also feels you need to learn some diplomacy."

"I'm afraid that's never been my strong suit."

"It comes with time."

Mary-Shane spent the afternoon finishing up Balsamo and the other obits. Wiz seemed quiet.

"Are you mad that they are letting me work city?"

Wiz turned in her seat and bunched her long drab dress on her knees. Her fists were knots. Her eyes swam in fury. "I'm sorry, Mary-Shane. I have nothing against you or your opportunity. I don't think it's jealousy for a woman 15 years older to be passed up, with a degree no less, even if it is in early child care and psychology. I feel like I've just had a shoe put up my rear end and I'm damn mad." Wiz picked up her huge purse, swept possessions into it, and said: "Please do me a favor. Tell Jules I quit"(Mary-Shane took a shocked breath)"and I'll give him a call tomorrow morning." Wiz started to walk away, then turned and regarded Mary-Shane with a long, strange look. "Mary-Shane, be careful." Wiz's eyes and mouth worked with some repressed knowledge. "This Smith story, stay away from it. Good luck with the police beat."

After Wiz had left, Mary-Shane exhaled through rounded lips, contemplating. Wiz had this degree and Mary-Shane had three credits garnered years ago during an abortive effort at college. Frank had taken her books on the front lawn and set them on fire before passing out from drugs. She could understand how the difference in age and education must bother Wiz. She hoped they'd be able to talk about it later. Reluctantly, she made the trip past Mart Willow's office to Jules's.

"She what?"

"She said she would talk to you about it tomorrow."

Jules waved his hand. "She'll calm down."

Kippy was in the pool when Mary-Shane got home. The apartment door was open and Mother sat in the shade. It was sweetly quiet when Mary-Shane, twirling sunglasses and clutching purse, jacket, and newspaper, walked in through the wooden gate.

"Hi Mom!" Kippy dog-paddled toward her, throwing off twirls of sun-jeweled water.

"Hi darling," she said. She tossed a life preserver and it was a near ringer around his neck but he caught it and threw it back.

"Hello, Mary-Shane," Mother said.

"Hi, Mother." Mary-Shane bent to kiss her mother on the cheek.

"I had to tell those young people in 1A and 4B to turn down their stereos. They were loud enough to be heard in the next county." She said this as though it were Mary-Shane's fault.

Mary-Shane shrugged and breezed into the house. "Can't help it, Mother." She threw purse and jacket down, then propped up the newspaper and fished a cola from the refrigerator. "Smith Murder Inquiry Continues," a front-page headline informed. There was a picture of Smith, taken a few years earlier during a banquet. The picture showed a pleasant looking white-haired man. Wiz's obit said his students had loved him.

"Come on, Mom!" Kippy yelled from the pool.

"I'll be right out," she hollered through the curtains over the sink. A fleeting pleasure crossed her mind, that this was her home. Hers and Kippy's. She had chosen THESE curtains over Mother's suggestions at the Fabric Store. That had been quite a few years ago now. She'd been in her early twenties, trying to cope with Kippy's cancer. She'd also been trying to cope with Frank MacLemore's death. In some ways it had seemed easier with Frank gone, an end to his drinking and abuse. Then again, having a child as a single mother was so hard, no matter how she loved him. She had to work, and she worried about him all the time, especially when she remembered all those night sleeping in a chair by his side in the hospital years ago before the miracle of remission.

She stepped into the bedroom, slipping out of her dress. In the light afternoon breeze that stirred the curtains, she relished the coziness of the bedroom. Sure it was a bit rumpled, the bed not made but just peeled open to air out. It was clean, and it was home. For a minute or two, absently still in heels, she dawdled in the closet entrance. She finished undressing, changed into her black bikini, and stepped into Kippy's room. The air was stuffy and she opened a window. His room had that Kippyness that she loved. It was a room steeped in twilight on the border between childhood and adolescence. The computer, stereo, football, and light weights (prescribed for his legs) suggested the beginnings of teendom. For all the rest, it was still the room of a child. There were stuffed animals with worn fur, model cars with fingerprints in the paint, balsa planes she had helped him build that had never flown well. There were marbles and pencils and baseball cards. Flags of the world in a San Tomas State University Grecians beer mug. And photos. Among them a tattered old black and white of Frank in his Navy uniform; he proudly held one year old Kippy while Mary-Shane stood behind them with a scrubbed teenage face and an unreadable expression somewhere between joy and sorrow.

"Catch!" She tossed the ball back and forth with Kippy, then cooled herself in the pool. Mother went inside to make dinner, puttering about Mary-Shane's kitchen with a hesitancy as though everything were in the wrong place and of the wrong sort. Supper ended up being hamburgers, silver dollar fries, and Brussels sprouts.

"Where did you get the Brussels sprouts, Mother? Surely not in my apartment."

"I brought a few groceries just so you wouldn't starve."

Mother added: "I'm going to wipe down all your dishes before I go home."

"No need to, honest." Mother was a pain, but during the hard times after Frank's death, she had been there every day to help out. Mother was a widow. Mary-Shane's Dad had died in an airplane crash when she was Kippy's age, about nine years ago. Mother had retired two years early from her job at the phone company to take care of Kippy while Mary-Shane tried her hand at a series of tedious jobs that didn't work out. The current arrangement was that Mary-Shane managed the apartment complex Mother had bought with the insurance money from Dad's settlement. She also paid Mother a small rent and covered her own utilities.

After a brief tangle of words, Mother agreed not to wipe all the dishes in the cupboard now, but sometime when Mary-Shane and Kippy were not home. After Mother had left, Mary-Shane did the remaining few dishes. Mary-Shane felt like there was a volcano inside her ready to explode. Kippy was watching Star Trek on TV. "Did you do your homework?"

"No."

"Kippy, you're not supposed to turn on the TV. until your homework is done."

"Oh Mom." The 'mom' was a moan. She heard crutches clicking, then silence.

Mary-Shane finished wiping the counter with a hand towel. "Have you got a lot?" Sometimes they would sit together and work on his fifth-grade grammar and arithmetic.

"I don't feel good." A truly, sincerely sad voice.

She swatted him with the hand towel. "Too many Brussels sprouts, huh?"

"I think I'll lie down for a while."

Mary-Shane frowned as he went into his room and closed the door. "Can I get you something?" Worry crawled like worms inside her gut.

No answer. A little while later, carrying milk and cookies in on a TV. tray, she found him fast asleep dressed in his socks and bathrobe. His skin felt hot and dry, and she contemplated waking him later on to take his temperature. Maybe it was an oncoming flu bug. Sitting alone in the living room, she started to watch an old movie, then felt alone. Sometimes, as busy as she tried to keep herself, as much of her time as she devoted to her only child, the terror of losing him overwhelmed her. And the fear of losing her pretty years, somehow, in this endless march of third-rate jobs. Tears surprised her, dribbled down her cheeks, off her upper lip, and she heard herself keening softly in the dark living room like an unearthly musical instrument, and buried her face in her hands. Tears forced their way between her fingers as she sobbed.

Chapter 7.

Dr. Boutros called her at the office. "No need to upset you, Mary-Shane. Dr. Wendt agreed that what we saw is probably a cyst. I think Kippy should come in for another X-Ray in about a month."

"Then you don't think it's cancer?" she whispered.

"No, I wouldn't think so at this time."

"But you don't know for SURE?"

Pause. "Let's have another look in a month and see if anything has changed."

Jules stopped by. "Any word from Wiz?"

"Not a thing," Mary-Shane said. "And I'm swamped with obits." She was angry, because she'd been unable to go on the police beat with Perry.

"Hang in there," Jules said walking away.

Chapter 8.

J. W. Washington was making his rounds (*whisk! whisk!, snap! snap!*) of the zoo and he came to the Pagoda. There, in the shade, he remembered the little blonde he had briefly spoken with that morning, and he wished she'd come by again. She had the scrubbed, pure look of one of those models with snowy smile, mint blue eyes, and halo of caramel curls, that J.W. often noticed on his wife's knitting magazines. Hell with the smutty magazines, if you wanted to see beautiful women look at knitting magazine covers. Today, J.W. noticed a shiny new padlock on the Pagoda door. Now wasn't that odd? Just out of curiosity, J. W. set aside his whiskbroom and scooper, fingered his belt for his heavy ring of maintenance keys, and approached the Pagoda. It was just one of the zoo's utility sheds. Inside were some shovels, picks, mulchers, weeders, rolled hoses, and the like; J. W. could almost do a mental inventory. Plus there was an underground water reservoir, and an old heater that no longer worked, from a century ago. Funny thing too, he hadn't been in there since remodeling started months ago. The key (marked "P" in J.W.'s laborious script) did not work on the new lock.

A snarling face surrounded by wild hair floated around into J.W.'s vision. "What are you doing?" It was Gilbert.

J. W. switched his pipe from one corner of his mouth to the other. "I work here, young man."

Gilbert's face grew redder. "I know that, old fool. I asked what you think you're doing at that door."

J. W. moved his pipe again, amazed. "I wanted to look into the Pagoda. That okay with you?"

Gilbert slammed a hand against the steel door. "I got a private contract to do work in there, and I changed the lock. I don't want anyone fucking things up in there, got it?"

J. W. lifted his pipe away and nodded. "Okay, if you say so, sonny." He considered arguing, but knew enough about Gilbert not to bother. *Whisk, whisk,* J.W.'s tools went, *Snap, snap!*

That evening, when darkness swallowed the zoo, when the night air was still except for the weird honks and groans of the animals, the Pagoda door creaked open. Gilbert stepped out, switching a toothpick from one side of his mouth to the other. He locked up and then walked to the Insect Hall while the something, the Pilot, sent urgent feelings from inside Gilbert's mind and soul. Gilbert walked inside the Insect Hall and stood quietly for some moments. The display cases—containing spiders, some dead and pinned, others wriggling and alive—glowed dully in the moonlight. Gilbert opened the display case as the Pilot urged him to. Gilbert didn't know or care whom the Pilot was about to destroy; there had been several killings in the past year, and Gilbert only knew that something big was on its way. After generations of first rewarding, then haunting and destroying the Burtongale first born men, the Pilot was about to fulfill its mission. Gilbert had not been told that; he just knew it, from a life of doing the Pilot's bidding, from years of having it inside of him.

The spiders stirred to life. They crawled around, agitated in a dim glow from no certain source. One by one they began dropping to the floor, avoiding Gilbert, then scurried off in search of the human being who had been snooping at the Pagoda, threatening the ship...

J. W. Washington had mixed feelings about working overtime this evening as he finished his sandwich and milk in the car and listened to a ball game. The money would help; but he'd miss the wife and kids.

J.W. put on his headset and turned on the Dandy Dan Dundee radio talk show. They were talking about football, his favorite sport, so he turned up the volume. He had been a football fan since his daddy had sat him on his knee at Home Stadium. J.W. got the golf cart ready to check all the ivied areas to make sure the sprinklers were fanning evenly. Later he'd empty all the trash cans in the main zoo office building with its cupola dome. He'd do the sprinklers first, because then he could listen to Dandy Dan Dundee talking about football. He'd save the trash in Admin 1 & 2 for last, because the buffer man came in at nine and they'd have coffee together and shoot the breeze for 15, 20 minutes.

J.W. Washington's ear speaker whispered a cheer of fifty thousand voices as the commentator revisited one of last fall's premier games. It was cool and pleasant in the zoo, with a little night moisture creeping in from the sea around San Tomas Peninsula. The park lights shed a yellowish glow. All street lights in San Tomas were sodium vapor by arrangement with the university observatory, to prevent fogging the night sky for the great telescopes peering into deep space.

J.W. drove his golf cart along Major Way, slowly checking the sprinklers. Here and there he got out to make an adjustment. Now he found a spot that was more difficult, in an island of ivy in the middle of Major Way. He found a sprinkler that had gone awry, shooting water over the pebbly drive instead of the ivy. He found no way to reach the sprinkler from the roadway without getting soaked. Gingerly, he stepped into the thick ivy, first one foot, then the other, waving his arms to keep his balance. To avoid being drenched, he crawled on his hands and knees toward the errant sprinkler. His fingers felt about under the ivy. Delicately, he marched his fingertips back and forth trying to assess a situation he could not see. He grunted heavily, trying to get comfortable lying on his side, for he was a heavy man, and no longer young. He felt a trickling sensation on his neck and brushed something away with his free hand. Glancing at his hand, he saw that the wetness was sweat, and he wiped his chin with the back of his hand. Then he concentrated again, closing his eyes, following his fingertips as they explored. First, there was the buried copper line; then a brass fitting where it came out of the ground; then a PVC plastic line. His fingertips walked to a PVC elbow that carried the water up into the sprinkler; and there was the problem... he could feel it with his fingers. The two screws, holding fast the strut that supported the brass sprinkler head upright, had come loose.

But he had the wrong screwdriver. Darn! He rose, avoiding the spray of water, and tip-toed out of the ivy to the road. Brushing his overalls off, he rummaged in the tool chest until he found just the right cross-tip screwdriver for Phillips head screws. Then he tiptoed back under the sprinkler, and, sitting on his knees, reached down with both hands into the ivy to try and blindly get the tip of the screwdriver into the head of the screw.

He felt an itching sensation on his back.

He freed one hand to swat over his shoulder without really looking.

The itch went away.

He put the hand back into the ivy. Sweat dribbled from his face, twirling, glittering down into the ivy. With his fingertips, he guided the screwdriver to the screw. As he did so, he felt something brush against his right cheek. At the same time, an odd tingling sensation coursed throughout his body, coming from his hands—an electric jolt, a stinging sensation. His first thought was that he had somehow encountered a short between the water pipe and some hidden electrical line, of which there were plenty in the zoo's antiquated construction. The tingling raced up his arms into his shoulders. Sweat exploded from his forehead. The feeling in his hands changed to a deep stinging pain in his hands. At the same time, a furry wriggling body brushed against his right cheek. In his peripheral vision, he saw a many black waving legs rounding the curve from his shoulder to his face. Tarantula! In a moment of frozen shock, he looked directly into its glittering black face, into its button eyes, saw its parted clamps ready to tear his skin. With a scream of pain and terror, he rose to his feet and brought his hands up to brush it away. He found that his hands and his sleeves were coated with spiders of all sizes and descriptions. They were biting, stinging, sawing through his skin. He uttered a choking cry as a hairy body tried to push between his lips. Already, the world had a darker, narrower focus as he staggered through the ivy. His shirt and pants tingled here and there as multiple legs ran quickly over his skin. He tried to beat them down with his hands, his elbows. He fell to the ground, rolling. Felt the squishiness. Lay on his back. His breath came in short, painful honks. His heart beat loudly, intently, as though ready to tear a hole in his chest. He saw, dimly, a man standing in the roadway. "Help me!" he cried out. The man was far away, but J. W. saw it was Gilbert Burtongale. Grinning.

A blanket of tarantulas covered J.W.'s face, and he closed his eyes; thought about football; thought about taking his sons to the ballgames next fall. Sure. They would go to a game. Why was he lying here feeling so woozy? At the ballpark? Hot dogs?

He was walking.

Huh? Walking down a long hallway of some kind. He looked at his hands and they were bright blue. Nearby, also walking, was a girl of 13 or so in a long skirt. Her long hair and skin were bright blue. She carried a blanket-wrapped bundle in her arms. "Hello. My name is Teresa. Did you die today too?"

J.W. looked at his hands again. "What did you say?"

"Don't you know? We died today."

J.W. hesitated. In the corridor ahead waves were breaking on a beach.

"Don't be afraid," she said. "We feel fine now."

They held hands and walked through the waves. Down into the sea. Fish swam around them. And through them. "You see?" she said. "Nothing to be afraid of. This little guy died today too." She opened the blanket, revealing a blue baby. The baby opened its eyes and smiled at J.W. "His name is Theodore. He fell out a window, but he's all better now." Ahead, too far to make out clearly, a gateway seemed ablaze with rippling sheets of fire. Just then some cold blue person walked reluctantly into the fire, pushed along by dark moving shapes.

Chapter 9.

In the morning, over breakfast, Kippy told her: "You had one of those screamers again last night."

"Huh?" She stopped in mid-croissant and blushed. For years, about once a month, maybe more when under extreme duress, she had variations on a nightmare whose contents were a closed, sealed secret. She might wake up screaming, sitting up in panic; or sleep through and have Kippy tell her she had awakened him. "Sorry," was all she could offer, but he seemed used to it.

Mary-Shane dropped Kippy off at St. Andrew's School. She watched until his mop of thick brown hair disappeared among other heads on the playground, then drove to work. Jules called her into his office. "Bad news. Wiz called early this morning and said she won't be back."

"No!"

"I'm sorry, Mary-Shane. It will take a few days, maybe a week or so, but we'll get a replacement. Meanwhile I'm afraid you're going to have to woman the obit desk all by yourself. When we get a new person you'll have to train him or her also."

"Damn."

"Yeah. I can empathize. I'll give you the freedom to help Perry in anyway you want, as long as it doesn't interfere with obits. I'm making you his assistant, and damn Mart Willow."

"That does make me feel a little better. Just give me a chance, that's all I ask." She thought, I will find a big story and write it down and be Hemingway and it will be good.

"Hey, there's more good news. Chatfield called from the zoo yesterday afternoon. Very impressed with you. Says he wouldn't mind helping you put together some color about the zoo. Want to do some stories?"

She took a moment to answer, remembering her mixed feelings about Chatfield. "Well, maybe..."

Perry stopped by to offer condolences about Wiz quitting.

"Great timing," she remarked as the copy girl brought a stack of death notices needing phoned accuracy checks.

"A little less chili pepper please," Perry said. He sat on the edge of the desk and cracked an apple. "Did you know there was another death at the zoo last night?"

"No."

"Yes. One of the maintenance men. They found him lying in the street, bitten up by spiders. I was just on the phone with the M.E. He says the stings caused a heart attack." Perry rapped a knuckle on the desk. "Well, assistant, I gotta run. Can't wait for you to get out there on the police beat."

Mary-Shane got to work. Doing obits alone was like rowing a leaky boat. The faster you rowed, the more water got in, or so it seemed. She arranged the piles of paper on her desk and tried to get organized. With the rhythm of cooperation between herself and Wiz gone, she felt overwhelmed. Each morning, ten or twenty death notices arrived, of which probably three to six required obituary newspaper articles. In other words, she had to write about twenty pages of meticulous articles every day before the two p.m. deadline. Woe if a name were misspelled, an address wrong, or a surviving relative not mentioned! Often, a death notice or obituary article required telephone time, checking details. Mary-Shane had been doing obits for nearly five years now, and it gave her a strangely serene overview of life and death. Sometimes she felt like a secretary to St. Peter or whoever unlocked the pearly gates. People died suddenly or from long illnesses or were murdered. People died young or old or in the prime of life. For example, one of the obits today was on a 13 year old girl named Teresa Avila who had died of leukemia. Another was on a little baby named Theodore Grant, who had fallen from a third-story window; with a name like that, he might have grown up to be a great lawyer, maybe even a president. How sad life could be. But she had her Kippy.

The obituary notice on the zoo employee who had died last night was phoned in by a relative late that morning.

"Would you repeat that name?"

"Washington. J.W. Washington."

She nearly dropped the phone. "I was just speaking with him yesterday!" Mary-Shane and the shaken relative exchanged observations about life, death, fate, and coincidence for several minutes more. Whisk, Whisk, she thought sadly. Snap, snap.

"Going to lunch?" Perry asked a while later.

"Is it that time? My God it's noon. Perry would you be a sweetie and bring me a sandwich?"

He was, and he did. They ate together in the hall on a windowsill. "Perry, I've been doing obits for a couple of years," she said as egg salad fell out of her mouth and she used her fingertips to stuff it back in. "It seems to me I've done several obits on zoo people the past year." He merely shrugged.

Still chewing, she hurried back to her desk. The clock was ticking. With every minute the 2 p.m. deadline loomed closer.

Ann Temple, Mary-Shane's girlfriend from school days, called at ten after two. "Hey Rat Breath." Ann and Mary-Shane long ago had exchanged special secret names. Ann's son Jeremy was a grade further along than Kippy at St. Andrew's.

"Yo Beagle Face," Mary-Shane said weakly, sitting back in her typing chair after having made the deadline by thirty seconds.

"Want to go out for steak dinner at Pepper's Steak House this evening?"

"Great idea," Mary-Shane said. "Let's make an evening of it." With that to look forward to, she brightened. She started playing with the computer while she ate the remaining half of her sandwich and lukewarm coffee. Suppose, she thought, I wanted to know how many people have died around the zoo during the last year or two, how would I look that up? Mary-Shane sat at the glowing screen. The keys clicked as she tried different directories and paths to access the information. At five, after calling Ann Temple to pick up Kippy, Mary-Shane was still working on the computer system. She saw Mart Willow walk into his office with (ugh) Gilbert Burtongale. Mart (bigger ugh) was Gilbert's uncle, and no doubt Gilbert was here to hit him up for some money again. The whole staff knew that Gilbert would yell his head off if he didn't get his way. The ancient woman, Polly Burtongale, made sure Gilbert always had his way.

As Mary-Shane pondered the computer screen, someone sang "He-e-l-l-l-o-o-o" right into her face and she nearly fainted. Gilbert. She stared at him, paralyzed.

He smiled charmingly. "I just keep running into you everywhere. I saw you at the zoo the other day, and now here." He looked at her closely. A *Dark Feeling* came over her. Don't you remember anything? his mouth said.

She shook. Words would not come out of her mouth.

His face looked luminous, as though she were shining on him. He licked his lips, and she noticed—yuck—white goo in the corners of his mouth, as if he never brushed his teeth. His eyes flicked over her skin with the speed of knives, as though carving off little bits of beauty here and there. "We are meant for each other." He licked his lips again. The ooze in the corners of his mouth made him seem hydrophobically mad.

She raised half her upper lip, exposing (she hoped) TEETH.

He raised his fingers. "Such pretty curls."

She brushed his hand away. "I have work to do."

"I'm sorry. Here I am, disturbing you while you do— what?"

"DEATH NOTICES," she said, trying to put a hint into it.

"You remember my name?"

She wished either he were gone or she could melt through a crack to get away.

"Gilbert," he said. "Gilbert Burtongale. I am going to own all this one day. But none of it matters. None of it." He made an apocalyptic face.

She turned away. Her fingers clicked on the keyboard. Her cheeks, as she stared at the screen, were hot points. She heard the swash of his clothing as he rose.

At 5:30, Mart Willow, Jules Loomis, and the staff all trooped past carrying their satchels and jackets, giving her surprised looks. Usually she was on her way to pick up Kippy about this time. Jules said, "They must be dying like flies out there." He passed her with a fond gaze.

The system prompted her through a series of menus. She tapped out the commands that would make the computer search through all the obituary articles for the past year, noting any that had the word 'zoo' in them, and printing on the screen before her the names and zoo jobs of the dead person(s). She waited while the cursor blinked on a dark screen. She was unsure this would lead anywhere.

"Processing..." the machine silently displayed. Still the cursor blinked. "Please wait..."

Then she sat up suddenly. The name "Washington, J.W." displayed on the screen. My God, she thought, it's picking it up. It's reading through the articles backwards, of course, and Washington was just entered today.

Folly, she thought. Probably just a blind alley. There might be one or two more, but probably nothing to interest anyone. "Smith, Johnathan, Non-Employee" the system displayed after "Washington, J.W., Maintenance." Her leg rocked rapidly forward and backward, a nervous habit of old. No more names, no more names, no more names, her mind repeated hypnotically as she tried to check her frustration.

Then the names winked into a column, one by slow one:

Appleworth, Mary Gift Shop

Jenkins, Ken Messenger

Andino, Rosario Biologist

End of Search.

"Holy Moses," she said. "It worked." Then the deeper implication struck her. "Five dead ones in the past year!" Already it dawned on her that here was her great chance. As scary and ominous as this whole thing seemed, she knew in her heart that here was the news story that would change her life.

Chapter 10.

Ann Temple brought her son Jeremy to Mary-Shane's apartment that evening. Kippy and Jeremy were astronauts in a computer game, shooting each other between the planets of an alien sun.

"We're going out!" Mary-Shane and Ann said. "Keep the door locked!"

"Okay," they singsonged disinterestedly, bleary eyes hooked on Captain Colorado, Space Hero.

At Pepper's Steak House, a billboard in the form of a giant menu advertised today's specials. Behind the billboard menu sprawled Pepper's: heavy beams smothered in ivy; lead-paned windows sautéed in shadows. Ann said: "Used to be Long Tom's."

"I remember." Mary-Shane looked up at the crossed salt and pepper shakers. "We met Frank MacLemore and Attila here when we were 18 years old."

"Can you imagine?" Ann said. "Knowing what we know now?"

Inside the restaurant, burgundy light glowed among oddly placed wooden pylons. Mary-Shane remembered that in its earliest incarnation this place had been an inexpensive family seafood restaurant. She tried to think—no, something was rushing her along, past fading images of her wild late teen years, into deeper layers of memory. Her parents had brought her here when she'd been a little girl.

"Mary-Shane?"

She felt Ann tugging at her sleeve. A cocktail waitress's airbrushed smile glowed white in the darkness. "Would you like cocktails while you wait?" the waitress said in a heightened voice, as though it were the second or third time she said it. Mary-Shane ordered wine. In the lounge, they sat on bar stools.

Ann sighed deeply. "We gotta lighten up here, Lull. What is this kinda glow you have tonight?"

Mary-Shane could still see Frank's pale young face, scruffed up with beard shadow, as he leaned toward her the very first occasion she'd seen him. They had been eyeing each other for about an hour. She could still see the hunger in his dark eyes as he inched toward her in the crowd. She remembered how her stomach had fluttered. She had not really cared that much for him at first. Until it had been too late. Once those love hormones started to circulate, it was Niagara wreathed in shattered water like smoke.

"We can always go somewhere else," Ann suggested.

"What? Oh no, it's okay. I haven't been here in a long time, but I don't want to have to leave anywhere because of old memories. C'mon, let's live it up." She raised her wine glass.

Ann raised hers, and they clinked glasses. Ann told about some software her company had just bought, and how she was enjoying using it in her accounting job.

"And I am going to write The Big Story," Mary-Shane said.

"I'm very excited for you. It's time you had some luck. You're intelligent, well-spoken..."

Mary-Shane interrupted: "...Have a nice ass."

"That too." Ann sniggered. She had a nice ass too, according to various sources over the years. She and Ann made quite a pair. They clinked glasses again. The hostess escorted them to the dining room. There, over flickering candles and mauve tablecloths, they ordered steak dinners.

"My parents brought me here once when I was small," Mary-Shane said.

"Wow, that's a priceless memory," Ann said.

Mary-Shane's father had died when she was ten. She grew silent, not wanting to drag the conversation into a sad valley. She kept the rest of the memory to herself. That memory was a sunny, semisweet piece of grayware, for her father had been killed in a plane crash over the ocean less than a month after that long ago dinner. Mary-Shane's troubles—with her mother, with herself, even with Kippy—had grown out of that tragedy.

The dinners came, and Mary-Shane and Ann ate hungrily. Mary-Shane was drinking her second glass of wine and feeling giddy. She remembered that long-ago day with her parents as though it were yesterday: Late on a Sunday afternoon. Time seemed to stand still. A big bar of sunlight leaned in through the window. My Dad was telling jokes and Mother was telling him to be careful I might understand but I was already laughing. Funny thing is they were clean jokes. Mother just didn't get them. "...Like this duck walks in the cosmetics store and points to the lipsticks. Says I'll take this one and that one and that one." Dad pointed at his nose. "And just put them on my bill."

Mary-Shane ate mechanically. She stared at the far table, her gaze truncated again and again by hustling waitresses. She tried to unravel time in her mind. She tried to remember first the lost world of Long Tom's, where in the haze of adolescent anger she'd seen herself as a Cortez in the jungles of newly discovered sexuality. Plunging deeper through the tunnel of memory—ah, there it was, the lump of pain surrounding Dad's death that had changed her life forever—and further back...to that place over there. How had it been? Not drab and dark like now or angry-smoky like the Long Tom's days... but simple, tidy, lit with light, secure, reasonable. Checkered table cloths a little girl would like, baby blue on white, with lacy frills. A fly circling over ketchup grown black and tacky on a wrinkled Spike's Family Diner menu... So that was the old name, Spike's Family Diner. She wanted to ask Ann if she remembered, but a half-chewed mouthful of steak was stuck in the corner of her mouth, laying a numbing choke-hold on the muscle there. One thing she remembered about Daddy was his eyebrows. They wobbled up and down when he told jokes. Funny, she had forgotten how fat he was. No not fat, just big and square with lots of extra flesh, but everything neatly tucked inside a clean shirt and a gray suit with wide lapels. He had pudgy white hands clasped under his belly. She hadn't realized how soft his fingers looked, as though soaked for hours in soapy water. But his eyebrows! How they moved up and down when he talked. His lips glistened wetly. His teeth glittered like pebbles. His tongue...

Mary-Shane put her fork down. She rose slowly. She took the napkin from her lap and meant to leave it on the chair but she felt it brush against her calf as it fell to the ground. A waitress excused herself and Mary-Shane nodded, barely noting the annoyed face.

"Mary-Shane. Mary-Shane! Mary-Shane?" she heard Ann's voice somewhere far away. All clinking forks fell silent. The laughing, talking, rustling of menus stopped, even a distant pounding jukebox fell silent.

"Daddy?" She stopped right before his table, pretty much where she'd sat that afternoon long ago, and looked up at him. Way up. His eyebrows waggled up and down. He bored into her with laughing eyes. His cheekbones glittered as though they had been made of glaze, like a doll's. His padded shoulders and chest heaved, no, bounced up and down. He reared his head back with laughter. Mother looked away, embarrassed. He slapped his soft white fingers on the table and turned toward Mother to see if she got the joke. Mary-Shane took a hesitant step forward. She reached out.

"Mary-Shane!"

Her heart pounded like an engine gone wild.

Closer, closer...

The eyes... ...the eyes... ...were empty as the black of space, devoid of feeling, drained of emotion... There was no speck of love in those eyes... The white fingers...

...fingers of death. The white powder of the undertakers was on them. Powder flaked and crumbled from the dark prune-like fingertips. Powder caked and piled up in the laugh lines at the edges of the face. Ceramic filled in the face that had been shattered and torn open in the airplane crash. The lips, the cheeks, the nose, eaten by fish, glittered now, a glass mask. But the eyes, oh the lovelessness in the eyes was what finally told her this was not her Daddy, this was nobody who had ever loved her, and she felt a *Dark Feeling*. Something was about to—Explode. Nothing would matter anymore. Hadn't—someone—awful—recently said that? Her mind reeled.

"Mary-Shane, are you okay?" Ann stood beside her, an arm around her. She was staring at a man in the checkered suit stared at her, puzzled. He had a coarse, kindly red face with droopy furrows.

Ann led her back to their table. "You were like in outer space there for a few minutes. I was like whoo-aa, where's this woman gone to? Welcome back."

"Thanks," Mary-Shane said. "I feel better now."

"Can I finish my steak or do you want to leave?"

"If all these people will stop staring." Mary-Shane picked at her food. The music picked up. Forks knives and spoons restarted their randomizations. Laughter and talk ballooned under the wood rafters. "Ann, I think I'm cracking up."

Eyebrow. "Oh?"

"I thought I saw my Dad sitting over there."

Fork. "Oh well, you were remembering." Mouth.

"Yes, but it was so real. It was like a nightmare, only I wasn't asleep."

Chewing. "You're under a lot of stress."

"I'll say. Look, maybe I'm really losing my marbles. You'd... you and Jeremy would look in on Kippy sometimes if I weren't here anymore, wouldn't you?"

Choke. "Mary-Shane! What ever are you talking about." Ann drank half her water. "Mary-Shane, maybe you are under a lot of stress, but I don't think you're cracking up. I've known you too long. Well, unless you've changed somehow the past few years, and I don't feel that. I remember how nervous you used to be when Frank and Attila were out drinking."

Attila had been Ann's boyfriend, Frank's favorite biker buddy. Mary-Shane could picture Frank and Attila, tangled in a bloody ball of flesh and torn clothing, pale dead faces staring out from the mangled steel of Attila's chopped Harley. She cringed, hoping this would not bring on another vivid illusion. But it didn't.

"So far this has been one really WEIRD evening," Ann said as they sat in her car outside. "You ARE going to be OKAY, aren't you?"

Mary-Shane touched her head with both hands. "I'm going to call my shrink."

"I think that's a good idea, Mary-Shane."

"I thought I was done with him years ago, but here I am again. Fucked up as always. Ann—?" She turned toward her friend. "You were with me years ago. What happened?"

Ann's face was dark and hard.

Mary-Shane gripped her friend's arm. "Please, if you know anything, tell me."

Ann looked like a different person, carved from stone. "It's just as well you don't remember."

Chapter 11.

Next day, Obits was a bitch as usual. She made her deadline and then called the M.E. No autopsies had been done on the four zoo employees; dead end.

Then she entered the newspaper's library, directly adjacent to where she and Wiz had their desks. A newspaper's library, known in the trade as "The Morgue," contained thousands of prefab obits on famous people currently alive. Background on nationally or internationally famous celebrities, politicians, and so forth had been provided by the wire services over the years. Generations of San Tomas Herald reporters had compiled data on locally known people, like the Burtongales—no inside skinny, no damaging info, of course, just p.r. When a famous person died, you printed a few paragraphs with the cause of death, added the canned info, and presto, you had a story that might be pages long, but instant in the making. Mary-Shane did not expect much information on the dead zoo employees or on theologian Smith, but it was worth checking. She slid microfiche sheets through the light and magnifying lens one by one: Washington, J.W.; Appleworth, Mary; Jenkins, Ken; and Andino, Rosario; but there was no listing for any of the names. Should there have been? She read her hard copies of the obits over again. Jenkins had been 49, Andino 53, and Appleworth 27. In fact, J. W. Washington had been 57. One thing they all had in common was that they had not died of old age.

She called the zoo. Dr. Chatfield expressed delight to hear from her. She asked: "I was going over some obits, and I noticed that five zoo employees died during the past several months, suddenly, in the prime of life. Do you feel there might be a connection? Maybe an environmental hazard?"

"Coincidence, Miss MacLemore. Pure and simple."

"It's a mortality rate like Waterloo."

"You're not planning to do a sensational expose, are you?"

"No, but even if I were it would not get past the editorial staff."

"I will be happy to escort you around the zoo if you'd like to do a nice series on some of the animals. The paper does it like clockwork about every three years, and it's time."

"Thanks, I appreciate that." She thought, hanging up, well, maybe some little stories might get me in the back door; but right now I think I might have a big story. She started contacting next of kin. Mary Appleworth's widower, John, a garage mechanic, was sympathetic but not very helpful. "I've got three kids, and it's all I can do to make ends meet. There is some insurance money due, and I was told by the lawyer to say nothing or I might lose the money. Sorry." He hung up.

Rosemary Jenkins, widow of Jenkins, blubbered a little bit. "They were pretty forceful."

"Who, Mrs. Jenkins?"

"The lawyers. They told me I'd have to keep my mouth shut or I could be sued and lose the insurance money."

Bulloney, Mary-Shane thought. "What's the name of the insurance firm?" But Mrs. Jenkins had hung up.

Jesus Andino, a doctor and the widower of Rosario Andino, hung up after providing the name of the law firm.

J.W. Washington's widow was too hysterical to make sense, so a sister spoke for her: "Yeah, there were lawyers in and out, you can be sure. They were talking a lot of money, but they said we got to be very careful who we talk to, or the insurance might not pay up. Who did you say you work for?"

Mary-Shane hung up.

The law firm was Kane, King, and Kahn. Mary-Shane looked their number up in the phone book.

"Burtongale Building," a receptionist answered.

Instantly, Mary-Shane knew where the law firm was; in that twelve story brick office tower, nearly a century old, owned of course by the family it was named after. "Please connect me with Kane, King, and Kahn."

"They have separate lines, Miss. Which one do you wish to speak with?"

Mary-Shane thought fast. "The one that's married to a Burtongale."

The receptionist said innocently. "That would be King. Just a moment please."

Amazing. The Burtongale family seemed to overflow with women, and the men they brought in all occupied points of power in San Tomas. She wondered who King was married to.

A woman answered. "Janet King."

Well, swallow my words. A cousin of Gilbert Burtongale, as anyone in San Tomas knew, but now the connection seemed more vivid to Mary-Shane. "Ms. King, I have a friend who recently passed away at the zoo, an employee named J. W. Washington. I was wondering if you were handling the case."

"Yes, I am," snapped Ms. King. "What is your interest in the matter?" Ms. King sounded like a thorough bitch.

"I was also stung by the spiders, but I didn't die. I lost the use of my left arm though, and I would like to sue."

A big long sigh. "Very well, Miss..."

"Chang. Phoebe Chang. Just out of curiosity, who is the insurance carrier?"

Hesitation. "American Canoga Insurance. Why?"

"Just wondering."

"I see. How soon can you come see us, Miss Chang?"

"How about this afternoon?"

"Fine." Sound of pencil scratching on paper. "Two o'clock?"

"Oh yes, that's fine."

"Do you know where we are located? Can you find us?"

"Yes, of course. Unless my condition gets worse. You know, blindness. Further paralysis. But I'll call in that case." Mary-Shane hung up. Tapped her pencil, staring at the phone. Then called Information to get number and address of American Canoga Insurance. Mary-Shane called the number.

"Burtongale Building," the familiar receptionist said.

Mary-Shane hung up.

She raced into Jules's office and closed the door. He looked up, puffing on a fresh pipe and raising quizzical brows.

"Jules! I think I'm onto a major story. There has been a string of deaths at the zoo, and I think they are being hushed up by the Burtongale family."

Jules listened patiently. "Mary-Shane, you can be a great reporter some day. There's one more thing you need to prove."

"What's that?"

"The common sense to realize that you work for the Burtongales and they will fire you if you so much as put a word of this on paper. Now go on, tag along with Perry and stay out of trouble."

But Perry had left for the afternoon and Mary-Shane was too frustrated to stay at her desk and get ready for the next day's obits. On a whim, she called the information operator in Oak Ridge, Tennessee and asked for the phone number of Whitbread Baptist Seminary. She spoke with a Dr. Philomel Crosby, Professor of Bible Studies. Mr. Crosby was a young man, and taken with her voice. "I'm fishing for a story," she told him. "The man died here, and it was all so sudden that we buried him without much of a story."

"Well," Dr. Crosby said, "we will miss Dr. Smith. He was something of a firebrand, to be sure."

"What do you mean, a firebrand?"

"Well, in his later years he became more and more taken up—some would say obsessed—with the idea of making Christianity as concrete as, say, science or mathematics. He wanted to PROVE"(she could hear the ringing of Crosby's voice in some church rafter)"that God and Satan are real."

"And this brought him to San Tomas?" she asked.

"It's a rather odd story."

"Try me."

"Dr. Smith was here a long time, and he did a lot for the seminary. One of the many legacies he left us was his Museum of Satan. If you're ever out this way, you should stop by and see it."

"What is in this museum?"

"Things of God and things of the Devil. Ordinary folks may scoff, Miss MacLemore, but good Christians take the Word of God quite literally. When he says there is a Hell, you better believe there is. But the good news is, when he says there is a Heaven, YOU better BELIEVE there is a heaven!"(how the rafters rang!)"In this museum, Miss MacLemore, the good Dr. Smith was gathering artifacts from around the world. Voodoo dolls from Africa, evil statues from several ancient empires, a Satanic Bible from England...well, you get the idea."

"You're putting me on."

"Absolutely not."

"This would make a lurid story, if a person wanted to—"

He said sharply: "We have had requests like that, but we stay away from them."

"I work," she said, biting her tongue, "for a legitimate newspaper. All I am looking for is a little background. So what does this museum have to do with why Smith was in San Tomas?"

"We have kept this out of the papers, Miss MacLemore, but Dr. Smith believed the devil lives in the San Tomas Zoo. How ironic that he died there the way he did. To bring Satan out of hiding, he took with him one of the artifacts in his museum: a wooden statuette of a West African rain devil. That's a demon who makes the animals in the jungle go into the villages and kill people. His reasoning was that if he could prove there is Satan, then there must be God. He was on a divine mission, Miss MacLemore, and maybe it was Satan who tore his heart out because he got too close to the truth."

"Thank you," Mary-Shane said. Another story Jules would quash if I even mentioned it to him.

"Did you want the correct spelling on my name?" Dr. Crosby asked.

"No." She let the receiver slip quietly into its cradle. The image of a rainy jungle, and beasts coming out to kill people, haunted her.

Chapter 12.

Saturday evening, Mary-Shane and Ann got together at Crank's.

Mary-Shane parked in the brightly lit, most fashionable part of Canoga Avenue. Several blocks over, the age-green copper spires of the Burtongale Building taunted her, lit by spotlights and flying a large American flag that gently luffed in the wind. Ann said: "C'mon, let's make eyes and have eyes made at us." Crank's was a popular dress-up bar along Canoga Avenue. They walked up granite steps to a warm oak doorway piped with shining brass tubes. Husky blond men with Crank's logo T-shirts and suspenders checked ID. "That's a nice start," Ann whispered to Mary-Shane while glancing back at a muscular bicep. A thin man in a business suit, too old and not right, said something charming to Mary-Shane. She raked him with The Icy Look, and the glitter went out of his smile, like a neon light with a rock through it.

"Not too crowded," Ann said. They found a small table set into the wall. A waitress in a mini-tux, tray held high, took their orders of house white.

Mary-Shane thumped Anne's back. "Good choice, Beagle Face. Glad we decided to dress up."

"Thanks, Rat Breath. Good to party a little again."

"You call this partying? Geez, I would never have imagined, when I was chain-smoking Camels and swilling beer with Frank and the boys, that in ten years I'd be sitting in a place like this wondering if I should sip Chablis or Burgundy." The interior was all mirrors, but cool because the light had an understated bluish brightness that made faces and hands appear fluorescent. Brass tubing arced among graceful potted palms. The mirrors, coated with art-deco figures in white latex, gave an impression of boundless space: trippy space, pounded by heavy speakers extruding a thick paste of metal-sounding music. Crank's was hip, and hip meant music without deafness. Talk, however aerated, was in. So was Looking.

"That one," Ann said, pointing. "There. No, there."

Mary-Shane finally saw him, a man with a nice smile who seemed entranced by his heavy blonde companion, listening to her every word. "Nice," Mary-Shane said. "He doesn't look scroungy, so probably no drugs. Trim, so he must work out. Isn't swilling his drink, hasn't scratched his balls."

Mary-Shane and Ann clinked glasses. The clinking caught the eyes of the man with the blonde, and a look of startled speculation crossed his upper face, changing the eyes, while the smile remained frozen. Watch it," Mary-Shane said. "He's a faker. He's seen you."

Ann was smiling across the room, nodding.

"Oh Jesus. I knew something was going to happen tonight. Fast work there, Beagle-Face."

Ann put her glass down with a knowing, secret smile. "I just enjoy the game a little bit. Try myself to see if I'm rusty."

"I'm going to the ladies' room," Mary-Shane said.

"Wish me luck. Hey whattaya know. He's telling her he must go to the bathroom." She pulled in her chin and made a deep Transylvanian voice: "Dahlink, I must go shake my hose."

Laughing, Mary-Shane escaped just before the guy returned; he glided in like a black and white fish, angling slightly toward Ann with an expressionless but appraising look at Mary-Shane. What a feat, Mary-Shane thought, he should be in a circus. How could a person present two different faces to two different persons at the same time? He curved in like a dolphin, fins laid back and relaxed as in a dancer's bow. With one side of his face he looked suggestively into Ann's eyes while with the other side of his face he sized up Mary-Shane.

She picked up her purse and threaded her way through the crowd.

That was when she saw Lt. Vic Lara of the San Tomas Police, whom she had met at the Medical Examiner's morgue, and her breath caught. Lara's eyes, like pencils shading in a drawing, started at her toes and moved up to her curls. His eyes had a warm, cocky twinkle, and his chin moved back in a smile. "Haven't we met somewhere before?"

"Maybe."

"Let me buy you a drink," Lara said.

"I'm with a friend."

"Now are you cold or just shy?"

"Oh why not?" Mary-Shane said.

"Great." He held the chair for her. Glasses came: wine for her, scotch for him.

"So we meet again," she said feeling witless. His eyes, when he looked at her a certain way, reminded her of old pain and she wished he'd quit doing that.

He moved a toothpick around on his lips. "I was kind of surprised to see you're on the police beat. Gets pretty gory."

"I quickly noticed that somehow. How do you deal with it every day, Lieutenant?" It occurred to her that this man could be a source of valuable information for her news reporting, not to be mention the big story she was developing—if only she wasn't so thoroughly scared of him and yet attracted to him..

"Vic. Call me Vic. Hey, do I get the feeling I'm being interviewed?"

She folded her hands on the table. "Do reporters make you nervous?"

He slapped his forehead. "Reporters. Naw. Pretty girls. Women who are sure of themselves and stare into your soul. Like you."

She laughed. "Very theatrical. Must be the Latin blood."

"Now there you've hit it right on the head. I'm Mexican-Puerto Rican." He made sawing motions with his forearms. "Salsa, baby. Sabes?"

"I like a little salsa now and then. Say if you trashed that toothpick I probably could see into your soul."

The toothpick sailed away in an arc. He opened his mouth wide.

She looked in. "Well, you have a lot of fillings..."

He snapped his mouth shut. "What are you, a dentist now?"

She laughed. "Just a struggling obituary writer."

He placed his hands over hers. "I was going to ask you for your phone number."

"You presume greatly, Lt. Lara. Here, I have something in my purse that I want to show you." She placed it before him.

"A tooth?" Vic asked, regarding the object.

She said: "I found it outside the zoo." There was a ringing in her ears, a rush of blood, and she wasn't sure why she was doing this.

"Oh?" He placed a new toothpick carefully in the "o" of his lips while his eyes appraised her. Again, that feeling scraped her soul. What was it Vic Lara did to her? He looked at the tooth but did not touch it. "Now why did you pick up this old thing? Isn't it better to let old things lie where they are?"

"You too, huh?"

"Wait," he said raising a hand as though he were cleaving a pound of truth. "Why were you wandering around outside the zoo?" His eyes looked surprised and interested.

"I wasn't wandering," she said, "I was throwing up."

He stared.

"I was grossed out by the smell of Smith's blood."

"You're going to be police reporter. Get used to it."

"I'm working on it, Vic. I'm with you here, aren't I?"

He stopped laughing. "You could do worse."

She whacked him. "I know. Stop treating me like a sister, will you?"

He reached for her hand. "Okay." He helicoptered close with puckered lips.

She felt starved and wanted to take him home to bed but she put her finger over his lips. "First things first, Vic."

He sat back. "All right, tell me exactly where you found this tooth."

"About a thousand feet from the entrance. On a bald spot of sand and scrub."

He nodded. "And?"

She looked at the tooth, confused. "I thought it might be important. A man murdered a thousand feet away. How on earth does an adult tooth..." She looked up, suddenly at a loss.

"You said murdered. This is getting very interesting." He yawned, still not touching the tooth.

"Blow it out your ear," she said. She swept the tooth into her purse and rummaged for the list of names. "I had something else to show you. I was going to call you. At work. Business only." She showed him her piece of paper. "I did some checking and found out that these people have died suddenly while working at the zoo during the past year."

He took the list and this time, his jaws genuinely slid apart. "How did you do this?"

Ann waved to her from a distance.

"Excuse me a minute." She hurried to Ann's side. "What trouble are you getting in now? And where's the shark man?"

"Oh, him. The dolphin. He was going to drive his wife home and then..."

"Wife! I had a feeling."

"And then he was going to come back for me. I told him to take a hike."

"Can you wait just a few minutes? I met a policeman I know and I want to ask him some questions about a case."

Ann laughed outright. Then she frowned. "You're serious. You, Mary-Shane MacLemore, are meeting with a cop to discuss a case."

"A murder. Hang in, I'll just see Vic for a few minutes."

"Oh, Vic is it now?" Ann ribbed.

When she returned to the bar, Lara was leaning his chin on his hand and looking down at the piece of paper. "Mary-Shane..." He swallowed hard. "This is classified police information. Where did you get it?"

"I looked things up."

"This is very sensitive information."

"For whom? The Burtongales?"

"Mary-Shane, I'm impressed."

"Oh?" She sipped her wine, secretly gratified that he was impressed with her research. Hell, she was.

He took her hand and squeezed it with just enough force to hurt.

"Ouch, Vic."

"Honey, don't look any further into this matter, okay? Please." He leaned close and she could smell the smoke and scotch on his breath. He glanced down at her hand and when he saw that he had hurt it he cradled it like a wounded bird in both of his hard hands and blew on it.

She got chills up and down her back. Her hair tingled on the nape of her neck. She pulled her hands away and hid them under the table, sealed over by her breasts. "Vic, I need a break. If I want to make it as a reporter, I need a big story. I'm not going to back away from this."

There was theater on his face as his gaze bounced from wall to wall as if trying to catch something elusive. "Madre. This woman cannot let things rest when I tell her."

"I am NOT one of your giggly little *mujeres*, Vic."

"So much I gather. With a name like a cowboy, nothing surprises me."

She ran through her standard explanation about her name, knowing it by rote so well that she knew when to stop for breaths. "My Mother was Doris Mary-Shane and my Daddy was Wayne Lull. I was baptized Mary Lull. Daddy thought that was so awful he stuck in Mother's maiden name, so I became Mary-Shane Lull. I dropped the Mary; and I've kept my married (widowed) name, so now I'm Mary-Shane MacLemore, and I like it that way."

He made a face. "Why not Martha? That's a nice name. Or Linda? You know Linda means beautiful?" He leaned close.

She leaned her face close to his. "You know Mary-Shane means mysterious, sensuous, and intriguing?"

He closed his eyes. "I could easily be convinced." He opened his eyes.

She gathered her purse. "Thanks for the drink."

"The number," he said.

"Oh yes." She tore a deposit slip from her bank book.

"Maybe we can work together," he said, folding the slip very carefully. "Maybe we can get our arms around this situation."

Chapter 13.

Wiz felt a quiet fury. Bishop Donald Mulcahy stood with his back to her, overlooking the basilica gardens as night fell. He started to light a fresh cigar but dropped the silver lighter, which thudded softly into the rug between his black shoes. Wiz's glasses slipped down along her nose. "For the last time, Bishop, I want to know if you'll get an exorcist."

"No!" He whirled and faced her. His steel rims glinted.

"I happen to know you've had an exorcist here for years. Why is it such a secret?"

The bishop rolled his gaze upward. "I don't care to debate theology with you this evening."

"Because you are just plain scared shitless?"

"I am scared. Yes. Scared to roll the Church back into the Middle Ages, back to a time when people were afraid to set foot out the door at night for fear there was a demon behind every rock."

Gotcha. "Isn't that how it is today, bishop?"

"Yes, yes, very clever of you, but don't you see, the demons today are human, just as they were in the Middle Ages."

Darn, turned it around. "Please!"

"Miss Chickowitz, I cannot offer my support."

"That does it." Feeling bloody anger beating in her ears, ignoring his mangling of her last name, Wiz pushed her glasses up for the third or fourth time. "People have died because of that thing in the zoo. I won't let this go on." Ignoring the last glimpse of him, darkly shaking his head, she stormed down the carpeted halls of the chancery and out the front door with a bang.

She found Jules Loomis still waiting in his car in the shadows of an ancient oak tree. He was just attempting to relight his pipe as Wiz threw herself into the passenger seat and pulled the door shut with a thump. "He said no."

Jules got the pipe going and the car filled with smoke. Wiz opened her window and made coughing noises and fanning motions. He said sorry and put the pipe face-down in the ashtray. He drove away slowly. "We figured that's what he'd say, didn't we?"

She shot back: "I was willing to give him a chance to listen."

"Are you sure you don't want to just tell the authorities what you think?"

"The authorities? That's the Burtongale family in this town. No thanks!" The growing night slid past, cool and deep with vegetal scents. Trees sighed in the wind, their dry leaves sweeping almost at ground level as though helping the roots look for water. Wiz waved briefly toward Jules after getting out. The dully gleaming sides of the Bronco, the shimmering opacity of the windshield, were a cipher. As she approached the service entrance of the zoo, she heard him start the engine and drive away.

A threat loomed; in response, a command crackled between the ancient stones with waves of blue light that roiled back and forth: Kill the angry one. Send our spirit into the night. Let it find what it needs to tear the soul from the angry one. High up in the cat house, a jaguar named Lilly stirred in her sleep. She padded out of her cave to listen. To try and sense what it was that had disturbed her. She slurped water from her pond. Stifling a cry of pain and rage, she felt as though something were tearing her apart into three pieces from inside.

Three shadowy jaguars pranced meaningfully toward the high walls. As their matrix rolled over, dying, the three copies of her sailed through the air in a fifty foot leap and landed on the street outside. Snarling. Tails twitching. Three black jaguars sliced through the darkness, searching. Their lean backs flowed with muscularity. Their loose, hungry bellies swayed with each leap, each jumping thump. Somewhere an owl hooted. The three cats ignored it, listening intently, smelling the air. Their eyes floated warily, drinking in the crazy light that was neither night nor day and charged them to manic pitch. Their tails flicked like whips. Their paws thudded imperceptibly, avoiding dry leaves and twigs that might crackle and give them away. Their feline faces turned from side to side, seeking...

No looking back now, Wiz thought. Dressed in dark clothing, she clung to the shadows under the trees. Heart pounding, she came to small utility door. Glancing right and left over her shoulder, she used a stolen (the Green Witches had connections) key and let herself into the loading area of the supply warehouse. Quickly, a blur, she faded among the trees.

She grasped the iron crucifix in the sash of her skirt, willing any stray evil spirits to confront her. Thus far, the night did not answer. Determinedly she reached under her belt and squeezed the contents of the small bag she carried: A gold coin, a silver coin, a smooth round pebble, a match, a vial of water, several chicken bones and feathers, a matchbox filled with the ashes of a small sandalwood cross burned on an east-facing hillside during a full moon.

She felt her feet carry her on silent night wings, like the messenger Mercury for whom the silver coin in her pouch was meant. From a small container she scooped a witches' paste which she rubbed on the tip of her tongue, leaving echo tastes of licorice and mint.

One after another, the zoo paths she took crackled as her toes barely touched the ground. She felt the White Magic and Divine Power sweep her along toward a great combat. She felt full of Jesus and the other gods. She felt drunk with righteousness.

Wiz felt danger and spread her arms. Let it find her. She grasped the crucifix in one hand and the small pouch of fetish items in the other. This was her plan: To summon the demon, then banish him from this place forever!

Wiz stopped. Had there been a thump, a crackle, like cats landing after a jump? She heard only the wind. But that was her signal to begin the combat. She began her ritual, drawing with chalk on the street. The chalk broke, and she barked her hand on biting gravel. On her knees, she sucked the scrape wound, tasting blood. So much the better! Wind whipped at her scarf. Her uncombed gray-brown hair blew around her head. She brushed it out of her eyes as she resumed drawing with a salvaged piece of chalk: The moon at the left hand of the Crucified, the sun in His face, a star on His right hand. That would be the star of Bethlehem. It would also be a minor solar emblem for Amon.

She began to pray: "Our Father Who art in Heaven, Hollow is Thy Name..." As she prayed she continued her drawings. The wind threw up a faint dust that hovered like a cloud filled with saffron light. Leaves, sticks, twigs were stirring, as if trying to arrange and rearrange themselves on the chalk markings. She huffed breathlessly, bending over the Sun.

She noticed that four demons were at hand. Three huge black cats leapt into the clearing, six forelegs extended all at once in a magnificent troika. And a ...man, swathed in a wind-roiled cloak... Knowing that the combat was about to be joined, Wiz laughed as they circled around. This was good already. She felt the power inside her. She was ten, twenty feet tall, holding her arms out like one crucified. The three jaguars and the man seemed separate but equal parts of a greater whole, a stage play of doom closing noiselessly in on her. Their silence was so eerie she was sure they were an illusion. She hunched down again to finish her Pentagram which would be a Star of David with a circle on the inside. As she did so, she performed the Rally. "Michael the Archangel, and all the hosts of Heaven, we summon you to protect us from Satan and all the evil spirits who roam the world, seeking the ruin of souls."

The black cats circled warily, two to one side, one to the other. Surely this man must be Satan or some very important devil. Then surely her spells were working! Elated, Wiz ignored the demons, knowing the devil liked to play with illusions. "Lord Satan, Dark Hand of Night, you are summoned to send forth your demons and evil spirits that are afflicting this place so that they may be defeated and cast out."

The cats leapt close like dancers.

Her heart thrashed so that it made her ribs shudder. She dropped the chalk and clutched her chest. But then wasn't this exactly what the King of Demons wanted? Staggering slightly, she bent over to pick up the chalk. The ritual must not be interrupted. She fell to her hands and knees, weakened by waves of darkness and nausea that filled her brain, alternating with more colorful waves of mauve, dull brass, wine red...

She tried to utter a cry, but it was stifled by several great weights hitting her all at once. Pain filled her, and she struggled to turn over onto her back, to sit up. She tried to wave an arm to fend them off. The arm was gripped painfully, torn back and forth in bone-jarring slashing motions. She smelled a rankness of spit and licked cat hair.

There was salvation at hand. There was a light that fell out of space. There was an explosion and the Book of Revelations opened before her. She cried soundlessly, reaching with a hand that wasn't there. She heard a tearing sound, and only dimly realized it was the sound of her own flesh.

She hovered in the air, safe now, and watched three black jaguars mulling over several dark bundles of rags. She was safe now, and could rest at last.

One by one, the cats winked out of existence. But the man put on rubber gloves. Why rubber gloves?

But Wiz was past curiosity, and turned away...

...rolling like a cork swollen in water...

...splashes...then darkness...

She was walking... down a long corridor... into ?a ship. Her hands, as she looked at them, turned bright blue. Ahead of her, one or two other bright blue persons walked toward...

"Hello," said a blue man with a nice smile. "My name is Freddy with a y. What's yours?"

...Several dark shapes loomed near a doorway shimmering with something like heat or fire. One by one, they pushed the numbly walking humans into the flames...

WE ARE SAFE NOW the pilot signaled to Gilbert.

Wallace Burtongale hurried out of the shadows carrying a machete and some bags.

Gilbert lit a cigarette and knelt by the body. Squinting, smoke in his eyes, he began by hacking up her arms. "The Pilot was in my head."

Wallace touched his son. "This has to end."

Gilbert hacked at her legs. The cigarette wobbled. "There are enough pieces now. It will happen soon. The ship will fly again. We will be free."

"What about this nosy little female reporter?" Wallace asked.

Gilbert looked up. He flicked his cigarette. "She's special," he said. "I get her last, as my prize."

Wallace expressionlessly held open a bag, and Gilbert threw in a foot.

A strangled cry awakened Roger Chatfield in his bedroom a block from the zoo, and he wasn't sure if it was his own or someone else's cry.

It almost sounded like a big cat. Or a woman; hoarse; a smoker?

He lay for some seconds in darkness, holding the sheet close to his chin, and groggily teetered between sleep and wakefulness.

He listened for another cry, but none came.

On the sleep side, he grasped questioningly after the fleeting after-image of... something... cats. The dream picture glared at him, then wrinkled into distortions like the folds in a curtain, then fell apart like dust in a sunbeam.

But it was four a.m.

No sunbeams.

He swung out of bed, rubbed his head, and then staggered off in t-shirt and boxer shorts to check on Rudy and Elisa.

The hardwood floor of 501 Lilac, one of the Burtongale family houses, was cold and unkind to his feet. He curled his toes up and walked on the balls of his feet. Never, he had vowed, would a man who had dug in the scorpion-infested sands of the Negev, who had used a shovel to fight off bandits swooping in on camels in the night, who had stepped into the throne-chamber of a dead king, never would such a man purchase slippers at the mall.

Elisa, 13, slept peacefully. Her hands and feet looked big and unfeminine, like the paws of a puppy that was still to grow. But her skin, even in the banana glow of the streetlight outside, looked smooth like honey. Her long mahogany hair lay like an open fan on the pillow. Her relaxed face presented ambiguous suggestions, from round infant cheeks to bony adolescent jaw to mature, hollowing eyes.

Rudy, 9, was also asleep. Perhaps the cry in the night had been his, for Rudy had always been a restless sleeper, and increasingly so in recent months. Whereas Elisa could almost climb out of bed in the morning and fold the sheets over and the bed was still made, Rudy managed to rumple up his sheets. Sometimes in his sleep, he even managed to pull the fitted sheet from under the mattress corners. He now lay on the bare mattress. He gripped his pillow against his chest with his fists. His head was upturned and his mouth was slightly open as though he were pushing himself up from a dream of drowning.

Gently, Chatfield covered his son with a blanket. He propped the boy into a more comfortable position with his head on the pillow. As he did so, the vacuous faintly alarmed cast of Rudy's cheeks changed to one of sleepy satisfaction. Nuzzling, he smacked his lips and settled into a deeper sleep.

Outside, a bird chittered in a bush.

Chatfield touched Rudy's blond crew cut and then stole softly out of the room.

Chapter 14.

Kippy dawdled over his breakfast. "You screamed again last night," he said with a mouthful of cornflakes.

"I'm sorry, I can't help it. Come on, we've got to get going," Mary-Shane urged. Feeling lazy and immobile, she bit off a piece of sugared and buttered raisin bread toast with one hand while twiddling a pencil in the other.

"You know, Mom, Fred Civitelli has been taking piano since he was six and now he's going to start a rock band. Can I take guitar lessons?"

She shrugged. "I'll tell you as soon as I finish balancing my checkbook."

The phone rang. It was Howard Berger. Her stomach twisted. "Mary-Shane, how have you been." He had a clear, intelligent voice, now with mixed shades of hesitation and desire.

"Fine, Howard. How's your cat?" She tried to remember its name, a beautiful Angora with silky white fur and a pretty little face filled with feline and female expressions.

He laughed. "Bitty? Oh, she's ... around. She was trying to avoid another cat and bumped into a rose thorn and got an abscess, so that just cost me a hundred bucks at the vet's. How's Kippy?"

"Fine." To think she had been intimate with this man. She hated his game: he seemed to always think of the two in parallel, his cat and her son. He seemed to be signaling, look, here's how well I take care of my cat, just marry me and you'll see how well I'll take care of...

"I called because I know it's time for his physical."

Damn you, Howard, she thought. "He's... fine. He's sitting right here and we're having breakfast."

Chastened, he said: "I figured you would be. I don't want to bother you at work, and you don't seem to return my calls."

"I can't talk right now, Howard."

"I understand." His voice thickened. "All right. Okay. Look. Here's the deal. Here's what I think. I'm going to ask you if you'd like to meet me for lunch."

"Thanks, Howard, but we've been around and around on this, and I don't want to hurt your feelings, but the answer is still no."

"All right, Mary-Shane. I'm going to cast off. Thanks."

Quickly she hung the phone up.

"Howard?" Kippy said.

She tore off another bite of toast, picked up the pencil, looked at the checkbook, and threw the pencil down.

"He's creepy," Kippy said.

"Thanks, Kippy. I needed that."

"I'm just trying to keep you out of trouble, Mom. If you marry someone, I've got to either leave home or live with the guy, so I've got a personal interest."

"I promised you, Kippy, I would never bring a man in this house that you don't feel comfortable with. Now put the lid on and get the lead out and get ready for school or no TV. tonight. Move!"

On the way to St. Andrew's Grammar School, they stopped for gas at a corner station. Kippy went inside to buy cupcakes. Mary-Shane paid, then went outside to pump gas.

The pump was slow. The numbers dribbled by, and she looked at her watch. Kippy was taking a long time. A blue van was parked at the next pump island. She hooked the pump handle on automatic and sauntered back, craning her neck to peer around the van.

The windows were opaque. Vague figures moved inside. Mary-Shane frowned, unable to locate her son's silhouette.

The pump clicked on, spilling numbers, and she kept an eye on it. She kept the other eye on the broad picture window.

No Kippy. How long could it take to buy cupcakes?

Click... click... click... went the pump. At last, the amount she had paid for. The pump slowed. It stopped. She pulled it out, replaced it on its holder, replaced the cap on her gas tank...

The van was still there. She dodged around it and between two cars.

Just then Kippy came out with his cupcakes.

Her heart sank. Gilbert Burtongale was with him, tall and wild-haired. Gilbert's eyes were filled with a crazed light veiled by friendliness.

"Hi Mom," Kippy said. He had just eaten one cupcake.

"Oh ho!" Gilbert exclaimed, seeing her.

Mary-Shane was furious. "Kippy, come on, we've got to hurry."

"Lady Luck strikes again!" Gilbert exulted.

This was no coincidence. He must have been following her. Men had done that before. Followed her around, seeking the excuse to casually fall into conversation. She could see it from his glance. "In the car," she commanded Kippy.

Gilbert stuck his hands in his jeans and shuffled up close, looking down at her, smiling. He said softly: "Come on, Mary, don't be hard on me."

For a moment, she forgot that her maiden name was Mary S. Lull. Then spat back: "My name isn't Mary."

"All I want is a chance. Think of all I can give you." Tiny amounts of foam or chalk or something slimy white, like runoff from a drainpipe, coated the corners of his mouth, making her gag.

She wiped the back of her hand against her forehead, feeling faint, feeling perhaps the onset of the *Dark Feeling*. She meant to say something piquant, but words jammed in her throat and she whirled, running back to the car.

"...least talk to me!" he was hollering with the first underlines of annoyance. His eyes moved from clever to hurt. She popped the clutch and roared out of the station.

"Did I do something wrong?" Kippy asked.

She shook her head. "No. No you didn't. I'm sorry I yelled at you. I think that man has been following us. He scares me."

"He does?" Kippy, mouth full of cupcake, turned his head. "Hey look. He's getting into that blue van."

"Yeah. So?"

"That van was parked on the corner by our apartment the other day. I know because he has a zoo decal on the rear bumper. Jeremy and I both noticed it. It's the panda one, the only one missing in my collection."

Chapter 15.

"Chalk marks," Roger Chatfield repeated in the morning as he strode into his office at the zoo.

"Yes, I thought I should catch you as you came in." Wallace Burtongale III poured coffee from the silver service. He was a short, pot-bellied man of sixty, with watery blue eyes and a ring of white hair around a burned red spot. His mouth curved down sourly. An aggressive Burtongale chin added vinegar. "Don't know the details yet. Someone broke into the zoo last night and drew weird symbols on the street near the pagoda." He yawned.

Chatfield threw his worn leather briefcase under his desk and sat down. He steepled his fingers and looked through them as if they were a gun sight. "Any dead theologians this time?"

Wallace shook his head as he took the lid off of a porcelain sugar bowl and click-clicked little silver tongs over the bowl. "Thank God, no. No bodies." Two lumps. Plop, plop. Wallace stirred. "This time however, it's inside the zoo. You know what that means. We cannot allow any snooping around. We can't get caught up in any scandal."

"Isn't that kind of paranoid?" Chatfield asked.

"No," Burtongale said. Relations between Chatfield and his boss had been deteriorating for reasons Chatfield could not put his finger on. Chatfield surreptitiously slid his upper middle desk drawer open an inch and just with the tips of his fingers touched the thick Kraft parcel he kept there for just such moments. It felt bulky and reassuring to the touch.

"Those are my and Miss Polly's explicit feelings, especially if that police reporter and nosy young woman come around again."

Roger sat back and laughed. "Wallace, they're from your paper. You own it. You own them. So squash the story. Isn't that what we always do?"

Wallace sat down wheezily before the desk. "I'm afraid there is one more piece of bad news, Roger. It's your favorite cat Lilly. The Peruvian jaguar."

Chatfield laid his hands on his desk, palms down, and sat upright. "No."

"I'm afraid so. The cat keepers found her dead this morning. No sign of struggle, poisoning, anything." Chatfield felt sick. Five years of work down the drain, the breeding project... "I'm sorry, Roger. I knew you'd take it hard."

Twenty minutes later, when Chatfield saw the cat, he closed his eyes. "Ouch." He felt as though he'd been hit. The cat had been a special breeder on loan from Peru. There was a whole wall of baby pictures of her, with her keepers, in the cat house.

"Call the vet," he said thickly.

"Already did," said a handler. "She's on her way to pick Lilly up for necropsy. Do you want us to, um, let you know—?"

"I'll be in my office." A tear stung each eye, and he brushed them away. He knelt down. The cat lay stretched out as if running, on her side, stiff with rigor mortis. The muzzle was slightly open and the tongue hung out, turned toward the ground. Her eyes were open. Faint wind stirred the tips of black hair. Back in his office, Chatfield put his face in his hands and thought about the future. "Dr. Chatfield," the secretary said over the intercom, "Are you back? I have someone on the line and I was just about to tell her to call back another time."

"I'll take it." He rose, slammed the door shut, and landed back in his chair. Disgustedly, he pressed the intercom button.

There was a pause. Then: "Hello?"

A familiar voice. Sweet somehow. Like a sour candy. "Yes," he prodded.

"Dr. Chatfield?"

He slowly began to smile. "Yes, how are you."

"Oh fine. How did you know it was me?"

He sat back feeling a flood of warmth. "Somehow I just did."

"That's nice," the MacLemore woman said with a surprised tone, pleased at being remembered. "I had a note from Jules Loomis that you wanted someone to do some color on the zoo."

"Yes, that was my suggestion. Suppose we meet over lunch."

Flustered. "I, well, yes, that would, I'm buried in, er, articles here, but..."

"What about tomorrow? My day here is rather full."

"Let's plan on it, unless something comes up."

"Thanks, Miss MacLemore. I'll look forward to it."

Funny woman, he thought pressing the button. She had hung up without another word. The room shook again as that pesky military plane murmured in low and thundered overhead before resuming its circling high up over San Tomas Peninsula.

Chapter 16.

Ears burning, Mary-Shane hung up the phone. There was something about Roger Chatfield she did not like, but she wasn't sure what it was that bothered her.

By eleven, most of the work was in. She had fifteen funeral notices and six articles. Of the articles, two were major stories (as obits went). The big one was Freddy Shaw (with a y), a city councilman. As Mary-Shane typed the formal, unimaginative notices and articles, her mind wandered in various directions. What was life? What was reality? Why did some people live to be ninety years old, and others only ninety days or nine years? She had nearly lost Kippy. She HAD lost Frank. Now these other obits. You became philosophical; doing obits was an overview, a final checkpoint on life.

The phone rang. Vic Lara. "Oh hi," she said, hearing that little spin on the i in hi that told her she was interested in him.

"I was wondering if we could meet for dinner."

"Not this evening. I have a doctor's appointment."

He pressed: "This is my only evening off. What do you say I take you dancing."

"We-e-ll..." She wanted to go slow.

"Say yes."

She laughed. "Yes."

"Great. Crank's? What time?"

"Crank's will be fine," she said still laughing. She was glad he made her laugh.

"Okay—I'll pick you up at your..."

"I'll meet you at Crank's in the bar," she interrupted to keep a distance. "Nine." She wrote herself a note just to be sure and resumed her work with a pleasant hum.

The phone rang. It was Sister St. Cyr. Mary-Shane was surprised; usually communication was by a note left in Kippy's lunch box. "Miss MacLemore, nothing big. You forgot to send ten dollars for Kippy's class trip next month. It was due today."

"Oh, sorry. I can bring it by on my lunch hour."

"Tomorrow will be fine," Sister said.

"No really. How is Kippy doing?" she asked.

Sister hesitated. "Well, I am a little concerned. Not worried now," she quickly amended. "Nothing dramatic, but his attention seems to be wandering. He got C's on three quizzes, and that's not like him."

"Do we need a conference?"

"Oh, not at all." Sister St. Cyr had a pleasant laugh. She told parents to remember her name was Sister Sincere.

A short while later, eating an apple, Mary-Shane wandered into the front yard at St. Andrew's. Stark light fell into the Victorian jumble of tomato-colored brick and almond-colored marble set behind a garden of trees and ferns. She had attended grammar school here. Alone in the courtyard, she stopped and looked up at the shuttered windows. The *Dark Feeling* swooped down over her—no, welled up from inside of her—and she dropped her apple. She reeled dizzily, sitting down on a low wall. *I WANT TO TOUCH YOU...* something inside of her said drooling. Marble gargoyles gazed down at her from leaded drain spouts. Horned goats, hissing serpents, grinning devils leered down at her.

Go away, she screamed inside. Go away! She looked down the tunnels of her blood, into the chamber of her brains, through the egg whites of her eyeballs. Get out of my fucking life!

I HAVE WAITED SO LONG... it said, but then drew away. Abruptly she felt okay again. She brushed off her apple, but saw a worm in it and threw it away in disgust. She walked down a dark corridor that smelled of floor wax and books. She paid the ten dollars to the school cashier, a chubby volunteer with a merry smile. As she left, she paused and looked back. Somehow oozing through the pores of the brick, children's cries reached her. She walked back. A Virgin of creamy nougat smiled down. Mary-Shane walked a little further and rounded the corner. Now the cries were plain. She looked down a slight incline past the school and saw milling blue uniforms on the playground. The boys' shirts and the girls' blouses made a constant semaphore of white through the leaves.

She resisted the impulse to wave, yell his name. Instead she kept to the shade under the trees so as not to be seen. There: around the basketball court. Shirts had the ball. Whack, whack, whack, went the ball as the shirt tapped it on the asphalt and decided on an opening.

Alone on the side lines at mid-court stood Kippy wearing no shirt. He was firmly planted on one crutch, leaving the other hand free...

Flurry of shirts and skins. Ball moved rapidly. Basket.

Kippy yelled "Yeah!" and waved a fist. His teammates pranced by and one by one slapped his upheld hand.

Mary-Shane waved her fist and whispered, "Yeah!" With a feeling of relief, she hurried to her car. Lunch hour was over (she'd forgotten to eat) but no matter. That was one healthy boy out there, yelling his lungs raw.

Having met her deadline, Mary-Shane gave Jules the high sign. He nodded, and she sloshed out into the drizzle. First stop, the public library, the information desk. "Hi. I seem to remember seeing, somewhere in the halls, a marble scroll or something that reads Burtongale Room." The young librarian called over an older lady whose kindly eyes swam like pickled eggs behind thick lenses. "Yes," the older woman said, "years and years ago when they built this building, there was a plan to have a room for Burtongale memorabilia and books. They practically paid for this library, I'm sure you know. Then, who knows, nothing ever came of it. The room is now part of the stacks, and off-limits. If I remember correctly, we keep magazines in it."

"But why the change of plans?" Mary-Shane asked.

The older woman shrugged. "I think they decided to keep all their books up in the mansion. They have a family museum up there, I'm told."

Mary-Shane went to a pay phone and looked up the number.

A woman answered (refined, cheery, British...). "This is Martina Strather."

"I was wondering about the Burtongale Family Museum," Mary-Shane said. "The library told me it's at the family mansion."

"Yes, it is, but it hasn't been open to the public in at least twenty years, and I don't anticipate that it will be. Miss Polly is very firm on that. Are you a scholar?"

"No, just nosy." Mary-Shane hung up.

Chapter 17.

Mary-Shane and Kippy ate pizza that evening. "Sister Sincere called me at work today. She was a little concerned."

"About what?"

"I'm not sure. You're daydreaming in class? You got low grades on quizzes?"

He chewed slowly and stared at her. "I got C's on some minor tests." His tone was clipped and tense.

She asked: "Are you spending too much time on that computer and not enough in your books?"

"No, Mom"(same tone she took with her own mother)"I didn't study because I had a headache. And she said the quizzes don't count if you get a better grade on the tests. You can substitute..."

"Okay, okay," she said. She knew she'd better chop this off before he felt confronted. "I'm just asking." She bit into her own slice. She pictured her mother's face: The boy needs a man in his life. Mentally, she threw a baseball at her mother's image to dunk it in a carnival pool.

Before her bedroom mirror, getting ready for her visit to the shrink, she noticed Kippy through a crack in the door. Who was this grinning, masculine, almost coarse young guy sitting on her couch watching football? What about the homework? She pulled on her nylons.

"Where are you going?"

"I'm going to visit the doctor."

"That sure is a lot of fancy make-up and stuff for a doctor."

"Okay, Sherlock, so I'm meeting a friend afterward and we may go dancing and I'll call you, okay?"

He looked at the TV, not answering.

She sighed deeply. Sometimes having a child was like having a parent. In some insane microcosmic crumb of thought she entertained and then resisted the idea of going out looking plain (which might give the shrink food for stark modern drama) and then dressing in the car behind a gas station as she'd done during her adolescence. Come on, Mary-Shane, she thought.

She checked herself in the mirror. She wore a gray wool suit with mid-calf skirt; dark blue hose; navy heels and strapless purse with attached gray leather gloves; tapioca silk blouse with pearl necklace and silk MacLemore tartan kerchief. I must go out more, she thought. Light make-up: her face was a good one, an agency had told her once, but sorry no models under 5'8. They had put her on a waiting list for faces, though (and called her for three auditions but nothing had come of them).

Dr. Stanislaus welcomed her into his leather-padded study.

She remembered where to sit: An indirectly lit alcove containing an office chair and writing table (stark) facing a couch (comfortable). Green plants, a microphone hanging from the ceiling, and a coffee table. Dr. Stanislaus brought to the writing table his file about her. He was a short stocky man wearing moccasins, brown corduroy trousers, and a lime colored bulky-knit sweater. His gray hair rose in a crew cut. He had a pudgy face with hints of coldness, though his brown eyes caressed disarmingly. "I haven't seen you in five years."

"I think I am losing my mind."

He did not seem fazed. "Why?"

"My son tells me I scream at night. Also, I think there is something inside my brain."

"What kind of a thing?" His questions were gentle, almost dreamily quiet and distant, but powerful; he coaxed her to retrieve from within her the pieces of a puzzle that would lead them to put a face on the things that frightened her.

"I'm not sure. A kind of presence. A *Dark Feeling* that comes over me sometimes. And I have really scary dreams, like about the end of the world."

"How often does this happen?"

"Once, maybe twice a day. Are you going to laugh at me?"

"No. I don't want to scare you, but it could be something serious like a tumor. Otherwise — ."

"Otherwise, I'm nuts?"

"You are undoubtedly under a lot of stress."

"You can say that again."

"Let's talk a little. How is your son?"

"There is a blip on his x-ray, but otherwise he's fine."

"A blip?"

"It may not be anything."

"You were married to an abusive man. He was tough, he gave the world the finger which you wanted to do. You told me that you would try to find a better man..." He paused. "Have you?"

She shook her head.

"You also felt tremendous guilt because of your son's condition, which medically was not your fault. You were going to put guilt behind you." She smiled, fleetingly. "You were going to look for the one thing you really, deep down in your deepest heart, wanted, and that was a decent man who would be nice to you and your son. You were not going to get all turned on by some biker, but you were also not going to go for the newspaper and slippers type." He grinned as he read from his notes, and she remembered offering him the analogy: You were not going to go for either a Doberman Pinscher type, nor a Pierre

Poodle type of man, but for a sort of a gruff, working dog guy like maybe a Labrador." He looked up. "What kind of men have you met?"

"I just broke up with a man named Howard Berger."

"Did you end it?"

"Yes."

"And?"

"He was stifling me. Possessive, jealous, insecure. He was a poodle." She added: "Kippy didn't like him either."

"I see. Well, you're probably right. He sounds like a poodle. So your search continues?" She nodded. "You are dressed up. Are you going out?"

"Yes."

"With a Lab?"

She thought hard, trying fit different dogs' heads and personalities on Vic Lara. "He's a cop. A wolf maybe."

"You used to dislike authority figures, especially cops."

"That was then. I've become an authority figure myself. Over one boy, anyway."

He looked at his watch. "Tell me about the wolf next time. You'll get a thorough physical tomorrow morning to determine if your problem has a medical reason." He wrote out an appointment slip. "This is important. They'll see you right away."

She felt her emotions slowly welling up. "I have been getting these *Dark Feelings*. And seeing dead people. I saw my hus-... my ex-husband at the zoo. And I saw my father in a restaurant." She told him the stories. "But I think it's like some outside voice or not a voice, a feeling, trying to play with my mind and not being entirely successful."

"Are you in trouble at work?"

"Yes."

"We have a lot to talk about then."

"Yes. Doctor—"

"Yes?"

"I feel like a cork about to pop out of a bottle. Maybe I'm trying to remember something horrible and I can't, because it scares me terribly, but I have to..."

He regarded her with a carefully composed stony-face. A troubled light haunted his eyes. "Can you remember anything at all?" His pencil was poised to write.

She asked: "Is there something you know that I should remember?"

He said nothing. The pencil remained poised. It was quiet in the room. A clock ticked. Finally he put the pencil down.

Mary-Shane's chest tightened. A *Dark Feeling* welled up. It made her feel numb. She fumbled in her purse. "There is something I want to give you." She rose, and, as if walking through water, placed the tooth on the table before him. "Please take it for me."

He stared at the tooth. "Where did you find it?"

"In front of the zoo."

"Do you remember where exactly?"

"Near the entrance." The words came from deep inside Mary-Shane. "Please. I want to give it to someone in authority."

He took a small envelope from his desk and slipped the tooth inside. "I will save it for you. We will talk about it some more."

Chapter 18.

At Crank's, Vic Lara leaned grinning against the bar. Music thumped and young bodies writhed. He dropped his toothpick. She ducked her shoulders and snapped her fingers. "You want to put your arms around the situation?"

"All ri-i-ight." He signaled the bartender for two more of something and then led her by the hand out to the dance floor. There they oozed to a slow tune. She liked all the songs and they danced hard to the fast songs. After about two hours or two margaritas, whichever came first, they left Crank's. Mary-Shane felt giddy.

Outside in the cool drizzle, under the glass ceiling of a bus stop, they sat on a bench. "You've got me puffing," he said.

"You ain't seen nothin' yet, honey."

"Who-o-o-o," he said with sly conviction.

She snapped her fingers and rocked. "Blowing off steam!"

"Are you about fed up with this police beat?"

"Yes and no." She folded her hands between her knees, looked down. "Derailed for now. Back on obits since Wiz quit."

"She quit?" The light inside him brightened, or was it just the shift of reflected streetlights as his expression changed to one of astonished interest. "Where did she go?"

He's working, Mary-Shane thought to herself, he's always working. "I have no idea. She was mad because Jules let me go out on the police beat with Perry. I've wanted to be a writer for a long time, Vic. I deserve a break. I have published some articles here and there in different little magazines. I am a published poet and author. I had a poem entitled Touch My Flower (Ignite!) in a U.C. Santa Barbara lit mag. Coupla recipes in a Chicago Polish-Italian newsletter."

He looked away. "We could still work together."

She gave him a sidelong look, hiding her suspicions. "Yeah, but not on this zoo deaths story, right?" She knew the answer already, before he spoke it. He was always working, and though he worked for the city, he might just as well have been Aunt Polly's private detective.

"Right."

Still, she was interested in him, for reasons she could not entirely fathom. She thought about this for a few moments. Something told her it was wrong to be interested in him, but she was drawn to him by some of the darkness inside her. "I figured knowing you wouldn't hurt."

"How's your tooth?" he asked.

"I gave it to my shrink."

"I'm glad to hear that," he said sincerely. He added: "Do you remember anything?"

"What do you mean?

"Years ago."

She felt blood rushing in her ears. Pain. Blocked.

"Sorry. Never mind." Rain drops pattered on the glass walls, making ads soggy. His eyes danced about as though following a complicated outline. His eyes grew large, glistening, and his jaws worked as though he were hungry. "You look beautiful tonight."

"Whoa," she said with new energy. "Down boy." She turned her face up to catch the cool wind on her throat. The smell of rain was delicious. She shook out her curls with both hands.

He lit a Camel, clicking the Zippo with macho smoothness. Orange light flickered on his facial bones and crevices like London during the Blitz. "There's a lot of undertow, Mary-Shane."

"Undertone?" She laughed, not understanding.

"Undertow. The water runs deep in this town. It's my business to know what goes on. This town is like dark water. It's cold underneath. There are things that go on that nobody would believe if you wrote them in a book. People who ordinarily wouldn't give you the time of day call you because they need you but they only tell you half the truth. Putting all the half truths together, you make quite a picture of San Tomas. Of the Human Animal."

"Vic, you sound like a newsreel."

"Sorry. I'm trying to tell you something."

"What?"

"I'm not so good with the words, but here goes. I think you're okay and maybe a little something could work out between me and you. You know, dancing, dinner... I make pretty good dough and I could show you a good time. Watch out for you."

"I really do appreciate that." She wondered if he were more of a Lab or a Pinscher. Poodle, no way. Only one way to find out. Go for it. "I think you're okay too, Vic."

"Want to go for a walk?" he asked.

"In the rain?"

"That's no rain. That's mist, drizzle." He ran to his car and came back with an umbrella. "For the faint of heart."

"That's what I like, a gentleman."

They walked together arm in arm. Along deserted streets curving down to the sea. There, at Catamaran Beach, breakers curled and crashed making the sidewalk shudder. "Storm out there," he said pinching his lapels together.

She huddled against him, glad for the excuse. His surfaces felt like knotty wood and twisted cable, lean and hard. He wrapped his arms around her and sought her mouth with his. She smelled old beer and sour cigarette smoke on his breath but it didn't matter just then. She'd find a way to diplo—

His hands stroked her back and buttocks, grasping handfuls of her, roughly. She pushed away, but he pulled her back. He opened his mouth like a wolf pup, in a snarl of hunger. She stood on tiptoe and thrust her tongue in, seeking his. He groaned with satisfaction and their tongues wrestled deliciously.

It rained briefly, seething in the crowns of California fan palms lining the shore. Fog horns moaned like distant dinosaurs. Over and over again, the sidewalk shuddered under the sledge hammers of the sea. Wind blew paper, leaves, loose objects. A cardboard sign did somersaults through street puddles, coming to rest flat against a dark restaurant window.

His hand began to explore between her thighs when she decided enough for the first night.

In the car, behind a windshield full of scattershot water, he said: "It'll be nice. You'll get stories Perry couldn't dream of."

"I'll have to get on the City Room staff first."

"Yeah, well there's time."

She thought about this with interest. She had not really thought the implications through. "You're gonna tell me stuff you don't tell Perry?"

"Yeah," he said flicking a glance at her, "Well, you don't think I take Perry to Catamaran Beach to make out, do you?"

She laughed. "You're wicked." She added: "I am waiting for that one big story, though, Vic. That one story will get me going because I want to make my career as a reporter."

The rain had let up by the time she was in her own car, driving home. She felt tingly, listening to the radio: "...Storm front from the Rockies is passing, leaving some showers through the night. Expect gusty winds, gray skies, occasional showers for the next three to four days..."

It occurred to her that she'd forgotten to mention the incident with Gilbert to Vic. Oh well, next time...

Kippy had finished his homework. He'd left it on the kitchen table for her to see. She checked and found that he'd done each math problem correctly. He'd left her a funny little note with a heart at the bottom: "Decided I better buckle down. My headache is gone. Please check my homework. (heart) Kippy."

She tiptoed in his room, covered his bare shoulder with a quilt. Touching his hair lightly, she bent over and kissed him.

Chapter 19.

This morning was her physical. She told Jules she'd be late but that she'd work doubly hard to beat the deadline.

Mary-Shane, wearing only panties and a cloth hospital gown, read magazines and waited through her physical at a private clinic overlooking the ocean. She got to sit outside on a private, screened patio between tests, shaded by an awning. The nurse practitioner mentioned to her that she had dark circles under her eyes. At first Mary-Shane was impatient. Then she realized that this was what rest really meant, and how little of it she'd had in a long time. She remembered some long ago yoga lessons and breathed deeply in and out. She tried to sit as relaxed as possible. And to explore her mind while she rested:

The ocean rumbled with a slow pulse beat, and she walked barefoot on a beach in her mind, wearing a bikini. It wasn't a scene from her imagination; it was a metaphor presented by the *Cold Thing*, and she willingly let herself into from curiosity. The day was hazy, and the sun burned milky-hot like a filament in a light bulb. The moon and the earth were like a heart beating, and the ocean tumbled through its phases like squirts in an artery. But it was scary—if the earth and the moon got too close to each other, they would squash against each other, go limp, and the whole music would stop.

The *Cold Thing* resided in the pebbly beach somewhere between a cortex (!where was high school biology when you needed it?) and a medulla, or was that an isthmus and some islets? She stubbed a toe of thought into the midafternoon tide pool of her consciousness. This was a motherly place with boulders of love and rocks of concern; the biting coral of girlishness lay far out on a reef. There were smooth river rocks every woman's soul flowed around: recipes, hurts, candle-making, ducks on a shower curtain, nagging mother, lost father... There! its shadow rippled on the fine sand, like the head of an eel: Did it have little crooked antlers on its head? Inscrutable, reptilian, feigning sleep, it dreamt of killing. She was sure of it. But why? What did it all mean? Why was she scared and curious at the same time, like her attraction to Vic?

"Were you sleeping?"

Mary-Shane opened her eyes. "What?" The white-clad technician handed her her medical file to carry to the next station. "You're done with X-ray, Miss MacLemore. You can go on to blood work now." The eyes softened. "Your X-rays look good, I'll just tell you off the record. The CAT scan is normal, but the doctor will call your doctor. It's lovely here, isn't it? Were you sleeping?"

"I may have dozed off a bit. It's so peaceful." But the *Cold Thing* lurked, and nobody would believe her if she told them. As she dressed, she realized she was light-headed and hungry. Time to find a deli, maybe get a chicken salad sandwich.

She thanked the medical staff and was glad to get out into the warm sunshine of reality.

It was good to be alive. It was good to be in the warm air as cars churned past and she could smell the heat of their tires, the vegetable-soup smell of lawns being mowed, the vanilla in a cone held by a passing child, the citrus aftershave of a young bodybuilder who leered at her. She trudged along the sandy sidewalk toward her car, enjoying the warmth emanating up from under her soles. As long as the *Cold Thing* slept— or was busy elsewhere— no *Dark Feelings*, no pain from it.

As she remembered the *Dark Thing*, she began to feel dizzy again. Somebody—whether it was Vic, or Dr. Stanislaus, or Father O'Malley—must help her get rid of this thing that had wormed its way into her very soul that day in the zoo. Somehow, too, she knew, somehow this thing in her mind had something to do with the deaths in the zoo, which had something to do with the Burtongales, which had something to do with her father, which connected to the ham bone, which connected to the thigh bone...

She shook her head, trying to clear the craziness away as the metaphor broke apart in her head.

The body builder looked at her strangely and then turned away as she held onto the rim of her car door with white-knuckled hands and made throat clearing noises. The dizziness abated again, but she didn't feel quite so happy anymore as after leaving the clinic.

A cloud had passed over the sun, suddenly turning the air leaden and gray.

She got to work at eleven and found that the entire resentful City Room of reporters and editors had been pounding away at obits most of the morning. That was like ten people at least, she thought with grim satisfaction.

Jules sidled by. He wasn't carrying his pipe and he had a funny dark look. "You heard from Wiz?"

She shook her head. "Not word one." She indicated with her chin the humongous pile of obits. "Christ, Jules, are they all out there dying by the truckloads?"

"I hope not."

"Have you found another Obit Queen yet?"

He leaned forward and placed his finger under his nose. "Shhh. I'm interviewing a guy tomorrow afternoon. You'll sit in, okay? Two o'clock. If we like him, we hire him."

"Oh Jules. That would be so wonderful."

"I thought you'd like that." He started to leave. "If you hear from Wiz, I want to know."

The Chatfield guy called and canceled, saying things had come up and it would be at least a week before he could really give her the zoo tour. But he promised to give her good color.

So instead she met Ann Temple for lunch at a French patisserie. Clouds were moving in from the sea. The air was gray, and inside the restaurant was an almost underwater light. A mirror on the wall seemed filled with quicksilver. Mary-Shane had a baked patty shell with steaming lemon-mushroom filling.

Ann spooned hot onion soup. "How's old flashy eyes?"

"The cop?" Mary-Shane licked her fork. "I went out with him last night."

"No."

"Yep. Had a good time."

"Is he as slick as he looks?"

"Stopped him at thigh one."

"Play that one slow."

Mary-Shane sighed luxuriously. "Well, I don't know what I want to do. He could be a little weird, I don't know. I'll see how it goes. But I intend to have some fun."

She spent the early afternoon digging through the back areas of the newspaper morgue, trying to find old scrapbooks maybe, or fiche, anything to learn more about the Burtongale family. It was hard to see in the dreary light, even with inside fluorescents on. A few droplets spattered the windows overlooking San Tomas. The spires of the Burtongale Building rode like ships in a sea of clouds. Tiny figures in anoraks stood on the roof of the Burtongale Building, reeling in the garrison flag while wind ripped at their clothes and they reeled like sailors on a pitching deck.

Mary-Shane threw her papers on the table and sat down. She felt like crying. Dead ends. All roads led to the Burtongale family, and all doors were closed. She could not go to Jules; she could not even leave her name with anyone for fear she would, as Jules put it, make more enemies. She went back to her desk, discouraged, and puttered around, cleaning up.

The phone rang.

"Miss MacLemore?" A man's voice. Nothing familiar about it. Very nondescript; grammatically correct at least; fortyish; possibly an authority figure. "Or should I say, Miss Chang?"

Oh chips she thought. Her stomach did a hiccup.

"You want to find out about the Burtongale family."

"I'm trying to do research for a story, okay? Who are you?"

"I could be a friend; help you; would you like that?"

She sat forward, tense and scared. "I'm not sure."

"Try me." (What was that echo she heard?)

"What do I need to do?"

"There is a restaurant right next door to the police station. I think you should feel quite safe there."

"When?"

"Let's say, five forty five."

She would have Kippy with her; Ann could not pick him up; she frowned... "Okay, let's do it." She could send him into the police station to sit with Vic, maybe.

"Just ask for Mr. Vecci. That's V, e, c, c, i. That's me."

The restaurant was Napolitano's, a pizzeria much used by both the police and by local businesses. She'd eaten in there a few times, but preferred Puffy's Pizza near her house because it had a thicker crust.

Mary-Shane luckily found a space fronting on the alley between the pizzeria and the police station. Dropping a quarter into the meter, she walked into the station with Kippy. Vic was not in, the receptionist patrol woman said.

Mary-Shane had Kippy sit down on one of the smooth wooden benches in the lobby, under pothos and arecas. "I expect to be back in a half hour, okay? You do your homework."

Low voice: "Okay."

Pinching her jacket shut against the drizzle, she hopped over puddles. The light was growing dim, like bluing in laundry water as the lid slowly closed. Neon glowed cozy in shop windows. Mary-Shane entered the restaurant and peeked around.

The restaurant was small, but it did a brisk business all day round, from the daytime breakfast lunch and dinner crowds to the all night requirements of police, fire department, and EMT people. It smelled wonderfully of breads and sauces, meats and sweets, and Mary-Shane was tempted to order a cannoli but she was too nervous. Standing on tiptoe, she looked around a knot of mechanics in blue overalls who held beers and chatted. In corner booths, families with small children worked on bowls of lasagna.

"Can I help you, Miss," said a thin Italian man with a small mustache and an accent.

"I came to see Mr. Vecci."

He nodded and went into a back room. Mary-Shane waited. She studied the display case of pastries off to one side. The tortes and marzipans looked delicious. Minutes passed. A middle-aged woman with heavy arms and lips came to work the cash register. Two sheriff's deputies from San Tomas County stopped in to pick up a large pizza. The cash register rang. More people came in to order. Mary-Shane looked at her watch again. First five, then ten minutes passed. She asked the woman: "Is Mr. Vecci coming out?"

"Oh yes, he'll be right out. Want some spinach bread?"

"That sounds divine," Mary-Shane said.

The woman cut something behind the counter, then handed over a still-warm piece of bread on a piece of wax paper. Mary-Shane tried it and made eyes. "Mmmm..."

"Here comes Mr. Vecci now," the woman said.

Mary-Shane stood back and stopped chewing.

The young slim Italian man came out, pushing a high-backed wheelchair. In the wheelchair, wrapped in blankets, was a husk of a little man who had to be ninety if he was a day. His skin was mottled like a pastry with chocolates and reds and blues. His hands were bunches of uselessly dangling fingers. His mouth was open, and his eyes stared mindlessly into space.

"Hey Pop," the heavy-armed woman shouted to the husk. "The lady's here from the state rest home. Y'have a nice vacation?"

Drool ran from the old blue mouth, the tongue protruded, and the eyelids gave a flicker of recognition.

Mary-Shane stood transfixed, as if some giant hobbyist had applied a drop of fixative to her head. Only dimly did she hear the woman ask: "Where is your assistant? And the ambulance?"

The door burst open. "Mom!" It was Kippy. He struggled with a crutch and the rattling door. "You'd better see this."

Mary-Shane stepped outside and put her hands to her mouth.

Her Mustang was up on blocks. The wheels were gone. The engine was gone. Even the trunk lid, the hood, and the driver's side door were gone. The rag top swung in windy shreds on the bare frame. The windshield had been removed. The seats were gone. Wires hung where the radio had been. The passenger side door was still there. Someone had used a power brush to remove a ragged swatch of paint, leaving a violent display of naked scoured steel. On it, someone had written in large white letters: NOSY BITCH. And in smaller print, evidently in some sort of laundry marker: "All you need to know."

Mary-Shane stood looking at her devastated car as total darkness fell. Kippy looked shocked, and she felt sorry most of all that he'd had to see this. To get him out of there, she hailed a cab. Then she bought them each a hot dog and soda

"Mom, why did someone do that to us?"

She looked up surprised from her self-pity, from the devastation of her own hot dog—a missile in an explosion of ketchup and mustard. "Someone was telling me I should stick with obits for a while." Now she'd have to borrow Mother's car.

Kippy answered the phone that evening and hollered in a cracking voice: "Mom! Phone!"

It was Lara. "Mary-Shane?"

"Yes," she said. "You sound like you're in a cookie tin."

"That's sweet of you. No, I've got a cell phone and as a matter of fact I'm standing in front of Flopsy's Diner on 101 feeling hungry and thinking about you."

"Did you hear about my car?"

"Yeah, I did." He sighed, as though she were a wayward child. "Are you okay?"

"I'm still a bit shook up."

"Want me to come by?"

"No. Thanks for calling."

"I'll check into it, Mary-Shane, see what I can do for you."

"Vic, do I need police protection?"

He appeared to think for a moment. "Probably not. Will you take my advice and back off from this whole mess?"

"Maybe."

"Come have coffee. I'll pick you up."

"Well—" she looked over at Kippy, who was busy with his homework at the coffee table. She'd always made a point of telling him ahead of time when she was going out. "I can't, Vic. I have to plan things."

"What's this plan things? Where's the party spirit I was hearing about last night?"

"That was after two margaritas and a lot of shanana. This is tonight. I worked all day, my car is stripped, I'm worried, and I'm tired. I can't leave Kippy alone. Not after today."

Chapter 20.

In the morning as Mary-Shane dropped Kippy off, fog filled the sunken entrance of St. Andrew's. The statues were frozen in desperate motions: they raised their crosses or folded their hands and looked up with pleading faces. Another gray, chilly day, the weather report said.

A ship of fog, a slice of the marine layer, since San Tomas was surrounded by the sea on three sides, sailed slowly in like a luff-rigged two-masted brigantine and settled in a shipwreck in that amphitheatre of weeping saints and crazed brick.

The morning was, as usual, a storm of phoned death notices, a race against time, a fight to even get to the ladies' room.

That afternoon Mary-Shane confronted Jules: "You know something about Wiz, don't you?"

In his office, he gave her such a stricken look that she felt sorry for him. She pushed the door shut with a sweatered elbow and leaned over his desk. "I had a feeling something was wrong when you were asking about her the other day."

He declined his head. His eyes were closed and his skin looked ashen. "If anything has happened to her, I'll never forgive myself."

"Jules, what is going on? What's wrong?"

He looked up shaking his head. "I don't know. What little I know, I can't tell you just now. Trust me?"

She stormed out. First a cover-up and now this. She tried repeatedly calling Wiz's home phone, with no luck.

That afternoon, Jules and Mary-Shane met in the personnel department. Joannes Berbere was an exchange student from Ethiopia. Small, with a broad bony face and a ready smile, he impressed Mary-Shane with his excellent command of the English language. He seemed self-assured and displayed his diplomas and writing samples. He was a graduate student in economics at San Tomas State. His wife was about to have their first child, and planned to quit her job as a bank teller for at least two years to stay home with the baby. Berbere beamed.

"How fast can you type?" Mary-Shane asked.

"I have been timed at 100 words per minute."

"Congratulations on your new job," Jules and Mary-Shane both told him.

"I'm so thrilled," Mary-Shane said over coffee at Vogelmann's.

"Me too," Jules said.

Jules looked nice in his light blue sweater, Mary-Shane thought. Vogelmann's was warm and cozy, smelling of German baking and freshly brewed black coffee.

She folded her arms together and leaned across the table. "I'm worried about Wiz, and I'm worried about you."

82

"I'm okay," Jules said buttering a roll.
"This is getting scary," Mary-Shane said.
"Tell me about it."

She called Vic and he met her. "I want to talk to you. About Wiz." They were in Vic's unmarked car. He kissed her passionately. She struggled out from under him, pushing his hand out from between her thighs. He lay back pretending to be unconscious. She swatted him. "Vic, be serious."

"What did you want to talk about?" he asked resignedly.

"I— This is not easy for me. My boss, Jules, whom I love very dearly, knows something about Wiz that he's not telling me and I figure with her missing every possible lead has to count."

Vic nodded, yawning. "You're right." He looked out the window as if trying to come to a decision. Abruptly, he reached over, opened the glove compartment, and pulled out a plastic bag. "We found these at the zoo." He dumped the contents on her lap.

Mary-Shane picked up a pair of glasses. "These look like Wiz's."

"There's no name on them, but I checked with your paper and then with the health plan. Her optometrist prescribed those, astigmatism and all. The optician's shop confirmed they made that style of frame for that lady. They are hers."

"Where were they?" Mary-Shane asked.

"In a drainage ditch outside of the zoo."

Tears misted her eyes like a summer shower, and she sucked in a couple of sobs.

"Okay." He slammed the shift into gear and drove toward the interior of the peninsula. "I think you are either crazy or very brave and if you wind up missing or dead or in the hospital with some kinda weird pentagons up your butt I'll be a sad guy."

He drove alongside the zoo on Canoga until the zoo wall fell behind. "I'm going to show you something." Vic slowed at the canyons outside the zoo. He pulled onto a service road. An arrow pointed above a sign that read ZOO MAINTENANCE//PRIVATE ROAD//KEEP OUT. "I want to give you an idea of the kind of crazy things I think Our Teresa has been involved in." Vic drove to the end of the service road, then kept going downhill along a leafy semblance of a path. She watched the shadows darken. Rolling over crunching pine cones, the car poked deeper into this forested no man's land. The path ended and the car stopped. They were down deep, maybe two hundred feet below sea level, in the canyon wilderness outside the zoo. The air was strangely cold, and mixed tree crowns (pine, eucalyptus, date palm) soared above in a floating gloom. He poked a fingertip at her chest. "Don't say another word until we're back at the car."

It was quiet down here, so still that when she stepped on a twig, she could hear the echo of its snapping bounce off an inky swirl of rock fifty feet away. Vic stopped. "Listen."

She listened. An indistinct murmur turned into the droning harmony of two silvery military planes flying in tandem. Evening sunlight glinted tangerine on their fuselages. "Just some Air Force planes," Vic said. "Seem to be having exercises lately. Wonder where they are based." Then he turned his attention to what was at hand. They walked into the darkest part of the woods. She stumbled a little because the path was uneven and the visibility bad. She thought she saw blankets spread here and there but once when she took a closer look it was a twisted piece of cardboard.

A bird broke loose, startling her. Vic gripped her wrist. "Come on, we've got to hurry before it gets dark." He used her wrist to turn her, and she, cringing at what she might see, looked straight into a horrifying death face in the bushes.

Its empty eyes stared at her. Its foul rotting skin looked shriveled. Both its open mouth, and the hole where the nose had been, gaped as if frozen in a last desperate breath. Its stained teeth grinned. Browned flowers were strewn on the makeshift altar under it.

Mary-Shane put her hands to her mouth. She gasped so deeply and sharply that her legs tingled. Chills ran up and down her spine. She was able to utter only a single word, a question, through her fingers: "Wizzie?"

Vic shook her from behind. "No. Look closer." She did. It was a mask of some kind. The dead brown skin was supermarket bag paper. The teeth were glued-on palm seeds. She squeaked hysterically. Relief drained down her body like shower water.

Vic pointed. "There among the flowers. There's some other stuff that had been glued on but fell off. Paper eyelids. Sea shells. This thing's been here quite a while."

In the cool piney air, deep down in the forest, she smelled something that was not right. Something burnt, like a fire gone cold, like meat left exposed too long. For a minute or so, she remembered the *Dark Feeling*. It swam up like a black smoke under the dome of her skull, obscuring the windows of her eyes. It surged like black water through the hidden canals of her body, splashing through the grottoes of her chest. Her heart pulsed once, twice, with a painful twinge like a small electrical current cruelly applied. She blinked rapidly.

The *Dark Feeling* ebbed as soon as it had come. There was another altar nearby. Its mask was made of a white paper plate with eyelets cut out. Common seashells formed an intricate design suggesting a frowning face.

Vic prodded. "Let's split. Hey, come on, let's get out of here." His eyes darted about. She noticed his right hand was under the left fold of his jacket, and the hammer of a large pistol stuck out. "It's getting dark, Mary-Shane. Once we lose the advantage of daylight..."

She inhaled deeply, then squeezed her nose shut and leaned forward to see what was on the second altar. Darkness was fast falling. It was getting pitch black down here, and she looked longingly up to the eucalyptus trees high up on the zoo ridges. Dusk inked the crude wooden structure built with obvious care by people who had neither nails nor paints. From the flat of the altar, among withered flowers, the flayed skull of a dog stared eyelessly up at her. Its teeth looked greenish and she realized that the skull had sat in state like this for a long time for moss grew from its muzzle in a furry tongue. Then the smell— underneath the altar lay two chickens, probably emigrants from the zoo. Their torn feathers lifted quietly in a faint evening wind. Their eyes had a cooked, bluish glaze. Their bones had been removed and protruded from a charnel pot nearby.

"OOOOOOHHHHHHH!" she groaned, pulling her hands from her face and letting her held breath explode outward as she staggered away. She pulled in delicious drafts of fresh, damp air aromatized by leaves and berries, by humus and bark.

Vic gripped her wrist and towed her along. "Ouch." Something in her arm crackled, and she tried to pull it away from him. She couldn't get it free so she ran forward to relieve the tension on her arm. In so doing she stumbled and fell on all fours. "Please stop hurting me."

Vic stood at a crouch, .357 magnum revolver in one hand, feet spread for balance, other hand palm out in a warding off motion. "Did you hear something?"

She scrambled up. Oh Golly Jesus, she thought, those Santeria people are going to skin us alive. Already she could feel the fish-gutting knife along her spine. Vic's eyes were wary slits as he started up the slope. "Wait for me!" she whispered desperately. Already it was so dark she could not make out the ground directly ahead. Somewhere up the slope, an amber street light glowed consolingly, but far, so far out of reach.

Vic was quicker and got slightly ahead.

Was he leaving her? She was too scared to call out again.

Behind her, twigs crackled.

Vic was a blur up ahead, and she struggled to catch up.

Behind her, feet ran, making dead leaves skitter through air.

Whoever, whatever it was, seemed to be running from hiding place to hiding place, watching.

She heard singing, and her skin crawled... Voices, singing, distant, barely audible under the wind...

She scrambled forward, banging her knee painfully on something (a rock? a tree root?). Limping stiffly, she used her hands and good leg to scrabble behind Vic.

The street light drew closer.

It was drizzling up here in the free, open world of normal people, with cars swishing through puddles, and shadows lying long in alleys, and neon lights cozy in the windows of otherwise dark little retail shops.

Vic bent down and grasped her arm again—gently. "There. It's okay now." He still held the revolver, but in a more relaxed manner as one would hold a brush or a book.

"You scared the hell out of me," she said rubbing her sore arm and wrist. "And you have a grip like steel pliers."

"Wait here," he said, "I'll get the car."

"Don't leave me—" she started, but he was gone.

She heard choir music clearly now. It was as though plugs had been pulled from her ears. The stained glass windows in the apse of the basilica of St. Thomas glowed in brilliant colors: sky, blood, custard... The windows seemed to vibrate with choir practice. Piercing voices—women, she thought, altos—had given way. Now Mary-Shane heard the operatic voice of a male tenor singing Jubilatio. The organ slammed out tiered chords in shuddering bursts. Like smoke from a chimney, the wind wrapped these praises in drizzle and spun them upward. An unseen jet labored in the swollen sky. Its whistling turbines swallowed the music.

Headlights swept by. "Get in!"

Near the edge of the botanical gardens, Mary-Shane spied a little girl with large eyes. The little girl, bundled in rags, was held in hand by a heavyset woman, also in rags, whose skin color was ambivalent under all the dirt. The woman carried a plastic bag whose volume and weightlessness suggested empty cans.

Vic waited as Mary-Shane closed the door and buckled up. As they drove away, Mary-Shane strained her neck to see the woman and the child. "Look at those poor people," she said.

He grunted. "Probably devil worshippers with the rest of them down there."

"Vic!" she said. "You're so hard!"

"Give me a break, Mary-Shane."

"I thought you were going to leave me. And look at me," she said, "what a mess." Her nylons were in shreds. Her dress was torn and ready for the rag pile. Her shoes were scuffed and muddy.

He said: "You don't appreciate the situation. I forgot how suddenly it gets dark down there. Know what? I think those people down there can see in the dark. Now maybe it's just 'cause some of them are Indians but that don't prove anything. I'm one fourth Indio myself but I see in the dark like I got brass plugs for eyeballs. You know what we call that section down there on the PD? The Jungle, that's what. That's the return to nature of all the people who couldn't make it in the civilized world."

Vic rattled on and she was beginning to resent his cool indifference. She kept thinking of the woman and the girl. She wondered if they had enough to eat. If those clothes were warm enough.

"I'll see you," she said getting out of the car.

"Hey wait—" he called after her but she ignored him. She slipped quietly in the apartment door. Her mother and Kippy apparently were not home yet. She did not yet hear the unmistakable whirring of Mother's fan belt as her aging boat turned the corner in stately slowness.

Mary-Shane sighed with relief. Leaving the ruined dress on the floor in her bedroom, she grabbed her bathrobe and pattered nakedly to the bathroom, apple breasts bobbling.

Hot water massaged her spine. She turned slowly, eyes closed and lips sputtering, rubbing her sore arm. Giving the shower a rest, she used her best milled soap, a mauve Jardin Primavera with lavender scent, to cover herself in thick lather. She reflected that Vic Lara was more of a Doberman and less of a Labrador. And she decided she would gather up some clothes and canned food to take to the street people. And she realized that, having once again felt the *Dark Feeling*, no matter how briefly, she was not finished with It nor It with her. She wondered if it was Frank trying to reach her. Was there, after all, a Beyond? Were there devils and goblins, to be driven away (but only so far) by choir music? She turned the water back on and rinsed off. She wished she could rinse her brain the way she was rinsing her skin. She rubbed her palms along the flat of her belly, then over the curve of her hip and along the firm flesh of her thighs. She felt to make sure the soap was gone from the hair on her venus mound. She held her breasts and looked down at the large caramel nipples and thought, Vic, you asshole, I think you blew it already, just by being you.

Chapter 21.

Perry Stein and his wife Matilda unloaded mops, buckets, buffer, cans of wax and boxes of detergent, near the back entrance of the zoo's administration building.

Desperate times called for desperate measures, and Perry felt he had to somehow get the story himself; nobody in this town told the truth and he could not wait to graduate to a bigger city and maybe a better paper.

He had printed up a batch of cards under "Matilda's Night Cleaning" and used them to obtain some night janitorial work in the zoo. That was another thing he figured he'd never need to do again once he got out of San Tomas, but for now with five kids, well, you did what you had to.

"Hurry, Hon," Matilda said as needles of water fell in a cold wind.

Perry did not need urging. His small round lenses were blurry wet. He wrestled the heavy buffer into the rotunda and there, while the roof pattered, knelt to examine the machine minutely.

"Whatcha doin'?" Matilda asked patiently. She was a big woman with heavy legs. Her gait was slow, a rocking from side to side, but she always got there anyway.

"Checking to see if any water got into the coil," Perry said lightly. He loved Matilda, and always spoke sweetly to her. Her hair was cut in a plain page boy. She had a wide solid German face with hard angles. Each time those strong lines cracked into a smile (shy or wise-ass or no shit or why don't you come and take me) Perry fell in love with her anew. She was the fertile soil, the lovely earth that had given forth five children and each of them in fine health.

"I'll bring in the little stuff," Matilda said.

"Okay Hon," he said frowning as he peered into an opening in the buffer's cowling. Holding it just so, a certain way and no other, he could see the coiled copper brushes and the colored wires for carrying the juice into that iron carousel. "I think it's okay."

"Don't go getting a shock now," she said someplace outside.

"Don't go getting a cold," he told her and hurried outside to help bring in the cleaning goods.

"Keep that soap out of the rain," she said grinning.

He grinned too. The thought flashed between them of how many suds a 25-pound box of soap could generate; they both knew, for during high school they had tried it in the park fountain. They laughed out loud together, beginning to sweat as they lugged in the rest of the gear. A lot of suds had come out of the fountain; had covered half the small park knee-deep; for hours, tumbleweeds of foam had torn loose bit by bit in the wind and rolled along city streets.

"This is a spooky place," Matilda said. Her voice echoed in the ceiling of the rotunda. "I wonder if it's haunted." She giggled, making echoes chuckle in the dome.

Perry opened the first door. "This is Dr. Chatfield's office. Now you just vacuum and dust, okay? I'll nose around and come back in a few minutes."

"This could be a great contract," she said, her pragmatic awe overcoming her fear.

"If it goes well, it might be," he agreed. He planted a kiss on her lips, which parted in a brief clinging motion, and he tasted the tip of her tongue. "You'll be okay," he assured her. "There are guards all over the zoo and there will always be someone within hailing distance."

She plugged in her small radio. "...weather story is more of the same, folks, a lot of drizzle..."

Perry stood in the doorway and looked into the rain. If nothing else, they'd make a few bucks. Who knew, maybe he'd catch a serial killer. He patted the camera slung under his poncho; better just see glimpse the killer and snap a few pictures and then run like hell. Perry grinned to himself. This job had been easy to set up. While he and Mary-Shane had interviewed Chatfield, Perry's practiced eye had roved about. He'd noted bubblegum trodden into the fluted tiles in the rotunda; coffee stains in Chatfield's carpet; cigarette butts lying against the corridor walls. Turned out the regular cleaning service had gone sloppy and been terminated several weeks earlier. Since then, coverage had been spotty. Well, Perry had assured the maintenance manager after showing him the gum and the stains and the butts, we can take care of that. He'd handed him the new card, Matilda's, not his own which Chatfield might recognize. The Burtongales would not take kindly to his attempt to get behind their facade.

Distant varicosities flickered in the sky. Dull rumblings blew in off the sea. It began to rain harder, and Perry folded his arms, squinting behind tiny lenses. Whatever was out there, he hoped, was getting good and wet.

Chapter 22.

Joannes Berbere, Mary-Shane found in the morning, was like a human teletype machine. The monotonous pace and the demanding exactitude of writing death notices seemed to suit him just fine. "Call me Spike," he said and his gold tooth sparkled.

"Oh," Mary-Shane said.

"I like the coffee here too." He stirred rapidly.

She resolved to ask him lots of questions about Ethiopia when there was some time, and she hoped her manner was friendly enough to convey this. Because what she really felt like doing was stuffing fifty pounds of paper down this throat and turning a crank to make death notices come out with speed and regularity.

Spike hummed as he typed. Waltzes, sonatas, cantatas, show tunes, hard rock, Sousa marches and salsa, he was a veritable radio. He had a wide bony face, large white teeth, and a happy jaw that seemed forever to bounce up and down going da-da, da-dum, da-di.

What a joy, Mary-Shane thought. "If you have any questions..."

"...I will be sure to ask." He had gentle eyes and an amused glow. His fingers chickled on the keys at an even pace and Mary-Shane just sat, watching with folded arms. Presently he seemed to well up with joy, and out came, ta-da, ta-di, ta-dum, as he ran through a medley of old Beatles tunes.

Rain pattered on the windows. Mary-Shane dawdled over an obituary article about a man who had polished machine parts at the same plant for fifty years. She stayed on the phone, safely looking busy, and taking notes. It was amazing not being in panic mode. Jules had instructed her to observe their new employee closely.

Spike hummed show tunes, rock songs, religious hymns, military marches.

Perry was on the road, and Jules was in a meeting. She could tell Spike was going to work out fine. She was anxious to get out and do some reporting.

Vic called wanting a date, and she said no.

Rain dribbled down the windows. She puttered about, arranging some oranges and walnuts in a basket on the window sill. She added some dried flowers in a blue vase. Her dictionary, thesaurus, and current novel (a thumbed library copy of Passions by Florence Risling Kiefer) stood in the sill, along with three pictures of Kippy at various ages.

She felt a little cold, so she wore a fuzzy pink sweater. Better cool than hot. The wet weather made her feel perky, almost more alive. She was able to leave work a little early. Vic was waiting outside. He persuaded her to have coffee with him at Flopsy's diner on coastal route 101. Lara poured black coffee. He smelled of subtle French lotion. "Are you okay, Mary-Shane?"

"Just tired."

"I'm sorry I made you mad the other day."

"It's okay." It wasn't, but life had to go on.

"Here, I want to share this with you." He placed a green leatherette notebook on the table.

She pulled it close. ADDRESSES was pressed in gold leaf on the cover. The pages were smudged from much use; one or two pages hung out like doors off their hinges. Johnathan Smith was written in No. 2 pencil on the first page, along with a phone number with a strange area code. She handled the book delicately.

"Go on, look through it."

"I feel like a trespasser."

"That's all right. You're doing police work now. No shame, no modesty, no delicacy. Get in there and see what you find."

She frowned. There was a San Tomas number, judging by the area code. "Wallace B....," she read. "That's the curator at the zoo, right?"

"Roger Chatfield's boss," Vic affirmed.

"Perry said he thought there was a connection. He said it wasn't just coincidence that Smith had his heart torn out and was dumped on the sidewalk near the zoo."

"Well, keep reading."

Mary-Shane flipped through, and as she did so she noted any local names and numbers. There were several. H. Hale...she looked quizzically at Vic.

"Harleigh Hale," he filled in for her. "Owns a bookstore on State 594, past East Canoga, almost in the mountains. An occult bookstore, I might add. We used to do drug busts there for paraphernalia years back when it was a head shop. Then it became a biker shop..." (Mary-Shane thought she vaguely recalled being in a place near the mountains one night when Kippy had been a baby; she had a black eye after an argument with Frank, and was cold and frightened riding in the back of Frank's old car; this flashed enigmatically like black and white photo stills from her subconscious but she could not put together a conscious thought about it; it slipped away) "...and finally this biker shop was bought out by Harleigh Hale. I personally keep an eye out, but we haven't had any real dirt on them."

Troubled by the tightness of San Tomas—no matter where you dug, either your past or someone else's peeked out with skeletal grin—she turned more pages. "None of the out of towners mean anything to me. I suppose the police are checking on them."

"Right, Chief. Every one, Chief. Thanks."

She felt her cheeks burn crimson. Then she started. "D. Mulcahy?"

"The one and only. I checked the number, and it matches."

"How could the Bishop of San Tomas be involved in this?"

"Doesn't mean he was involved, but it also doesn't mean he wasn't involved."

She flipped through but did not find any more names. Was Mulcahy now also a suspect?

"You missed one."

"Huh?"

"Under the k's."

She turned back with wetted thumb and scanned a fairly dense crowd of out of town names and numbers. "Oh no!" After several passes, her eyes found what they had been unwilling to see:

Terry K. (nnn) nnn-nnnn...

The phone number swam before her eyes as she tried to focus on her friend's name.

"Have you seen Miss Chickowitz around? We've checked every lead, Mary-Shane, and I'm afraid that I have to tell you the lady is on the missing persons list."

"Her name is Kcikiewicz." Mary-Shane pronounced it for him: "Terri Tsha-ki'-vitch. Low on the first syllable, high on the second, swoosh on the third." Mary-Shane had a mental photo in which Wiz was sitting at the obit desk looking up and smiling at some joke. Sunlight played in her laughter. But if you looked closer, you saw that the odd play of shadows, like a photographer's closing shutter, never completely left her eyes.

Mary-Shane dreamt of Frank that night.

Riding on the back of his Harley. Wind streaming through her hair. Both of them smiling at some joke while sunlight honeyed their faces. Lovingly, she tightened her embrace and pressed her cheek against Frank's back. Downshifting on a narrow road among grapevines, Frank eased the bike close to a fence. Mary-Shane reached over and managed to snag a bunch of grapes. They tasted tart and sweet. Juice ran down her cheek. Frank turned and smiled at her. Only it was Vic Lara's face on Frank's body.

She sat up in bed because someone was crying.

Kippy.

She was out of bed and running. Tangled in her sheet. Stumbling. Bumped her knee.

"Darling are you all right?"

He turned a light on and looked at her. Rubbed his eyes. "I must have been dreaming."

She tried to catch her breath. "Me too. I thought I heard you crying."

He held his head. "I had this weird dream about being in a... a zoo, I think. Or a farm. Or maybe it was a giant submarine under the ocean." He let her sit beside him and hug him. "I was trying to find the way out but I couldn't. It was dark all around except..." (he turned haunted eyes to her) "...except there were these faces looking at me. I think they were like big grasshoppers or something because they had these..." (he made circular motions with his hands around his face and couldn't think of a good description). "And there was this devil." He looked stricken. "He had a nuclear bomb."

She patted his back. "I think you should just go back to sleep. You'll be surprised how easily you'll slip away."

"Thanks, Mom."

"Good night," she whispered and closed his door.

She stopped in the kitchen to draw a glass of water. Then she padded to her bedroom. She set the water glass down and yawned. Stretched.

Before she got into bed, she went to the window to close the shade a bit more.

And froze. There, parked against the opposite curb not far down the street, was a blue van glistening with rain. Quickly she closed the curtains.

Chapter 23.

On Saturday, Mary-Shane and Kippy went for a long drive up the coast. They picnicked on the beach and a light rain forced them to run for the car. Mary-Shane felt relieved to be away from San Tomas. On Sunday, their ritual: Breakfast at a diner, then Mass at St. Cosmas, visit to Mother for lunch, and finally the afternoon free. Mary-Shane, stopping at home to pick up a forgotten $10 bill and Kippy's comb, planned to go to a rainy-day matinee with Kippy (Captain Cosmos and The Galactic Secret; oh well, she couldn't take Kippy to see Love Secrets of Suburbia, so guess what had to give). She listened to her phone answering device.

At first she did not recognize the thin voice that hovered somewhere between frail and brave: "Mary-Shane, I must speak with you urgently. Please call me as soon as you can. Okay? Oh, and this is Father Lawrence O'Malley of St. Cosmas Parish. The number is..."

She called, and a very elderly but spry voice answered. "Father! This is Mary-Shane. I'm returning your call."

"Oh yes, my dear. How have you been?"

"Well, to be honest, up and down."

"So I gather. And Kippy?"

"He's okay. Five years in remission. You remembered us!"

Father Lawrence had been the Catholic staff chaplain at the hospital during Kippy's illness. He had spent a lot of time with the boy. "How is the sacramental life?" Father Lawrence asked.

She flushed. "Well, we don't always make it to church. When we do, it's to St. Cosmas."

He said: "I had a rather odd request from Bishop Mulcahy. Don't know entirely what to make of it. He wants me to hear your confession. He specifically said to offer you the Eucharist."

She felt stunned. "What brought that on? And why?"

"Could you do an old man a great favor? Stop by my house soon and we could talk about it. Like this afternoon?"

"This evening," she promised.

It was still daylight when Father Lawrence greeted her at the door of the small rectory and led her to the equally small living room that was cluttered and dusty, its furniture old, the doilies suggesting some of the elderly parish women came to clean once in a while. On the mantel piece stood one of those tall glass bubble clocks in which brass balls spun and rocked back and forth, a delight for the imagination of an earlier century.

Father Lawrence, wearing a shiny old cassock that tended toward gray rather than black, was thin and ascetic-looking. His bony nose and rocking-chair jaw

94

looked fragile. Here and there, the rice paper skin was speckled with something rose or chocolate or ink blue. He folded his hands over his knees, exposing a wide brass wristband and a timepiece whose lens was battered to a snowy consistency with nicks and scratches that seemed to suggest time for him was no longer of the essence. His intelligent brown eyes seemed ready to leap from their bony caves. His lips, compressed in a smile, acquired a troubled shape as she told her story.

He raised a hand. "Let me begin by saying that everything we will talk about will be covered by the seal of the confessional. That means it's between me, you, and God. I can't tell the bishop, the pope, the police, or anyone else a word you tell me. Even if you were the worst murderer in the world, every priest is so bound under penalty of eternal damnation in hell. You can feel safe sharing your heart with me."

"I'll try," Mary-Shane said.

He put on his mauve stole, prayed a moment, and waited.

"I don't know what to say," she told him.

"Try."

Haltingly, she recited every indictment she could think of. I have been angry because... I had lustful thoughts about... I haven't been to church because... She ran out of ideas.

"Is there more?" he gently asked. He had his eyes closed and hands clasped, and had not looked at her.

"I can't think of a thing. Wait." She covered her face with her hands. "Something deep inside of me feels sick. There is something inside of me, a terrible something. Or someone. And there is a memory that is there, that wants to come out, but it's very ugly, and I wish it would come out, but I won't let it. I think I murdered someone, or watched someone get murdered, I don't know which. I'm seeing a shrink and..." (she began to cry) "I don't know how much longer I can stand this!" She, rebel, wild one, slid down on her knees and buried her face in his lap.

He stroked her hair. "God loves you very much, Mary-Shane. Reach down, pull this thing out, hold it under the light, no matter how shameful or dirty it is. God will forgive you without any conditions. You must trust me. That is the truth."

She labored hard. Her breath came in dry heaves. But the awful clot of memory would not loosen from the arteries of her soul. She wanted so badly...

He put his hands on hers. There was surprising strength, almost a desperation, in his grip. His eyes stared into hers and she could smell his breath (chalky, sour).

"Father, I want to know about the time when Frank died. I don't remember anything. If anyone knows, you do." The clock ticked slowly and loudly.

"Try to remember, my child." The brass balls spun and swung hypnotically. The air was like tap water. The gray light was severe. Mary-Shane's heart pounded.

"You need to keep up your sacraments, my child. They stand between you and the devil. They stand between life and death."

She licked her lips. The words croaked out. "Yes, Father."

He closed his eyes. Prayers flurried from his lips and she could tell this was no ordinary confession. The words were slurred and rapid. They lacked novelty but were instead an engine of formulary and incantation centuries old. They had been spoken when the legions still rode out from ancient Rome, had been spoken when Byzantines ruled from their high walls, when medieval crusaders butchered each other in Europe, against alchemists and witches and sorcerers, whispered in every city and on every continent of the world. The whispering went on and on calling upon the three persons of God and all the saints, male and female, as well as the many classes of angels and archangels.

She almost grew drowsy. His grip on her hands never relented, and her skin began to sweat. Names fell around her in a chalky sour-smelling snow fall. Strange ancient names of men and women, boys and girls, who had been torn limb from limb by lions. She could almost imagine the sound of chains, the smell of hot gory sand, the roar of a hundred thousand cruel throats under a sky colored mother of pearl. They had lived lives like she or Kippy but in other places and other times. They had been pierced by miraculous wounds or healed without medicine or had walked out of flaming ovens. They had died and were immured and sometimes after fifty years could be unburied and their flesh was undecayed and the air around them filled with a smell sweet as rose petals. Others had been turned on the rack, dragged through muddy streets, tortured in rainy towers. Or subjected to any of the dark madnesses humans could perpetrate upon one another. He called on them now asking the power of their holiness to push back the snarling teeth of the demon. "...I, Lawrence, priest, adjure you, Satan and all evil spirits if you are present in this child of Christ, depart immediately to your place of damnation.

"And I, Lawrence, in the name of Jesus Christ," he said raising his hand in the sign of the cross, "absolve you from all of your sins, in the name of the Father, the Son, and the Holy Spirit." At last the heavy grip lifted from her hands. "Mary-Shane, I have just performed an ad hoc exorcism, and you have received God's forgiveness. Do you accept the divine reconciliation?"

She though about it. "Yes." She felt safe and pure, like a child with simple beliefs. She could almost imagine Mommy and Daddy coming in now to take her home. But the *Cold Thing* was still there. And the terrible memory, a blur with no name, a blot of pain at the core of her soul. Father Lawrence held up a white wafer the size of a quarter. "This is the body of Christ, Mary-Shane."

She recoiled. What is this? snarled the eel in the pool at the back of her brain. A brief vision flashed: *A jackal face with five horns.* The sunlet from the pagoda floated up.

Father Lawrence looked troubled. "Mary-Shane, God has cleared the slate for you. He asks you to accept Him. We do this in remembrance of Him, as he instructed."

She said: "Father, I don't think the slate is clean. I can't." She shied back from the shining white wafer.

"Trust me," Father Lawrence said. Sweat erupted in big droplets on his forehead.

She stuck out her tongue.

He looked at her closely. His hand trembled as he laid the wafer on her tongue, and it made a little sizzle, melting. She tried to pray, with all of her heart, but God's door seemed closed, and she swallowed the tiny bit of mush convulsively.

Father Lawrence rubbed his thumb gently on her forehead. "Mary-Shane, I want you to pray every day. I want to see you in church every Sunday. And I want you back here in a week. We need to explore this a little further. The bishop asked me to report back to him, and I'm uncertain how to tell him about our meeting this evening. Are you sure you're all right?"

She stood up and straightened her skirt. "I think I'm okay." But she wasn't sure, deep inside. He let her out, and it was clear he was hiding his uncertainty. "Come back next week," he urged. "I will," she said, noticing that the flowers in his garden were huge, like faces hungering for something, as she left to go to Mother's house.

"The BOY is not FEELING well," Mother said in her kitchen.

Mary-Shane put her gloomy meeting with Father Lawrence behind her as she commanded: "Kippy, stick out your tongue."

He did.

Mary-Shane glared over her shoulder. "See, Mom? It's pink. Not coated at all. He's healthy."

"I feel kind of tired," Kippy said.

"Did you sleep last night?"

He considered. "Yes and no. I slept, but there were these dreams."

"Again?"

"Yes. It was like a horror movie, and I knew it, so it wasn't particularly scary. It was more like a dull headache." He rubbed his chest. "Or heartburn or something."

She shook her head. "Mother, I would like you to stop making us feel like hypochondriacs."

"Hypochondria is self-inflicted!" Mother glared back. Her head was covered by blue-silver hair in curlers like the head-chargers in some of Kippy's plastic creepy monster kits.

"Oh what's the use?" Mary-Shane said throwing her hands up and striding into the kitchen shoving chairs out of her way.

Mother gathered her things. "You should be grateful to have me."

Mary-Shane was ready to walk out without saying goodbye.

"We are, honest," Kippy said.

Chapter 24.

On Monday, jack hammers and car engines ripped through the morning's sunny peacefulness as Mary-Shane crossed the street to the Herald Building. She was running late as usual, and luckily Mart Willow was not in his office as she rushed to her desk. But then, Spike had things under control. He smiled and handed her a phone message note. This land is my land, this land is your land... he hummed and went back to the death notices.

Mary-Shane spent a hectic day riding with Perry. They covered a fire in East San Tomas, a double murder in Canoga Heights, a riot at a union picketing line by a meat processing plant in Fairview, and a speech about crime by the mayor.

That evening, with Mother's ("See, where would you be without me?") borrowed car, she and Kippy drove home. There, looking dusty but apparently rebuilt, was her Mustang. It was totally restored, except there was still no radio, and in place of the defaced passenger door was a new, yellow door that did not match the car's green paint. There was an envelope on the driver's seat, containing her keys, and a note from Vic: "Here is your car. Hope it works okay. I wheeled and dealed with someone who owed me something. You don't owe me anything. I would like to see you again, and I'm sorry I made you mad the other day. Vic." The new license plate read: WARNED1.

Ann and Jeremy came over for dinner that evening. Ann had the afternoon off and she'd made meatloaf, mashed potatoes with chicken broth gravy, and as dessert, banana custard in graham cracker cups. Ann and Mary-Shane talked at the kitchen table. The boys played video games in the living room. Jeremy had brought "Galaxy 7000: Captains of Thunder" and the boys took turns chasing and killing each other as spacemen or hideous monsters dwelling in star caves. Whatever those were.

Later, Mary-Shane walked Jeremy and Ann out to their car. She waited while they loaded plates and bowls into the back seat and got in. With a kid, going anywhere was like planning a safari, Mary-Shane sympathized. Under the familiar loquat tree that shed so messily on the crew cut lawn, familiar light ambering the mild night air, the *Dark Feeling* hit Mary-Shane. It welted her between the eyes so hard she reeled back. Had she not managed to grasp a loquat tree's hard trunk, she would have keeled over into the hedges. Ann and Jeremy waved as the car pulled out. Ann did a Y turn in the middle of the street. Each leg of the Y was punctuated with a rattle and a screech of the old transmission. At the last leg of the Y, Ann shifted into first gear. The car was dead stopped and Ann leaned out to wave. Only it wasn't Ann. It was Wiz. Her face looked pale and her eyes were filled with vacant sky.

The car slid away. Mary-Shane staggered toward the brush cherry and threw up. She washed her face and hands at the garden hose. Then, gripped by a terrifying urge from the *Cold Thing*, she stood stiffly and dropped belly-whompus into the pool. As she sank to the bottom, she contemplated opening her mouth. What was the use? She opened her eyes and glimpsed the flaking blue latex paint on the surfaces in the pool; and the tiles, inset at regular intervals near the surface, with yellow and red flower motifs on dark-blue enamel. Then her chin banged against the bottom. Ouch. She bounced slightly, rolling like a log. It would all be so quick, so welcomingly dark. She floated. The water was warm from having steeped in sunlight all day. So cozy. Final. And easy. No more of this thick sludge of life she was painfully squeezing through. A chill breath (of the living, rustling, whispering, everynight world) did feathers up and down her back.

NO!

She balled her fists and yelled. The yell came out as a bubbling choking noise and she stood in the pool trembling. Something, someone, had just tried to kill her. Her feelings were a washing machine of rage, pain, invasion, humiliation, penetration. She had just been raped and she seethed for revenge. The *Uncaring Thing* slipped away like a snake backing into the hole in the back of her mind. She pulled towels from the wrought iron railing—she and Kippy had left them to dry yesterday—and tripped into the apartment. "Are you in the tub?" she hollered.

"Yes."

"Are you okay?"

"Yes."

She went into the kitchen without turning the light on. The kitchen still smelled steamy and soapy from dishes being done. She rummaged in her purse. Not finding her mirror, she dumped the purse. Some of it went on the table, some on the floor. She pawed through the contents and found her cosmetics mirror. Damn, a scrape on her chin. She'd worn a few of those thanks to Mr. MacLemore. Washing her face at the sink with cake soap and a dish rag, she sputtered and looked at her indistinct reflection in the dark window. No more Miss Nice Guy, she thought. You wanna fuck with me, I'll find you and I'll make you wish you never heard of me. She lowered her head and put her hands to her face. What am I doing? she thought. What, am I nuts? This isn't Frank MacLemore I'm talking to. This is some Dark Thing that's risen up from hell. It's his spirit. Frank's come back to haunt me. No, I'm really off my bean now. My coconut's gone mushy. I'm slipping on the great banana peel of mental jock rock. The lights are on but nobody's home.

Hearing the door open, she quickly straightened. She looked at her reflection again. Determined. I don't believe in any of that supernatural crap. I'm under a lot of stress and, and, and...

Kippy stepped out on his crutches, and she whirled to face him, half expecting Frank. In the odd lights seeping from outside, he did look a little like his dad. But the softer lines, the beautiful saucy eyes, those were hers.

He looked her up and down. "You're dripping. And what happened to your chin?"

"I slipped and fell into the pool," she said. She went to the bathroom and put toothpaste on her brush.

Kippy slipped into an easy chair. He toweled his hair. "My legs. They ache like. It think it's the weather lately always changing."

Mary-Shane dropped her toothbrush in the sink, where it bounced around clattering before she finally caught it.

Chapter 25.

She told Dr. Stanislaus about her fall into the pool. "I feel something in my head. I felt it when I nearly drowned myself. I feel it now. It's always there."

"A personality?"

"I'm not sure. It's like an eel coming out from under the rocks deep in the water."

"So it's a snake or an eel?"

"I'm not sure. I don't see a creature, I just think there's one."

"So maybe it's just an analogy."

"Maybe."

"Then we'd like to know what it's an analogy of."

"Yes. Am I suicidal?"

"You are under a great deal of stress. It seems to me you are afraid. You seem afraid of people doing things to you, not you doing things to yourself."

"Then, on Sunday, I was examined by an exorcist."

"You were what?" The gray walls around Dr. Stanislaus grew smoky, or was that just her vision blurring?

"I was interviewed by an exorcist." She told him about her meeting with Father Lawrence.

Pause. "I see." Another pause. "And how to do you feel about that?"

"Scared."

"Of the devil?"

"No. For my son's health."

"So it's the old fear."

She laughed. "Popping up in new ways?"

"What do you think?"

"I wish I were so sure."

He never spoke her name. "Tell me about the exorcist."

"Are you going to laugh?"

"No."

She told him. He drank it all in without expression.

"I guess you hear the wildest things."

He looked up at her. "What do you mean?" His eyes bored into her.

"I meant, this all sounds crazy, right?"

He changed the subject. "Your physical turned out fine. No brain tumors or anything."

"Can I ask you a question?"

"Shoot."

"Does it bother you in any way that a patient of yours seeks spiritual help as well as medical?"

"The mind is still a mystery. If it helps, do it."

"You don't think I'm flipping my frying pan?"

"I don't think so. I'm still working on extreme stress as a hypothesis. Are you getting your sleep nights?"

"Are you serious?"

He tapped the microphone. "Patient answers no."

Chapter 26.

The next day, Mary-Shane loaded a bunch of Kippy's old clothes into the trunk of her car. On midmorning break, she bought a nice thank you card and mailed it to Vic. She was thankful, but she kept the card as free of undertones or overtones as she could. Didn't want him reading anything into it other than thank you. Spike ("...it's a long way, to Tipperareeeee....") was really catching on. His good eye for detail delivered her of death notices. They got the obits put to bed on time and then had the luxury of preparing for tomorrow's rat race.

The copy girl brought the mail to each desk. She dropped a package on Mary-Shane's. Mary-Shane opened it and found a book and a note. The note was from Father Lawrence: "You were asking about the B's. I remembered that I had this. I'd like it back, please. Best, Father L. (Remember your daily prayers!)."

Wow, she thought, delicately inspecting the old volume. It was an 1895 edition of "Wallace Burtongale II, A Life of Adventure, As Told By Annabel Burtongale." The heavy covers were done in swirly reds and yellows, with faded leather edging. She sat on the edge of her seat, held the book between her knees, and flipped through it. There were pen and ink drawings, finely executed in lined shadings like patent office pictures of machine parts: A camel and an Arab boy near a pyramid; a paddle wheel steamer on a river lined with palm trees; an explorer in pith helmet (Wallace I?) in a violent moment shooting a lion; a sphinx in glossy black stone surrounded by turbaned workers with haunted eyes... Quickly, she pressed the book shut and slipped it into her lunch bag.

That afternoon she left an hour early and drove to the Jungle, the wood by the zoo where she'd seen the primitive horror masks. She sat near the maintenance road leading behind the zoo and waited. The sight of the woman and small child had torn at her conscience. She had a box of blankets and clothing in the trunk for them. Rain drops pong-ponged on the car roof while she kept her gaze fixed on the leafy canopy of the Jungle. The basilica was dark and silent.

While she waited for street people to appear, she wrapped her legs in a blanket and munched chocolate-malted-milkshake-flavored popcorn still warm from the take-out stand. Coffee latte in a foamed plastic cup steamed on the dash. She flicked idly through the radio stations, finding no music for this moment. She turned the radio off, content to listen to the rain. Forced into idleness, she walked through the city of her mind, visiting places of which people generally did not think during their busy lives. These were not generic crossroads like 'work' or 'home' or 'play,' but nameless side streets of the self, of long-ago joys and fears. Some of them evoked a hazy inner smile, others an endless drizzle of tears. Somewhere in that metropolis of her psyche, sprawling now miles below as if glimpsed from a jet, was the nested conspirator who had made her city lights flicker, flicker, darkly, sickeningly...

That was it, the microscopic Mary-Shane, pedestrian with a suitcase and a windblown skirt, said to herself on a street corner with no name, in a city called Mary-Shane, that was it! The power station... If she could find the power station, she could find what was browning out her lines...it was the answer to all her questions!

Transposing herself once again to the amorphous jet window, she tried to project her comprehension over the utility grid far below. She tried to recall the *Dark Feeling*. Tried to home in on its source. But there was no lump in the snake, no bubble in the straw, no feeling anywhere on the grid...

TIME TO LAND.

Wait, one thing. A brief message. A phone call. A radio signal. A something. The echo of a smile. A wriggling sun.

WHAT?

She cried "Huh!" and sat up because all around the windows of her car there were faces. She surveyed the scattered popcorn in her lap. She realized she had fallen asleep and had a dream; something about flying and about being lost on foreign streets and about the sun on the pagoda (wiggly limbs, smile that made her shudder). All her sudden realizations in the dream were lost. She was as far from the answers to all her questions as ever. She looked at the twisted, deformed faces staring in at her while they pressed their fingers on the glass like minnow bellies. She rolled down the window a half inch and gulped mouthfuls of wet air faintly soured with unwashed-body smells.

"Are you all right?" asked a narrow face with an open sore in blond chin stubble.

"I'm fine," she said. She recognized them now: the street people she'd come to help. She rolled down her window, aware it was a gesture both brave and foolish. Vic would lacerate her if he saw her doing this. They crowded around their leader and she saw they were men women and children of all races and ages. Their sodden rags clung to them, here and there colored with false gaiety by a bright logo like 'Wild One' or 'Party Animal.'

"There was a woman with a little girl. I saw them the other day."

Eyeballs exchanged telepathic glances. "That must be Mabel Stork and her little one, Evvie," the blond man said as though speaking of a neighbor. "Hey, anybody seen Mabel?"

"Who?"

"Mabel Stork."

"Oh, she gots the little—"

"Yeah, man, she de lady dat... ."

"She's working the Mission up around Canoga," said a knowledgeable voice. The ragged ones were hard to distinguish from one another. Mary-Shane thought of Charles Dickens's novels and thought what am I doing here? Is this a time warp? People like this don't exist anymore. Is there a Ripper among you, dear folk?

A dark face floated in. He had one good eye; the other lay shut as though asleep. Dreadlocks lay heaped over the ears under a green yellow and black tam. He grinned: "Moonboy here. You nice lady. I read your mind." He had a lilting Jamaican accent.

She thought What are you doing here in the drizzle when you could be home where it's warm smoking ganja?

He nodded as though in conversation. "Jah! No work here no more. You think this is bad you should try them docks in New York and over Port Elizabeth way."

She stared at him thinking about the woman and the little girl.

"Ah," he said, "Mabel Stork and little Evvie now." He turned his face so the good eye could scrutinize her from several angles. "You not the police now, are you?"

She shook her head.

"You been seen here, the folks was talkin' about." He reached a long bony hand into the car and she stared down at the ebony fingers, half expecting them to go for the buttons of her blouse. Instead, they moved toward her hand. She looked at his fingers, then at the pink tongue straining between his teeth, then back at his fingers. And realized what he wanted. She handed him the big styro coffee cup. He lifted it like a chalice and drank until he made a gratified groan. "Ahhhh!" he said and handed it to the next one. "Here, Christopher Marlow, drink."

She watched the blond chin stubble, the Adams apple bobble, and wondered how old is that kid, sixteen?

Moonboy grinned. "You bring good coffee. You no cop, you too soft. And dumb." The grin faded like a light shut off. "You got something for Mabel Stork?"

Her hand sneaked to the window crank. "I have some clothes for the little girl. Or any other children with you. And I can get more," she added with the desperate thought if only they let me go.

Moonboy laid a hand on the window as if to hold it down while he looked left and right considering.

Her heart throbbed fearfully.

"All right," he said. She felt his power, and realized she was getting a reprieve (but from what? the altar down below?). "You leave the things with me. I see that Mabel gets them. And Evvie."

She handed him the trunk key. Darkness was falling, and no way was she getting out of this car.

"You come again," he said in a booming voice. "You no cop. You bring what you can because" (he pointed down into the Jungle) "we all cold. And hungry," he emphasized. "Bring food."

"In cans?"

"Yes, cans. Anything."

"Hey, steaks!" someone squeaked.

"French fries & catsup!" another shouted.

"Filet mignon with mushroom caps."

"QUIET," Moonboy said. She heard and felt the trunk slam shut. The key materialized and she plucked it away. "Thank you," Moonboy said. "You ain't stuck on the cop, is you?"

She glared at him, her cheeks burning.

"He got nice hats, and a gold ring, and sharp shoes he like to kick a man with, and always de pressed suits." Laughter erupted behind him.

"Thanks," she said. "Listen, it's been swell, but I really just wanted to give the stuff to Mabel and the little girl, okay?" She turned on the engine and felt reassured by its steady power. "Me gotta go now, okay Louie?"

He waggled his head. His eye looked daunted. "You a saucy one." Shadowy figures cleared out of her way. She turned the wheel and rolled forward.

"You come back with food!" she heard shouted as she drove off. The voice was filled with desperation.

As she drove down the familiar streets toward home, her eyes stung. Her hands were trembling so badly she had to pull over in a well-lighted gas station and just sit for a few minutes. She would never tell anyone about this. You could have been raped or murdered, she could picture her mother saying; or Vic. Why do you do these things, Mary-Shane?

Because I can be a real asshole at times, she thought. Kippy would have lost not only his Dad but his Mom also. She started the car. I meant well, that's all. As she glided past the open work bays of the gas station, she heard mechanics laughing (oh welcome all the familiar sounds of life!) and a radio blared old rock tunes.

That night, after Kippy had fallen asleep and she herself was tired and ready to slip away, she sat in her living room and brought out the old book Father Lawrence had given her. The book lay heavy in her lap and the words and pictures floated in a haze as she skimmed through it, too tired to really read. Annabel Burtongale had written by way of introduction:

My grandfather, disenchanted with the life of business and commerce laid out for him by his father, went East to Yale and studied Oriental History. Not satisfied to be merely book-learned, he set out in 1862, while that most tragic of Civil Wars ravaged our nation, to explore in turn each of the great empires that had given birth to our own civilization.

My grandfather made, in all, seven journeys by packet that took him to the now slumbering mounds and monuments of Sumer, Akkad, Ur, and Babylon in the Tigris-Euphrates river valley; to Palestine where David and Solomon, and later Jesus, walked; to Egypt, where once Pharaohs ruled; and finally to the West of Africa, where the camel caravans from Sudan and from the Atlas Mountains of Morocco meet the Congo jungle trade routes at the fabled outpost of Timbuktu.

My grandfather, as I shall relate, encountered the suspicions of modern viziers and grandees, as well as the ignorance of primitive people living upon the ruins of forgotten greatness, at every turn. On the island of devil worshipping witch doctors in Togoland, he barely escaped with his life, having coveted a stone idol too dear to its pagan worshippers to let any man part them from it.

But from Egypt he did bring, in his last expedition, from the haunted temple ruin of Blessed Mason Imhotep on the First Cataract of the Holy River, the fine Black Sphinx that stood until recently in the entrance to our family's zoological garden. And it is to this sensitive issue that I must ultimately turn, for in a precipitate act of impulse, my grandfather ordered the cursed statue, that weighed some twenty tons and had been shipped across sea and land at great cost, dumped at sea off San Tomas...

Troubled, Mary-Shane wanted to read further, but tired, she yawned, slipped the volume shut, and fell asleep on the couch.

Chapter 27.

Jules Loomis called her into his office about mid-afternoon the next day. "Mary-Shane, Wiz's body has been found." He looked bereaved.

"No." She felt her face drain.

"Some hikers found her bones in a shallow wash deep down in the woods outside the zoo." Mary-Shane sat down and wept. Jules offered her a tissue, but she shook her head. Tears sailed off to both sides. She found a hankie in her purse.

Perry took her along in his car. Tears of rain dribbled along the windshield as Perry pulled into the by now familiar morgue building. An assistant M.E. opened a shiny drawer. This was, as she had imagined and not found when coming to view Johnathan Smith's remains, the chilly room with the stainless steel drawers and cruel drains set in the concrete floor. A large plastic bag slid out on its drawer. Behind it were several smaller bags. "Jesus Christ," Perry whispered over and over.

Mary-Shane wished Perry would shut up. The assistant M.E. undid the metal snaps on the bags and they fell open. "God!" Mary-Shane cried out as the skull's empty eye sockets stared at her. She recognized the slight yellowish unevenness of the front teeth. There had breathed life and laughter so close to her. In her mind, like Hamlet over Yorick's skull, she could clothe again those poor bones with lips and nose and twinkling eyes. She could reach out and touch the dear eyes. Help the glasses back up that always slid down. Caress the mouth that spoke with such hurt and fury, yet also with comfort and advice while she sat opposite Wiz sharing a joke or a yogurt. The assistant M.E. was saying: "...evidence she was torn apart by something or someone with large claws and a short, powerful stroke, like that of a big cat. Not long afterwards she was carried some distance in a sack (we have fibers) and cut up with a hatchet..."

Mary-Shane's eyes throbbed. The evidence of her senses told her this was very much real. Devils didn't have handsaws. But they might have claws. Where did one check such information?

The assistant M.E. buttoned up his grisly sacks. His pale hands worked carefully as though he were sealing lunch bags.

That afternoon Mary-Shane called Vic from the office.

"Hi, sugar," he said.

"Hi." She wasn't ready to call him sugar or honey or anything. "Vic, I went and saw the body."

"Miss Chickowitz?"

"Yeah. That's Tsha-ki'-vitch. She was my friend, Vic. Who did it?"

"I'm sorry. I don't know."

"Why did they do this to her?"

"Who's they, Mary-Shane? Do you know? I don't."

"Vic, we know she was dabbling in the occult."

He sighed deeply. "I keep telling you to butt out."

"This is more personal, Vic. She was my friend."

"You see how she ended up. Want to JOIN HER?"

"Thanks for the car," she said quietly and let the receiver rattle to rest in the switch hook.

"How is the new guy doing?" Jules asked.

"Spike? He's a human teletype machine."

They regarded Spike who sat upright at his terminal, typing away while humming a complex symphony. At the moment his lips were making 'bup-bup-bupbup' trumpets.

"I'll learn all about classical music this way," Mary-Shane said.

"At least you manage to keep your sense of humor." He left unsmilingly, but gave her a fond glance over his shoulder.

Perry stopped by. "Mary-Shane," he whispered, "There's some kind of a feud going on in that family. I don't know between whom exactly or over what, but Jules and a bunch of others are on one side and Wallace and probably Polly are on the other side. This time, Jules's bunch seems to be winning, at least for now."

"Maybe that's why Jules was able to move me over with you," Mary-Shane ventured. "Am I being used? Are we?"

A Mr. Belmont called her.

"Who?" she asked irritably.

"Peter Belmont," the older man's voice continued patiently. "Terri's boyfriend. She used to speak of you very fondly."

"I'm so sorry," Mary-Shane said.

"Thank you. It's hard on all of us. Are you a Believer, Miss MacLemore?" There was such sticky, hidden insinuation in his tone that she became flustered. "Yes?"

"A Practicing Believer?" he said, paring closer to the bone of whatever he was driving at.

"I'm a— sort of semi-practicing Catholic," she said.

"Oh." A pause. "I see." His voice became once again merely pleasant, opaque. "There is going to be a small get together this evening at our apartment. Not exactly a funeral such as you're used to, but a send-off if you will. A memorial. How shall I put it—?"

"No need," Mary-Shane said. "I'll come. Where is it?" She'd never been to Wiz's apartment. She'd never shared in Wiz's private life. All she knew was that somewhere there was a garden and in it were old yogurt cups, with sprigs of this and that growing out of them.

Perry could not go with her; neither could Jules; but she resolved to go. So once again Mother had to pick up Kippy.

Mary-Shane found the yogurt cups all right. They stood in tilty rows in a small window plot outside Wiz and Peter's apartment. Attached to each cup by a weathered clothes pin was the paper packet in which the seeds in that cup had come. All herbs, Mary-Shane noted, some with weird names. Some of the packages seemed to come from Mexico, from Europe, even from Africa and Asia.

The people were, as she had expected, odd. What else? She remembered Wiz in her dowdy clothes... But nice people, once you got past the extra-bright smiles and the soft, insistent hand shakes. It wasn't creepy, exactly; but she felt as though there were a tremendous secret, and she was the only one at the memorial who didn't get it. In the end, she could not wait to leave. She stayed an hour, and in that time she felt as though cats were rubbing against her psyche.

Chapter 28.

Next day, Mary-Shane and Perry went where Wiz's body had been found. Great billowing rain clouds rolled in from the ocean. The sky was pen and ink colored and about as stark. Dotted with police cars, the mouth of the Jungle looked less formidable. The basilica looked small and gray. Uniformed police moved about in small conversations. Forensic people had a van pulled up and were examining the burial site inch by inch for clues. Several figures in drab clothing stepped from the bushes. Mary-Shane's heart leapt when she saw Mabel Stork and Evvie. Mabel had a dull look.

"Did you get the blankets?" Mary-Shane asked. The little girl's face was dirty but her cheeks looked full. She had circles around her eyes and as she hid behind her mother's skirt she coughed deeply, rackingly. "The blankets," Mary-Shane repeated.

Mabel's grimy face turned toward Mary-Shane. "What," she said flatly. Mary-Shane realized the human being before her in castaway clothing was probably insane with no business on the streets or in this Jungle or worse yet dragging a small child with her.

"I gave some blankets to Moonboy for you."

Mabel hooted as though this were a joke. Evvie coughed again and Mabel wrapped a freckled ham arm around her.

"Your little girl's got to be seen by a doctor," Mary-Shane said. All the years of worrying about Kippy welled up in her. She wanted to take Evvie in her arms. As she felt this she realized how much she'd always wanted to have just one more child, a girl.

"She'll be looked at by a physician," the policewoman assured Mary-Shane. Mary-Shane watched sadly as Mabel climbed into the police car. Evvie's large eyes, floating amid Mabel's skirt, remained fixed on Mary-Shane with an intense pleading. Or was it warning. Or was it simply insanity? As she stood there with Perry, they heard a whistling sound that grew into a scraping sound and grew until she got frightened. The ground was shaking. She looked at Perry, but he was looking up. A shadow darkened the already somber sky. Perry whistled. "That's a big one, huh?"

A jet aircraft, so massive and sprawled it did not seem possible it could fly, crawled overhead slowly and ponderously at about two thousand feet. Air Force stars were clearly visible on the wings and fuselage, as were small windows for peering out.

"A C-5A Galaxy cargo plane," Perry said. "What in the hell are they lugging around in our skies?"

That afternoon Mary-Shane left work a few minutes early, determined to find Vic Lara. She was having a change of heart. Maybe she should buy him dinner. She was happy that her car was back and maybe she'd give him one more chance. She left messages at his office, and received no reply. She'd tried dialing his car phone, and received no answer. A female Sergeant Somebody at police headquarters assured her he was working. Mary-Shane figured he'd probably be someplace near the zoo or the Jungle.

It was getting dark, and beginning to rain again. The windshield wipers kept a beat as she cruised along looking for his car. Leaves and papers rattled across the street. Palms bent their green crowns. The rain fell hard and straight, banging on the car roof. Visibility was down to a few dozen yards. She nearly gave up.

Then she saw Vic's car. It was pulled up at an odd angle, one wheel on the curb. She pulled her raincoat over her head and got out. "Vic?" she called. "Vic?" Her voice sounded thin. The air rattled loudly with water punching the street and the sidewalk. "Vic?" Each time a gust of wind cut through, the water turned white like sheets of glass thread.

The dark car stood at an unnatural angle pointing toward a copse of trees. Three of its doors were open, the driver's and both rear doors. Worried, she sloshed through the overflowing gutter. Her feet grew chilled, her shoes soaked, her stockings gritty with roiled sand and debris. "Vic?" She peered into the car. Nothing out of place that she could see except... the lock on the shotgun rack was open and the shotgun was gone...

"Oh my God," she whispered. Something had happened to him.

Lightning forked overhead like veins and arteries full of neon. Thunder followed almost immediately rolling around and growling bearishly, slamming against her ears. She held her hands to her ears and looked about frantically. The raincoat fell away and she barely noticed.

Lightning flashed, then thunder rolled close; lightning again, then thunder.

Amid winks of lightning, she spied something beyond the trees. Dancing? Singing? A small globe of lemon light dimly flashed about and kept changing shapes. "Vic?" She hurried through knee deep grass that tore her nylons and gashed the soft skin of her calves.

Lightning: a figure jumping.

Lightning: a pair of arms waving in supplication.

Thunder: and in it a man calling for help.

She climbed up a minor grade and emerged between two giant pines. Except for the wildly gyrating bubble of light, it was blind dark. She heard voices in the prattling rain and could not make out the words but she could feel the intensity of emotions. Even as she formed the word Vic her lips fell slack and she sank down on her knees at the sight. It was as if her body was giving out. What she saw next was like a defective movie clip, visible only in short stark frames of lightning and whenever the globe of light found a target.

Vic Lara, dressed in starchy clothing now saggy and soaked, held a shotgun on three street people and was whipping them with a long steel flashlight. It was, she recognized, one of those heavy police flashlights designed to double as a nightstick. The men were bleeding and crawling dimly begging for mercy. Mary-Shane held her hands over her mouth not knowing what to do. Should she run? Her legs felt paralyzed. Should she call out his name, ask him to stop? He might turn and shoot her, for he was in such a frenzy that his mouth hung open. Whipcord strong, he kicked and beat the men.

Lightning, lightning, thunder!

The heavy flashlight whacked one man's back so loudly that each slap, each dull boom of steel on bone, jerked Mary-Shane's head from side to side as if she herself were being beaten.

Lightning, thunder!

Rain streaming down her face, she rose and screamed his name. "Vic!"

He turned, swinging the shotgun around ready to fire, and for an instant she looked death in the face. She saw his face only twice for a fraction of a second as lighting flashed. Horrified, she saw who he was, what he had become. His eyes were like black holes filled with insanity and she wondered if a man had to be drunk to do something like this. His mouth was a slit of fury. There was a gash on one cheek where something had raked him. His skin lay stretched over his bones as though part of some alien anatomy.

The lightning gone, she stood blinded and transfixed in the powerful beam of his light. Somewhere thunder growled. The rain streamed down. There was a moment of waiting, of imbalance, of dread, during which she heard the rain, and her choppy breath chugging piston fashion in her throat, and the deep racking sobs of the two conscious men.

Then the light swung away. It fell first on the man who lay unconscious. Then on the man still trying to crawl away holding his bloody head. Then on the untouched man who now was in turn on his knees with folded hands.

They were just boys, Mary-Shane saw. She screamed, "Vic Lara, you motherfucker, let them go." She screamed again in a voice that fought thunder: "Let them go!" The third time her voice cracked and nothing came out of her mouth. She beat the air with her fists.

He turned away and barked: "All right you fucking clowns. Now get this. I'm gonna be up your assholes and down your necks every minute until you deliver the son of a bitch who's down here killing people. Before you're next, assholes. Got that?"

Mary-Shane heard no more because she whirled and ran. She heard him behind her. "Mary-Shane!" he yelled.

She ran heedless of the cutting grass. "Mary-Shane!" he yelled again. She ran across the sidewalk. Past the skewed police car. Splashed through the overflowing gutter. "Mary-Shane!"

Her car was on the other side, locked... she slowed to fumble with her keys... She heard a loud click behind her. The shotgun. She whirled in slow motion, knowing she was going to die. Of course. She was a witness. He was aiming to blow a hole in her the size of a tunnel. As she turned she fell, landed hard on her butt.

He stepped into the light of a street lamp. The shotgun lay over one forearm, open and impotent. "Mary-Shane," he pleaded. It was good old Vic Lara again. Easy going, smiling. He extended a hand from twenty feet away in an offer to help her up.

She backed away, rising. She shook her head. "No, Vic, no. Don't come near me. Don't ever touch me again."

"But Mary-Shane, I can explain..." His voice had that purr to it. His teeth gleamed in the streaming rain.

Mary-Shane got the car door open, hunched like a madwoman, fumbling. "Don't you ever, ever, ever come near me, do you hear?"

He stood watching as she drove away. She looked back once more. The body was Vic Lara's but the face was Frank MacLemore's.

Safe in her car and headed home, she realized she'd lost her raincoat. No matter. Let the street people have it. It was a good price to pay in tuition for this rare opportunity to spy directly into a man's secret soul and come away having seen the devil.

Chapter 29.

A gentle, whispering rain sifted through the leaves outside Mary-Shane's apartment and fell splat splat down among the arecas and chaemadoras in the garden box.

"Kind of a drippy yucky day," she said wiping down the kitchen table. Secretly she was relieved, because her mind had been made up for her about Vic. No more.

Kippy sat by the living room window. "I kinda like it. I'm watching the raindrops fall into the pool."

She looked over his shoulder into the pool. Hypnotically, circles appeared, grew from dots into stove rings, then were overlaid by new dots turning into concentric circles.

She swatted him with the dish towel. "Got any homework?"

"I did it all last night. Me and Jeremy Temple worked through all the math problems. I really like the geometry problems because you can visualize..."

My son the nerd, Mary-Shane thought happily. Frank would— she paused in mid-dish, as a thought suddenly occurred to her. Frank had hated educated people. He had considered himself street smart, an alumnus of Hard Nox U. She remembered that Frank and his buddies had actually gone out while still in high school, big raw football players, and looked for San Tomas State University boys to beat up. Frank, she figured, would have always been angry at Kippy. Would have beaten him, beaten his son the way he had beaten her, the way he himself had been beaten by HIS father...

"Mom!" Kippy said. "Mom! You're going to break the dishes."

She stopped and took a deep breath. She realized suddenly that she had been banging the plate against her knees. Wiped her arm across her forehead. "Sorry." Frank, she thought, you're better off dead. It's best for all of us.

Kippy was still watching t.v. at eleven a.m. The kitchen and living room were done. Windows gleamed, tables looked bare and new, dishes stood stacked, brushes were at attention in the dishrack.Mary-Shane thought enough and abruptly ended her housecleaning.

She undid her apron and tossed it into the clothes pail under the bathroom sink. "Kippy? Tomorrow it's supposed to be bright and sunny. We're going to the zoo tomorrow, okay?"

" 'kay." He watched Captain Colorado of the Space Patrol zap several Denebian Greelings.

"I don't want you to sit and watch tv all day. How about we go to the mall for ice cream a little later?"

" 'kay."

Captain Colorado, having rescued the Aldebaranian princess, reassures her that her kingdom will now be safe. In answer to her tearful plea, he says he cannot marry her because he must return to his lonely patrol of the Spaceways accompanied only by his talking dog Ray and his telepathic parrot Kibble. As the music crescendoes, credits roll...

"What a jerk," Kippy said.

Mary-Shane frowned. "Huh?"

Indignant, Kippy waved his hand. "In real life nobody would go flying around in space with a dog and a parrot if they could live in a palace and like maybe, well, you know, *FOOL AROUND* with someone like old Princess there."

Mary-Shane plopped down on the couch. "Yeah, well who knows maybe he knows something we don't. Like maybe she's a nut with the credit cards. Or she talks all night. Or who knows."

"Yeah," Kippy said grinning, "or she might have B.O."

"I wouldn't doubt it." Mary-Shane flicked open the paper and looked under movies.

Kippy went into the kitchen and the mixer briefly went "whrr!"

She fluffed the paper. "Hey, here's a movie we can go see tonight. Journey into Fear." It was a remake of the Eric Ambler classic, and several of her favorite actors were in it.

"Naw," Kippy said in the refrigerator as he looked for something, "I'd rather see that space movie."

She looked up and down and flinched when she came across a large and lurid ad for the bug-eyed monster saga Invasion from Galaxy Five. "Oh Kippy," she lamented.

He slammed the refrigerator door and stuck a can of frozen orange juice into the electric can opener. "You don't have to go with me. I've got a new friend at school who's just nuts about space stuff."

"Oh?"

"Yeah. His name is Rudy Chatfield. He's only nine but he can run the mile in seven-twenty and he's dynamite under the hoop."

"Rudy who?"

"Chatfield. You know. His dad's gonna give us free passes to the zoo. I can probably get you in at a children's rate." He made a face. "Just kidding."

She took two deep breaths and leaned over the back of the couch. "You're going tonight? with this kid? whom I haven't met?" (And don't want to meet, she thought, if he's got anything to do with the zoo).

Kippy licked the spoon, having just let the glob of frozen concentrate go plop into the mixer. "There's a further angle here."

"I can't wait."

Kippy measured cans of water into the mixer. "He has a sister named Elisa who is dynamite. She can ice skate backwards."

"How old is this Elisa?"

"Thirteen."

"Ah-hah! He goes for older women."

"She's real pretty. Two eighth graders got into a fight about who could carry her books to the bus."

"I thought you were more interested in model cars and dinosaurs and all that neat stuff."

He spread his arms. "Hey, do you think I'm a fool like Captain Colorado? Seize the month!"

"That's Moment," she said and turned to her paper.

The mixer fell silent.

She thought about Roger Chatfield in his airy office with the light pouring in like cream. I'll bet Elisa's real pretty, she thought.

Mary-Shane and Kippy met the Chatfields near the Bijou 6-Plex amid a sea of yelling kids.

Mary-Shane shook Dr. Chatfield's hand. Kippy paired off with Rudy. Rudy was a fast-moving blond comet of a boy with a bang on his nose and a cut on one knee. He wore his hat backward, his jeans jacket half off, and three colors of sneaker laces.

Elisa was a tall, caramel girl with long mahogany hair. Her clear white sclera and blue irises were startling. She carried herself maturely and demurely but had humor in her dimples, one before each ear and another in the center of her chin. So this is the first of a long line of beautiful women who will steal my son from me, Mary-Shane thought. Lord, but she IS beautiful. Elisa politely followed the conversation between her Dad and Mary-Shane, but her eyes wandered after Kippy. After a while she whispered something in her Dad's ear and he nodded. He gave her twenty bucks and she wandered off to shop.

"We meet again," Chatfield said in that kindly voice that made Mary-Shane want to wring his neck.

"So we do, so we do."

"Can I ask you for coffee?" He pointed to a nearby Donut Shoppe.

"Well—"

"If you're in a hurry, I understand."

"Okay." It would be rude not to. Besides, he was a tall good looking man. Not a Pinscher like Lara. Not a poodle either, she deduced from the hard knots in his arm. Arm? What was she doing? He'd casually extended his arm, European style, and she'd slipped herself around it as though they'd been going steady for decades.

Mary-Shane, she thought, are you nuts? This is a married man. Are you about to have your first extra-marital affair?

She felt her cheeks burn. Should she pull her arm away? Would it anger him? Or should she keep it like that but stand a half a foot away? Would he think she was cold? Or should she press against him like a damn...

He interrupted her flustered course of thoughts by holding the door open and ushering her into a place that smelled like heaven.

No, leaven. Sugar, dough, coffee..."Uuhhmmmm..." she said.

Killer donut special, a sign said, *67 cents.*

He too inhaled. "I love that smell. I don't drink or smoke or have any similar vices, I work out every day, but this smell drives me to crime. The smell," he said, "of warm, freshly baked...tantalizing..."

"KILLER DONUTS!" they said together and laughed.

She pulled her arm away under cover of jollity and took a window seat. He came back minutes later with a tray of coffee and donuts.

"I really shouldn't," she said holding up a glazed, multi-color sprinkled, raspberry filled donut.

"Join me in sin," he said.

He was a nice looking man with thick dark hair. He had strong hairy arms. Chest hair poked over the V of his open, blue-white pinstriped shirt (very expensive, she thought, longing to reach out and touch the material). His dark eyes (like Elisa's) were mature and kind and intelligent. His skin had the same caramel complexion as Elisa's.

"I thought we were going to do some zoo color, Dr. Chatfield," she teased in her practiced way, drawing out the syllables over him like the meshing of a net.

He appeared flustered, looked down. "I'm sorry. Call me Roger, will you? I meant to call you but, well, frankly, with things at the zoo the way they have been..."

"I understand," she condoled. "My friend was murdered there just a few days ago."

"Oh Jeez, I'm sorry. That would be Miss Chickowitz."

"Tsha-ki'-vitch. Terri. Yes. Now be sure and quickly correct me and say it was outside the zoo, not inside, with your fabulous safety record."

He swallowed hard. "I don't blame you for the way you feel. No, I've stopped thinking that way."

She froze in mid-chew. "Honest?"

"Yeah."

They ate in silence for a few moments.

"Isn't it ironic somehow," Chatfield remarked, "that our children are at the same school?"

"Quite a coincidence. San Tomas has over thirty private schools. It has more private schools than many cities have public schools, including San Tomas."

"You should write a tour book."

"Maybe I will."

"Rudy and Kippy seem to have really hit it off."

"Yes. Maybe we can have Rudy and Elisa over for cookies or dinner sometime. If you and your wife don't mind."

He looked startled. "I'm sorry. I thought you know. My wife died in an automobile accident three years ago."

Mary-Shane felt blood drain from her cheeks.

He laughed. "That's why you were holding your arm so stiffly. I thought you were having neurological difficulties. I was going to recommend a specialist—." He winked. He knew what she'd been thinking.

"I was. I am." She collected herself. "What about you, Mr. Zoo Mensch? Did the thought ever cross your mind that I might be, like, heavily married?"

He laughed. "Yes. But I checked."

"With whom?"

"I ain't gonna tell."

"You better, Roger Chatfield."

"Sister St. Cyr."

"God no."

"God yes. I tried to play it straightforward. This new friend of Rudy's seems to come from a nice home. Do his mother and father live nearby? Well that old bird—"

"—Sister Sincere, I call her—"

"—Good name. Sister Sincere looked through me like a sunbeam through glass. She has those twinkly eyes the color of—."

"—Nickers—," Mary-Shane said meaning the marbles.

"—Yeah, knickers," he said, "and she winked and told me not in so many words that you were single and quite possibly unattached."

"You are making grave suppositions," she admonished.

"How about dinner or a movie sometime soon?"

"I'll think about it," she said.

He looked at her through the hole in a donut. "Tuesday at seven?"

That would be the evening with Dr. Stanislaus. She'd feel free and refreshed. "Eight thirty," she said. "By the way," she added, "do you know much about the history of your zoo?"

"Some," he said, puzzled.

"Do you know anything about a statue, a black sphinx maybe, that stood in the main entrance at one time and then was dumped out at sea?"

He frowned. "Where did you hear that?"

"Oh, just some casual reading."

He had a closed, careful look. "There are some old stories. But I only came here ten years ago, and they're nothing but rumors. You don't believe in horror stories, do you?"

She grinned. "Try me. I read all the time. Horror stories too."

His look was rueful. "I'm a scientist. I close my mind to weird tales. Don't let rumors carry you away."

Chapter 30.

During the night, Mary-Shane put her hands over her mouth and drew in a deep breath of horror. It was dark except the street light near her bedroom window cast a broken film of beery light on the window sill. As she awakened, she felt adrenalin run like a shower of needles up and down her legs. Sweat made her hands slick as she removed them from her face and stared, puzzled, into her palms. Same reflected amber glow. And silence.

Only a memory of the nightmare remained, leaving a crawling feeling along the piano keys of her spine. It was a memory of walking down endless corridors that were dark on both sides, and being terrified because she felt eyes on her back. There was something... *a ship*. A sunken ocean liner? The Titanic? Her father's face... And Frank MacLemore yelling, yelling, sending his fist into her face... She sat up in bed and held her head like a vase, letting reality flow back in.

After a while, she padded across the living room and listened at Kippy's door. He was snoring. She stumbled into the kitchen, poured herself a half glass of water, and slipped back into her bed. After wrestling the pillow around for a moment or two, she fell asleep.

Chapter 31.

On Sunday, Mary-Shane and Kippy went to St. Cosmas. She sat where Father Lawrence would notice them as he puttered over his chalice. After Mass Mary-Shane and Kippy had brunch at the airport tower diner. Airplanes were Kippy's favorite, next to race cars and trains. His favorite, he made sure the world knew, was space ships but any launching pads were just too far away in the great big world. So the comings and goings of Cherokees and Piper Cubs had to do.

Mary-Shane was using a slice of bacon to push an oozing yolk on a slice of toast when Kippy declared: "Mom, I'm going to be an astronaut when I finish my Ph. D. in Physics."

"That's nice, dear."

"I'm going to be the first disabled astronaut." He toyed with his donut, making of it a rotating space station. "We'll have to fight our way through Congress on that, but I'll convince them that an astronaut doesn't need much in the way of legs if his arms and brain are strong."

They visited Mother as they did every Sunday. Mother's tone of voice played a singularly masterful woodwind of irony, whose reed had been pickled for so long in a brine of admonishment, blame, and silent accusation: Howard Berger, Mother said, no longer calls me about you. Mary-Shane smiled to herself privately as she stepped out onto the raised front lawn to look at the garden she had once planted as a little girl. It was something she did every Sunday, arms outstretched, teetering in high heels and tight dress on the rocky terraces overlooking Mulberry Street. Daddy had given her the packages of seed, had helped her carry potting soil in her child's wheelbarrow, had shown her how to notch the rows of soil, how to mark a straight line with a string between two pegs that could be turned tight, how to drop the seeds evenly, and then to cover them so the birds could not take them. They'd planted rows of peas, spinach, and tomatoes (all the things you don't like but they're good for you). They'd planted patches of strawberry, raspberry, boysenberry and mulberry. They'd planted a big pizza wheel of spices too. They'd planted an orange tree, a lemon bush, a black walnut tree, and aloes large and small. Shortly afterward, Daddy had died in the plane crash and she'd cried and cried out in the garden wishing he'd come back, but there was only the wind, blowing in the leaves. Layers and layers of pain had forced into the root system of her heart. Not only would he never come back, but there could never be another Daddy. The pain of his abandonment crazed her, made her wet her bed at night. She hated Mother for undoubtedly Mother had driven him away. Why else would he not come back? Ah, and poor Freddie. Freddie had been the hamster Daddy had given her after a trip to Farmer's Market in Santa Ysidora. Feed and water him every day, Daddy had said rubbing the thin blonde hair on her bony forehead.

Now Daddy was gone and she would sit for hours and stare at Freddy. Freddy at first circled in his cage, sniffing curiously. Then curiosity turned to worry. His large pink snout would raise to her beseechingly. Where had the good life gone? Where are my pellets, my water, my fresh straw, my finely shredded cedar bark? She sat depressed and stared, a frozen girl like a statue at St. Andrew's, and said to him in her mind: Daddy, I will take care of Freddy if you come back and take care of me. In the end Freddy grew disinterested and simply stayed where he'd lain down. "Mary-Shane!" Mother had hollered bursting in on her, "So this is where you've been hiding. Oh get away from him, he's sick, get out of this house and play with the other kids, I won't have you moping around, it drives me up the wall to see you sulking around like that." That evening, secretly, she'd taken Freddy from the trash where Mother had dumped him along with the egg shells and coffee grounds, and she'd given him a tearful burial in the middle of her spice garden where all the spices of heaven and earth met in the vortex of the great pizza wheel Daddy had designed for her. She had lost her challenge to heaven. And never again would open her heart so totally.

She nearly fell over, for one of her high heels got stuck in the soil. She wobbled onto the cement and marveled at how her mind seemed to be loosening its clog of old memories.

"Mother...?" She lurched around the corner on her high heels, waving her arms to keep from tripping as spaces between rocks caught her heels. Then she heard the creaking of Kippy's old swing. Stepping hard a few times to make soil fall from her shoes, she walked clicking neatly along the concrete walk along the house. Open mouthed, she stood unseen and watched Kippy and his grandmother. They were down in the fenced in play area whose hard-packed earth had not thrown forth seed nor blade in twenty years. Mother, not Kippy, was riding on the swing. Laughing. Whooping. Up and down, back and forth. Her drab dress flew in the wind. Her mottled hands clutched the chains. Her lined face was raised smiling and open-eyed full of girlish joy.

Kippy, holding on to the supporting bars with one arm, was pushing her. Faster, faster.

"Rockets away!" Mother yelled.

On Sunday afternoon, Mary-Shane took Kippy to the zoo. "What were you doing there with Grandma?" she probed, but was unable to get anything out of him. She concluded it must have been something spontaneous...

"You look very, um, official," she told her son.

"Mixing business with pleasure," he said proudly carrying the new leather briefcase Mother had given him for his birthday. He was to do a report for school. It was to be on a subject of his choice, using the technique of description from direct observation. He had picked the zoo. He was going to write about six zoo animals (why? because, he explained, things came in six-packs) and part of that was going to be a paragraph describing each animal from direct observation.

My son the professional, Mary-Shane thought proudly.

It was a warm, dry, pleasant Sunday. The zoo was crowded. Lots of tourists. Mary-Shane found herself doing a lot of waiting around while he wrote meticulously in a black and white marbled notebook. She stood in line for an iced tea and reflected on her figure. She kept thinking about the rainy evening Vic Lara had beaten the three homeless men. That gnawed at her conscience.

She hated waiting in line. As she stepped from one foot to the other, her gaze drifted around the zoo. She noted the central kiosk, where every half hour a puppet show on environmental themes was presented. She whistled in recognition, while her skin crawled. Where the stage now stood on its elevated stone pedestal, about ten feet by twenty feet, an ancient Burtongale had once placed an archeological treasure from Egypt. Then, going mad, he had it dumped into the sea before he died.

And as Mary-Shane considered these things, she felt the *Dark Feeling* coming back. Instinctively, sensing danger, she looked around for Kippy and her mouth went dry.

Kippy had the tip of his tongue captured between his teeth and was frowning over the notebook. He scribbled, stopped, frowned, scribbled, stopped, frowned.

It wasn't the full-blown *Dark Feeling*, just a faint trace of it. A sense of something alien extending its consciousness into her mind the way oil spread over water.

People nudged her to keep moving with the line, and she responded like a mannequin whose limbs are made of hard rubber.

Whatever it was, it just wanted to see if she was still there. It was cold and sluggish, as if just awakening from a deep sleep. There was only a cold Presence touching her soul.

"A dollar!" the pimply boy yelled for the umpteenth time.

She dropped quarters on the counter, took her tea, and turned.

"Your change!" he squeaked in a ridiculing tone, and several other counter kids tittered as though she were a drunk.

She ignored them and walked toward Kippy. As she did so, the *Dark Feeling* went away and she felt okay.

That evening, she again attacked the volume written so long ago by a lone voice in the Burtongale clan. The dead voice floated up to her in the living room:

...There were rumors that my grandfather had gone insane, but I wish to indicate the contrary. There were logical and scientific explanations for each of the deaths that occurred among zoo workers. Nonetheless, the fact that the deaths seemed to cease once the Black Sphinx had been dumped at sea caused a proliferation of new and ignominious theories regarding my grandfather's work. Furthermore, the fact that he died unfortunately senile fueled cruel rumors that must be laid to rest once and for all...

As Mary-Shane sleepily closed the book, she felt a thrill of unease, something dark and stabbing about her own past.

Chapter 32.

Above the zoo, the full moon glided like a ship with tattered cloud sails. A ship on fire.

Perry Stein unloaded the buffer with extra care outside the lesser rotunda of Admin 1 & 2. Beside him Matilda sniggered.

"What's the matter, honey?" he asked.

She flicked a dust pad. "I always giggle when I feel creepy."

Perry stopped and took off his glasses. He carefully wiped each of the small lenses on his shirt tail. Then he replaced the glasses on his nose and stepped to the edge of the cone of light thrown from the lesser rotunda. "You're right," he said, "I can't think of a creepier place at night than a zoo." As if in answer, several low, full sounds echoed through the trees from someplace deep.

He stared up into the black tree crowns and swallowed hard. Yellow light glittered on his glasses. Some of the sounds, Perry could have sworn, were not of this earth.

High on a ridge separating the Jungle from the zoo, two shadowy figures dug silently. Their arms moved rapidly and their rags fluttered. Inches away, the alarm-rigged fence hummed electrically. The two men worked fast, ducking out of sight each time the guard jeep passed on the access road just inside the zoo. Moonboy gripped Christopher Marlow's arm. "Be careful, unnerstan'?" Moonboy's single eye stared with the same singularity as the moon above, sharing a lunatic light.

Christopher Marlow shook his blond hair and a smile opened a crack in his youthful beard stubble. "We'll all be eating pig tonight, bro."

Moonboy cackled and clapped Christopher Marlow's shoulders. "You watch the boar, is what I tell you. The she boar be sleeping around her young. She be surprisin' quiet, you hear? You don' hear her until she be runnin you down and THEN boy do you hear all manner of snorting and yelling!"

"I'll be careful," Marlow said. He lay on his back and held his breath. The corded sinew in his abs tightened, glistened. In a moment, in a heartbeat, he was inside the zoo without having touched the fence.

"Walk true!" Moonboy whispered after him.

"Oink oink," Marlow said. But Moonboy had disappeared. The ridge curved empty in the moonlight.

While Perry spread paste wax on the central floor, Matilda opened Dr. Burtongale's office and nearly dropped her duster.

"Come in," said a kindly voice.

Matilda clutched the duster to her full bosom. "You nearly scared me to death." She felt Perry's reassuring presence right behind her; he always hovered close by to protect her, especially here.

"I'm Dr. Burtongale," the old man said removing his glasses. "I hope I'm not in your way."

"Oh no," she said, "I'll be in and out before you know it. Say, you're working late, aren't you?"

"That makes two of us."

His dark shadow fell before the pagoda, and the 300 pound gorilla sniffed curiously. He easily sorted through the dozens of smells, everything from the feather of the emu to the horns of the wildebeest, the leaves of the oleander to the berries of the chinaberry tree, the penetrating urine of the flamingos to the pond scum of the Southern Malaysian Duck. What he had come to find was not near yet. But was coming. And would be soon. He raised cupped hands and tapped them lightly under his breasts in anticipation.

Two other hulking shapes joined him. They loomed with silent, efficient menace on the open street near the pagoda. At the sound of an approaching guard jeep they melted away into the forest, then reassembled as the jeep's exhaust faded. They continued to stand on all fours, waiting. One of them had found a baseball bat, which he rested on the ground in a grip relaxed but ready. What they wanted was coming. Their special sense told them so.

Chris Marlow paused often. He had thought this would be simpler, but then what in life was? Was this really any different from breaking into an office building and trying to outwit the prowling guards along miles of shiny waxed corridors? Buildings tended to be full of weird noises too, like things flapping suddenly that made you jump but turned out to be the wind in a fan blade.

Why should this be different? He slid down an embankment making leaves crash softly. He waited and listened. Tiny hooves pattered away. A feathered thing shifted, fluttering, in its sleep. A hunting owl hooted. He stole along the edge of the road, ready to duck for cover if anyone came. He hoped there were no foot guards, or if there were, that they had loud feet.

"Thank you," Matilda said, pulling the door shut.

"Thank you," echoed Dr. Burtongale with a broad smile, removing his glasses and then putting them back on as the door closed.

"I'm done, darling," Matilda sang. "Perry?" She stopped and frowned. Small things dropped, acorn by acorn, on the roof. The air in the rotunda rustled as though spirits were chasing one another in the darkness under the ceiling. Mural-bound dinosaurs flashed wicked teeth and stalked forward with raised claws.

"Perry?" she wailed, dropping her duster.

In his office, Wallace Burtongale put his glasses down and rubbed his eyes. The grandfather clock chimed a melodious 'Big Ben' and ended with twelve drawn out 'dong's. It was midnight. Wallace sat back in his plush, high-backed leather chair and placed his hands on the arm rests. He closed his eyes and listened. The clock ticked, and its well-made machinery turned in its lubricated bed. The silence in the room was so profound that Wallace could hear the gear wheels inside the clock, magnified by the priceless hard West African Ash from which its cabinet had been made a hundred years earlier. He heard the tiny collisions of gear teeth, with no more force than a fly's wings beating together, and then the oily smack as the gear teeth separated again to make another full circle and touch again.

His breathing became long and shallow, as though he were asleep. But this was not sleep. He turned his unseeing face up as if to hear above the microscopic racket inside the clock cabinet. His mouth became pursed and harsh. There were terrible shadows inside his eye sockets. His fingers gripped the arm rests. His breathing became part of the machinery of the room.

The three gorillas began silently to move.

Their shadows and the shadowy bodies throwing the shadows danced indistinguishably under the chill bluish light near the pagoda. They made only two sounds, both so faint as to be almost indistinguishable from the general sounds of the zoo at night. One was the click of a rolling pebble here or there as a calloused palm or a carefully bent finger displaced it. The other sound was an occasional soft cherrywood *boing* as the baseball bat bounced lightly against the road surface.

Chris Marlow listened to the subtle sounds of the zoo and felt his spine shiver as though dead fingers had strummed a harp. Each time he passed a habitat, and its unseen occupants snorted or shlushed or snarled in their sleep, his heart nearly gave out. He was bathed in sweat. This was a little different maybe, he reflected after all. In an office building, no matter how unsuperstitious you were, every creak, every bang, every rattle immediately became a movement of evil spirits. But then you got whatever you were after, and once you hit the pavement outside among cars and people and flashing neon lights, you could laugh about it. Here, the noises were really made by things that could tear you apart and eat you in seconds. All that separated you from them was a shallow moat and a flimsy steel railing.

Some of the unseen animals were small. Others were not.

His heart nearly stopped when he stepped so close by a hippo that he felt its hot breath on his cheek. He had startled it in its sleep and it bounded up. Its breath shot a stink like rotten vegetables and hot runny shit. As Chris Marlow stood frozen, its heavy footpads danced about and made the ground shake. Chris was still trembling after the hippo had stopped running about.

Not much farther now. The boar compound was several enclosures further up on the right. Chris Marlow reached into his raggedy jacket and pulled out, foot by foot, the rope.

"Hi Baby," Perry grinned.

She closed her eyes and let out a breath. "Perry my sugar, you don't know how scared I've been wondering if anything happened to you."

"Now, now..." He took her in his arms, relishing the bigness, the softness of her, her faintly sour female sweat smell and the waxy smell of lipstick on her smooth young face.

"I was just straightening all the kinks in the buffer cord, three hundred feet of it, using the whole parking lot outside.

She pressed her cheek against his. "Always tell me when you're going outside, okay?"

"Don't be scared. Guards are all over the place."

Chris Marlow wasn't sure if he saw them first or if they saw him first: three huge guys, one of them with a nightstick or a bat or something.

Chris ducked into the bushes. His heart was beating so hard it seemed to lunge against his ribs, like an animal trying to escape a cage. He held his hands to his sore chest and looked out over the bush.

There were— he could not see properly in the weird light. How many? Three? Two?

Why were they not moving? Had they seen something? Were they waiting for other guards? They looked funny, like guys dressed in gorilla suits. What was this, a joke? Maybe a fraternity prank. Sure, an initiation.

Silence. Their heads and necks loomed darkly against the moonlight, and Chris began to get the feeling that they were not part of a prank. There was no giggling or shoving. Whoever these guys were, they were about serious business.

One of them was looking directly at Chris.

Hey, it was one thing when these guys were across the moat and behind bars. It was another thing when they were right there in the street with you.

No, it couldn't be. There must be guards around. Or maybe these were the guards and he wasn't seeing their uniforms right in the light. Sure, they were wearing football ponchos like those huge linebackers sitting on the bench on a rainy afternoon. That was it.

He cleared his throat. "Okay, I give up." Man give me a fucking warm jail cell. And some thick bars. I love it. "I'm in here. I don't have no weapons." He threw the rope out.

The shape had not moved. Eyes glittered intently.

"Jesus Christ, man, don't look at me that way." His lips beat against each other as he began to blubber. His pants got warm and wet as he peed all over himself. "Please..." he wailed and held his hands over his ears. "Please..." He stood like a small boy waiting for his irrational mommy to come and beat him like she did so often when she was drunk. *Why, mommy? why? what did I do? I promise I promise I'll never do it again oh please...*but mommy never backed off from a good beating. She would always stop yelling and have a look of concentration, lower teeth gripping upper lip. The strap would fall again and again and again on his naked skin, and his wails and the whipping leather would be the only sounds in his terror. "Oh please," he blubbered. He stood naked and had shit himself. Shame, shame, shame. The warm stinky oozed down his baby thighs and patter pattered on his bruised toes.

They moved now, hulking forms, lacking humor. Their mouths were open, revealing sharp white teeth, tusked incisors. Run? They were coming from three sides.

He was frozen with terror. *No, mommy, no no no!*

Poopy on the floor. Bad, bad!

They were all business, walking on their fours. Hairy fingers curled on the street. Knuckle, foot, knuckle, a determined rhythm. *Boing, boing* rang the bat softly, bouncing on the street.

You stinking little fucking son of a rat bitch. I'll kill your grimy ass if your father doesn't kill you first.

No, no, he cried. *I promise. Promise. Promise.*

But she never stopped when it came to this moment. The bat went up. The fists went up. He held his ears and screamed, hot tears trickling down his cheeks. He remembered nobody ever came to help him, but he screamed anyway.

"Did you hear that?"

Matilda and Perry stopped and looked at each other. His impulse was to run out and see who or what had made that sound.

In his office, Wallace Burtongale's eyes flew open. There, the sign that it was over. He rose and with a shaky hand used a handkerchief to wipe sweat from his forehead.

He opened a desk drawer and removed a laptop computer. He closed the drawer and let himself out of the office.

"I must have been crazy to bring you here," Perry said.

An office door opened, and they started. Dr. Burtongale walked out and locked the door. He carried a briefcase or something. "Good night," he said pleasantly without looking at them. His face wore a distant, eager look.

"Good night," Perry and Matilda echoed.

"Did you see the look on his face?" Matilda whispered.

Perry stepped to the door and looked out. The zoo was oddly silent, as though all its denizens were either dead asleep or else deadly alert and listening for danger.

"Close the door," Matilda's voice shivered behind him.

Wallace Burtongale walked through the security lot. He nodded to a young night watchman, who nodded back. "Just heard a scream," the night watchman said.

Wallace smiled at him. "You must be new here."

The man muttered: "Two years. But you don't never get used to the sounds they make out there."

Wallace found the particular green and tan golf cart that was his favorite. Placing the laptop computer on the seat beside him, he drove off. He stopped at the old pagoda-shaped utility house. The light played ripples on his face as though he were under water. His expression was eager. His eyes were big. His teeth showed in a hungry humorless grin. He unlocked the door to the Pagoda. His grin faded before he could enter.

WE ARE REPAIRING THE SHIP, the Pilot said. *YOU WILL SEE, WALLACE, WHAT A GREAT THING.....*

"You can take me," Wallace said. "Let my son go."

YOUR SON IS PART OF THE PRICE.

"No! It has to end here. Take my mind, what's left of it. Like you've taken generations of us. Let Gilbert go."

GIVE ME WHAT YOU HAVE BROUGHT, the Pilot said greedily.

"Yes." He knew he would not be where he was in life were it not for the Pilot. He thought of his father, dying insane between padded walls in the Burtongale mansion. He thought of his son's wasted life. He thought of his own coming depression and insanity, the fate of each Burtongale heir.

Wallace set down the laptop. His footsteps crackled on the hundred year old tile floor. He flicked on a light, but the bulb popped and darkness once again shrouded the claustrophobic interior. No matter. A shaft of moonlight leaned inside, lending a metallic light. Oil tank, generator, gas turbine, wall meters, gadgets bulked all around as he put the computer down in the middle of the moonbeam. He unzipped its cover and popped up the display window. The internal disk drives hummed like tiny toys, and a bluish light glowed from the window. The system display came on:

READY

Wallace closed and padlocked the door. Then he drove down the road. The first thing he saw was the baseball bat. It was slimy with clotted blood and stray hairs. Wallace removed the hose from the back of the cart and found a faucet by the side of the road. First he washed down the bat. He threw the bat into the back of the cart. Then he began to wash down the gore.

"Hello, Father," said Gilbert behind him.

Someone DID come to help Christopher Marlowe.

He was walking along a corridor toward the sea, and nothing made sense, but then had anything ever?

"You look sad," said a bright blue woman offering her hand.

"Are you an angel?" he asked, taking her hand which was chilly but firm.

"No," she said in a mixture of sadness and relief. "My name is Jane Callahan. My suffering is over, and I take it yours is too."

"Are we going to the Good Place?" Christopher asked.

She shook her head and smiled quizzically.

Chapter 33.

Dropping Kippy off at St. Andrew's, Mary-Shane got to work fifteen minutes early. She was sitting at her desk sipping coffee, eating a donut, reading the paper, and combing her hair when Perry waved from the City Room.

Spike walked in, big grin on his face and a bounce in his step. "Good morning, good morning! Ta-dum, ta-dee!" He sat down and started typing.

Mary-Shane clapped him on the back. "Yo spike, what's it today, Sound of Music or 1812 Overture?"

He smiled and kept on typing: "Jane Callahan, 43, after a long illness, at Mother of Angels Episcopal Hospice, San Tomas..."

She grabbed her coffee and followed Perry to Meeting Room C which was along Mahogany Row not far from the Burtongales' luxury offices. Perry closed the door and sat down. He looked haggard. She sat down beside him and offered a bite of her donut. He shook his head. "I did a dumb thing, Mary-Shane. What's that you got there?"

"Raspberry Sludge with a Party Sprinkle Sugar Coating," she warned, "yum. Want some?"

He shook his head.

"Don't know what you're missing." She took a bite and said with her mouth full: "You look like hell."

"I feel like it," Perry said. He stared down at his fingers which were scarred and detergent-dried. "I took a night cleaning job at the zoo."

"Hey, that's pretty smart, I think!" She stopped chewing as infinite possibilities for information gathering flashed before her. She pictured herself and Perry riding on giraffes at night, wearing cameras and peering over the treetops for a murderer.

He shook his head. "No, what I did was I took my wife with me. I thought—I don't know WHAT I thought. We always do the cleaning jobs together. But there was something screaming horribly..."

"Probably a chimpanzee singles bar at closing time," she offered, chewing merrily.

"Stop it, Mary-Shane. I realized I could have gotten us killed. Don't laugh. Try being there yourself at night..."

"...Okay," she said brightly.

He buried his face in his hands and shook his head. "I just don't know what to do now. I will never take Matilda there again."

She took a deep breath. "I did something too. I caught Vic Lara beating three street people on Friday evening. He had a shotgun on them and was working them over with a heavy steel flashlight. They were all bloody." As she told him, her light air gave way to a feeling of rage.

135

Perry held his head again. "Oh Christ."

"He let them go when he saw me. I called him every name in the book and took off."

"Great. No wonder he was short on the phone this morning."

"I'm sorry, Perry."

"You're going to get this whole newspaper shut down."

"Perry," she squeaked, "damn you. He was beating them. They were crying. They were bleeding."

"I'm sorry, Mary-Shane. You should have seen him work over the winos on Canoga Avenue when he was a plain old salutin' dick."

"Can't we go to the police chief, Perry?"

"I wouldn't recommend it."

"I'm going to report what I saw. He was beating them."

"No."

"Yes."

"No."

"Yes, dammit. I've got to do something."

"Mary-Shane. Listen. Vic Lara is where he is because he's a personal friend of Miss Polly Burtongale. Did you know that?"

"I don't care."

"Think about Kippy's medical insurance."

"Dammit."

Back at the obit desk, Spike had finished typing death notices and was assiduously cleaning house. Her own desk looked like Nuremberg after the Oktoberfest. His desk looked as though it had been newly built and just delivered.

"How do you do that?" she asked. She eyed her dying tulip, her fuzzy dice, her papier-mâché duck (from Kippy in fourth grade), her pile of women's magazines (with slushy romances hidden on the bottom), her nylons box full of pot-pourri, and last week's apple.

He handed her a sheet of computer printout. Pride sunned his cheeks. "My first article," he said fidgeting as though he were afraid she might disapprove. "Jules seemed to like it. Even Mr. Willow grunted and I think nodded although I'm not sure because I was afraid to go into his office."

"I heard that." She flicked the paper upright and read: "Adolph The Gorilla, 15, was found dead last night of an apparent heart attack... Is this a joke, Spike?"

"Not a bit. Jules thought it would make a warm human interest story on page one of the local news. Unfortunately I have only been here a week and so, per company policy, do not merit a by-line."

She whistled. "You'll be City Editor in a matter of weeks. Keep it up." Adolph (what a name, huh?): "...found dead of a heart attack in his enclosure at the Burtongale Zoo. Assistant Curator Dr. Roger Chatfield said he was speaking for himself and the entire zoo family, both human and otherwise, in expressing profound regret at their friend's passing. Dr. Chatfield said that Adolph had been adopted by missionaries in Kenya as an orphan just weeks old. His mother had been shot by poachers and dismembered for trophy use. Dr. Chatfield said Adolph had a reputation as a quiet, easy going primate. Blah blah blah...said Adolph brought joy and will be sadly missed. "Good going, Spike. Nice article. I weep for Adolph."

She persuaded Perry: "Let's go see the occult bookstore." She had told him about Vic and the address book.

Perry relented, offering to drive. "Why do you want to go there?" Perry asked as they floated along in an ambiance of detergent, chlorine, and sponges. Mary-Shane's skin crawled suddenly. The *Dark Feeling*? Flashes: Screams; beating; Frank; eyes of anger, eyes of terror;: and Mary-Shane screaming, as she clutched the baby.

"What's the matter?" Perry asked.

"Nothing," she said quickly. She wasn't entirely sure why she wanted to go there, but she knew she needed someone along for courage. She sipped take-out cola as the car purred toward East Canoga and the Santa Ysidora foothills.

A knot formed in her stomach. The only time she ever went this way was to buy Kippy's special orthopedic shoes. The late afternoon light was wan, false; rain clouds strained thin, cool sunlight. "I get really nervous going up this way. I used to live out there with my ex-husband before he was killed. Things were really rocky toward the end." Her head felt heavy, and she rested it on her knuckles, elbow on knee. "I don't remember..." But she perked up. "I need to see the place. Maybe talk with the guy. After all, he was in Smith's address book."

Perry grinned. "Okay. I need a diversion anyway."

Mary-Shane did a light makeover in the sun visor mirror. East Canoga turned into State 594. The pampered town streets of San Tomas gave way to wider open spaces with a country western flavor. Irrigated flowers and greenery changed to sun-dazzled sand, rocks, and shrub. Houses and businesses were mingled without zoning, and stood farther apart. A thing dropped tended to lie about for a long time, as evidenced by dusty, discarded items like a kitchen sink, a car engine on a pallet, a dog house lying on one side, a soup plate that looked more like it lay untouchably near the Titanic rather than on the desert floor. There were more pickup trucks, cowboy hats, roadside horseback riders. State 594 wound uphill into the Santa Ysidora Mountains. Perry and Mary-Shane were not going that far.

"I'll be..." Perry said as he powered down into second gear and the car crept onto a dusty square that doubled as lawn and sidewalk for a tumbledown house. The house had been worn to a gray pumice color by years of unremitting sunlight. A picture window in front displayed the sign "Harleigh Hale, New Age/B&W Arts," along with a black cat, a candle snuffer, some dried flowers, a picture of a smiling sun with octopus fins for rays, and a row of books. Perry turned off the engine.

A sign on the door read: CLOSED. They walked up to the window. The cat turned out to be stuffed, the candle snuffer had a skull face on it, and the books had titles like Dark Secrets, Love the Night, Santeria, Black Magic Revealed, Thus Spoke Satan. They each ogived their hands and peered inside. Mary-Shane made out dark shapes: A stove pipe like an upside down L; walls lined with books; a Nazi flag; a skull on a cookie box; and an old-fashioned wooden floor radio that resembled a small juke box.

As she stared hard at the radio, tracing its lovely old lines with an admiring eye, a greenish skull from hell flew at her. She shrieked and jumped back.

Perry grabbed her shoulders. "What is it?"

"Something came right at me." She pointed, then wrapped her arms around herself and tried to seem small. She took a deep breath and turned toward the window. A bird juggled himself into better position to look at her. Mary-Shane laughed. "It's a goddam parrot."

"Can you beat that?" Perry said shaking his head.

A green-yellow parrot held the grimy curtain rod in his claws and turned one eye toward them. "Do you think he's hungry?" Perry asked.

She shook her head. "His tummy's nice and round, his feathers are shiny, so are his eyes, and his claws look healthy." She added: "My friend Ann Temple had a parrot for years. We used to feed him fruit."

"You have surprising pockets of expertise," Perry cracked. "So what happened to the parrot?"

"Ginger? He caught pneumonia and died."

Perry looked shocked. "Parrots do that?"

"They're a lot like people. Don't have an original thought, and repeat all kinds of blather."

Perry peered inside again. "I think his dish is over by the skull on the cookie box. Looks half full of water."

"Then we can stop by again. After calling first."

Back in the car, she was glad to get away. Something, something, something teased her memory. About Frank MacLemore. A black and white mental photo. Violent. And this place...?

"Well, it's been fun," Perry said merrily. The twinkle in his good eye mocked her gently. Mary-Shane began to feel a very strong Dark Feeling, and she was silent all the way back to the paper. Perry gave her concerned looks, and his humor fled, but he said nothing.

Chapter 34.

That evening, over a slapped-together dinner of macaroni and cheese, Kippy asked her worriedly: "Mommy"(when did he ever call her that? when he was his little vulnerable self?)"are you okay?"

She waved him off, feeling a wave of darkness. "I'm fine, baby." Panic pressured her, that cork again, ready to blow, and she fought to keep control.

"You look pale, and your hands are shaking," he said in a hushed voice.

"It's probably the beginning of the flu," she said, starting the dishes.

Kippy disappeared into his room. He'd been doing that more and more, hunching over his computer with those Captain Somebody games. Mary-Shane felt relieved to be alone with her panic.

The universe seemed shrunken, a tunnel vision of terrible starkness bordered by panic. She poured out tears into the dishwater bubbles. I don't understand what is happening to me, she thought, and I've been fighting so long to keep it all under control, but now I'm losing it. I'm losing it! They are going to take my Kippy away from me.

She felt restless when she was finished cleaning the kitchen. Thoughts wrung through her mind: How sad Adolph died; poor Roger Chatfield; something about the tooth; an old man staring eye to eye with her holding out his hand for something that could not be denied much longer, something very very urgent... The parrot's face kept flying up close to hers, opening and shutting its mouth...

In a near trance, she peered into Kippy's room. He sat at his terminal like a statue. The screen played a horrid white light on his face.

She left a note: "Sweetheart, gone for a ride. Back soon." With pen in trembling hand she formed the letters and left the note on the kitchen table. If things went as they had lately, she would return and find him asleep, head on his arms, monitor glowing while unguessable assault ships flew in from a hostile galaxy.

The night air, once she was in the Mustang with the top down, was cool and refreshing. What am I doing? a part of her thought. It was the sick part that worried about losing Kippy. Not the other sick part within that part, the part about the cancer, but the other sick part, the part about being an unfit mother. He (who? the cop!) was going to have Kippy taken from her. What is my mind doing? she wondered as she drove east on Canoga, into East Canoga, and finally into the foothills where State 495 began. It was like a drive into the past, into a black and white movie of a very bad time that she'd shut out of her mind.

She drove to a liquor store with wind singing in her ears. She put money on a worn counter among candies and cigarettes and lotto tickets and plastic beef jerky jars. "A half pint of Old Wanderer," she said. Why am I doing this? she thought as the clerk nuzzled off to look for the booze. Because that is what Frank and Attila did the night we went to... *Oh God no, please don't let me relive that*! The liquor was brought, innocently, change was made ("hey, lady, don't forget your money here!") and she was back out into the night holding the paper bag with the bottle in it. There was in her ears a seashell wind.

She drove to black arts store under whirly-wheel stars. The cold air cut. Silence and loneliness were a heavy blanket. She held the package uncertainly. She was in a film and now there were bits and flashes as the film came to an end, just before it was about to tear loose from its reel. She was in the backseat of Franks' car with Kippy and Ann. She had forgotten to buy Frank's booze and he was really mad. He was more mad because, because...something about money. And Charlie Best. The door had opened. Charlie and Harleigh had stepped out. There were frantic explanations. Frank took the tire iron from Attila and threatened Charlie. There was a man(who?who!) in the backseat with Mary-Shane and he now got out, grinning meanly.

Mary-Shane took a few hesitant steps forward, unscrewing the top. She caught a (ugh) disinfectant whiff of whiskey. She set the bottle down near where Frank, had she stepped back in time, could have reached down with one hand and picked the bottle up, drunk from it, maybe not done what he had done next. The tire iron rose, fell, rose, fell, in a spray of blood...*Mary-Shane, in the back seat, screams and covers Kippy protectively with her body...*

Numbly she drove home, crawled into bed, and winked out.

Chapter 35.

On Tuesday morning Mary-Shane woke an hour early and could not get back to sleep. Her sleep had been full of tooth-achy pain. She could not remember what she had dreamed about.

She considered the Burtongale book lying on her living room table, but was too tired to get up and read it. After lying in a steely morning light, thoughts rushing in disconnected circles, she rose and took a shower. Hot water runneled down the gulley of her back and quickened her a bit.

Kippy came to the table tired and grumpy.

She made pancakes and sausages. Toast and jam. "How are your legs?"

"Okay."

"You said the other night they hurt."

"I think I'm just coming down with a cold."

Spike seemed happily at work that morning. She still checked every day, fearful that it had just been a good dream and she'd come in one day and have to do it all by herself again. Somehow, Spike managed to do the work of two people.

Perry offered to take her along on his beat, but she shook her head. She puttered quietly editing Spike's obits.

"You seem different tonight," Dr. Stanislaus said at his table. A gray light swirled over his head, vague and undefined like smoky daylight.

She clutched the seat rest and struggled to breathe, to swallow, to remain intact.

"Would you like a glass of water?" he offered.

She tried to let go, but no tears came. Instead, her facial muscles felt stiff and numb and she spoke with difficulty: "I am losing my mind, doctor. I need help."

"I will help you," he promised. "Do you think you can relax? My other evening patient canceled, so we have time."

She pointed angrily at the microphone. "Are you taping this for the police?"

He shook his head. "The books were closed long ago. You don't have to worry."

"But Vic Lara came and talked with you about me."

"Yes."

She held her head. She was going a hundred miles an hour and the floor was a blur under her. She was coming apart. Her heart fluttered. Things inside were crumbling inside. The walls were cardboard and folding, wetly, after long rain. She heard herself sobbing. Felt tears streaming through her fingers. Tasted salt, the sea in her eyes. Let tear drops fall on her lap. Heard her own high-pitched voice quaver: "I loved Frank."

"I know you did." He remained behind his bastion, but he looked awkward, ready to leap to her assistance.

"I can't keep it inside any longer. You won't let them take Kippy from me, will you?"

She could not see him, but heard his voice as one heard another ship's horn in a storm: "Of course not." He had placed tissues nearby and she dragged a string of them out to wipe her face. She sobbed, then looked to see what he had placed on his desk.

A tooth.

The past was open now, a big cave, still partially shrouded in darkness. Memory wanted to keep its sick secrets hidden but she wanted to shine a light into every crevice.

"It's okay," he said gently. "You had a hard time, and the police were pretty rough on you and Ann. But it's long since over."

"I get to keep Kippy?"

"Of course."

She composed herself. Yes. Of course, how simple it all seemed. "I've done okay?"

"Nobody could have done better."

"I've been trying really hard since I got out of detention."

"I know you have."

She sniffled. "I remember... Frank and Attila came back from a big deal. The cops had our shack in the mountains staked out, but I got word to Frank and they were clean the first time Vic showed up with his goons. They tore the place apart but we were clean." (The cozy shack, the logs burning in the stone fireplace, the diapers strung out to dry, the little crib in the corner with the broken rail from Frank hitting her and she slipping, banging her head...but also the love they made, wild, while mountain wind sighed outside...)"Then someone"(who?)"asked Frank to help with a really big deal"(what?)"and he and Attila got a lot of money for bringing in this thing"(a thing?)"in a truck..."

"Do you remember what was in the truck?" Dr. Stanislaus asked.

She shook her head. "It was parked outside the book shop. You know, that Satanic book store..."

He nodded. "Harleigh Hale and Charlie Best's place."

"They were partners," she said. "And Charlie was supposed to pay Frank that night. We were all going to go party someplace. Frank had a stash of grass and pills someplace, and on the way we even picked up some beer"(she remembered the crackle of tires as Frank pulled the big old car into the liquor store parking lot; he made some rough joke and Attila laughed; Frank dark-haired and sensuous, sexy but flinty, and Attila blond scraggly biker tough...)"and then we went up there."

"Was the truck still there?" Dr. Stanislaus asked.

"Yes. There was someone there to pick it up"(she remembered a shadow, sitting in the seat beside her, tickling Kippy's baby chin: who?someone she hated and despised, someone really awful)"no, it was someone who rode with us."

"Do you remember who that person was?"

She tried. "No, I can't seem to pull it out. It's almost there. Someone awful. But then so were most of the people we hung around with." She remembered the trips into Mexico. The fights Frank had gotten into. A guy in Juarez left for dead. A lot of O God... "No wonder I feel bad about myself."

"You'll feel better once you get this out," he said.

"We got to this place, I mean Harleigh Hale's place, and there they were, Harleigh and Charley. Sounds like a song, huh? I had Kippy, he was just a little baby, and Ann was there. Yes, that's it, but there was still someone else, this awful—"

"A man?"

"Yes, an awful man. Frank and I and Ann and Kippy we drove up there and Attila was driving the truck behind us, that's it. Charlie Best had the money and was supposed to pay Frank. Then this awful guy was to drive the truck away. Only Charlie was drunk, he had lost some of the money or so he said, and Frank started to beat him up."

"What were the other people on the scene doing?"

"Well"(she could smell the gasoline air, the mountain wind, the grass, the wood smoke coming from Harleigh Hale's chimney; but this awful other man remained a shadow)"Ann and I and Kippy were in the backseat of Frank's old gas guzzler. All we wanted to do was go party. Then the money problem came up. Charlie Best didn't have all of it so they started beating him up"(Charlie was on the ground, crying out, holding his head, and I began to yell at Frank to stop)"I tried to stop Frank but it got worse. Harleigh Hale came out with a gun but they took it from him and beat him up. Frank took the tire iron and... and..."

Dr. Stanislaus waited silently.

"...And finished Charlie off. I saw brains on the ground"(gray, glistening, like gelatin tinged pink, and nearby the fluffs of white hair still attached to a shattered skull)"and I..."

Dr. Stanislaus waited.

"...And I was just crying and screaming. Frank and Attila threw the body in the truck and dumped it at the zoo. Where I found the tooth recently."

"And the truck?" Dr. Stanislaus asked.

"The awful guy drove it away, I suppose. Least, that's what I figured afterward."

"You have no idea what was in the truck?" Dr. Stanislaus asked.

"No. But it wasn't drugs. It was something... from a museum... I have no idea. In those days I didn't know or care."

Dr. Stanislaus tapped the microphone gently, idly. "Okay. Let's fast forward. The body was found. Harleigh Hale testified in court that he came out and found his partner dead. The police, and I am speaking of the young detective in charge of the investigation, namely Lara, assumed he was lying under threat of harm. Without Hale's testimony, the case would have come to nothing. And it did, anyway, because Frank and Attila were killed a few days later in a motorcycle accident. The odd thing about that was that the brake line of Frank's Harley had been severed, so it looked like another person was involved. Maybe your dark awful man, whoever that was; the police were never able to determine who he was. And you don't remember?"

She strained(someone grinning; big and disheveled;selfish;an asshole, Frank had called him,who was he?)"I cannot remember. I do remember Vic Lara came into the shack again. He had a warrant and he was looking for Frank. He came in and kicked things around. I was holding Kippy and I was scared he would hurt him. He took Kippy and put him on a table. A police woman came and took Kippy away. Vic drove me to the lockup. In cuffs, for Chrissake. I'd forgotten all about that 'til now."

"I know," Dr. Stanislaus said. "I told him to keep you under control. Forgive me. You'd been on drugs. You were hysterical. I was afraid you might— throw yourself out of the car or something."

She sobbed, choking, for a while, unable to speak, remembering the sickness of that day. Gradually she wiped her face with tissues, finding the last tears. "I've served a long sentence."

"Years and years," he said brightly. "Isn't that enough?"

***

She found Kippy asleep at his computer. Galactic war games were flashing, and she turned the machine off. Gently, she led her little boy to his bed and tucked him in. His hair was tousled and his skin was baby-fine. She laid her cheek against his and listened to his steady breathing. She stroked his cheek and kissed it. Then she gently closed the door and got ready for bed. She crept into bed and slept like a baby.

Chapter 36.

She felt tired the next day, and called in sick. Made herself a large mug of tea and watched soaps, wrapped up in a heavy quilt on the couch, until she fell asleep. She awoke when a big plane droned in low overhead. Probably one of those skywriters, she thought, turning in the thimble of her blanket.

Splash...she still had this other with her, this *Cold Thing* under its rock in the water in her brain, and why? Because of what was on the truck that night when Frank and Attila and (???) beat Charlie to death...

After showering and eating, she drove to see Father Lawrence. He welcomed her at the rectory door. "I didn't think you'd be back so soon."

She wore jeans and her sweat jacket. Hands jammed in the belly pockets, she sidled in, welcomed by the warmth of his kitchen. An elderly woman was just finishing up some dishes. "Come into the study," he said. They sat cozy while the clock ticked. She said: "I started remembering things, Father."

His face went pasty. He folded his hands and lowered his forehead. She knew what that meant. He was starting the clock again; seal of the confessional; but that was okay, she had nothing to feel guilty about. Not anymore. She told about her session with Dr. Stanislaus. While she talked, he retrieved the box containing the sacred hosts stacked like poker chips. "What did the doctor say?"

"He said it was a healing process."

"Then let us hope it is. Come, say your confession." He prayed silently, then waited for her to recite ("I had impure thoughts ten times." "I yelled at my son." "I stole a pen from the office." "I ate lunch in the morgue, that's the library." "Father, I can't think of anything really bad I did.") and then he absolved her. "Are you ready to receive the Body of Christ?"

"I am." Afterward, she asked: "That was a test, right? If I were possessed by demons, I'd be rolling on the floor foaming at the mouth, right?"

He patted his palms together lightly. "Well, I don't know. That would be the Old Thinking. Very straightforward. Then there is the New Thinking. We've all gotten a lot smarter and more sophisticated, and maybe the Devil has too." He opened his palms, having no direct answer. "So we'll have to work together to see what is going on with you."

"What do you think, Father?"

He smiled kindly. "You're remembering terrible things and it's upsetting you. Dr. Stanislaus will help you work it out."

She drove home. The apartment was empty and for a moment she imagined this would be what it would be like if Kippy were gone. She pushed the dreadful thought out of her mind. Taking the portable phone along just in case, she drew a bubble bath and slid in to soak. The warmth lulled her. She lolled, wrapping bubbles around herself. Sitting with the old book about Wallace Burtongale III, adding hot water every few minutes to keep the bath hot, she did not get much reading done. She'd forgotten her date with Chatfield. Feeling guilty, she called on the portable phone. Roger Chatfield's recorded voice sounded calm and nice.

"Hello, Roger? This is Mary-Shane. I'm sorry I wasn't able to keep our— wasn't able to meet with you. Some things came up today and I had to leave work early. It was all very frustrating and I forgot to call." She couldn't think of anything else to say so she hung up. There. And if he didn't like that...

She sat back and soaked. She tried to think of pleasant things, like seventeenth century poetry or recipes. Yes, recipes, lots of them with butter and sugar and egg whites and spices, lots of spices... But where, half dozing, did she drift? Back to the office of Dr. Stanislaus. Back through the dark corridors and onto the couch. He sat again looking somewhat like a late-night talk show host with the microphone hanging over a bare table. It was so stark in that room. So much like a blank sheet of paper, waiting to be written on. But wait! There... in the ceiling that was not really a ceiling but a nest of reflections like a spider's web made of glass...

..faces...looking down...watching...

The phone trilled in her ear and she sat up with a start, splashing water all over. "Mom! Are you there!" It was Kippy on the recording device. She reached for a towel. "Mom, Ann's mad at us for being on the computer all the time. She's sent Jeremy to bed and she wants you to pick me up right away."

Mary-Shane dripped a trail of suds into the living room, and the cool night air nipped her behind. She threw herself over the table to reach the answering machine just as it was about to shut off. "Hang on, Kippy. I'm coming right over!"

Chapter 37.

On busy Canoga Avenue, San Tomas's main street, a man fell down. A few people stepped around him. A couple of rowdy college kids jumped over him. Then people started to gather around. Some were a dinner and dancing crowd, some intellectuals from UC San Tomas, some into sports judging by the slim bodies on the young men and the firm calves on the young women. Sensible people who, seeing a drunk on the ground, avoided getting their shoes dirty. Some were compassionate, others just curious.

A distant siren wailed. The man on the ground was neatly dressed and did not appear to be drunk. An off-duty intern kneeling by him found no outward sign of stroke, heart attack, or convulsion. In fact, there was a strong pulse, but very slow.

The ambulance pulled in with a dying wail. The crowd parted. Doors slammed. Gurney wheels chattered loudly. Equipment came in a heavy box. "What do you think?" the senior EMT asked while his partner worked on the prostrate man.

"No idea," the intern said.

The junior EMT looked up. "It's like nothing I've ever seen before. This guy is either in a coma, or else just sound asleep. His pulse rate is thirty beats per minute but strong "

Inside the zoo, Perry Stein stepped outside to roll up the long cord now disconnected from the buffer. It was tedious work, and he sweated as he tugged, wound, tugged, wound, each time throwing another coil of cable around the heavy ball on the ground. Their night's work was mostly done. He'd buffed the main corridor in an hour and seventeen minutes flat. Each night he timed himself. The quicker he got done, the longer he and Matilda could sit in the truck and wait. And listen. And hope something happened. But nothing ever seemed to happen, and Perry was deciding this was just a good little side income. He heard the steady whine of Matilda's industrial vacuum cleaner as she finished up the offices. Perry loved her dearly, and he would not let her out of his earshot. With a series of yanking and looping motions, he got the cord wrapped up in a heavy ball at his feet. He squatted to lift the cord, keeping a straight back. He had a good grip and was about to lift when the sound of the vacuum cleaner inside changed.

He stopped, puzzled. The vacuum had a music all its own. It played low notes on the thick carpets, high notes on patches of tile. Each attachment had a pitch and tenor of its own; they were like instruments in an orchestra, and Perry knew them each, for he had worked side by side with his wife for years.

This was a sound he'd never heard before. He left the cord and went in the building. As he tore the office door open, he found the vacuum cleaner upended and whistling in empty air.

"My darling!" He threw himself over her. "Sweetheart, what happened?" Her head lolled as though her neck were broken. Wailing he jumped up and scrambled over the desk throwing aside papers and books. He skidded to the phone and dialed 911.

"Emergency," a man said.

"My wife," Perry gasped, "I don't know what's happened to her!"

On State 594, Harleigh Hale slowed his pickup truck and prepared to turn into his property. For a moment he paused and looked around for possible intruders; and saw nothing. Stars shone clearly overhead. Hale hummed to himself as he drove up to his book store. He turned off his headlights and gathered his newly acquired books. The curtain parted and there were those claws, that beak, that silly look of anticipation.

"Hi, Winky!" Hale said in a high voice, waggling a little finger. "Hi Winky! Daddy's home!" Effortfully—for he was a heavy man, 300 pounds before breakfast, and sixty years old—he grasped a bundle of books under one arm and slid out of the seat. He slammed the door and massaged his saddle-sore butt. The bird chattered. "Just a minute, Winky! Daddy will be right in!"

He stopped and admired the store. The sign read, "Harleigh Hale, Bookstore/B&W Arts." Wasn't much, maybe, some folks might think, but he and Charlie had built the place from the ground up years ago. He'd kept his silence all these years about Charlie's murder, but Gilbert hovered, waiting for him to make a mistake.

Harleigh unlocked the door, slipped inside, and quickly re-locked it. The parrot fluttered up and landed on his shoulder. "Did Winky have enough to eat? Is Winky thirsty?" He shuffled over to check the bird's dishes. The two white porcelain bowls were nearly empty. There were white droppings on the side of the table. "Daddy came home just in time. Daddy was at the Cross County Book Fair, Winky. Daddy got some nice new books." The floor creaked and rocked under Harleigh as he walked among the display tables. He sneezed his way through a dust cloud and opened the refrigerator. His bed, his TV, and his toilet were in the back room, separated by a wooden door and a short corridor that smelled dank. He took out a jar of seed and rumbled back across the room, past the Nazi flag, past the skull by the cookie tin. "Here, Winky. Daddy's got some seeds..."

The parrot sat on the sill and burped.

"Oh, gottum a tummy, huh?"

Winky turned his head and took in an eyeful. He blinked several times and his forehead had a puzzled shine. Harleigh chuckled. That old parrot was the best friend a man could ever have. Tonight he was just so tired. No surprise, given the long drive during the day's heat, bringing those books from a desert roundup of witches. "Here, Winky." The parrot fluttered onto Harleigh's shoulder. He slipped Winky a cracker. "Might even be time to hit the road again for a while, eh old bird?" They'd done it after Charlie's death eight years ago. Frank and his cronies could not have known that a small piece of their precious museum haul had wound up in the store. Even though Frank and Attila had been murdered, Gilbert was still around. In any event the stolen object was too hot to fence.

Without changing his clothes or washing, Harleigh lay down on his wide bed. Its sturdy wood frame barely creaked under his huge weight. In the darkness he held one hand to his forehead and tried to think his thoughts away in order to sleep. The parrot rustled nearby, gnawing under his feathers.

Strange. There was something in his mind. His skin crawled. It was a cross between a *Someone* and a *Something*, and it made him sit up. Panicked, he got a drink of water. It, whatever it was, was there in his mind like a speck of dust on your glasses or a bleb on your nose. He banged his hand upside his head as if he had water in his ear. Nope. Still there. A grin? evil? He was about to sit on the bed when a *Dark Feeling* came over him, a picture that was a grinning cross between a sun and an octopus.

The last thing Harleigh perceived was a dry scraping on his window sill. There was an old pear tree out there. The tree had survived here in the mountain desert all these years, shriveled and leaning against the house. A gnarled limb, like a skeletal hand, rasped back and forth on the window sill. That image, and a thought, and a worry floated together in Harleigh's mind as he keeled over backwards and sprawled on the bed. The thought was that finally his family history of obesity and stroke had caught up with him. So this was how one died? A blur of images flashed before him like a photo album blowing in the wind (his life;his daddy;his mommy;ice cream;a bicycle; a girl...) all to the accompanying scratching on the window which was surely Death's metronome. His worry was that Winky would be all alone and did he have enough food and water?

Harleigh opened his eyes. The scratching had stopped. He was in a dark place (underground?) (hell?) full of eyes, faces. Gargoyles. One stuck its tongue out. If this is death, he thought, at least I'm still me. Water was all around. Harleigh looked down at himself, amazed. His skin looked cold, bright blue. Fish swam around his head in graceful swirls, dancing scarves. "Why Harleigh! What a pleasant surprise."

Harleigh gaped. The person walking toward him with extended hand was none other than Charlie Best. His dead friend. "Charlie, are we in purgatory or something? Or is this Hell?"

Charlie's grip was cold, reminding Harleigh of pickles in the fridge. Charley's skin was bright blue. "Naw, old buddy. It's a ship, near's I can figger. Come on, some folks you gotta meet."

Harleigh followed fearfully. There were catwalks suspended in midair, or was it midwater? Distant figures walked on them, veiled and blue. "Charlie, how is it we can breathe here? And how do we get out of here?"

"I don't know that we ever get out of here. I've been here a long, long time, Harleigh."

Harleigh recoiled in shock as two figures stepped from a mist. Frank... Attila... "Charlie, you guys are all dead!"

They looked at each other and laughed.

"...Then if you're dead... what am I?"

Chapter 38.

Crystal eternity: More stars than alphabet soup in a black bowl. Gilbert, in his van with four heavily armed companions in fatigue uniforms, tooled downhill from their hiding place in the Santa Ysidora Mountains. The desert wind grew weaker over the mountain peaks. The air grew still, and the stars twinkled. There was little traffic on the state highway, and one could hear for half a mile a clang of gear teeth as Gilbert downshifted near Harleigh Hale's place. After a brief inspection, the van pulled up alongside Hale's truck.

The house was pitch dark. Gilbert and his companions checked around back. Gilbert knocked on the door, softly at first and then loudly. No answer. No sound, not even wind. They burst into Hale's place, fully expecting a shootout. They advanced with stabbing flashlight beams, M-16's at ready.

There was a flutter, a screech, a scream. A gunshot.

The air was filled with feathers.

"Hold your fire!" Gilbert shouted. "It was only a damn parrot. We want Hale." They found him in the rear on his bed.

Gilbert found no pulse. He slapped Hale's cheeks. No response. He straightened up. "He's dead. Let's get on with it and get the hell out of here." Gilbert wanted what the old man had stolen from Frank and Attila. He hadn't known then, but Dad had recently clued him in . This fat old bastard and his cheating buddy had kept the smaller item. And now the Pilot wanted that. The Pilot wanted every piece of itself.

Gilbert and his companions searched the house. He heard the methodical sounds of books being loaded in pillow cases and crates. Floor boards were torn up. The stove crashed through the window and landed outside. Skulls, nazi flags, cookie tins, everything went out the windows. The stars twinkled like a skyline without structure. There were thumping sounds as books and other contraband were loaded into the van.

"No luck."

Gilbert nodded slowly. He was disappointed, but not unhappy. He was glad to see Hale gone. "Burn it," he ordered.

There was a raw petrochemical tinge in the air. The men backed out, shaking gasoline cans. Hellish sparks shot up into the air. Dry wood exploded in flames. The men tossed their cans and ran toward the van as the air behind them went Whoosshhh...! They were far away into the mountains when they heard the distant wail of the first siren. Looking back, Gilbert smiled. Already the flames were dying down. It looked like a tiny match going out. *But fire danced in Gilbert's eyes.*

Chapter 39.

When she returned to the office on Thursday morning, Jules told Mary-Shane that Perry was at the hospital because something terrible had happened to Matilda but nobody was sure what.

"Oh no," Mary-Shane said.

"Yeah," Jules said fighting his pipe with shaky hands. "You're the crime reporter until Perry returns. You ready?"

She nodded distantly. Something was quietly wreaking hell in her town and part of it lived in rental space # 1 at the back of her brain. Part of her felt like standing on the roof and shouting: Something has taken up residence in my brain and you're all next!

"Mary-Shane, snap out of it. I know you're shocked. We all are. But the show goes on." He handed her a sheet of paper. "There's a list. Stop at the DA's office for a copy of the Mazzini indictment. The police chief's office for a statement if you can get it. And for heaven's sake if you bump into Lara, DON'T ask him how the zoo investigation is going, okay?"

Mary-Shane and Jules visited the hospital around six to see how Matilda was coming along. Mary-Shane loathed hospitals because of Kippy's cancer. You hold a limp hand, you cradle a feverish head, you comfort a crying boy. But mostly you sit and wait while he sleeps, drugged to the limit. How many times, when the hush is on the night and the only sound is the mousy squeak of a nurse's shoes, do you lean forward on trembling hands, lay your ear by his mouth, and listen to find out if he is still breathing?

As Mary-Shane and Jules trod along the corridors of Burtongale Memorial Hospital, a chloroformed silence inlaid the chocolate-colored floors. It was supper hour, and a beefy bready aroma steamed off of aluminum carts parked at angles in the halls. Outside in the liberty of the healthy world, the sun lay low over tree crowns, and its last rays weakly printed vanilla lozenges into odd corners.

Mary-Shane saw them in the waiting room: Three boys and two girls, all under ten, and Perry. The three boys wore white shirts and bow ties and sat squeezed together. The two girls wore flouncy dresses and shiny black shoes and clung together on a creaky chair. Perry sat in a stuffed chair. His face was in his hands, and his elbows on his knees. He looked up with an expression of grief and fatigue.

"What happened?" Mary-Shane whispered.

The children were silent. They stuck together and twisted stiffly from long sitting. They stared with haunted, pleading eyes. Perry blew his nose in a paper towel. "I was just outside for a minute. She was inside Chatfield's office. Next thing I know, the vacuum cleaner's upended and she's...like this."

"Any prognosis?" Jules whispered.

Perry shook his head. "Technically she's in a coma. Physically they've been unable to find anything wrong with her. All her vital signs are down, but steady. It's just as if she fell asleep."

Late in the day, Mary-Shane picked Kippy up. He seemed quiet. Or was it sullen?

"Are you okay?"

No answer, and it went like that most of the way home.

As she pulled up in the parking lot of the apartment complex, he held out an envelope in fingers grimy from basketball, inky from writing.

"What's this?" The seal of St. Andrew's School was on it.

"It's a note," Kippy muttered. He rubbed his nose and sniffed.

"Use a handkerchief," she said. He reached for the tissue box while she read: "Dear Miss MacLemore: I have felt the need to write you a note. Kippy is sleepy and inattentive in class. He is argumentative and does not seem to get along well with his peers. Please call me so we can set up a meeting with Kippy's teacher. Thank you. Sister St. Cyr."

"Kippy," she said lowering the letter into her lap, "is something bothering you?"

"No!"

There is, she thought, but what? Hormones? Puberty? "Okay, sweetheart, let's just go inside and have a bite to eat."

"I'm not hungry."

"Okay, well maybe take a hot bath."

Inside, Mary-Shane prepared dinner (hamburgers, mashed potatoes, carrots) and a desert she knew Kippy really liked (coconut custard in graham cracker cups).

"Are you running your bath water?" she shouted over the clatter of some dishes she was washing.

No answer.

"Supper's ready," she said wiping her hands on a dish cloth.

No answer.

She knocked on the door. It slid open a few inches.

He turned to her with a face contorted with fury. "Are you spying on me?" he snarled. His teeth were bared, upper lip curled back dripping with spittle. His dark eyes flashed with feral light, as though touched by the aurora in some echoing arctic wood rather than the cold bluish computer screen. His hair stood out in hackles.

Mary-Shane staggered back.

"Get out!" the wolf snarled.

Mary-Shane turned and ran. The *Cold Thing* laughed under the rocks as Mary-Shane splashed through. She dropped the dish cloth. She upset the wooden tray and custard cups went flying. She tripped in the hot custard, burning her knee as she went down. She scrambled to her feet. Flinging the door open, she ran outside. Pounded down the stairs. Past the pool. Out to the parking lot. And there she leaned over her car. She held her hands to her mouth. And drew in great sobs of air. Hot tears coursed over her knuckles and splashed on the hood. Her eyes burned. And her soul hurt.

The *Cold Thing* was amused.

I'll show you, she thought. She ran around the side of the house. Slipped on gravel. Fell. Skinned her calf. Gravel hung in her scraped skin but she ignored the burning hurt. She could not see distinctly in the darkness. She slammed the flats of her hands along the wall, seeking, seeking...

...and found the breaker boxes, one for each of eight apartments. Blindly, she marched her fingers up along the breakers until she found the right one. She pushed the master switch for her apartment to the right.

She heard a snarl. Kippy? Then a yell.

Somehow the breaker slammed open again.

The yell turned from frustration to a howl of satisfaction. It was not Kippy's voice. Could not be. And yet maybe it was. She used both hands to snap the breaker shut again and held it. Somewhere she heard a sound like lots of machinery powering down. The darkness deepened, but somehow with less bite. Carefully she eased her pressure. The breaker stayed shut.

A car pulled into the drive, and by its headlight she caught a glimpse. The breaker looked black and swollen. It smelled faintly like burning rubber.

Sniffling, wiping her tears, she shuffled back to the apartment. She gently brushed away bits of gravel sticking to the wound on her calf. "Ouch, dammit."

The apartment was dark. Ominous. A face appeared in the doorway. Mary-Shane stopped. Hands grasped the door frame. Hair stood on end. His eyes were frightened. His lips quivered. "Mommy!" he wailed. "Mommy!"

She ran to him. He collapsed crying against her, head on her shoulder. "I'm sorry," he said sobbing.

She rubbed his head, rocked him, held him close. "It's okay, sweetheart, it's okay now."

She felt the *Cold Thing* watching slyly, and loathed it. She held her son close.

"I don't know what happened, Mom." Kippy began to control his sobbing and once again became the ten year old instead of the frightened little child. They went inside where it was dark.

"Is it okay now?" Mary-Shane asked while Kippy picked up his crutches that lay near the door.

"Yes." He seemed sure of that, at least. "We were playing the Space 3000 game on line," he said.

"We?"

"Me and Jeremy," he said in a confessional voice. "And the others." He hung his head.

"What others?"

"I don't know. Other kids, I guess."

"You'd better tell me all about this." She led him into the living room and they sat down.

"Well, Jeremy's mom bought him this modem about a month ago. He logged into a bulletin board that had games on it. They were free games that you could download. So we took a couple. And this one was really neat." There was an afterglow of excitement in his eyes. "We had a lot of fun..."

"...And then," Mary-Shane said, "things got out of hand."

He rubbed his temples as though there were something painful in his head. "I don't know. Space 3000 is where a giant ship is traveling through the galaxy for thousands of years and there are thousands of creatures frozen inside. The rules are complicated but basically every once in a while someone accidentally wakes up from being frozen. Then the monitor rats hunt him down to keep the place clean. But if he makes it to the city in the ship, he's safe."

"City in the ship?" Mary-Shane echoed.

"Yeah, well, I guess this is a huge ship. I never thought about it much, but I guess it's probably..." (...he stopped and thought...) "...about five miles wide and ten, twenty miles long."

Mary-Shane grasped his shirt front gently in both hands and shook. "Kippy, there is no spaceship. It's all a delusion. Now tell me, is it gone?"

He held his head and looked at her. He frowned. "Yes."

"Are you sure?"

"Yes."

"Absolutely sure?"

"Yes. Let go."

She went into his room with a flashlight and disconnected the computer. She took the modem, wrapped it in its cord, and stowed it under the kitchen sink between the scouring pads and the cleaning fluids. She threw a pile of dishrags and rubber gloves over it and slammed the doors. She went outside and pushed the breaker open. She went inside, hugged Kippy, and tapped his forehead with her index finger tip. "No gremlins up there?"

He grinned. "No."

"Good." She patted his cheek lightly. "Come on." She took him to his room. There, she plugged in the computer and turned it on. The blue-gray screen lit up. READY, it said.

She unplugged the Web connection. She erased everything on the hard disk drive. "Anything on floppies?" she asked. He reached into a drawer and produced a handful of floppy disks. She reformatted them one by one, turning them back into blanks without a shred of data on them. She reloaded his word processing and BASIC programming software for him. "Got any homework to do?" she asked.

"Sure do."

"Okay, get to it. And then a bath. And then bed."

He hugged her. "Thanks."

The old Kippy, she thought, closing the door gently. She made herself a strawberry milkshake and stood in the moonlight watching ripples cross the pool below.

Somewhere, a printer chirred. Mary-Shane, frowning, took her milkshake inside and went into Kippy's room. He was fast asleep, mouth open and hair mussy on the pillow. The computer screen glowed softly, and there was a word displayed on it: WARNED2.

She went to the printer and looked. Sure enough, it had spat out the same word: WARNED2. The *Cold Thing* stirred fitfully inside her. Her milkshake lost its flavor and she set it aside. How much clearer could the warning be? Okay, she thought, I'll back off completely. Put me on obits. I give up. The threat now was against her son. And that overrode any desire to crack this hideous story. I give up, she thought at the *Cold Thing*, I quit. I won't risk my son. Checkmate.

Chapter 40.

Kippy had gotten into a fight at school that morning.

"Kippy," Mary-Shane said as she met him, foregoing her lunch hour. "This is the second time I need to speak with Sister."

"I'm sorry Mom." Low voice. He ran off to the playground.

Sister St. Cyr wore the white habit and headdress of the Poor Sisters of Mercy. "...About Kippy's behavior," the nun said. She tented her hands on the desk. "Miss MacLemore, I'm always grateful for an interested parent."

"Well, I try to keep an eye on things."

"He's a fine boy," Sister said. "I've seen the tension in him. Well, I'll bet you haven't had a nice vacation in a long time. I recommend you take off for a day or so. Go to the mountains. Get away from it all and just be together."

"That's a lovely idea," Mary-Shane said. "But I can't afford to take a day off."

"The weekend then," Sister said grandly. "Ah the countryside! Do you know what I do on my vacation?"

"No." I can't imagine, Mary-Shane thought.

Sister rose and pointed to framed black and white photos on the wall. "I go to Montana and go horseback riding. That's me, there, in the dungarees and plaid shirt, roping that calf."

Mary-Shane whistled.

Sister grinned. "I'm a farm girl. Born and raised in Montana. 4-H Clubs, the works. Believe me, I know what I'm talking about. You take your son and escape from city life for a while."

At the office, Spike nodded as she walked in and plopped her things down. He was in the middle of the crescendo of the 1812 Overture, and he made body English with his hips at every sputter-lipped cannon salvo.

Mary-Shane carried her coffee to Jules's office. In passing she noted that Perry's desk had not changed; a foamed plastic cup of tea still stood where he'd forgotten to take it with him on the fateful day of Matilda's collapse.

"Hi, Mary-Shane." Jules looked blue around the eyes.

"Jules, you look like you were up all night."

"I can't sleep well anymore." He threw his pipe down and rose. "Always thinking about old Wiz. And now Matilda. What's going on in this town?"

She did not have the energy to tell him about her secrets, the *Cold Thing* and the *Dark Feeling*. Leave those for Dr. Stanislaus.

"You'd better get out there," Jules said. "Murder and mayhem and you're the police reporter."

"Thanks." She heard the irony in her voice.

"People are dropping suddenly all over town. I want a story."

"I'll do what I can. Where do I start?"

He hollered after her: "That's your problem."

There were notes on her desk. Call Roger Chatfield. Call Mother. Call Dr. Stanislaus. Call Father Lawrence. "Jeez, Spike, you're a human switchboard, huh?"

Spike was between performances. "You have a busy life."

"You may be right. How are they dying?"

"It has been slow."

She sifted through the notes. "Yeah, well it comes and goes in waves."

Roger Chatfield. She left a message at the zoo.

Father Lawrence. Oh hello, Mary dear. Just checking...

Dr. Stanislaus. ...to verify your next appointment...

Mother. Mary-Shane, dear, haven't heard from you and I thought I'd just call...

Why hadn't Ann Temple called? The bitch. Easy, Mary-Shane. Maybe I'll call her this evening. Yo beagle-face. What's up.

Mary-Shane began phoning. There were twenty-four people lying in comas in area hospitals. Drop Disease, some of the medical people were calling it. These otherwise healthy people suddenly went into comas. It was as though their minds had temporarily left their bodies; hopefully they would somehow return.

The phone rang. Roger Chatfield. "I thought I might catch you."

She smiled. "Nice to hear from you. I'm sorry I missed our date the other night. Things got really out of hand."

"Maybe you heard—we lost one of our gorillas?"

"Adolph. I'm sorry."

"I was thinking, Mary-Shane, I know this is rather forward of me, but maybe you'd like to bring Kippy and we could all go camping this weekend. I'm taking Elisa and Rudy up into the Santa Ysidoras. You and Kippy can have your own tent. Privacy of course. Ahem."

She fiddled with a pencil. Her heart raced. "Yes, Ahem. Well... do you think Kippy could keep up? Camping, hiking, I mean..."

"We'll make it work. We're old hands. I take the kids up there probably once a month when it's not too cold. The Good Outdoors, you know."

"Sounds like fun!"

"I think you'd enjoy this."

"Roger, you don't know how perfect your invitation is right now."

"We all need to get away."

"Are you a mind reader?"

"Saturday morning then. We'll pick you up at eight."

She put the receiver down with the tiniest of clicks, not wanting to disturb the peace she felt. She imagined herself roping calves, and the thought made her smile.

As she picked up the afternoon dispatch package from the PD, she called to check in with Jules, all very routine. Jules informed her that Harleigh Hale's place had been torched Wednesday night, and Harleigh Hale's charred bones found in the ruins.

Jayzuz! She wished she had a helicopter as she drove east. Visions of Frank raising and lowering the tire iron over Charlie Best's blood and brain spattered head eight years ago crept into her thoughts, and she pushed them aside. She pulled up near Police Line tape stretched over saw horses. Harleigh Hale's truck was blackened, on its back with its roof flattened.

A sheriff's deputy waved to her to stay back. Mary-Shane showed her press badge. "What happened?"

The deputy, a pretty blonde, shrugged. "Don't know. We may be looking at arson, but nothing is official yet until the M.E.'s report comes out."

"Any evidence of foul play?" Mary-Shane suspected that Harleigh Hale had been murdered; she had an idea who the best suspect would be: the man she had erased from memory.

The woman shook her head. "The Fire Department is still investigating and until they are done this is a restricted area."

Mary-Shane took out her company camera and snapped some pictures. As she circled around the back, she heard a noise coming from a clump of bushes. She turned and saw a pale little face staring out at her. "The parrot!" She started toward him, but he ran.

"I think that's Mr. Hale's parrot," Mary-Shane said.

"I'd better call the county animal shelter."

"Such a beautiful bird. What will they do with him?"

The deputy pointed with her chin. "That ole boy's been hurt somehow. Look at the mess on his right wing."

Mary-Shane looked. The bird's curiosity had gotten the better of him. Afraid though he might be, he had hopped around the side of an old mesquite stump. Now he eyed the two women like a distraught little old bald man, and a green one at that. His facial expressions ranged from foolish to pitiful, and the big rings around his eyes suggested only, please somebody pick me up and feed me, oh please. He cocked his head to one side.

"They'll put him to sleep, I bet," the deputy said.

"Did you hear that?" Mary-Shane asked the bird. She put down her camera and walked toward the bird. He kept stepping backwards to run away, then always turned toward her and took a hesitant step forward. Mary-Shane knelt about ten feet away and clicked her tongue. She held out her hand and snapped her fingers.

"*Waaak!*" the parrot said.

The deputy, who seemed to have a heart after all, walked over with her lunch box. She took out an apple and some cookies. "Here, you little shit. Probably your last meal as a free man." She told Mary-Shane: "I just radioed the animal shelter. They'll pick him up within the hour."

"And they'll put him down?" Mary-Shane asked.

The woman shrugged, hunkering beside Mary-Shane with her fingers entwined and a look of sympathy. "He'll never fly again."

"The poor little so and so," Mary-Shane said.

"Hi Winky Baby," the parrot cawed. He raced by, fluttering his good wing, grasped a piece of apple in his beak, and retreated to a safe distance.

"His name must be Winky," Mary-Shane said.

The deputy rose and dusted her pants off. "Yeah, well..."

"I'd like to take him."

"The animal shelter..."

"Please!"

"I'll call them back and say the bird died."

"Bless you."

Winky made another pass, grabbing the rest of the apple. He devoured it, regarding Mary-Shane with one side of his face. His expression was irresistible.

"Here, Winky," Mary-Shane said.

The parrot hopped over and took a cracker. He retreated only a foot or so, staying within reaching distance. She made no move toward him.

"Hi Winky Baby," he cawed.

"You want to come home with me?" she asked. "Kippy will fix your wing. He knows how to do that stuff. And then maybe someone in Kippy's school will take you. Oh, we'll find you a nice, nice home."

"Hi Winky Baby," he cawed and hopped onto her wrist.

The deputy hollered: "He's officially dead. Get out of here with him, will you, before my supervisor shows up?"

"You bet," Mary-Shane said.

Mary-Shane saw that the bird's left wing was shattered, much of it missing. What was left was a suppurating stump and some tangled bits of feather. She thought she saw a shotgun pellet embedded in some swollen pinkish-blue flesh, but the parrot would not let her look too closely, and she did not just now want to raise the issue with the deputy.

Waving thanks as the deputy shook her head, Mary-Shane drove off,.

Quickly racing home, she borrowed a large bird cage from Mrs. Abrahamson in 6A. Mrs. Abrahamson kept finches, but many of hers had recently died from colds, and she was still too angry at them to buy replacements.

Mary-Shane set Winky up in the kitchen. "Water, crackers, some apples, oh and here's celery..."

"Winky Nice Boy," the parrot cawed, "Winky Nice Boy."

"Yes you are." She raided her shelves and her refrigerator. "Maybe tomorrow when we see Mr. Chatfield, he might know what to do with you. That's it, Winky! You are in like flynn. If nobody else will take you, I'll seduce Roger into finding you a little roost at the zoo!" With that she fled out to the car and back to work.

Chapter 41.

Wallace Burtongale frowned a lot lately. Of course he could not confide in anybody (only Miss Polly had some inkling, he was sure), but things were going so well for the Pilot, so badly for himself and Gilbert.

Two evenings in a row, two shipments of computers; this shipment was from Korea and consisted of a mixed bag of hand-held accounting terminals, several dozen standard PC's, a passel of laptops, a hundred complex scientific hand calculators, and a half ton of ten gauge insulated copper wire in fifty pound loops. Wallace made ten trips in all, and the Pilot was pleased.

The Pagoda now had a slightly more pronounced glow. The old machinery and the oil tank were dimly visible like coals in a furnace, only this fire was not warm, red, and flickering, but cold, white, and immobile. Wallace took his time unwrapping the new arrivals. As before, plastic peanuts and wrappings were snapped up by a wind out of nowhere. The walls and the ceiling were beginning to look fluffy white as though a pastry chef had decorated them with whipped cream. Already the Pilot was putting the copper wiring to work. Tracks of wire snaked through the foamed plastic.

Thump-a thump-a thump-a went the shadows and the white light strengthened.

At the corner of Canoga and Seventh, where the streets changed from "shoppy" to residential, a grandpa was taking his six year old daughter home from a music lesson.

The girl had been abused at home and luckily her mother's parents had been willing to raise her. The girl's mother had gone mentally around the bend and was peeling paper flowers in a nursing home (he loves me, loves me not). The father, a rock musician and cocaine addict, was always away playing gigs. That was fine with the little girl because with Daddy not here he could not hurt her, though she always woke in a cold sweat screaming at night and Mommy just slept on. Now at Grandma and Grandpa's house she got enough to eat, she had nice clothes, and things were okay. Except, ho-hum, she had to go to school every day instead of watching cartoons with Mommy.

The music lessons were fun. She carried her violin proudly and held Grandpa's hand. They were just talking about doll houses. "...And I'll have a Mommy Doll and a Grandpa Doll and a Grandma Doll and maybe a doggie doll," she said.

"And no Daddy Doll?" Grandpa asked gently.

162

"No," she said curtly. They came to a red light and waited for the little glass man to change to white. The little girl was watching cars fly by (such a carousel of red and white lights!) when she noticed that Grandpa's grip had weakened.

"Grandpa!" she was going to chide, you always hold my hand tight when we wait to cross streets, but instead she let out a scream, for Grandpa had sagged to his knees. Wind ruffled his white hair over his reddish bald spot. His mottled face looked bluish and his tongue protruded slightly between peanut-brown teeth. His eyelids were drooping. "Grandpa!" she screamed, shaking him, but he fell down at her side with a thump, and she was sure he'd banged his head.

Being a girl who had to take care of herself, in the make do way of little children, she stayed by her Grandpa. She never let go of his hand. She jumped up and down waving. Thus she flagged down a police car. Then came an ambulance and they took Grandpa away. He was still alive, they told her. Just sleeping. Oh she said and felt relieved. Grandma would be glad to hear at least that. The policeman drove her home.

Clouds were gathering in a far corner of the night sky, away from the moon.

Under the full moon, Guard Johnny Gep locked the gate of the utility lot and prepared to make his round with his time clock. Strange, Dr. Burtongale was driving back and forth again with all those boxes. Not that Johnny Gep was one to question his superiors. Seventy years old, this had been his formula for survival. Smile like hell, keep your mouth shut, do what they tell you, and collect your paycheck. Lotta younger men couldn't understand that.

He whistled merrily as he marched down Zoo Lane toward the central kiosk. That was key station number one. You had to climb up the grass to get to the pyramid and on rainy days you got your shoes wet. He ought to know. He'd been doing this for thirty years since he'd retired from the Army as an E-6 laundry platoon sergeant.

Key station number two, the east refreshments area.

Key station number three, the east restrooms.

Key station number four, back of the security office.

Key station number five, the Pagoda (brightly lit again, for the fifth night in a row; must write that up again!)...

He heard an animal snorting as he turned the dangling key in his clock, where the key number would be embossed on a paper disk, proving he was here at such and such a time. He thought he felt the ground shaking.

For thirty years he'd listened to the weird sounds of the zoo at night. He often told people, if you want something weird, if you want to shiver down to your bones, spend some time in a zoo at night. You'll hear noises you swear didn't come from this earth. Johnny Gep was used to the noises, and he knew most of them.

Now he frowned. The sound he'd heard was of one of the larger animals. But there were no larger animals within earshot.

There it was again. A short, deep chortle, like gravel being blown through a wooden pipe. Johnny Gep stopped near the Pagoda and set the heavy time clock down. He tilted his head down and listened.

There. *Bork! Tadump, tadump, tadump!*

Then he heard rapid crashing noises, like foot pads on ivy and brush. The echoes carried around the area, so it was hard to tell where the sound was coming from. The ground definitely was shaking.

His skin crawled. Shivers ran like sharp fingernails up and down his spine.

For a moment he recalled his younger years, when he'd worried about the impossible. Like one of the bigger animals breaking out, or a female in heat breaking; ready to charge at rocks and trees in a fury, not to mention at a lone unarmed man.

Something moved in his stomach, and he figured it was probably his chili dinner, hopping from his large intestine into the small.

He bit his lip and wondered what to do. Play it safe, was his motto.

On the one hand, quit the clock round and go back as quickly and quietly as possible. Say you heard something like a big animal snorting and crashing around loose in the brush. Become a laughing stock. Maybe get written up.

On the other hand, just go ahead and finish the clock round. There were only three keys left anyhow. One near the elephants and rhinos up the road, a second near the ostriches and emus on the south side, and the third at the maintenance depot on the way back to the utility lot. It would take just ten more minutes.

He made his decision. It was quiet out there, and he pushed away from the Pagoda. Walking briskly and looking often over his shoulder, he kept to the shadows by the side of the street. Far up ahead, between street lights, he could already see the huge rocks around the elephant enclosure. Nothing could get out of there.

He heard the snorting again, like steam being released from an engine.

He felt the ground shake under his feet at the same time that he heard the rapid crashing noises and his bladder let go.

Jesus, Mary, and Joseph, this was for real.

Slowly he felt his trouser legs get hot and damp as he urinated freely. All were survival mechanisms, the eggheads had told him over the years. Puke, shit, piss, dump anything you're trying to digest, and run as fast as you can.

He knew what was running around before he saw it. Or them. Somehow one of the black rhinos had gotten loose. They were one of God's most angry and combative creatures. They would charge at anything if it came close enough or in any way threatened them.

He considered: there was a phone back at the Pagoda. Should he break off his round and hurry there? Somehow, his reflexes took over for him. He didn't sweat it much, knowing he'd never been real clever in the thinking department anyway. By the time this thought registered, he'd already dumped his time clock and was trudging back as fast as his ancient legs would let him. Luckily he was small and light—the years had evaporated all the beef and brawn off of him, he liked to say, finally leaving more brains than brawn.

Even at that, he was too noisy.

He heard the snort behind him, heard the rasp of hoof on asphalt, the thunder of hoof on grassy road shoulder, the scatter of gravel under a powerful running leg.

Charging at him, the size of a Chevrolet, was a two ton rhino. Its double nose horn was lowered ready to strike.

Johnny Gep looked about. There was no tree suitable to climb into, even if he had the strength.

But there was a rock...

Even as the beast bore down on him, he walked as fast as he could, away from the road and up a slight embankment that surrounded a group of boulders. As he slithered up the embankment, the rhino's charge carried it past on the street not fifteen feet away.

He heard its tough pads slither in a long crunch of tortured gravel as it sensed his location and braked. He let out a wail of terror as he went over the shoulder, up onto a small rock, then a bigger one, and finally on top of the big one which luckily had a flat top.

The rhino crossed the road and charged up the bank in a welter of leaves. Dust still drifted in the air as the animal stood looking at him. It rocked its head from side to side and snorted. Then it charged away.

Whew, he thought. Gone.

No, he heard the pattering of hooves, the snapping of twigs, felt the thunder in the ground, and there it came again. It ran toward the boulder, stopped almost within snout's reach of him, and huffed in frustration. He saw the deathly intention in its eyes. He felt the stink of its hot breath on his knuckles as he clung to the rock. How far could rhinos jump? he wondered, for the first time in his many years at the zoo. He'd seen a female elephant in must, once. Must was the elephant's version of heat. The animal had tried to kill its mahout, and was attempting to trample its way through a steel fence, until it broke a leg and had to be put down. The rage in this rhino was on that level. Johnny screamed in mortal terror. The rhino repeated its tactic, running away, then charging back, and stopping in frustration. Sooner or later, he sensed, it would solve its problem. This rhino was not going to give up, he knew it. It was almost as though something had gotten into it. Some possession. Some demonic force. Johnny couldn't figure it out.

He flattened himself fearfully. He watched as the rhino passed time and again in its charge. What made it more frightening was the sensuous way it rocked its bulk from side to side with each powerful springing step.

It tried a couple of times to jump onto the boulder, but ended up sliding down. Then it would stand looking at him, so close he could count the folds in its eyelids. He shrank back while looking into tiny hate-filled eyes.

Then there were two—no—three rhinos charging around in a circle. What in the hell? Had the alarm not gone off? Had the whole rhino group gotten out? But how? How could these enormous beasts have gotten over a ten foot moat eight feet deep and then yet over a four foot stone wall? Impossible, yet here they were milling around like soccer players, waiting to kick his ball into the next town.

He prayed. Oh Lord, let someone hear. Let Dr. Burtongale maybe have his cart out tonight like he sometimes did...

Oh no, now what?

The three rhinos waddled up to the boulder and began to push with the sides of their heads. Their heads alone were each four feet long and weighed as much as a motorcycle.

Johnny Gep lay flat on his belly and hung on with his fingernails. Again and again the boulder shuddered as their combined mass thrust against it.

Slowly, slowly (his life flashed before his eyes) the boulder moved. With a groaning sound like distant thunder, then a tumbling sound like an avalanche, the boulder went over. As it went over, he first slid, then fell, into darkness. For a moment, the darkness smelled sweetly of damp grass. Then the blackness closed over him with the weight of a huge boulder. He heard his bones snapping while his nose inhaled a last whiff of moss, then blood, then nothing.

He walked down a long corridor toward some sort of flaming gate. Dark shadows moved there. Figures walked toward the flames, and the dark shadows thrust them in. Dreamily, Johnny Gep noticed a bright blue baby crawling alone in the corridor. It had left its blanket behind. "What are you doing here?" he said and picked the baby up. It cooed at him, smiling. "Come along, little fellow," he said holding it close.

Chapter 42.

"Why am I doing this?" Mary-Shane said wiping sweat from her forehead as she raced from one task to another: Finishing the dishes, making the beds, packing her knapsack and Kippy's, feeding the parrot...

Elisa and Rudy Chatfield knocked at eight-thirty. "Sorry we're late," Elisa said. She had serious, confident brown eyes and a graceful way of standing with her hands folded behind her back. Long dark hair fell over her shoulders. Rudy, blond, sturdy, a two-fisted boy, radiated agreement.

"It's okay," Mary-Shane said, "we're just barely but not quite ready. Can you have your Dad come up a minute?"

"Oh let me! I'm gonna I'm gonna I'm gonna!" Rudy shouted and ran off, fists and knees pumping the air. A minute later, Roger Chatfield stood in her kitchen looking tanned and gorgeous and twirling his aviator sunglasses. "That bird," he said, "needs to get to a vet or he'll die of infection." Winky had not touched his orange. He sat in the bottom of Mrs. Abrahamson's finch cage. "He's in shock," Roger said. "Fortunately, we can get him to the best vet in town." He captured the bird, who fluttered weakly, and lifted him to his chest careful to keep the beak pointing away. "We'll stop by and leave Mr.—"

"Winky," Mary-Shane said.

"—Mr. Winky in the care of our zoo vet."

Mary-Shane closed the drapes, left a light on, and locked the door. Getting away! It was exciting to be with Roger Chatfield and she felt no apprehension as she'd felt with Vic or queasy avoidance as with Howard. Chatfield marched off with broad back and sturdy legs. His legs, she noted, were tanned and had the knots of a bicyclist. What am I getting into now, she wondered, picturing herself puffing along behind him on a 50-gear *turismo* special. Why did women reincarnate as someone different with each man they met? Maybe he liked to read. They could reach out from arm chair to arm chair and touch toes... stop it, Mary-Shane, you're slipping into delirium!

They left Winky at the zoo. The van climbed uphill on State 594, past the burned out waste that had been Harleigh Hale's bookstore.

Two military jets played tag high up. "Seeing a lot of those lately," Roger said.

As they puttered away from San Tomas in Roger's VW bus, Mary-Shane felt a wonderful lightness come over her. For the first time in weeks, the *Cold Thing* was not only quiescent, it was gone. She sat back with her bare feet on the dash, sipped a cola, and listened to Roger's stories. He'd been everywhere.

In the back was a swirl of kid activity.

First the mountains were just hills with potato boulders on them, the way the antediluvian sea had left them eons ago; then there were mountain table lands of green forest where the bus crawled noisily under the shade of linked tree crowns; then the desert sprawled before them like a smoky mirage done in crayon, all shades from grape to orange.

Mary-Shane sighed luxuriantly. Wind lifted her hair. She wore sunglasses borrowed from Roger.

Roger had grown up in Ohio. He'd gotten his Master of Science degree in Archeology from Georgetown University near Washington and had dug for buried cities in Jordan, Israel, Egypt, and Iraq. Then he'd switched from Archeology to Zoology, earning his Ph.D. from Washington State University. There he'd met Susan Burtongale, middle child and oldest daughter of Wallace and Margery Burtongale. His face betrayed some of the loss.

"She was a beautiful woman," Mary-Shane said.

"How do you know?" He thought she was jesting.

"I saw her picture on your desk that day when Perry and I—"

"I remember the day. I'm surprised you would notice such a fine detail."

"I'm surprised YOU remember the day, Roger," she teased.

The VW bus clattered up and down hills and under tree crowns like a toy. Mary-Shane looked at her reflection in windows and mirrors and gazed at a strange woman who looked as though she'd been airbrushed. Dark sunglasses, so you could not see the eyes; but one eyebrow had a quizzical or skeptic arch. A pretty face, even when plain and without makeup, changeable with mood and light, capable of making second string in three different facial beauty ads.

The stranger's face looked calm and composed, (until she saw herself and almost burst out laughing; she knew she had never actually been that studious and self-possessed).

Roger heard her snicker and half glanced toward her. "Huh?"

"I just saw my reflection. I look like a nomad."

"You look nice."

In midafternoon they reached the state park.

The kids whooped with relief after the six-hour trip. Mary-Shane liked being the mother figure for a carload of kids, given there was an acceptable father figure to go along with it. She took a last look at the stranger in the reflections; was it like this, she wondered, to have a husband and a family and do regular things? For the moment it felt good.

Roger parked his sunglasses atop his head and drove a few hundred feet, bouncing, very slowly, until he found a good camping space. Their space was almost completely sheltered behind bushes and tree trunks. With the bus parked crosswise at the entrance, they had an area twenty by twenty feet to themselves. In one corner was a barbecue pit and chimney of cemented blocks.

"The bushes are like walls," Elisa said deliciously, rubbing her hands and making eyes at this privacy.

"Yeah, and the outhouse is on the other end so we can smell the pines," Rudy blared. His blond hair stuck up like porcupine quills. Mary-Shane noticed his shirttail always hung out no matter what he was doing. Kippy, only a year older, was a neater, quieter boy, but they seemed to get along.

"What can we do to help?" Mary-Shane asked.

Roger said: "I'm used to the equipment and I work pretty fast by myself. Give me a half hour."

Mary-Shane took the kids to the Overland Museum, which was a huge single-room log building overlooking miles of tree crowns. A woman ranger, with a gun and campaign hat, used a stuffed specimen in a corner by a potbellied stove to explain how bears hibernate. She pointed out that it was not yet winter, and to watch out for any bears that might approach campsites looking for food.

Over the faraway hills were charcoal colored clouds.

When Mary-Shane and the kids returned, Roger had popped out the VW camper top. He'd opened the rear and made a shelf for food and drink, covered by a tarp on four aluminum poles. He'd set up two tents in the clearing, one near the bus and the other about fifteen feet away. The one near the bus, he said, was for Mary-Shane and Kippy ("to be closer to the latrines"). The other tent was for himself, Elisa, and Rudy.

"I'm starved," Rudy shouted.

They grilled up some hot dogs, hamburgers, and baking potatoes. Working together at the barbecue, Roger and Mary-Shane had Another One of Those (Wonderful)(Scary)(Melting Together) Looks.

Thunder grumbled.

The wind grew brisk, and rocks had to be placed on napkins.

They all ate hungrily.

"I fobot how womerfum hamburbums ban tafte outdorf," Mary-Shane said.

"UUmmmm," Roger agreed, nodding toward the dark clouds approaching. Pine boughs swished back and forth. The air got cool and damp. It got real foggy and scary so the kids huddled in blankets in Mary-Shane's tent and giggled.

"What if a bear comes?" Mary-Shane asked him.

"We zip up the tents and hope for the best."

"Oh Daddy!" Elisa cried flying into his arms.

Kippy and Rudy each took a crutch and made fencing motions.

"Not to worry," Roger told Elisa. "These bears only look for people with out of state license plates. It's a matter of professional courtesy from the bears." He released Elisa. "Ready for the Last Roundup?"

"What's that?" Kippy asked.

"I escort the whole crew to the potties and after that it's lights out."

They had two oil lanterns between the five of them. Roger carried one, Mary-Shane the other. The two lanterns glowed in the fog. The kids giggled, clutching their towels and toilet kits tight.

Elisa was very precise about her pretty teeth, and now she seemed extra introspective. "Mary-Shane..."

"Hmm?" Mary-Shane brushed, and had a mouthful of mint foam.

"...You like my Daddy, don't you?"

Mary-Shane nodded.

Elisa rinsed her brush at the coldwater tap. "I think you and Kippy are very nice. Daddy was friends with a lady. She wasn't very nice to me and Rudy, and she broke Daddy's heart for a while there. You won't hurt him, will you?"

Mary-Shane spat out. Sucked in a handful of cold water. Gargled. "Elisa, I like your Daddy a lot but we only just met and..."

But Elisa had run out into the night.

There was a lantern in the fog.

"Roger?"

"Yo."

"Hurray, it's you." She gave him a squeeze. "It's nice to know you're out there with your lantern."

He squeezed back. "Like your lantern too."

They clinked the lanterns together like champagne glasses.

Elisa's face hovered concernedly on the other side of Roger, her big dark eyes sweeping over Mary-Shane still brimming with that question.

Rudy and Kippy came out of the men's room. Rudy was flipping his soap dish repeatedly in the air and catching it. Kippy was treading carefully through the smelly puddles outside the john so as not to slip a crutch tip.

"Captain Colorado!" Rudy yelled and ran in circles around the group.

"Mom," Kippy said when they were alone in their tent, "are you going to go out with this guy?"

Time for honesty. "Maybe." She waited for an answer while the pine boughs dripped in the fog. The tent was zipped up from the inside and the heater made it toasty. Mary-Shane and Kippy occupied sleeping bags head to toe with a space in between for their folded up clothes.

"He seems okay," Kippy said.

"I think he might be," Mary-Shane said.

"We can get free tickets to the zoo while it lasts," Kippy said.

Mary-Shane was dreaming in her mummy bag about a library. A nice big stuffy library with rows and rows and rows of books. Outside it was snowing. Yes. A cozy picture with a mellow little porch light far off in snow among trees. Something frightening outside, but Roger was there to protect her... She heard a faint noise, like tin banging on stone. The endless vistas of books disappeared with a frightened poof. Kippy was sleeping thickly and she could tell he was okay. There, that noise again. A tinkling sound.

She sat up and groped for the flashlight. What if it was a bear? She made an opening just big enough to peer outside. A faint glow came out of the fog on the far side of the bus. She must get Roger...

...but by the time she was out of the tent, wrapped in a blanket and listening, she heard him whistling softly. She smelled burning coal.

She walked to his tent and peered in. Two heads, two snores, two kids fast asleep. No Roger.

She walked around the bus. "Roger?"

He was sitting with his back to the bus, tending a small fire made of a handful of coals between three stones. He looked outdoorish and quite comfortable. He grinned. "Hey, I thought you were fast asleep." How handsome he looked with the firelight playing on his chiseled features and white teeth.

"You woke me."

He rose, threw away the twig he'd been bending, and approached her. She clutched her blanket tightly around herself. "Good," he said, took her in his arms, and kissed her. She drank in the feel and the taste of his mouth like a thirsty person takes in fresh water. She could not get enough. She let the blanket fall away as she reached up to pass her arms over his shoulders and pull herself closer to him while their mouths worked thirstily together. She moaned lightly and hoped with part of her mind that the kids would not hear and with the other part of her mind that this would never end. Just her, and him, and the little fire, and the world full of fog.

"Tea," he said as they sat together and watched the little pot, waiting for the water to boil over the stones. "Darjeeling, with that like orange zing to it."

"Just the right thing at a moment like this," she agreed. They sat close together under her blanket. She kissed his neck. "This is a very nice moment."

He squeezed her close to him. "Very nice. Maybe once in a lifetime. I mean we can go camping again, but who would guarantee we'd have another fog like this?"

She unbuttoned two of his shirt buttons and rubbed her fingertips on his chest. "We could try a bunch of times. Law of averages says we might get a nice big rainstorm."

"Naw, we'd have to stay in our tent. No fun."

"No fun," she agreed pulling his chest hairs.

"It might be cozy," said with a tone that suggested if he could he would stand up and overturn the tubs of heaven to shower her with any kind of weather she desired.

"I like the fog," she murmured. "Thanks, Roger."

"Water's about ready," he said. He threw in a metal ball.

"One of those gadgets," she commented.

"Tea infuser," he said.

"I thought you were just going to toss in a tea bag like I would have."

"Naw. Gotta do some things right. I learned to drink tea from the Jordanians, and they learned it from the Brits. Let that stuff steep 'til it's good and dark. Then you got yourself a cup of tea."

"I'm going to go right out," she said, "and buy several infusers. And throw my tea bags away."

They listened to the tea water bubble and looked into the fog hoping maybe what? to glimpse a star? He patted her knee, put his arm around her. "You know what I have in my desk drawer?"

She shook her head. "An elephant gun?"

He gripped her hair and shook gently. "Do you know that when you laugh sometimes you sort of tinkle like a chime?"

She said, "I didn't know you were so what is it, romantic. When I first met you, you seemed stuffy."

"That's my official Burtongale persona." He rose, stuck a hand in where she'd undone the shirt buttons, and offered a Napoleonic pose. He said in a thick Wienerwald accent: "Zere is nozzink, nozzink, nozzink atoll happening in our zoo."

"Roger?" she started at the sound of an engine.

He sat back down and poured tea into his cup. "Ummm?" He sipped, grimacing, then offered it to her.

"Thanks, I'll wait 'til it's cooler." She listened intently.

"What's the matter?" he asked.

She shivered, pulling the blanket close. She heard the engine clearly now. A pair of headlights swelled up in the fog. A boxy looking vehicle drew near—a van. She cried out.

High beams exploded, showering them with light. A van bumper glimmered sullenly.

"Hey!" Roger shouted, waving. "Get that light off of us!"

Mary-Shane felt paralyzed. The van.

"Hey!" Roger repeated.

The high beams flicked off. A pair of yellowish low beams glared at them a moment longer. There was a crunch of gears, and the van slowly backed off. Somewhere, it turned and was driven off.

"Hey, you're shivering," Roger said.

"I'm jumpy. I'm sorry," she said.

"Relax," he said, cupping her face in his hands.

Her teeth chattered. "I'm okay now. What was it you keep in your desk?"

"Ever since Susan's death," he said, "I've kept my resume in the middle top drawer. I keep it updated and ready to send out, complete with references, lists of things I've published, excerpts, and so on. It's in ten copies so far, stamped, addressed to my favorite ten universities, and ready to send. All I have to do is walk to the mailbox and my life changes."

"I bet they'll all want to hire you in a second."

"Well, it's pretty competitive, but I have strong credentials."

"To run another zoo?"

He shook his head. "Never again. This has been nice, but I've thought of going back to digging." He handed her the cup. "Then I keep thinking of the kids, and I think I'll just take a teaching position somewhere."

"That could be fun." She sipped her tea. "Ow-wow-wowwie, that's hot and bitter."

"You should see your face. Sorry, I wasn't thinking. I can go get you some sugar."

She imagined her tongue would steam for ten more minutes. "I'll pass. I probably couldn't sleep after a few teaspoons of that."

"You'd be surprised. You could drink ten cups of coffee and this air would put you under like a narcotic. You look scared. Do I do this to you?"

She shook her head. "Don't mind me. " She did not want to spoil the moment with explanations. "But you sure do help me relax."

"Let's relax over our tea," he said.

She slipped close. "Would you do something for me?"

"What?"

She murmured: "Please hold me."

He held her tightly. She closed her eyes and pressed her cheek against his chest. She slipped her arms around him and held on. It was the first time in wow-how-long that she just felt utterly safe and at ease and happy in a man's arms without wanting to push away.

He kissed what he could reach of her face, brushing curls from her forehead.

Resting an elbow on his lap, she reached up with the other hand and pulled his head close to kiss him.

He set the tea aside. "Have I passed some sort of screening?"

She toppled him over backwards and sat on his chest. "Roger, you are a fine specimen of a man. I want your best kiss, and then I've got to get in and go to sleep or I'll die all day tomorrow. And you'd better get your rest too." She gripped his lapels in her fists while he looked up at her. She bent close, letting her breath warm his face. "I warn you though, Roger Chatfield." She brushed his lips with hers. "I have been a woman denied too long."

The next morning, Mary-Shane and Kippy both slept late.

A burst of sunlight exploded in her face.

Rudy blared: "Hey, get up, Dad says it's almost lunch time."

"Tell him I said his middle name is Hitler," Mary-Shane said. "Now close that flap before I bite your arm off."

Zip went the flap. Darkness returned.

"Mom," Kippy groaned.

"Hi ho," she said rubbing her eyes.

"I think they put something in those pine needles. I feel like I was drugged."

She turned over and positioned herself to crawl out of the sleeping bag and out of the tent. "It's called oxygen. You learned all about it in school. Eighth element on the periodic table."

Kippy yawned and rubbed his eyes. "I slept too long."

Mary-Shane unzipped the opening. "Rudy!" she called.

Rudy stood like a hesitant squirrel out of reach.

"I was just kidding," she said. "I won't bite your arm off. Come here."

He approached.

"What's for lunch."

"Deer meat," he said.

Mary-Shane frowned. Was it possible? Had that incredible man gone hunting already and bagged something? In a state park? Oh lord, there probably DID have to be something wrong with him. "Isn't that poaching?" she asked.

"No," Rudy said, "we buy a season ticket."

"You mean permit."

"Yeah."

"What if I don't like deer meat?" She feared to offend.

Rudy shrugged. "Well, there's always frozen hamburger patties."

Boots came crashing close. "Mary-Shane? Are you two finally awake in there? It's ten thirty." Roger wore his chef hat and chef apron. He held a pot holder in one hand and a frozen patty in the other. "How do you want your burgers? With bacon or..."

"Ha ha ha!" Rudy yelled and ran off.

"What's gotten into him?" Roger asked.

She rolled her face on her arms, then looked up. "He had me going that you went out and poached a deer and we were having it for lunch."

Roger looked puzzled. "But I did. We are."

She stared at him.

He blinked.

She threw her pillow at him and he ran off and she chased him. "You're full of it, Roger Chatfield! Full of it!"

It felt good to holler a little. She stamped about and unkinked her back. Seeing Rudy peer from behind bushes, she called: "Okay, Rudy, you can come out. Good joke."

He stepped out, and Mary-Shane tucked his shirt tail in for him. Elisa, who was doing place settings at the table, said: "Rudy go wash your hands. You too, Kippy. Go on."

Mary-Shane turned and saw that Kippy had emerged and was standing with one crutch, scratching his head and yawning. "Go on," she told her son, "wash up. Eating will clear your head."

Sunshine dappled the grove of trees. A blaring boom box marred the perfection, but was driven away after a minute or two. Butterflies chased along the wind-driven flowers. Leaves rustled and whispered all around. Birds warbled. The air grew warm and dry, smelling of grass.

The kids went for a hike.

"I was afraid about hiking..." Mary-Shane said.

Roger put his hand on her shoulder. "Don't worry. Rudy will run off and be inconsiderate, but Elisa will match Kippy's pace and they won't go far. I drilled her."

"Thanks. Just watch out. He'll get mad if he thinks you're doing him favors."

"Kinda like his Mom, huh?" After a glance over his shoulder, he took her in his arms. "Another stolen moment alone."

She stood on tiptoes, wrapped her arms tightly around his neck, and French-kissed him. As she did so she squirmed and pressed her breasts against his chest.

He breathed thickly and said in surprise: "No bra." He reached down and touched. His fingers felt sensuous and her nipples felt raw and aroused.

"Surprise." She'd known that sometime that day, his fingers would brush against her. That she would let him.

He said: "I want to kiss those very slowly, very carefully, and very very sensuously."

She touched his nose. "I can hardly wait. But not on this trip, Roger."

They sat down on a high rock with the blue expanse of a lake spread before them and the kids were crashing around somewhere below in the woods, but they held hands and looked into each other's eyes. "Ever since Susan died," he said, "I've wanted to pull out of that Burtongale crowd. Oh, but the job, and then the kids... You know my biggest fear is that Miss Polly would sue me for custody of the kids and somehow win. I know it sounds crazy but those people have a lot of power all the way to the state house and the courts, and you never know. I couldn't give them up."

Mary-Shane said: "I know what you mean. I nearly lost Kippy and I would die if anything ever happened to him."

"I'm glad he's okay now," Roger said. "He's a wonderful boy."

"Your kids are really neat too," Mary-Shane said. "Rudy looks like he can be a handful." She remembered how he'd let her tuck his shirt in. "But he can be managed."

Roger nodded. "Mary-Shane, this is all a dream. I'm going to wake up and it's going to have been nothing more than a nap at my desk. Wallace Burtongale will come in like a big blowfrog and announce that he's tired and going home early like he does every day lately."

"Ha, ha. So that's what you think of your boss. Well Mart Willow must be Wallace's good buddy."

"They are," Roger said. "Mart is married to Miss Polly's daughter Janine, who is a surprisingly decent sort."

"I heard Wallace's wife died a long time ago."

He nodded. "There are some weird stories about her, but that's before my time. You cannot get an honest answer about the Burtongales."

"Have you had much to do with Gilbert?"

There was a flash of annoyance in his eyes. "That stupid..." but he was unable to finish his sentence.

Rudy, Kippy, and Elisa stood in a line watching them, eyes trained like guns on a brigantine.

Roger continued to hold Mary-Shane's hands in his. "Come on over, kids," he called. "They might as well know," he whispered.

Mary-Shane's heart beat thickly. She tried to kid, but her voice was a stammer: "What, that we are holding hands?"

They yelled "Yay!" and climbed on the rock and piled on Roger and Mary-Shane. Elisa hugged Mary-Shane and kissed her on the cheek. A lingering toothpasty glance reminded Mary-Shane: (Don't hurt him, okay?) and Mary-Shane held the girl tightly.

In the late afternoon, the air cloudy and gray, they drove along the coast singing songs the kids all knew from videos, and the parents by osmosis. The sun lingered thinly. The sky was a mother of pearl color. Sea gulls squeaked like rusty winches. The wind smelled of rain and fish.

At one point she said: "There's something in the air down in San Tomas. Something..."

Rain drops formed on the windshield. His gaze was distant. "You know we lost that jaguar the other week. And you read about Adolph, right?"

"Yes, the gorilla."

"We lost a white rhino called Buster the other night. We found him keeled over dead as a stone the other morning in his enclosure. No obvious cause of death. Probably massive heart failure, same as the others."

"What's going on at the zoo?"

"Nozzink, nozzink. Seriously, if there's a story, I'll give it to you."

"That's okay but Miss Polly will quash it."

As the van tooled downhill, past the charred bookstore, night fell, and lights floated like lost ships in the rain. Drains overflowed with water, and waves moved across gutters.

Roger and the kids dropped Mary-Shane and Kippy off at the apartment complex. Mary-Shane hugged Rudy and Elisa. Mary-Shane stretched out to kiss Roger. He whispered: "I'll call you."

"I'll be waiting," she whispered back.

The *Cold Thing* was back. She could feel it. But it was asleep. Or busy. Bumping heads gently, playfully with Elisa, she lowered herself from the bus. Kippy was already unlocking the apartment door. She waved without turning back and heard the bus chatter away into the night.

"Did you have a good time?" Mary-Shane asked rubbing Kippy's hair.

"Yeah. Moooom, please! Stop that."

She wandered into the kitchen and started putting away odds and ends. "I think," she said, "we'll make the bottom of the hall closet our camping closet. What do you think?"

He shook out his socks.

"Not on the rug!" she yelled.

He balled them up and tossed them toward the bathroom. On a good day, with the door open and the door under the sink ajar, he could land small objects in the laundry basket from his room. "Are we going to be doing a lot of camping?"

She sensed his drift. "Well, we could also put our emergency stuff in there. You know, civil defense."

"Mom, I saw a movie where these people are wandering around in rags after the world is destroyed. We could get ready for that. But do we have guns, or do we just rob them from stores after the end of the world?"

"Take a bath and get ready for school tomorrow!"

"Are we going to go camping again?" he shouted from the bathroom.

"YES!" she hollered back. Yes, I'd really love to.

Chapter 43.

Obits were coming in right and left, and Spike was busy. Mary-Shane sat at her desk thinking warm thoughts of Roger Chatfield as she pored over the night police log. Jules sent her to cover a fire on Montclair Street. She drove to watch the red engines roll in. Men and women in silvery suits bumbled about with axes and hoses. Thick honey-yellow smoke filled the air, smelling of wood and what? A vision floated lazily in her memory: A cabin, covered with snow, smoke curling lazily from the chimney in a panorama of mountain peace, but it was not a calming vision; rather, it made her stomach knot up and her mind flutter...

The smoke turned black as a wall fell in and tires began to burn. A special Fire Department tanker truck laid down a viscous cloud of gray foam, putting out both the fire and her inner vision. She remembered to interview the battalion commander. This would make a nice piece: technology overcomes disaster.

Jules liked the story when she turned it in. She did not have long to bask. Eating lunch with one hand and typing with the other, she tallied the night's murders, rapes, suicides, and so on. She prepared the City Roundup article, a daily feature about The Violence We Live In.

At one, the copygirl made her rounds and dropped off a stack of interoffice envelopes at Mary-Shane's desk. One caught her attention. It was addressed simply "Police Reporter" and had been submitted anonymously. Mary-Shane spread the contents before her, yellowed clippings from various places and times with things highlighted in yellow marker and those things seemed to say Burtongale a lot. She grew afraid, remembering WARNED2's threat against Kippy. Nevertheless, she skimmed through the clippings with compulsive interest and with growing puzzlement as to who might have sent them.

SAN TOMAS (Special to the Herald). Dr. Wallace Burtongale proudly announced today that his son Gilbert finished his fourth year at Mainwether Academy, and will be attending the University of California, San Tomas in the Fall as a freshman...

ALTA LOMA (Allied Press Service) Police are investigating the mysterious deaths of two freshman UCST coeds at their off-campus apartment. Police say their hearts had been severed and the scene was a grisly one...

SAN TOMAS (American News Service) Police are investigating the motorcycle deaths of two reputed drug dealers, Frank P. MacLemore and James "Attila" Hunter. Det. Lt. Victor Lara of the San Tomas Police said that both men had been sought in the tire iron bludgeoning death of Charles Best, a local drug dealer and occult bookstore partner a week earlier. MacLemore's young widow, free on bail for child abuse charges, appeared hysterical in her courtroom appearance...

CHICAGO, Ill. (AP) Marshall Goldberg, Curator of the Abramowitz Orientology Museum at the University of Chicago, announced a major art burglary. Two guards had been brutally murdered by mysterious burglars who took artifacts from among the museum's many priceless objects.

The Yoreni Stone, a rough sculpture in iron ore, was taken by either two or three men, police are not sure. The sculpture had no intrinsic monetary value, Goldberg said. It had been brought to the U.S. during the 1920's by an anthropology professor and UC alumnus. It came from Ivory Coast in West Africa, where it was rumored to have strange and violent effects on native villagers. Another object, a small stone plate from Africa...

Mary-Shane stuffed the clippings (there were more of them) back into the envelope and into her desk drawer. Should she tell Jules? Or keep quiet? Who was putting her up to this? The risks seemed to great for her to leap blindly into any further investigation. But the clippings stirred up old pain; somewhere, a cabin lay cozy and solitary, covered with snow, and dribbling smoke, but horrible...blood running out from under the front door and down the steps...?

Chapter 44.

That evening, she noticed that Kippy seemed to be spending more time at his computer again. When she checked in on him, he was keyboarding a homework assignment. She worried about his eyes, but felt too overwhelmed to challenge him. At least, it kept him out of trouble; for now...

Roger called. She broke into a broad smile. "Well, what a surprise."

"I wanted to thank you for coming camping with us."

"I had a wonderful time. Kippy did too."

"Maybe you'd like to do it again sometime?"

"I think we have no choice. Kippy has already set up a camping part in his closet."

"I was thinking about you today."

"You have crossed my mind once or twice too, Roger."

"That has kind of a warm tone, the way you say that."

"Sounds kind of warm to me too. Make more calls like this."

He laughed. "Let's plan something soon."

After they had hung up, she sat back with a warm and fuzzy feeling that quickly turned into a warm and scary feeling. What if (a thousand things)? After Kippy was asleep, Mary-Shane sat in the living room with a mug of hot chocolate. She was unable to sleep, and the old Burtongale book from Father Lawrence lay open by the TV. She picked it up and flipped idly through. What if, somehow, he too could not handle someone with a special child...? Or if she wasn't educated enough? Or...?

Wallace Burtongale I, she read, had abruptly ended his explorations and settled in San Tomas to be a prominent citizen in this and that. He had taken a rudimentary botanical garden and expanded it into what would, by Civil War standards, become one of the leading zoological gardens west of the Mississippi River. She found a brittle news clipping, brown with age, that someone had long ago inserted. Startled, she read:

CHICAGO (Hearst News Service)—The annual Congress of Zoological Associations ended today with an award ceremony at the Shawnee Gardens Lodge. Participants, recently returned from the War with Spain, noted the unfortunate death recently of a prominent member who will be sorely missed. Wallace Burtongale of San Tomas, California, passed away while residing at St. Elizabeth's Hospital in Washington. Dr. Burtongale, who was very active in zoological affairs, had been suffering from a state of complete mental and physical exhaustion resulting from his arduous travels in Africa. Members of the family indignantly denied rumors that Dr. Burtongale's sanity had been affected by his

The clipping ended there, the rest lost in time and eternity. But someone had written long ago in fountain pen or quill (the forked nib's quick strokes were evident:) "Went insane!" and this was underlined. Mary-Shane studied the truncated article, wondering if Father Lawrence were aware of it.

Hearing a sound outside her window, she folded the book away and rose. Looking out the window, she saw a shadowy figure crossing the foggy street to a parked van glistening with condensation. Her heart missed a beat or two. The man, whose features she could not make out, opened the rear door of the van and got in.

Heart pounding, she stared at the van. A glow seemed to emanate around it. Terror rose in her soul. What if Roger came to think she was crazy? She had not really let him in on the things that were going on inside of her. She stared at the van, feeling angry (a snowy mountain cabin: what was this thought?) and the van just sat there unmoving, perspiring with condensate in the fog. If she could SEE the man, then she'd remember WHO the third man was with them the night Charlie Best was killed. Impulsively, she threw her robe on and ran outside with bare feet. Wet concrete and grass felt icy cold to her bare feet. In the drizzle, as she ran into the street, she saw two blood-red taillight swirls as the mysterious van slipped into the night.

Chapter 45.

Wallace Burtongale unhappily stepped from his office, locked the door, and walked toward the rear utility lot in the zoo. What if the ship flew away? What then of the Burtongales?

The full moon rode on a raft of clouds.

With a soft whine, the cart carried Wallace out of the utility parking lot. He drove to the maintenance parking lot which lay deserted and padlocked in moonlight. Wallace found the air/sea container from Japan, arrived earlier in the day.

The seals and straps took a few minutes; he did not have the right cutters. The doors swung open easily and he began loading box after box of generic computer equipment onto his cart. As he worked, he thought about the nightmare his life was.

He drove across the zoo. A familiar feeling of well-being wrapped itself around him like a narcotic, overlaying his depression, as he entered the pagoda. A light of indeterminate color oozed out of the walls. The light reminded him of blots on an old photograph. One second its tinge was greenish, the next second it might be bluish or white, or even flicker off for a moment.

The Pilot had lived in the back of his mind for as long as he could remember. The secret knowledge was passed down through the generations from one Miss Polly to the next Miss Polly. The oldest son carried the Pilot and when he died it went to his son, in whom the seed of the Pilot was already planted. But the Miss Pollys had Knowledge about what had been brought from Africa so long ago. The Pilot did not speak words to Wallace. It spoke *Feelings*. It had always been that way, and he never questioned it, though he knew he was Different From Other People. That had been drilled into him since childhood, as it had been drilled into Gilbert; ...that You Did Not Tell Anyone. The Pilot welcomed Wallace to its sickly radiation. *WE ARE GROWING STRONGER...WE ARE PUTTING THE SHIP BACK TOGETHER...*

Wallace stepped forth carrying the first of tonight's laptops, and the Pilot was pleased. Already the few he had brought were tied together and glowing. It was a faint glow, for the screens were turned dim as possible. What the Pilot needed most were the chips and the data buses inside. Already, a conductor had seemingly grown out of the air—bits of wire, patches of crystal or quartz, scraps of cloth with metallic threads woven in, anything that could carry a faint pulse. And there was a little throbbing, like a machine, already a little louder...

On command, Wallace poured out the plastic peanuts. A wind kicked up inside the pagoda. The dessicant light flickered. Power was marshaled from elsewhere. The peanuts began to tremble. They levitated ever so slightly. And then, with only the faintest whisper of a whoosh, they skittered away to disappear in the licorice darkness among the pumps and other machines. There were explosive sounds, like popcorn popping, and Wallace hunkered down, covering his face. He peered between his fingers and saw the most amazing sight. The plastic foam forms lifted into the air and then exploded. A light grew inside the pagoda as energy was marshaled from other places. Lines began to appear on the walls, like fishnet, only made of plastic foam melted to a chewing gum consistency and then sprayed onto the cold stone. And even as this went on, metallic threads began to snake through the plastic foam lines. The Pilot was rebuilding his ship.

Five, six more times Wallace made the trip. In the end, all that was left was a tall stack of flattened cardboard boxes near the pagoda. The maintenance crew in the morning could be ordered to retrieve them and they would ask no undue questions. Reluctantly, like an addict coming out of a fix, Wallace backed out of the pagoda when his work was done. He stole one more glance inside. The glow in the pagoda was more pronounced now, because there was more conducting lineage. And even with their screens dimmed as if they were asleep, all the laptops attentively faced in the same direction toward the darkness among the pumps.

As Wallace stumbled toward the golf cart, the depression hit again. He knew that once the ship was reassembled, the Burtongales would not be needed any longer. And the Pilot would have no mercy on them.

Chapter 46.

All day Tuesday, Mary-Shane was bothered by a sense of anxiety. She tried to review her life and found that everything was such a mess, it was hard to sort anything out. She wanted to put things in places—Kippy (ok) here; Mother (status quo) there; job (a dreadful feeling in the stomach) here; love life (ah, maybe a glimmer of something positive?) there; *Cold Thing* (yooohooo, ooohh where aaaarre youuuu?) here.... but when she got to that set of hidden doors, one of which had been unlocked by the tooth, she found that her mind wanted to knock down all the order she had just struggled to create—slam all the doors open, let the truth shine forth. But what truth?

Dr. Stanislaus, that evening, said: "How do you feel?"

"Terrible."

He nodded. "You did extremely well last week. Have you remembered anything more?"

"I was hoping there isn't any more," she said.

"Maybe there isn't," he agreed. "What do you say we go in and find out for sure?"

"What do you mean?"

"Hypnosis."

She shrank back, afraid.

"If there is something else you are hiding from yourself it's all in there already and all we have to do is face it. It's the only way to make it go away once and for all."

"Will it," she asked miserably, "go away if I face it?"

He had her lie back and led her through a few yoga relaxation exercises. When she was very still, just a mind floating in a room of neutral light, his voice sounded quietly like distant commands in a spaceship: "We are going to go in a little deeper now, and I will be with you the whole way..." He had her imagine walking down a long aisle in a great big school room, to a black board. She took chalk in one hand and an eraser in the other hand. Then, beginning with the capital letter A, she was to write first the capital letter and then the small letter. Then she was to write the next capital (B) but not before erasing the last capital (A). Then she was to write the next lower case (b) but first erase (a). Before writing C, she must erase B. And before writing c, she was to erase b. And before writing D, she was to erase C...

Somewhere between J and K, or was it K and L?, she stepped through some sort of door or sank through some ice or floated up through a ceiling...

Where are you? Dr. Stanislaus asked.

"I'm in a cellar." She smelled mustiness all around, damp sand fouled with rodent turds; she tasted blood on her lip and felt the fear deep in her gut.

Tell me about the cellar, Dr. Stanislaus said.

But she was too numb to talk, too much afraid. Frank's hard, strong fist was on her torn blouse collar. In his other hand, shiny and merciless...

Tell me about the cellar. Are you alone?

"Oh God no." She sobbed, she wriggled, she cried out and raised her hands. "Frank has a gun. He already hit me with it. And he says he'll shoot me."

Your husband Frank? came the distant voice.

"Yes! Yes! Why did I forget this? He's insane! And I'm too young to know any better. I thought I loved him."

What did you do that made him so angry?

"I... I... I said I was going to the police."

Why?

"Because... Because... of the baby."

What baby?

"I don't know," she wailed.

Was it Kippy?

"Yes... No... Another baby."

Try to remember. Reach for it.

"A baby!" she wailed. "A dead baby!" Mary-Shane sat straight up and screamed. It was pitch dark. She held her hands over her mouth.

...Please hang on. Hang in there...

"No no no no!" she screamed. The dead baby was in her arms. Mabel Stork smiled, a dirty evil smile glad at her pain and shock. "N-n-n-n-n-O-O-O-O-O-O-O-o-o-o-o!" she screamed beating her fists against the wooden beams in the cabin, the white cabin, the white cabin, where the air was so suffocating...

Dr. Stanislaus's voice floated over like a light of comfort: You are quite safe. We are close to where we need to be but now you have to make the decision. Do you want to go on?

"No."

Okay, then I'll lead you out and we'll talk about it. Maybe you'll want to try again some other time. Push it all away, please. Just push. It will move away.

She pushed, and sure enough she was out in the snow and then in the sunshine, rising like a balloon... but she did not feel good; she remembered catechism and looked down at the state of her mind and it was like having a dirty soul; it was like realizing for the first time that you really need a bath... "STOP," she said, "STOP. I want to go in. I want to get this over with. I don't ever want to go through this again. I need to know."

Very well. Can you pull it all back?

She tried. "No, not quite."

Very well. Let yourself sink down. Go back down. Go back in.

Like a stone, she sank back into those painful waters.

Why was Frank threatening you?

"Because..."(she saw vividly: Frank's old car)"we were driving up to the mountain shack to see..."

Whom?

"I can't tell or he'll kill me."

Frank is dead. He can't hurt you.

"Maybe the other one will"(that face... who?)"the one whose name I'm never supposed to mention. He might kill Kippy."

Try working around it.

"We were driving to a mountain shack to deliver something in a coffin"(Attila laboring along behind them in the rented Haul-a-Way)"and collect money."

Kippy was with you?

"Yes."

Was there a dead person in the coffin?

"Ummm..."(dead person?)"...no. Not a person. A thing, Black, that's all I remember."

A black thing. You saw it?

"Yes"(black; half melted; rock?)"it had no shape but it shone a little.

Okay move on.

"Frank and Attila"(breath coming in steamy rags, snow on jeans, leather jackets, cccold up here!)"go around the front and I follow holding Kippy. A wooden door opens and we go into some kind of kitchen. It smells weird like food with all the wrong spices. And there are weird things on the walls. Devil things. I'm thinking this dude is really weird, man, but we can live for a half a year on the money we'll get from him."

This dude is who, the one you can't name?

"Yes the guys sit down at this table. Frank and Attila wear guns under their"(thick leather, hard oily smelly)"jackets. I suppose the other man was too. Then Kippy shit his diaper. Frank turns around"(snarling, eyes lit with anger)"like Get that asshole out of here."

Why did you go along? And why take Kippy?

"We had no heat in the cabin and Kippy had bronchitis."

Oh.

"Yes so this guy points to a door. I go through there"(cooking? what smells like that?)"and this big lady"( )" points to a table where there are diapers and things. Cool, I think they have some kind of nursery here. Funny, you don't hear any babies."

Oh God.

Mary-Shane drew a deep shuddering breath. "So I start changing Kippy. Then as I'm looking for powder, this woman picks Kippy up like she's going to rock him. I turn my back for one minute and when I turn around she's GONE. Kippy cries. I heard him outside and I flew out the back door. The woman was walking away fast, and ME AFTER HER. She gets to this car. Some people get out and hand her a bundle. Suddenly there are two bundles. Two babies"(GIMME MY BABY OR I'LL KILL YOU BITCH)"she turns and hands me this baby and right away I knew something was wrong. It was dead"(where are my sobs today? who weeps for this poor soul, this little flower?)"I peeked to make sure, there was no life, no kick no movement, meanwhile Kippy was wailing and these people this man and woman got into the car with him"(SCREAMING: GIVE ME MY BABY OR MY HUSBAND WILL KILL YOU AND TORTURE YOU I WILL REMEMBER YOUR LICENSE PLATES)"All I had to do is threaten them with Frank and the woman rolled her window down"(a look I will never forget: absolute, cold, disdain: Is it really necessary to carry on like that? GIMME MY BABY OR YOU DIE, WITCH. At that a smile fogged the glass of her face, faintly.)"The husband was waving for her to hand over Kippy. I'm still standing there holding the dead baby. His name was, OH GOD"(Stevie; a little name stitched into his nightie; weeks old?)"

Take a few seconds. Pause, get your breath. Only go on if you can. I can always bring you out right away.

Mary-Shane took a deep breath. "I can't stop now"(There was a faint glitter between the ice-white eyelids, tiny slivers dead eyes a message: don't let them take your baby too)"No, I have to go on. I MUST. For a second I thought it's all over and this WOMAN was just smiling at me, a real ice queen, holding Kippy"(like something she had decided she did not want to buy at a sale)"

Can you recall who any of these people were?

(No)"No, but I wouldn't tell you if I did. Frank said he'd kill me and Kippy too"(the gun the cellar the blood but I didn't care I was just so glad to still have my baby I'd do anything—anything)"Finally she handed Kippy back to me"(Really, dear, don't carry on)"she said not to carry on but the husband yelled something, We don't want any trouble, and he gunned his car and they flew out of there"

The license plate...

"No chance. I ran back past the house and got into Frank's car. I locked the doors and pulled out the other gun he kept under the seat. But nothing more happened."

What happened to the dead baby?

"I don't know. The woman took him from me. All I remember is Frank hit me. I said I was going to the cops. When we got back to our cabin he took me down into the under-shed and said he would kill me if I blew it for all of us. I promised never to tell."

I think we need to back out. We've done enough for tonight, don't you think?

"Doctor..."

Yes?

"I think they ate the baby."

Push it away. Let it go. Come back up. It's over.

Dr. Stanislaus moved to help her but she was quicker. Somehow, the sweet-salty cooking-smell remained in her nostrils. She ran for the john and vomited, vomited, until her head felt like splitting and her jaw ached. Coughing yellow stinging slime, wiping ropes of dinner that dangled from her nose into the whispering potty that oddly and comfortingly vibrated like a seashell with the hum of traffic in the street outside, she groaned between attacks. Dr. Stanislaus handed her fresh clean warm soaked towels and she got herself cleaned up.

She released her grip on the cold slippery bowl edge and washed her hands and face at the sink.

"Who was the other man?" he asked.

"I can't quite pull it in."

"Is it a man?"

"Yes."

"Old or young?"

"Young. Back then, anyway."

"White, Black, Hispanic?"

"White."

"See, you remember a lot. It's all there, waiting to be pulled out. I could call Lara right now and they'd have a police sketch artist here..." He looked at his watch. "No, by the time we got that all set up you'd be beyond this hypnosis. Let's let it go until next Tuesday."

She rose, ready to leave. "And find out who those people are, stop them from taking any more..." She ran outside, unable to say the word. Babies.

Chapter 47.

"Mom, you've been acting weird lately." Kippy lifted the bowl and slurped the rest of his cereal and milk. She stabbed a sausage with her fork. "I'm sorry, sweetheart. I've been seeing my shrink about some old things, and I'll tell you some of it one day. Please trust me, I'm going to keep my cool."

Kippy folded his hands on the table. "I will help you all I can." She laid her hands over his. "That's awful sweet of you. What you can do to help me is to keep your room neat and do your homework and be the good boy you have always been."

He squeezed her hands. "I love you, Mom." She felt hollow, a tree wounded by lightning, but things would be okay if only she hung on. "I love you very much, Kippy."

Wednesday at work: Fires, murders, accidents, mankind at work. She went through the motions as best she could. She sat in meetings and smiled and nobody knew how she felt just now. At times she seemed to slip back under hypnosis and tell Dr. Stanislaus: "I'm packing all these little pieces of painful memory and stacking them by the door for the mail man. I am going to mail them to Timbuktu." And he would say: "Good girl, Miss No Name. Keep working at it. Push it away. Push!"

She stopped in to see Jules. "How is Matilda?"

Jules looked gray. "Same, Mary-Shane. Perry doesn't move from her bedside. You look kinda frazzled yourself."

"You noticed."

"Same old vinegar." Shaky fingers fiddled with a pipe stem.

She took Kippy to Mother's house, where he was to do his homework and then watch a space movie. She met Vic in a dark, drafty bar and they sat far apart in a booth nursing steamy coffees. "Vic, I've been seeing Dr. Stanislaus."

"I know."

"You've been watching me like a hawk, haven't you?"

Vic looked somber. "Yes."

"You never quit working that case, have you?"

"No."

"I should be mad at you for snooping on me, but I'm not."

Vic put a bottle cap on the table. Old Wooffentooth or whatever. "When I saw you put the whiskey bottle outside Hale's place and drive away, I knew you were on the track."

"When did you know I was starting to relive the past?"

"When you said you were going to see Doc Stanislaus."

"You all worked together, huh?"

Vic stirred his coffee thoughtfully. "Maybe if you remember it all, you'll be healed. About the other day."

"Yes," she said. "Why?" Why had he beaten those men?

He stirred. "I've been after this Satanic ring for years. There is a connection to the Jungle, but I don't know what. I showed you the altar, right? You don't know how many times I've been close, but they are so well organized, they always manage to cover their trail."

"Why do they do it?" She meant the Satanists, and she knew he knew that was who she meant. She thought of the well-dressed couple and shuddered. We don't want any trouble. She felt sick.

He shrugged. "Maybe some of them really believe in all that hokey. Most of them are too shallow to know any better. They're in it for the thrill. They are so dead inside that it's the only way they get their rocks off."

"I wish I could tell you where that cabin was, Vic."

He considered that. "The PD and some other agencies covered big swatches of those mountain ten years ago. We knew from Miss Temple that there was something—you were closed up tight as a clam—"

"Frank threatened me."

"—I figured as much, even back then."

"That baby's name was Stevie."

"Let it go, Mary-Shane. He's been dead ten years. The world is hell. We have met Satan, and he is People."

"I recognized one of the people, Vic."

He looked startled. "What?"

"Mabel Stork."

"Holy shit." He stubbed his cigarette out. "Mary-Shane, they've still got Mabel in county detention. I might be able to get her out. Make a deal with her."

"I'll come along."

"No you won't."

"Yes I will."

He gave her a long stare. "I guess, Mary-Shane, you're part of this whether I like it or not. You've been part of it from the start, without you even knowing."

She nodded. "To the bitter end, buddy boy."

In the three short days since Mary-Shane's camping trip with Roger, the rainy weather in the mountains had turned icy cold. The snow level had descended to three thousand feet at night. A black fog roiled in serpentines along State 495 as Vic's car rumbled along on blocky snow tires. Night fell early.

"The roads are still clear," Vic said, "otherwise I wouldn't even try this. There's more snow forecast for tomorrow, so we might just luck out this evening."

In the back of the detective car, separated by a bullet-proof plastic shield, sat Mabel Stork. Mary-Shane, morbidly curious, stared into Mabel's face, trying to rediscover that dirty gleam in the eyes, the mean grin, but Mabel was a blank.

"She's been around the bend a couple of times no doubt," Vic said. "Probably been on her way down hill for years."

"And Evvie?"

Vic shrugged. "Poor kid. She'll get farmed out to a foster home."

Mabel's fist smashed against the plastic. Rage was in her eyes.

"Yeah, you can hear me really good when you want to," Vic said as though he were speaking to a caged animal that would bite if released.

God, Mary-Shane thought, Hard Vic. What had she, however briefly, seen in him? "Maybe this wasn't such a good idea," Mary-Shane said. She felt scared.

"I got us a one-time deal with old Mabel back there, Mary-Shane. Give it a chance, okay? If she helps us find what we're after, I let her go." He gave her a Look. "Mary-Shane, deals are cut all the time. It's how things get done."

Mary-Shane sat back miserably and let the achy fabric of the past envelop her. This was a lot like something that happened before. She'd come this way in the dark with Frank and Attila and the other man... So many question marks in her mind! Once Vic left State 495 and started crawling up and down hilly curvy little mountain blacktops rimed with thin snow, Mary-Shane was utterly lost.

Mabel's fist smashed the plastic again.

"Give her some coffee," Vic said indicating a thermos. Mary-Shane passed a dented steel cup through a slot in the plastic and Mabel's hard fingers took it. Was there a look of smoldering recognition in the woman's eyes, an ember pile of hellish light?

Mary-Shane poured herself and Vic plastic cups of coffee. The bitter aroma was comforting. "Vic, does this have anything to do with the Burtongales?"

"Why do you ask?" His gaze, scanning the night, was opaque.

"Everything lately seems to." She slurped hot coffee, winced, and blew over the surface.

Vic shut the engine off. The hood banged, cooling. Snowy gritted lightly against the windows. The wind had a lame howl in its throat. Mary-Shane pulled her coat tight, staring at the forest of pines waving in the darkness. The sky was a milky glow above the dark skyline of trees.

Vic opened the driver's side door. "You can stay in the car if you want to," he told Mary-Shane.

"Not me, I'm not moving an inch from you." She slid across the seat after him.

Vic pressed something hard and warm into her hand. She looked down and saw that she held his heavy revolver. Vic rattled his shotgun loose from the dash. With flashlight in hand, shotgun on elbow, he stepped outside. "Easy, Mabel old girl," he said unlocking the back door.

Mabel, bundled in clean though castoff charity clothing, bounced out like a ball. Mary-Shane tried to keep Vic between her and Mabel as they trudged uphill on crunchy snow pack. The revolver, no longer warmed by Vic's flesh, drew the cold to it.

Somewhere, a hound or a wolf keened, hills and valleys away, rippling over Mary-Shane's spine. The keening was taken up by other canids farther away, in a relay of warnings. Suddenly, Mary-Shane remembered the curve in the road where Attila had parked the truck with the [???] in it. "This is the place," she whispered to Vic, who did not answer. "I think," she added. Mabel stood stock-still.

There! Mary-Shane recognized the sloping roof, lacy with snow. The blunt chimney. "This is definitely the place."

Vic sniffed. "Someone had a fire going in there not too long ago."

"Vic," Mary-Shane whispered, but he ignored her. She wondered why he hadn't cuffed Mabel. Mabel watched, hare-like, still.

Vic turned the flashlight on. He was all concentration. He approached the worn blackish wood door, shotgun still cradled. Mary-Shane followed, holding the revolver. Her hands shook as she held it pointed at the ground before her.

Vic gave the door a kick. On the second try, its lock snapped and it swung open. The flashlight stabbed inside: The familiar table, the stone fireplace, the door leading to...

Vic sniffed again, backed away. He trudged silently through calf-deep drifts outside. They went around the back. There, Mary-Shane put together a vague memory of the nightmare landscape where Kippy had nearly been taken from her so long ago.

Vic kicked in the back door. The flashlight beam picked around inside. Another hearth. A long shelf (for diapers?). A rusty cooking pot. "Place looks abandoned," he said quietly. He sniffed carefully. "There's been a fire here recently. A hunter might have stopped in the last few days, made a fire, then moved on." He stepped closer to the entrance.

A kind of hypnosis drew Mary-Shane alongside him. There: this had been where she had laid Kippy down. There on that bench where tonight snow twinkled, having fallen through a hole in the roof. The place was glacial inside. Dead.

The flashlight beam meandered up and down stone walls hung with daggers of ice. Meandered back and forth, and finally came to rest on some Things on the mantel piece.

"I'll be damned," Vic said.

Mary-Shane drew a deep breath, looking at a picture of herself. It was a picture of Mary-Shane, ten years younger. Smiling like the sun. There were other pictures: Mary-Shane and Frank, he holding her in one arm and a rifle in the other, and looking cocky woodsy mean. Attila and Frank on their motorcycles on a summer afternoon. And another person. A tall man with a beard, holding a baby. Kippy? Mary-Shane took the flashlight, aimed its beam, stepped closer.

"You know what?" Vic said. "Someone has built an altar to you."

"Get out." But the evidence of her vision betrayed the common sense of her mind. Yes, there among carefully garlanded pine boughs, was somebody's altar to the past. With dreadful fascination, she shone the beam directly into the face of the man holding her baby. Those dimples. That beard. Those crazed hungry eyes...

Someone screamed.

As if in slow motion, Mary-Shane and Vic turned.

Another scream.

The flashlight beam dipped, then rose again.

The light shone directly into Mabel Stork's face. She was running, a bundle (how could she move so fast?) of clothing hurtling at them like a missile. Her eyes were black with hate. Her teeth were bared like a zoo animal's. Her cap fell off, and stringy gray hair fluttered sweatily. A rusty ax, forgotten by some wood-chopping camper, waved over her head as she raced directly at Mary-Shane.

P O O O O M M M...

went the shotgun, jerking in Vic's arm.

Mabel faltered. The black rage in her eyes melted into confusion. Then she came again, ax swinging.

P O O O O M M M...

the shotgun thundered again, blowing her out the door and into the snow. Vic ran after her, stood over her aiming the shotgun at her head, but Mabel lay dead still in the snow.

"Jesus Christ," Mary-Shane said. Her heart fluttered, and she was seeing in waves of black and white. She felt faint.

"Easy," Vic said, stepping back into the ruin. He took the gun back from Mary-Shane.

"That's him," Mary-Shane said in a voice that was little more than a strangled whisper. She pointed to the picture of the man holding baby Kippy. In the picture, she recognized the hearth of Frank's cabin, miles from here, Frank's shack, long since fallen down and reverted to the forest. "That's the third man who helped kill Charlie Best."

Vic shined the light close. "Gilbert Burtongale," he said. "I thought so all along, but I never could prove it." He turned warily, scenting like a hound. "He was here not too long ago. This stuff is fresh. He must cherish those memories. Did you let him sleep with you?"

"Fuck you," Mary-Shane said.

"Well?" Vic's eyes glittered coldly, and the shotgun hovered in his hands.

"No, you asshole. I hated him. Besides, Frank would have killed both of us if I had." It all came back to her: "We were cold and hungry and along comes this rich kid asshole. We let him stay with us and for a couple of weeks he paid for coal and food. His eyes were on me all the time, and I think Frank was about to cripple him. Then he came across with this idea. Frank and Attila were supposed to pull a big job for him. Something he wanted. So they let him stay some more." Mary-Shane grew angrier by the second. "He used to FONDLE me with his EYES. I couldn't STAND it. He wanted to ball me in the worst way. But then everyone wanted to. You too, Vic. You tried to make a deal with me too after Frank was killed."

Vic lowered the shotgun. There was no denial in his eyes. "That was a long time ago," he said. "You were wild and sweet. Could you blame me?"

Outside, Mabel Stork's bluish face was already frosting over. Her hands were folded together oddly, as if in final prayer.

Vic said: "Mabel was one of my dead ends. Mabel Stork was a nurse, long ago, down the coast near L.A. She left her job right about the time a baby named Stevie Koenig disappeared from the maternity ward. Mabel was a Pediatric ICU nurse, so we never did pin anything on her. But other babies had disappeared in town, including two of her own. She split when things got hot. Her mind was going, I think, and she wound up in the Jungle with her one baby that she kept. Evvie. Come on, I'm going to take you home. And I'm going to look for Gilbert Burtongale." He walked around the body, one foot mounding snow over it like a grave. Then he headed for the car.

Mary-Shane trailed along on the crunchy snow. "You're the Burtongales' pocket cop, aren't' you? You've covered for them and they've covered for Gilbert and meanwhile you got yourself promoted to lieutenant."

"Shut up," he told her.

"How much longer are you going to cover for them?"

"I told you I'm going after Gilbert." He stopped. "Unless, of course, you don't want to testify."

She stood frozen. "Damn you, Vic. You know I'm afraid for Kippy."

"Okay," he said, "well then don't holler at me if you're going to keep covering up for Frank and Attila and Gilbert yourself."

They descended from the mountains, into the warmer, wetter coastal climate. It was drizzling in San Tomas. At her apartment door, Vic said: "You can't run from him."

She sorted her thoughts. "I HAVE noticed a van hanging around the neighborhood..."

"He owns one. I checked."

"And I HAVE been bumping into him, and he HAS been making those sleazy comments... Oh God, Vic, I need protection."

"I could put a lot of heat in here, but it would tip him off. I don't want to scare him away, I want to draw him in."

"You are not going to use me and my son as bait."

"Let's make a deal. You move in with your mother a couple of days. I put detectives in here to wait for him."

"What on earth does he want from me?" she wailed.

Vic stuck out a finger, catching a small white thing like a feather drifting through the air. He examined it briefly (a cinder? a snowflake?) then flicked it away. "Gilbert is insane, and he's stuck on you. Not only that, he's uncanny, Mary-Shane. I kind of figure"(his eyes had a strange glint, something outdoorsy and wild to them)"Gilbert followed us and saw us at his shrine."

Chapter 48.

Mary-Shane packed a few things. She wanted to take a long hot soak in the tub to wash away pathetic Mabel, the shack, most of all her strange sick satisfaction at seeing Mabel meet justice. *Am I becoming like Vic?* There was a phone message from Roger: "Please call." She started a pot of soup while she dialed. She drew the drapes over the curtains and turned on a lamp.

"Hello?" Roger said.

"Hi, it's me," she said unbuttoning her blouse, cradling the portable phone under her chin. The sound of his voice, so strong and calm and sane, made her smile. Mabel kept coming, kept getting shot. Mary-Shane shut it out of her mind.

"Oh Hi Me," Roger said.

She tugged off first one sleeve, then the other. It was cold in the apartment, and her nipples hardened under the flimsy bra. "It's good to hear a friendly voice."

"Amen," Roger said.

She dropped her wet jeans. "I'll tell you about it some time." The tea kettle whistled and the microwave dinged.

"Mary-Shane?"

"Ymf?" She had a mouthful of mushroom bits and crackers.

"I called to ask you to dinner tomorrow night. Think you can come? And bring Kippy?"

The house on Mulberry Street was buttoned up tight. Rain lashed its windows. Wind tore at the trees outside, banging limbs against the walls. *What about the Cold Thing?* She sat on a third floor potty with a crossword puzzle and shivered. The seat was cold and made her bottom goosepimply. Outside, rain splattered endlessly on concrete by the trashcans. When she was a little girl she'd come up here when Daddy was home from his sales trips and the downstairs bathroom was busy. It had been a happy, secure feeling. After Daddy died and things got dark, she'd come up here to be alone, trying to pretend that Daddy was really home again downstairs. Mother had called her a lunatic. She'd started dating and sleeping with guys and met Frank...old, old, old history. Cold. She hoped that now Evvie would be free and have a happy and safe life. And even the *Cold Thing* (it was still there, yes) slumbered; no, it was too busy elsewhere to bother with her.

Alone, after Kippy and Mother had gone to their beds, Mary-Shane wished Roger were with her. She'd liked the way he'd held her and she meant to ask him again. She slipped between the cold sheets and cuddled in a ball, hands between her thighs. She was still tense from the evening's unbelievable horror. Gradually, her own warmth massaged her. She thought about Roger. She reached down and touched her hair sleepily, then noticed wetness. Her finger moved sleepily. She sighed. Well-lubricated, her fingertip moved up and down, slowly, the pressure each way on her clitoris causing a wave of arousal to move through her gut. Another storm front was moving in. She yawned. It was that time of year, and good to be indoors with a fire and a book if you couldn't be in someone's arms. Yawn! Whose arms? Dinner with... Rain spattered against the window in slow rhythms. Warm under the covers, finger becoming leaden with sleepiness, she rose to a small climax (woke herself with a faint cry) then tumbled wetly down the hill into sleep.

Chapter 49.

An owl glided over the night zoo, using a brief respite between rain showers to hunt for a mouse. Lightning flashed dryly, illumining heavy wet tree crowns and slick roads.

Wallace Burtongale locked his office door behind him and walked across the dark, whispering floor under the lesser dome of Admin 1 & 2. He went out into the night, pinching his yellow slicker close. A wing fluttered behind him, and he jumped; just an owl!

He loaded boxes of computer equipment. The cardboard grew soggy as new rain started to fall, but no matter; these computers were needed only for their innards.

The cart crunched over gravel. Its single headlight threw a wavering football of light through flogging rain drops. Besides a glass or two of brandy, another spirit (the Pilot) filled him and he felt the Pilot's sense of purpose.

Wallace smelled the damp loam, enjoying it through his fear. Approaching the Pagoda, he noted that the White Stuff stretched like waterproof thread along the paths, droplets beading on its meerschaum-like surface. It was as though some power company of spirits was laying lines for a new city (or ship), and their logic was incomprehensible to humans. The narrower strands resembled the weavings of a spider. The thicker strands looked like melted candy or foam tossed by the tide in lumpy ropes. He heard the flutter of wing again. The closer he got to the Pagoda, the thicker the strands became. By tomorrow, employees would be reporting it. He considered closing the zoo on some pretext; then laughed silently into the streaming wind because soon he would be free, one way or the other. Nothing would stop the ship.

The hard foam was so thick around the Pagoda that Wallace had to leave the cart fifty feet away. He walked over queasy slopes of dried foam, carrying box after box to the door.

The padlock, rimed white, resisted at first, then yielded as a surge of warmth struck it from the growing power in the Pagoda.

The door swung silently open. Wallace shielded his eyes in the glare. Thumpa, Thumpa, went the earth deep down and echoes rose through the well of machinery. Dozens of computer screens tilted toward him like faces trapped in white cowls of foam.

GOOD...YOU HAVE DONE WELL...

Wallace opened the boxes he had newly brought. As he tossed aside the foamed plastic packing materials, the existing foam began to bubble like acid, absorbing the new stuff. On a wall conduit, an owl watched as, one by one, Wallace took out about thirty black boxes with high-powered computer chip arrays and leaned forward to deliver them into the foam.

From somewhere in the earth or the sea came a faint thumping sound of machinery. The machinery (or was it a pounding heart?) seemed glad to get the new food. The black boxes sinking into the foam contained untold gigabytes of processing capability. The black boxes disappeared in fits and gobbles as the foam made a mouth around each.

NOW, the Pilot said, followed by a pause that might have been an electronic megaburp, *ALL SWITCHES ARE ON AND WE CAN POWER UP. THIS IS A GLORIOUS MOMENT FOR..MY..RACE...*

"I want to be free," Wallace said.

It laughed.

"No!" Wallace said. Having done this last task, he was alone and terror gripped him. He was a little boy and he did not know where his mother was.

Wallace heard a scream, a flutter. The owl keeled over, fell with a plop, stiff before it hit, and the foam gobbled it. Suddenly, the room was filled with owls. Wallace screamed as they flew into his face with vicious beaks and round yellow eyes. He tried to get up, but they were big. They weighed his arms down. He felt pain, disembodied somehow (shock?) as they tore open the arteries in his neck...

White foam bubbled. The machinery in the earth thumped on, stronger and louder every minute. The foam made crunching noises as it sucked in Wallace's earthly remains chunk by chunk as a dog gobbles its food.

Wallace Burtongale walked down a long ramp into the sea. He heard singing, saw bright undefined light all around. He looked down and saw that he was Cold Blue. Faces floated all around. His fathers welcomed him. And all the Aunt Pollys who had kept things together over the past century...

The hidden machinery thumped louder and more insistently, and his heart with it, as he walked down the long corridor to his destiny and the destiny of an entire world. To the ship in the sea.

On Thursday morning, Mary-Shane went to Jules's office. "I want to be put back on obits."

Jules threw up his hands. "Aw Mary-Shane, no way. Perry is still out taking care of Matilda. I don't have anybody else."

"Jules, my son and I are in danger. I may just leave town."

"Let's compromise. I'll honcho the police beat for now. You just do the leg work, especially the Daily Log. You stay away from this zoo story and anything related to it. After all this blows over, we'll take a fresh look at things, huh?"

Roger stopped by in his Porsche and took Mary-Shane to lunch. They bought sandwiches at a seaside deli and ate with the top down on a sandy road overlooking curling breakers. He said: "I don't know what's going on. Wallace hasn't shown his face in two days. Miss Polly calls just about every hour, beside herself."

"There's bad news in this town, Roger. Let's run away."

"Together?" His eyes teased.

"I don't know," she teased back. "I'll have to check my social calendar." (Which was empty, but he wouldn't know).

He bit into his sandwich. "Still coming to dinner today?"

She crunched on a pickle. "Our hot date at the zoo?"

He winked. "I like that little, what did Perry call it, chili pepper about you."

"Jalapeno." She kicked off her shoes.

"I bet behind that vanilla goddess you're just a kitten."

She stood up on the seat, looking out through the sunroof. A beautiful view of the sea. "Right," she admitted. "A lost one." She held her dress against her legs with one hand so he would not be embarrassed by (what was it today?) her pink bubble-gum briefies. She liked this man; he appeared to go for elbow room when pinched. No Howard Poodle, he; nor Pinscher Lara. Inspired, she asked: "Do you like dogs?"

"I have two dogs."

"Poodles?"

"Be real."

"Pinschers?"

"We've got an English sheep dog and a Labrador retr—."

"Whoopee!"(He looked puzzled)"What's for dinner?"

That evening, Mary-Shane and Kippy drove to Chatfield's house. "How quickly it gets dark out now," she said as she pulled into the driveway. "Are you okay, Kippy?" Kippy sat beside her, still in his school uniform, hair neatly combed with tap water. He looked full of anticipation, and Mary-Shane wondered if it was more for Rudy or Elisa. "Do you think they're home, Mom?" he breathed, looking ready to feel hurt.

How odd; she felt a numb excitement, almost fear, as she regarded the dark house. It was shuttered and looked closed in upon itself. Pines and junipers clustered like smudges. Mary-Shane felt like an intruder walking to the door.

Then: Someplace deep inside the house, colors moved. She saw big steel letters spin, recognized the computer-animated logo of the Evening News. A porch light flicked on, like an orange dropped in water. A screen door shook. A dog barked huskily and his echo fell like axe strokes on neighboring shutters.

"You look like a pair of orphans," Roger Chatfield said.

Mary-Shane burst into a smile. "I feel like one!"

Bumping the screen door open with his shoulder, Roger lifted in their bags. Kippy sidled past Roger. Mary-Shane and Roger stole a quick kiss, a dry brush of upper lips.

Rudy, in oversized bathrobe and clumpy cowboy boots, and Elisa (wearing makeup! Mary-Shane gasped) in neatly ironed jeans and shirt, crowded around Kippy.

"Just in time for dinner," Roger said. He wore shorts, sandals, and terrycloth shirt.

The dog was Woofer, an English sheep dog who seemed to navigate by sonar because of the hair over his eyes. He looked like an explosion in a mop factory as he attacked Mary-Shane in turning motions. "Get Woofer outside," Roger ordered, and Elisa came for the dog. Woofer's tongue hung out of the shag as she dragged him away skidding. He made no effort to help, but sat staring at Mary-Shane.

"That's Tweeter in there," Roger said, and Mary-Shane dimly perceived another dog face through several layers of glass doors and windows. "She's a black lab. She's staying outside because she missed her flea dip this morning. Now we'll have to get them both dipped again." Roger flopflopped back to the stove, armed with a spatula.

"Can I help?" she asked. Getting a blank look from him, and looking around, she set the table. Everything seemed to be in the wrong place (heavy plates up high, little plates down low) but she kept a zipped lip. Roger was a good cook. She pushed up close behind him, touching her hand to his side. She inhaled deeply: Oniony burgers, garlicky tomatoes, parsleyed mashed potato leftovers browning, candied carrot logs. He freed one arm and cranked it gently around her neck, pulling her face to his ribs. She pushed away. "Later. The kids..." Inwardly she longed for Later.

He held the pan over the stove en riposte, spatula curled over the back of his head, and said: "Let zem eat boigahs."

At the dinner table, everyone was smiles and jokes. Steamy rolls were passed, butter was daubed on, forks and knives swished. Rudy and Elisa had placed

Kippy between them and were passing everything to him. "Seen that stuff floating around outside?" Rudy asked with a full mouth.

"Looks like snow," Elisa said.

"Looks like plastic foam snow," Kippy said, "fake Christmas stuff."

There was, it turned out, Almost Later before there was Later. Almost Later was in the den watching a Peanuts special. Rudy and Elisa sat on the floor, Kippy between them. They had a thick nest made of folded blankets, and a large comforter to keep them warm. Woofer and Tweeter had food and water and yelped innocently in their sleep behind the house. Mary-Shane and Roger sat at opposite ends of a long hard leather couch. Small flames licked in the fireplace but the den was cavernous and chilly.

"Gggggg," she said shivering, wrapping her arms around herself. He brought her a blanket, which warmed her. The Peanuts special was sweet and silly and warm.

By the end of the Almost Later, Elisa kissed everyone goodnight and drifted off to sleep. Rudy gradually keeled over and Roger carried him off to bed. Mary-Shane used the remote to turn off the TV. Kippy crawled over and put his head in her lap.

"You might as well stay over," Roger said bringing pillows.

"Better go brush your teeth," she told Kippy, too tired to make a pretense of protesting his offer.

Kippy gathered his crutches and rose. Did he know? she wondered. Once or twice early on with Howard Berger, Kippy had gotten this look. "I'll show you where the bathroom is," Roger said starting to rise. But Kippy pushed Roger back onto the couch. Kippy laid his head on Roger's chest and embraced him silently. Roger hugged Kippy, rubbing his hair. So that's why he was so anxious outside, Mary-Shane thought guiltily. The boy needs...

After all three kids were in bed—Kippy in Rudy's room with Rudy, Elisa alone in hers—Mary-Shane and Roger sat on the couch. Now it was Later. "This is v e r y y cozy, Roger." She shivered deliciously as rain prattled on windows.

He rose. "Want to watch a movie?"

"Sure." Oh god, she thought, here come the Swedish three-way flicks. Here come the love aids. Here come the hot wet moist sucking... if he's like that, I'm outta here!

The VCR whirred softly. Alfred Hitchcock's North by Northwest. "Oh God," she said meltingly, "my favorite movie of all time."

He unfolded more blankets. "I hoped you'd like it."

"Too bad we don't have any popcorn."

Something in the kitchen made chortling noises. Then: Ding ding ding. A salty buttery smell spread. He brought a tray and a large bowl. "It's low salt, hope you don't mind"("Roger!") "The cans are root beer."("Oh Roger!")"Hope you don't mind. I cannot imagine a movie without popcorn and root beer"("Oh Roger it's wonderful!"). He put some blanket around her. He wrapped the rest around himself.

"Mmmmm..." she said. She welcomed his strong, hard body next to her. It got warm (finally) and she stopped shivering. Toot toot, beep beep went the Manhattan traffic of 1959. She rested her cheek on his terrycloth shoulder. It got warmer. By the time a confused Cary Grant was standing in the United Nations holding a knife and being framed for the murder of the diplomat at his feet, Mary-Shane and Roger were spooning. She wrapped one arm around him and watched, just eyeballs looking over his neck. It was then ten of ten.

There was a distant thump. She jumped, tightening her grip on him. "What was that?"

"Relax. This house has many thumps, and I know them all. That's the oak branch hitting the north eaves. That means the wind is over thirty miles per hour. I'd better go check all the windows."

"Stay," she said. He did.

Eva Marie Saint was just seducing Cary Grant on the train. The Pullman compartment looked cozy and private. Roger and Mary-Shane twined tongues, exploring. His hand caressed her shoulder, the long firm curve of her waist, the sharp edge of her hip, the fullness of her buttock and thigh. His tongue flicked gently in her mouth, and hers flicked back hungrily. Her hands explored the smoothness of his back, the cordedness of his muscles, the flatness of his belly. It got suffocatingly hot under the blanket and they threw it off. She threw her chin back and moaned. Her hands locked in his hair. He opened her blouse, used his teeth to slide her bra aside, kiss her full breasts. She moaned. Her thick nipples puckered hard. She felt his tongue sliding in the soft valley of her belly button. She reached down with both hands, grabbed his belt, and undid it. The 1959 train chattered toward the mountains. Their breath rushed in and out in tandem. She threw her arms back and wailed softly, listening to the patter of the rain and the slapping of his hard body against her soft body.

The 1959 train chattered into a long dark tunnel. They came together, crying out and reaching for each other with lips and fingers and nipples while his chuffing rhythm broke in climax.

It grew silent in the house. Overhead, rain pong ponged on the roof. They lay together for a long time. She stroked his hair gently while he lay with his cheek on her belly.

"You sound like a fish," she murmured.

"Love your belly," he said kissing it.

She hugged him and pressed a kiss on the rim of his ear.

He crawled up. "I may be in I love with you."

She touched a fingertip to his nose.

Chapter 50.

Breakfast at the Chatfield home was a quiet milling of sleepy bodies around the kitchen serving counter while Roger cooked. Later, Roger and Mary-Shane found a few moments alone in the hallway while the kids waited in the driveway. "I'll take Rudy and Elisa to school with Kippy," she offered.

He kissed her. "Okay. When do I see you again?"

She wrapped her arms around his neck and laid her cheek against his chest. "When you like."

"This evening."

"Yes!" They looked into each other's eyes. "I'll talk with Kippy," Mary-Shane said.

"I'll talk with Rudy and Elisa," he said. "You two could spend a week." His eyes lit up. "That's it! You can't go home yet. You don't want to stay at your mother's. You don't have a friend who could... Say, it's perfect. We'll take advantage..."

"What about the danger?" she asked.

"I'll get us under surveillance. I'll have all the locks changed. And we'll put you in the spare bedroom next to Elisa."

After dropping off the kids and picking up the morning PD pouch, Mary-Shane arrived at the City Room. Jules, looking gray and swamped, accepted the photos and press releases with barely a nod. He was hunched over his terminal, laboring on a story about the disappearance of a zoo employee named Johnny Gep.

"Jules, can we talk for a moment?"

"Sure." He looked up reluctantly.

"I'm not sure how to begin, but here goes. Somebody has been sending me news clippings." She laid the envelope on his desk. "It's gotten too scary. Somebody wants me to be involved, and I don't want to be."

Jules frowned as he pored over the clippings.

"Jules, it wasn't you, was it?"

He looked up. Laughed. "Are you kidding? It's all I can do to keep myself, not to mention you, out of trouble."

"I figure if I pass these things along to you, you'll know what to do with them. I'm just curious about one thing. How come you knew about Wiz getting killed?"

His expression was pained. "She was a white witch. I didn't take it seriously at the time. I was trying to give her a crack at police, same as you. It was Mart Willow's wish. She had me take her to the Bishop, then the zoo."

"She did seem a bit weird," Mary-Shane agreed.

"If anyone owes it to stick his neck out now, it's me."

"You were just being a chauffeur."

"I was her supervisor."

Mary-Shane rubbed Jules's shoulder.

Mary-Shane took Kippy to a deli near St. Andrew's for lunch. "Kippy, did you enjoy yourself yesterday evening?"

"Yes, I sure did."

"You know that we're supposed to stay away from our apartment for a few days because of that horrible Gilbert. Would you rather stay at Grandma's or at Rudy's?"

His eyes grew wide. "Wow, let's stay at Rudy's."

"Okay," she said feeling glad inside. "Dr. Chat— Roger and I are getting to be good friends, and..."

"You guys are lovers, huh?"

She felt her cheeks glow.

Kippy laughed. "Mom, come on, it's just like the movies. You two are like lovesick sheep."

"That's lambs, Kippy." They ate quietly, and she wondered at what age she had known what lovers were. Or did.

On her way back to the paper from a false alarm fire, she stopped on Mulberry Street. Mother seemed different somehow. "Hello Mary-Shane, dear. So nice of you to drop in." Mother and daughter sat in the sunny sewing room and ate salads. Mother had that new bright look, like someone converting to a very strict religion.

"Haven't heard from you in over a week, Mother." Mary-Shane licked mayo from one finger with a smack.

"Oh yes, well I've been busy and I figure you've been occupied." Mother's teaspoon went ding-a-ling-a-ling in her coffee cup. "Have to leave you young people your own way, you know."

Mary-Shane shook her head. This, from her mother? "I just came from a fire." She used fork and toast to heap eggs, ham, cheese, and romaine into a vinegary load.

"Oh how exciting. Have you been promoted?"

Mouth full of salad, she said: "It's up in the air."

Ding-a-ling-a-ling, went the spoon like a train bell, and Mother did not even correct her about talking with her mouth full.

"Mother, are you.. okay?"

"Why of course, dear. Never felt better."

Mary-Shane left feeling bewildered. As she drove away, she gave a last glance. Sure enough, Mother had picked up the garden hose and was smiling and waving. Was there an extra brightness about the house?

She called Vic before leaving the office.

"Nothing yet," Vic told her. "I've had people in your place for two and a half days and our man hasn't shown up. How's life at Mother's?" His tone told her he knew.

"Oh dry up. I sure wish you'd catch this SOB so Kippy and I can move back in." What am I saying? I'd die if there weren't this excuse to spend a week with __. Suddenly she felt abashed that strange men were in her place, perhaps looking in her underwear drawer and who knew what else.

Vic said slyly: "Roger Chatfield contacted me this morning. Very, very confidential. He wants a surveillance unit near his house, but he does NOT, I repeat NOT, want Miss Polly to know."

"Oh? Vic, you have such a way of always making things awful. Yes, I stayed at Roger's house last night."

"Relax, I'm just teasing," Vic said. "I was a bit pissed, is all, that I had two guys by your mother's house last night and you weren't even there."

"So? If he's stalking me, he could think I was there."

"I'm pulling the two guys from your mother's to Roger's. We don't have hundreds of people."

"I never expected you did," she bit back. "Vic, just catch the fucking guy and stop giving me a hard time." She hung up on him. What a pain.

The phone rang. "One more thing, Mary-Shane. Don't get too cocky. I'm looking for at least two missing persons, including Wallace Burtongale and a guard from the zoo. Gilbert's out there and when he's ready he'll come after you." This time, Vic hung up on her.

Roger slipped the door shut after the kids were asleep and took Mary-Shane in his arms. She pressed against him. His hands roved down her back and rested on her buttocks. She stood on tiptoe and kissed him.

He said: "I've waited for this moment all evening. Just to be alone with you. To hold you." He slipped into bed while she looked for a bathroom.

The master bedroom was a long, narrow, low-ceilinged attic, a pleasant room, brightly paneled in maple. Padding nakedly about, she found lots of closet space; a lot of it empty and, from clues like a tipped over white shoe, she deduced it had probably been Susan's; how sad. In a closet, in a chest marked "Susan Burtongale," she found some high school pictures of a sweet, pretty blonde with serious eyes who vaguely looked like a Rudy without the blare and the porcupine quills. Feeling like an intruder, she let a plastic-wrapped yearbook slip away after a brief glance. The trunk was full of things a magician would use to entertain: A top hat, a black wand, a tangle of silk kerchiefs in all colors, a bag of dice, packs of playing cards, a picture of young Susan dressed up in front of an audience just as she lifted her hat and bowed; how poised, Mary-Shane thought; how sad. She closed the trunk, shut the closet door. Lots of mirrors. She turned this way and that, inspecting her figure. Still firm. Jiggly breasts. Roger lay naked on the king-size bed watching her. She peeked into the bathroom. Holy Moses, it was as big as her bedroom at home and done in honey colored marble and blue and white tiles. She tiptoed in to pee. An oversized bathtub, like some king's sarcophagus, stood in the middle. A shower enclosure was in one corner. Two sinks with mirrors on a wall. A door led into another room. There was a double sauna, now cold; probably part steamy room and part dry room when hot. "The whirlpool spa is outside," Roger hollered. "In the garden. Seats twelve."

"Wonderful," she said and her voice echoed among the tiles. She slid into bed and welcomed his warmth. The bed had a three-tier headboard with book racks; stereo controls; wine rack now empty save for three dangling glasses; a caddy for last-minute removal of watches, rings, wallets, earrings. Rain pattered and splattered outside. It peppered the window panes while they made long love. Satisfied and sleepy, they cuddled together. The clock in the darkness shone: Four a.m.

Groan.

The house was dark. And silent. Starlight showered photons that collided exploding with their ghosts in waxy wood floors.

A floor board creaked, and Kippy, who had been half asleep, opened his eyes wide. He was thinking about his Mom and Roger. Kippy wished Roger could make her happy. He knew how stubborn she could be, however, and what he liked about Roger was he did not try to make her be someone other than she was. Howard Berger had made her uncomfortable, and she'd tried to fake it pretty well. In the end, Kippy was glad to be rid of Howard. Roger was different. He was neat. So far. Again the floor board creaked. Kippy half sat up and listened. Someone was breathing in the hallway outside. Kippy reached for the baseball bat on the floor. "Hey!" A forced whisper.

Kippy rolled up his eyes. "What do you want, Rudy?"

"Hey, I'm on the shell with Jeremy." Shell meant computer.

"You're supposed to be in bed."

"We're doing a game. I thought you'd want to get in."

"Rudy, my Mom would kill me if she knew I was back on that."

Rudy drifted into the room, his pale skin and straight upstanding hair transfigured to silver. "They're asleep."

"Have you been watching them?" Kippy sat up, angry.

"No, listening. They were horsing around upstairs but now my Dad's in his bed and she's in the guest bedroom by Elisa."

"Rudy, you're a sneak."

"You're no fun. I thought having a brother would be fun."

Kippy bit his lip. Mom hadn't really said it, but he and she must be kinda careful because it wasn't their house. Roger must like her a lot to have her and Kippy stay here.

"Come down for a minute. Or pack your crap and go home."

"I can't, asshole. Your Dad's keeping us here. You think I want to hang around your crummy house? And with YOU?"

Rudy shuffled to the door. "Chill out."

"I hope your dad's asleep," Kippy growled as he used a crutch tip to slide his slippers close in the dark.

"He's cutting Z's," Rudy said.

"Okay." Kippy used his wooden crutches, that didn't make any clicking sounds, and they went down the stairs one creaky step at a time. Mr. Chatfield turned over in his sleep with a loud groan, and the two boys froze on the stairs. But he resumed snoring, and they tip-tip-tipped down to the first floor hall. Elisa's door was closed, and the boys assumed she must be asleep. You could tell, Rudy had already informed Kippy; if her light was on, she was reading or doing homework or maybe jabbering on the phone with her million girlfriends; if her nightlight cast its stain under the door, then she was asleep. Kippy followed Rudy along the dark corridor. A few times the rubber tip of his crutch squeaked on the floor, and both boys froze and listened.

Nothing. Outside, wind soughed nervously in tree branches. Inside, a floorboard creaked, a snore filtered around, a dog snuffled in his or her sleep. "Here," Rudy whispered. He pushed open a door Kippy had not known existed. There were doors leading to broom closets, preserve closets, storage closets, piled rooms of books and chairs and sheets. But this was an unused room filled with old dust. An electric bulb hanging from the ceiling cast a fuzz ball of 40 watt light. The room smelled of mildew and rat droppings. Three old wooden chairs stood in no discernible order. On an otherwise bare table stood a glowing computer terminal. The terminal was plugged into the room's only electrical socket; it processed data using a single line to a hole in the floor. "Whew," Kippy said, "what is this place?"

Rudy looked proud. "It used to be a storage room, years ago. The door was locked and nailed shut when Lees and I were babies so we wouldn't go in here. I just pulled the nails out and Dad doesn't know a thing."

Kippy felt a twinge of fear at making Mr. Chatfield mad and maybe screwing things up for Mom. "We shouldn't be here, Rudy."

"I live here, I know the rules. You do what I say."

"I don't know." Kippy looked up at the ceiling, where spiders hung. "Where'd you get the computer?"

"Well, I couldn't use the one in my room or Dad would get suspicious. Then Jeremy told me how to fix up this old black and white TV set that was in the attic. It's simple. All the input and output is done through Dad's system, but since his is linked to the research institute at the zoo, the Web connection and processing are done on their system. Doesn't use much power; nobody will ever know!"

"Didn't know you were such a computer nerd," Kippy said.

Rudy looked proud. Just then the steady white light on the screen flickered. Letters in large pica type began to scroll out, and Kippy read: "Captain Colorado calling the Space Cadets!"

"Oh no," Kippy said, "that's how we got into trouble before."

"Yeah, Jeremy told me all about that," Rudy said running his fingers over the keyboard like a maestro. "This is different. It's all cleaned up now. This is the real $89.98 Captain Colorado Game from a store, not the screwy one."

Kippy inched forward for a closer look. Already, enemy fighter ships were massing around Altair. Kippy licked his lips. "Move your battle station around," he said.

"I'm trying to move all five of them," Rudy said busily. He was working two joysticks and a keyboard all at once. The keyboard clicked, like careful footsteps. Rudy's tongue was between his lips with concentration. Two of the enemy fighters were slowly peeling away.

"Careful," Kippy said, "they're going around behind Altair. They'll come out at your back."

"I can only do so much at once," Rudy protested.

Kippy slid a chair next to Rudy's. They manipulated the joysticks and made adjustments on the keyboard. A faint draft stirred through the room, bringing with it white specks no bigger than sugar grains.

Chapter 51.

"It is about time," Gilbert told his father's head.

The head stared back in shock.

Gilbert smiled in the semi-darkness of the Burtongale Building, where cruel gryphons perched on the high spires under inky clouds throwing a pelting rain. He rifled through his Dad's phone list. "You old fool," he muttered, "you almost gave the game away before I could get my dear sweet girl." Rain rattled on the green copper roof of the spire as Gilbert dialed the newspaper. The night operator answered, sounding tired because it was near morning, and her daytime relief would soon be there.

"This is Wallace Burtongale," he said.

"Oh yessir!" the woman said in a suddenly awake voice.

"Please ensure that the following message is put on the desk of Mary-Shane MacLemore in the Obit Section of the City Room. Are you ready?"

"Yes! Yessir!"

"Miss MacLemore," Gilbert dictated, "I regret recent events and wish to help you with a story. Please come to see me this morning in Room XV, East Tower of the Burtongale Building. Just come right up when you are ready. I will be waiting for you." He thanked her and hung up, thinking of how he would touch her. How she would feel to his fingertips. "I will be waiting for you."

Chapter 52.

Monday while it was still dark, a rain storm rolled in from the Pacific, coating San Tomas Peninsula in smoky gray clouds. Traffic was slow as Mary-Shane took Kippy to school. Cars had their lights on. The statues in the schoolyard looked pale, mouths oooed, cheeks hollowed, in outrage at being wet and cold.

At the paper, Mary-Shane borrowed a blower and dried her curls in the ladies' room. Nine a.m., time to make the run several blocks over to the PD. Should she drive her car? Walking was out of the question, because rain was beating down. More clouds moved in and it got darker.

As she put on light makeup, she noticed Jules in his fishbowl office. Jules was looking at a piece of paper, which he stuffed into his pocket with an upset look. A moment later he was on his way out. He wore a hat that shadowed his face. The collar of his raincoat was up. He almost took the door with him.

"Jules!" she called, thinking to get a ride. But he did not hear. She chased him down corridors while putting on her raincoat. She started to worry, and did not call again. She ran down the crowded main stairway ten steps behind him, buttoning the nylon rain helmet (Andre Feuille, very in) that made her look like one of Kippy's space ladies.

Shoulders hunched, Jules shambled along the spattering sidewalk. Mary-Shane phoomphed her umbrella open and followed. It rained so hard she thought the umbrella fabric would tear. Jules looked like a soggy mushroom stub, walking, holy crap, he wasn't getting into his car, he was sloshing through the puddles like a robot. Mary-Shane bounced over the puddles, flew around pedestrians and trashcans, risked death by speeding bumper and angry horn, as she followed him, and gradually his direction became evident.

Looming ahead in the mist was the Burtongale Building, and Jules headed straight for its Gothic maw. Mary-Shane remembered her phone calls, and the ensuing wreckage of her car, and felt a twinge of fear. But if Jules were in trouble, she must help him.

The Burtongale Building was a brick and marble relic of the 1890's. A block large, it resembled a brick standing on end, twelve stories high. On top were pointy spires sheathed in green copper. Shreds of fog drifted from dark window to dark window. Some of the windows were round, like eyes. At each third story was a ring of marble, done no doubt by the same sculptors who'd cobbled together the courtyard at St. Andrew's. Armored angels with swords stood ready to defend Burtongaledom. Gargoyles squatted, cheeks in hands, and projectile vomited fresh rainwater. Cherub babies floated in heaven offering lilies to Greek-looking ladies. These ladies had plump asses, wore nightshirts, and looked like they were high; the Muses, Mary-Shane recognized as she got closer. Each muse stood on a globe wrapped in a ribbon, and you could make out names on the ribbons: Clio/History; Erato/Love; Urania/Astronomy; what went on in those old Greeks' minds? Mary-Shane wondered; or for that matter in the minds of the dotty Burtongales of a century ago. Then: Over the entrance was a bigger figure, a woman with a shroud over her head, and her head sunk into her palms, her invisible but tortured face clamped between banana-sized fingers: Memory, it said simply, as though that spoke for itself. Mary-Shane thought of her ordeals at Dr. Stanislaus's. Rainwater (tears?) waterfalled from Memory's fingertips. The heavy brass door pinched shut behind Jules entered it.

Mary-Shane splashed up the stairs and entered the past century; well sort of, except for the newsstand in the corner selling lotto tickets, OffRoad Thrills Magazine, UCST pennants, and Cruel Death rock posters. The newsstand was the only genuine source of custard-yellow, homey, Mom-like light. The rest of the place was like a gelotype of a Depression rail terminus; a black and white stipple of milling murmuring figures whose cigarette smoke rose into a bluish haze under watery skylights. Jules was nowhere in sight. Mary-Shane went to the receptionist in the middle of the lobby. She recognized the whispers there from her earlier phone conversations; all the whispers converged here, a world's worth, from men and women pouring up and down the stair cases and across the vast floor. The reception podium was womanned by three elderly ladies. "I'm looking for Mr. Loomis," she whispered. Her voice seemed to have turned itself down to Low.

"I can't hear you darling," writhed a lipsticked mouth amid wrinkled putty.

She cleared her throat. "Mr. Loomis."

The woman pointed to the east stairway. Mary-Shane ran and just caught sight of Jules's hunched figure before it disappeared around a turn. Mary-Shane ran after him. Up, up, up. Around, around, around, dizzyingly, dodging bodies. Feet rattled on peanut-brittle marble. As she went up, the bodies became fewer and then it got quiet. She slowed, listening. Heard a squeak of wet shoe leather. The slam of a metal elevator cage. The whine of an engine, shudder of a greasy cable. She ran up; the stairs continued; but the elevator door opened on the stairwell, seemingly without sense, between floors. PRIVATE, a sign read. A brass pointer above the door, black with age, moved across a spectrum from XIII to XIV to XV and stopped at XVI. There were (she worked the Roman numerals in her mind) sixteen floors? Not twelve? The elevator rumbled. The pointer dropped back down to XIII and stopped. A few men and women in raincoats (dry; out for early lunch?) walked down the stairs giving her curious looks. She banged on the elevator door. The lift rumbled open, a worn wooden box with a plain seat and a bare bulb, 25 watt. She pushed open the accordion gate and entered. The door rumbled shut; the accordion gate snapped shut. She regarded the four knobs marked XIII XIV XV XVI and hesitated. Go right up to XVI, as Jules had? She was chicken. Okay, compromise. She pushed XIV. The elevator rumbled up about ten feet and stopped. The door opened.

She stared through the accordion gate and gasped. Across a cigarette-smelling corridor with Art Deco pictures were a row of high, narrow windows. The windows and their wall tilted inward and were slightly curved; she understood why, immediately: She was in one of the spires above the building! An elderly man, so white he might never have seen light of day, trudged by. Mary-Shane froze, terrified that she might be noticed and tossed; worse yet, lose her job at the paper. The albino-like gent wore a baggy dark suit and carried some hoary ledger under one arm. His eyes had a vacant look; did sixty years in the spire of the Burtongale Building do that to you?

Mary-Shane pressed XVI; hell with it; go all the way. The elevator rumbled up ten, twenty feet and stopped. The door rumbled open, and again Mary-Shane gasped. Several men in fatigues stopped what they were doing and stared back at her. She recognized Air Force from the wavy upside-down white on blue chevrons with the star in the middle on each man's arm patch. Several had no arm patch but little shiny lapel bars; those must be officers. It was cold up here in the last teeny story before the spire turned into a pencil point. That was because the windows were wide open and you could see across miles of turbulent charcoal colored clouds, and a rainbow far away, and piled high white mountains of cloud. Gulls screamed as they flew by. The airmen had set up an array of instruments. She saw glowing screens, radar blips, sine waves. She saw telescopes aimed at the earth, the sky, and the sea. She saw that the men stood ankle-deep in I wires and cables of every color.

"Who are you?" one man asked. "Restricted area," another said. A third started for the cage. Mary-Shane pressed XV and the door rumbled shut; the man got his arm out just in time. She heard shouting above as the elevator slid down a story and stopped.

The door rumbled open and again Mary-Shane gasped. Jules lay in a pool of blood, crumpled on an oriental rug in the middle of a still-small, but larger than XVI, room. She tore open the accordion gate and ran to the body. "My God. Jules!" She knelt by his side. There was blood on his head. He looked pale and did not seem to be breathing. Nearby lay a fireplace poker, its pointy end gory. A tuft of Jules's hair was stuck to it. In adrenaline slow motion she touched his carotid pulse while her other hand reached for a phone on a wood and leather desk beside two jars, each of which held a human head in it. "Hello? Hello?" (No pulse).

"This is the main desk," a lady pronounced.

"I'm in the east spire on floor fifteen. There is a man here who is dead or dying. Get help up here."

"That area is off limits," the lady intoned.

"Will you have mercy and just send the police, you cow?"

"Someone will be up shortly to aid you."

No pulse; no... She rolled him over, opened his raincoat, and started CPR. He had eaten onions with breakfast. She was still pumping furiously when ambulance attendants rushed in carrying a first aid box between them. Jules moaned. He opened his eyes, looked at her, and whispered: "Sorry..."

She shrieked. "Jules! I thought you were dead."

"I thought OUCH"(he touched his gash; through pooling blood, among islands clots, the white of his skull showed)"I thought I was dead for sure."

"What are you doing here?"

"Shush, lady," said one of the attendants, "this guy's in and out of shock." Jules's lips were blue indeed, and his eyes glazed. He touched her shoulder urgently, lips trembling. "Mary-Shane... I'm sorry"(why, Jules?)"really really sorry, didn't think...it would go this way. Ask Vic. Forgive..."(Jules!) He slumped backwards.

"Out of the way!" the men said. They wrapped Jules in blankets, placed him on a stretcher, oxygen mask on his waxy face, and carried him out. "He'll be okay," the men assured her as the door closed. There wasn't room for her, so she waited in the small room. Her knees knocked together, and she looked around for a place to sit, maybe some water to drink. Sure enough, there was a kind of ancient wet bar. She filled a heavy, fluted glass with tap water and sipped. Only then did she have the time, the presence of mind, or the courage to look. Two gallon compote jars sat side by side, wide-mouths with rubber seal and clamped glass lid. She regarded the faces with revulsion and pity. The first was that of a white-haired old man. His blue eyes were wide open; flat; lifeless like those of fish on ice at the store. His mouth was slightly open, a bit more on one side or the other, as if he were about to remark about some subject of great surprise. She remembered Vic Lara's lecture about dead people's expressions and was not so sure. The other was a younger head. Its eyes were closed and looked as though he'd gone down with a pair of shiners. The mouth was closed, perhaps in a last sob. She recognized the Viking hair, the beard stubble, the herpes sore on the chin: Christopher Marlowe, Moonboy's pal from the Jungle.

She stared at the enigmatic, silent heads. They were unable to tell her anything, so she backed away for an overview of the place: Someone's office. Opposite the elevator shaft was a cold fireplace. The poker holder lay tipped over on the rug. Light filtered in through four stained-glass portholes; the pictures were of grinning naughty 1890's girls, but the light was the color of beer from narrow, shuttered windows in the inward tilting walls. She snapped open one Venetian blind and looked down upon the street far below, dizzying. A gull streaked past.

Walking to the desk, she found a pile of news clippings. Burtongale, they all seemed to say. So this was where the Mad Clipper had been preparing those packets she was getting. "Hudson's Auto Body, 13051 State Route 495," read a yellow copy of the receipt for her car. And in a shoebox were several license plates. She looked through them. WARNED2. WARNED3. URDEAD. Someone here had bats in the belfry, and it wasn't her. She pulled a packet of state DMV vehicle registration certificates out of the shoebox. She looked through them, and a pang shot through her: Frank MacLemore, each said. Application for Vehicle Registration Approved. Each of them... yes of course, the car had been Frank's at one time.

The elevator door opened, and she whirled, clutching the papers to her belly but they fell on the floor. Vic came out of the elevator. He was just snapping the security snap on his holster. When he saw her he stopped; his long coat fell shut, hiding the gun. His eyes took in the jars on the desk, but focused on her, on the papers at her feet.

"Vic, I think you guys have some explaining to do. Why all this?" She waved a hand over the desk. "Why the GI Joes upstairs? Why Jules here on the carpet? Why Wallace Burtongale and Christopher Marlowe in aspic?"

"Easy, easy," he said raising his hands and coming closer.

"Don't easy me," she said in a low, furious voice. "Just tell me the truth, okay? Why the DMV? Don't mess with my life any longer."

Vic scratched his head. "Let's have coffee."

Secure in a nook at Vogelmann's, with coffee and Danish, Mary-Shane accused: "Jules told me to ask you."

His fingers were smeared with butter and he licked them. "Mary-Shane, you're gonna think I'm nuts but here goes. You know those planes you've been seeing? Guys in vans?"(she nodded)"The government's been in town for the last three months or so investigating strange magnetic forces. The Navy and the Air Force are both especially interested, because they have some ultra-secret low frequency communications equipment. Suddenly they started getting weird signals, interfering with their own. All over the world they got these signals, and they track them down to little old San Tomas here. So they bring in the vans and the planes and the little guys with the thick glasses and curly hair, and before you know it we have ourselves a circus going on. Meanwhile, we've got people dying at the zoo, as you discovered. They were dying from simple heart failure up 'til three months ago, but then it changed; people dropping in comas. And meanwhile Gilbert's friends with the cloven hooves are stepping up their parties around town. I wonder who brought the two heads up for review. I'm still missing a few pieces of the puzzle, but yes, I'd say it's probably all tied together. Your buddy from the zoo is part of it too."

"Roger?" She felt all color drain from her face. She saw Vic's satisfaction, and hated him more than ever. "What does Roger have to do with all this?"

"They all know, Mary-Shane. Chatfield, the Bishop, the Burtongales..."

"Know what?"

He looked at her with eyes like steel marbles. "I'm gonna tell you this, and if you breathe a word to anyone, I'm going to never mind your salsa or peppers or whatever, I'm gonna make tiger snacks out of you. They all know, Mary-Shane, and I guess you have a right to know. There is an alien space ship buried somewhere around here, or in the ocean, and the government is quietly going nuts trying to find it."

She laughed.

He gripped her wrist.

"Ouch, Vic!"

"Sorry." He let go.

She eyed him furiously, rubbing her wrist. "I've had dreams about it. There's a bomb or something. And I hope it blows up in your car! With you in it."

Vic ignored her jibe. "There are signals coming from somewhere in the ground or the sea in our little town, and they are full of chatter. But it's not American chatter and it's not really of this earth. It's data, it's analog, it's real-time, almost like"(he paused, straining his memory and understanding)"almost like tests you run when you're putting together a very complex thing like a space shuttle. Or fixing it."

"The government thinks it's aliens," she intoned in a you-got-me-now voice. Her mind mega-processed, trying to remember any aliens she might have seen lately. The little old man with the ledger? "How about you, Vic? Are you a Martian?"

He brushed her flippancy aside. "Mary-Shane..."

"And who clobbered Jules just now?"

Vic looked contrite. "I talked him into this."

"This had better be good, Vic."

He raised his arms in a W of innocence. "The situation just arose and a quick decision was needed. Jules called me and said he had been handed a strange note that came in to the night operator. Wallace Burtongale asked you to stop by his office this morning. Jules was worried about you. He knew you'd been getting clippings from someone."

"Wallace?"

"Who knows; depends on how long he's been pickled. I traced the clips through the company messenger service. They were coming from up there on Ex-Vee East."

"What is Ex-Vee East, Vic?"

"This room. Wallace Burtongale's private office as corporate chairman of Burtongale Inc."

"Which owns American Canoga Insurance and Kane King Kahn Attorneys, among other things?"

"Oh you are sharp, Mary-Shane. That's why Wallace tried to reach you."

"The old fart in the jar?"

"The very one. Maybe you can get Roger Dodger to explain that to you. Oh by the way, while looking for Wallace, I passed by your favorite building at the zoo."

"Roger's office?"

"Oh sly wit. No, the Pagoda"(she raised her eyebrows)"which is now about drowning in some kind of white shit that the government boys are flipping their lids trying to analyze. Has Rodger Dodger told you any of this?"

"Stop calling him names. No."

"Then he's a secretive fella, and you'd better watch yourself."

"Thanks," she said bitterly.

Vic said: "I suggested that we let you come here"("Vic, you prick!")"sorry, and me of course hot on your pretty little heels"("you son of a bitch!" She banged her fist on the table)"sorry again, and Jules agreed. Then, give him credit, he changed his mind and decided to go there himself."

"Expecting what?" she said, a hot tear in each eye as she snapped her purse shut and turned to get up.

"Well, one person comes to mind"(Gilbert, she thought) "although thanks to Jules's humanism we may never know.."

"You were in on the license plate scam," she said. "And my car getting stripped. You and Wallace. You made a fool of me." Her great story! The story that was going to make a career—suddenly it looked as though she'd be on obits for ever, if she was lucky at that.

He made a W with his arms again. "For your own good. Wallace was a good man in his way. He knew about Gilbert's passion for you. Now we know for sure he also knew about Gilbert's other activities. He didn't want to see his son fried, but he wanted to meet with you; warn you."

"Are you sure?"

Vic shrugged. "It's the best I can come up with."

"You filed for several registrations in Frank's name, using your connections with the DMV, and you were going to give me..." She frowned. "Did you have anything to do with the computer that night?"

He looked baffled. "Huh?"

"The second warning," she said.

He shook his head.

"Vic, I'm really pissed at you." She told him about Kippy nearly being a wolf and snarling at her and she dousing the breaker to snap him back. But there was a doubt now in the back of her mind about the warnings. Vic had faked one, but who had done the second?

Vic looked increasingly alarmed. "Mary-Shane, keep him away from any electronic stuff like computers, okay? Something is acting out there, maybe trying to cover all San Tomas with a grid of wires in this foamy stuff, maybe trying to signal to outer space, or who knows what?"

"So you never did give me a second warning," she said, still angry at him anyway.

"No. I was about to, but I couldn't find the right time. You're always zipping around in your car, trying to solve things the whole government can't seem to piece together." He stirred his coffee, his face aglow with reflectiveness. "Did you know? All the Burtongale men go nuts about age forty or fifty. Gilbert simply started earlier."

Mary-Shane rose. "Good luck with your case." She took a deep breath. "So long, Vic."

He looked apologetic. There was one thing about his look that gave her satisfaction; it was one she'd seen in several men she'd walked away from: a look of undying regret that he would never, ever know what she was like between the sheets.

Chapter 53.

She called the hospital before leaving the office. Jules was going to be released that evening, they said; did she want to be connected through to him? She hung up.

She picked up Kippy ("Mom, are you okay?" "Yes, darling, I'm just very angry at a few people right now." "At me?" "No, darling, I'm very happy with you." "That's a relief. I thought Sister Sincere called you." "About what?" "I broke a window. It was an accident. I was just—" "Kippy, zip your lip and tell me tomorrow. I don't want to hear any more today, okay?")

The rainstorm let up, leaving a pearly sky. The streets were drying as she tore into Roger's driveway. Roger stepped out, wiping his hands with a dishcloth. "Barbecued beef," he started to say.

"Roger, you level with me right now or You-And-I is history."

He paled, his joy shaken.

She told him the day's events, down to Vic's insinuations. "I have been used, and I am tired of it. Roger, if all this"(she waved her arms at the house, at the sky, at the earth)"has been another pathetic effort to use me somehow, to lure aliens out of the earth or spaceships or whatever, I'm going to lock you in a room with Vic Lara for two weeks and not feed either one of you"(she said the next with her fists balled, chin forward, standing on the balls of her feet)"and see how long you last!!!"(she paused for breath) "Furthermore I will pack my son in the car and leave here, never to speak to you again!"

He looped the dishtowel over his neck and hung his fists from its ends. "Mary-Shane, I figured if I told you half of what's been going on you'd think I was nuts and you'd leave me. I love you, and I don't want to lose you. The kids"(she saw three pale cookie-like blobs with raisin eyes hovering in a window)"all love you. For the first time in a long time, Rudy and Elisa have somebody who tucks them in, I mean other than me, a mommy person, and Kippy has someone, a daddy person, he can sit next to and watch TV and ask those endless questions boys ask." He added in a faint voice: "Please." She deliberated silently for a minute. "Please?"

She flew into his arms. "I believe you."

"I guess," Roger said, "I'd better call Miss Polly and tell her about Wallace, if Vic hasn't already."

Jules wobbled out of his office. There was a big bandage around his head. "Mary-Shane, talk to me. I'm sorry."

"Jules," she said, "pissed off is not the word for how I feel."

"Okay," he owned up.

"I made up my mind last night. Life is too short. I'm tired of the way everything works or doesn't work. I'm going to be a reporter for real. I'm just warning you."

He looked into his mental files. "You're right. You have been kept unfairly dangling."

"How about, I've been used."

"Yes," he said meekly.

"You go in your office and stay there," she said. "I will bring you a story."

He looked at her shrewdly. "Looks like you're going to go for broke." He shrugged and turned to leave.

She ignored him as she word-processed: "A series of unexplained deaths in recent weeks at the Burtongale Memorial Zoo has police officials puzzled. Among the prime suspects currently being sought for questioning is 40-year-old Gilbert Burtongale, a drifter of no certain address..."

She backed up and deleted that paragraph, replacing it with: "No suspects have thus far been officially named."

She paused and thought about her life, her career, Kippy's medical coverage. Then she typed on:

"Police and U.S. Government officials have been investigating mysterious waves from San Tomas. An unnamed city official theorizes there is a connection between the murders and the puzzling appearance of a dry snowy-looking substance all over the city. The latest victim may be"(Mary-Shane MacLemore, she was tempted to type, then decided she might be a victim but not the latest)"Dr. Wallace Burtongale VI, curator of the San Tomas Zoo."

She paused for breath, as though she had been shouting. She looked through the white pages of the phone book. Then she dialed the Burtongale residence at Number One Canoga Avenue on a hill overlooking the ocean.

"Hello?" the woman with a British accent answered.

"Hi. This is Mary-Shane MacLemore. I'm the police reporter for the Herald. I'd like to speak with Miss Polly."

The woman said: "I'm sorry, that's just not possible."

"Please."

"I'm afraid that will not be possible." Mary-Shane heard someone on the other end whisper authoritatively.

"Who are you?" Mary-Shane asked, vaguely remembering.

"I'm Miss Strather, the House Manager. What they used to call the Butler. As in The Butler Did It."

"Did you?"

Miss Strather laughed. "No."

"Maybe Gilbert will be in later."

"I sincerely doubt it, Miss MacLemore. He doesn't come around much, I'm afraid."

"I'm doing a megastory here, Miss Strather, and I don't know quite where to begin or stop. But I assure you I will get something with a beginning, middle, and end down on paper giving the who, what, where, when, why, and possibly the how."

"Oh dear..." The next moment, Miss Strather evidently had the phone taken out of her hand. A firm, old-old lady's voice came on: "Who is this?"

"Mary-Shane MacLemore, Herald. Police Reporter."

"What are you calling about?"

"Who is this?"

"Polly Burtongale, young lady, and I'll have you know there's a standing rule, no calls unless they go through Martin Willow."

Mary-Shane swallowed. "He's not here."

"Why don't you wait until he gets back."

"Miss Polly, people are dying in town. Your grandson is after me and may want to kill me. Your son is dead. There is a whole lot going on, and I'd like to bring it all out into the open."

There was a silence. "How do you spell your name?"

Mary-Shane was tempted to either hang up or else spell m-a-r-z-i-p-a-n, but she diligently spelled out her real name.

"Thank you. I have no comment at this time, but somebody will get back to you."

"I'm so grateful."

The click and dial tone hurt Mary-Shane's ear.

Mary-Shane hung the receiver up and put her head in her arms.

"Pardon," Spike said.

"What?" she said into her elbow, voice muffled.

He slipped a clipping before her. It was an item from the classifieds. Thinking of a career change?

"Thanks," she said. "I'll hang on to this." She resumed typing. An hour later, she marched into Jules's office. "Jules, I forgive you because you tried to protect me. You were not using me like the monster Vic Lara. Here is the story. Print it or I resign. Fire me, I don't give a rat's ass."

His face turned white and his eyebrows rose to his hairline. "Okay," he said, "this is your story." He looked as though he were holding a grenade.

"I wrote the truth. You can toss it, edit it, publish it, whatever. By the way, I called Miss Polly."

He winced back as though hit by a steel ball. "Ow, Mary-Shane, you really know how to go all the way. What did she say?"

"No comment. But someone will get back to me."

Jules had his pipe apart on the desk. He put the story among the pieces and regarded it as though it might give him cholera. "I will not place this on the desk of Mr. Willow," he stated, "because Mr. Willow is not here. Thus it goes to the compositor on my say-so. You might as well go find a cardboard box, because I suspect you will be packing. Are you sure you want to go through with this?"

Her legs felt like rubber. "No." She heard a quaver, and was surprised it was in her own voice. "Something has to give, Jules." She knew she could not take much more. Her wagon was coming apart at the axles. "Publish it."

"Okay," he said. She noted some empty cardboard boxes in the hall next to his office.

Chapter 54.

That evening, she sat on the couch in Dr. Stanislaus's office. "How do you feel?" asked the doctor, scrupulously avoiding use of her name.

"Pretty good." She looked up and damned if it didn't seem as though the ceiling was swirly gray again.

"No more mental intrusions?"

"Down to a dull roar."

"How is your love life?"

She told Dr. Stanislaus about Roger Chatfield ("Not a pinscher, not a poodle, maybe a shepherd.")

"Ah. Function is important. A shepherd, you said?"

"Maybe one with a tail at each end and no head."

"Humor! Splendid. We are making progress. These are the creative moments. Would being shepherded make you feel good?"

She felt embarrassed. "Now I know what I like in a man. Where there's smoke there's got to be fire. There definitely has to be fire in my man. That's why I like the Dalmatian type. Lots of spots, a red hat, boots made to run, a partying animal."

"Is a Dalmatian just fun?"

"I've never had one."

"No, but do you imagine it would be a just for fun animal? Or do you see some utility? Could he be coming to the rescue? Could he be supportive? Be both shepherd and Dalmatian?"

She laughed. "I honestly don't know, Doctor. You may be weirder than I am." But she understood his efforts to engage the dark underbelly of her mind with shapes and concepts you could play with in the light. If he was amused, he did not show it. "Next week then, same time?"

"Okay, but... Dr. Stanislaus?"

"Yes?"

"Are you from outer space?"

Pause. "The patient exhibits humor." Dry voice. He tapped his microphone nervously.

"I keep thinking I see faces up there," Mary-Shane said pointing into the gray mist. Dr. Stanislaus stared at her. Slowly, he said: "The patient's keen perceptions mar continuation of the experiment."

"We're on the Enterprise, right, and any minute now Mr. Spock is going to step out and make that face, right?"

"We should switch to Plan B," Dr. Stanislaus said.

Mary-Shane gaped. There was a sound like a switch being thrown. The ceiling changed colors. Now it was clear glass. A plain lemony light bulb shone through.

224

And several faces were looking down at them. They were Zorillian faces, horrid distortions of the human physiology rendered hideous by years of living close to the nuclear furnaces of Fermaria. A door opened in the wall, and two men in business suits stepped out. As they entered the subdued but normal and restful light of the treatment room, their features lost that alien look and assumed more of a U. S. Government look, which was nearly as grotesque, but nowhere near as efficient as the maniacal Zorillians. (Hell, when had she read that novel? She must have been twelve. And maybe it wasn't Zorillians but Floridians. But who cared?).

"I'm sorry to startle you," Dr. Stanislaus said, "but you were too clever for us. Now I see no alternative but to let you in on our little secret. Meet Dr. White and Dr. Black of the Centers for Disease Control."

"I don't believe it," Mary-Shane said as they bent politely to shake her hand.

"They really do work for the U.S. Government," Dr. Stanislaus assured her.

"No, I mean the names."

Dr. Black, a white man, shook her hand. He had a long neck with a big adams apple, and a small crew cut head. He had a face like a boy, with no beard shadow, though the wrinkles put him in his early forties.

Dr. White shook her hand. He was, indeed, a very dark-skinned black man with thick cheeks, stout shoulders, and twinkling brown eyes. His hair was a close-cropped shiny mat. He smelled of expensive musky perfume, as though he wanted to go dancing.

Mary-Shane clapped her hand to her forehead. "You know, of all the places to finally at last lose the last remnants of your cotton picking sanity, why does it have to be in my shrink's office?" But she was secretly glad governmental things were being done.

Dr. Black said: "We're here to investigate."

"I met your Air Force counterparts yesterday," she said.

They exchanged looks. "So we heard."

"Is the world going to blow up?"

Dr. White smiled. "You've been having really, really bad dreams, haven't you?"

"There's no indication—." Dr. Black began, but was interrupted.

"What we should tell you," Dr. Stanislaus said. "You are not the only one. This phenomenon, whatever it is, seems to involve telepathy. The San Tomas Association of Psychologists has recorded at least forty cases of patients with manifestations such as yours in town in the last few weeks."

Mary-Shane said: "I'd better call the exorcist and see how business is on the other side of the Great Debate."

Dr. Black said: "We know of at least ten people who claim they have something like an eel living in their brain. Sometimes it's a fish. Sometimes a kind of underwater dinosaur. Always in the brain and underwater."

Dr. White cut in: "Lately, we've been getting two or three octopi with a sun's face..."

Mary-Shane squealed, covered her mouth. "Me too!"

"...and one parrot," Dr. Black said.

"Did he have a broken wing?" she asked.

"No." Dr. Black looked at her. "We are looking at all the angles. For example, does the perception of underwater translate into some sort of pressure on a certain part of the brain? Does the fact that it's in multiple patients mean it's an epidemic, perhaps a virus that goes to a certain spot and sits there causing edema, etcetera, etcetera."

Dr. Stanislaus said: "So you see, you are not alone."

"Also," Dr. White said, "we need to find out why people all over San Tomas are dropping into this coma. Perfectly healthy people, most of them; it is as though a part of their mind has left their body and gone for a walk someplace."

"You should feel good too," Dr. Black said, "to know that you are advancing the cause of science."

Chapter 55.

Next day at work, Mary-Shane stopped to chat with Jules. He looked glum. And grim. And tired. "Mary-Shane, Mary-Shane, Mary-Shane," he said. He'd apparently given up on the pipe. Its pieces lay on a ceramic tray on the bookshelf. "Good job on the story. I want you to do a follow-up today."

"Thanks. Jules, I can't believe you're going along with me on this." Her story was on Page One under her byline. She'd copped ten copies of the paper, planned to frame one. Her first page one byline. Jules gulped black coffee. "I haven't heard from Mart yet, but it will be quite interesting."

In the afternoon she thought about Evvie. Now there was a poor kid with not a soul in the world. She called the City, got the runaround, called the County, and eventually learned that Evvie Stork had run away. She phoned: "Vic, where could she have gone? To the Jungle? To Moonboy? What if the Satanists get her? Even Moonboy was scared of them."

"All right," Vic said. "I'll do some checking. Still mad?"

"Yes. Call me if you hear anything." She hung up.

She sat with her hands over her eyes, remembering the baby Stevie, and considering joining the police so she could become a detective and work on Satanism cases. She took off early and stopped by to see Father Lawrence. Same drill; she accepted the Eucharist and felt okay. I am not to blame for the hell in the world. "Father, I am worried about Mabel's daughter Evvie. She ran away from detention. She could be in the Jungle and I'm afraid Gilbert and his crowd might get her."

The priest nodded. "The Devil's work is never done." He held a sacred host in his palm and looked lovingly at it. "I understand what old Johnathan Smith was trying to do. I wish I had his courage. I'd like to face Satan holding one of these."

"Father, the girl—?"

"Oh yes. Well, you might call Miss Polly. They have—"

"Miss Polly?" She laughed. "I tried that already."

"You don't know how involved Miss Polly is in causes. Especially children. As you learn more about the Burtongales, you might see how hurt Miss Polly has been in life."

"Do you know her?" Mary-Shane asked.

He smiled faintly. "Seal of the Confessional."

"My God," Mary-Shane said, "then you *know*."

He turned his face away, old, pale, illumined by faith and furrowed with a lifetime of listening to the best and worst of humankind. Mary-Shane was dumbfounded. She knew she would never get the information out of him. She wondered if Vic had already stood just as stymied outside this locked door that hid many of the answers she was looking for. Did the Bishop know? Did the Vatican? Was that why Mulcahy was so impenetrable? "Father," she said, "there is still Evvie. She has nobody to turn to."

He scribbled a phone number down. "That's Miss Polly's charity. It's called Liberi, which means 'children' in Latin. Give them a call. They may still be open."

Mary-Shane glanced at her watch. Roger picked the kids up in the evening. How nice to have someone to share things in life.

She used Father's kitchen phone.

A British voice answered. "This is Martina."

Mary-Shane did a double take. "Miss Strather. Mary-Shane MacLemore."

"Oh yes," Miss Strather said. "I have no comment."

"No, no, I'm calling about something entirely different. A young girl. Evvie Stork."

Martina paused. "I've heard her mother is, er, missing."

"Yes." Mary-Shane resisted the urge to tell her she'd seen Mabel die. "I heard Evvie ran away and I was worried about her."

"I share your concern." After an awkward pause, Martina added: "I happen to know that Child Protective Services have located her and she is now in a foster home."

Mary-Shane said 'hm' to herself. Now how had the Strather woman known this? Had Vic told Miss Polly and Miss Polly told Martina? Strange, how all this machinery meshed together in this town, and after growing up here she was just beginning to really see the net.

"Did you want to stop by?" Martina asked.

"I was hoping."

"You can call me Martina. Yes, stop by for a few minutes."

After a brief drive across town, Mary-Shane entered a new concrete building not far from Kippy's school. The stairwell still had a faint sour odor of lime, and the steel handrail was painted red. Liberi. Moments later, Mary-Shane sat in a book-jumbled office.

A graceful, willowy woman, mid-thirties, entered and offered her hand. She had an English accent. "Miss MacLemore?"

"You can call me Mary-Shane, and I'll call you Martina."

"That's perfect." Martina's face lit up as she went to her desk. Mary-Shane sat in an armchair before the desk. Martina was unexpectedly attractive. A head taller than Mary-Shane, she had silky hair and a narrow clear-skinned face. She had that gap between her upper front teeth, and the tip of her tongue kept bumping against it as she spoke, almost but not quite a lisp. She had bright blue eyes and moved gracefully.

"I thought you were the, um, Butler," Mary-Shane said.

Martina laughed. "I enjoy doing a little volunteer work in a good cause, and Miss Polly approves."

"So you manage estates."

"An interesting profession, at least I think so."

Mary-Shane was full of questions. "Any kids of your own? Hope I'm not being too forward?" There was a purpose to this visit, but she suspected neither she nor Martina knew exactly what it was. Maybe they just wanted on some subliminal level to walk around each other, kick the other's tires. Ah, women, Mary-Shane thought to herself, what is it about us?

Martina smiled opaquely. "This volunteer work fills a few hollow spots in my otherwise busy life."

"About Evvie."

"Yes," Martina said shuffling papers awkwardly. "Well, we did have a contact with Mabel Stork earlier this year. We sheltered Mabel and Evvie at our Canoga West Mission. I looked that up while you were on your way here."

"Does the girl know her mother is dead?"

Martina looked startled.

"I assume you knew." This was a reach, Mary-Shane felt, but that old instinct was just in there digging away.

"Yes I did know," Martina admitted. She looked downright flustered.

Mary-Shane considered. "I'm wondering if she—well, her mother was involved in some really criminal activities, and I wonder if Evvie could somehow produce a clue. I mean she's just a kid, but—."

"Why don't we leave that up to the local police?" Martina said rather sharply.

"Fine. Well, you see, as police reporter it's my job to be one step behind the police. Now if I were a step ahead of the police at some point, then all we'd have to do is about face, and then I'd be behind him again." The thought of Vic and she doing such a dance struck her as hilarious.

"Him," said Martina. "You mean your friend the detective. Mr. Lara." It was a question.

"I guess it must have slipped out that way."

Martina's face took on a strange cast, as if she were going to explode; or as if she knew things she wasn't telling Mary-Shane, which was in any case why Mary-Shane was there fishing. "This Lieutenant Lara. Would you consider him an accurate, reliable source of news?

Mary-Shane pondered about that. "He can be difficult at times."

"Yes, he rather seems the type."

She remembered both evenings in the woods by the zoo, the one where he'd nearly left her, and the other one, the rainy one, when he'd beat the three homeless men. "Scary, too."

"I had that impression myself."

"But his police work seems topnotch. Are you concerned about the quality of information he brings to Miss Polly."

"Among other things, yes."

"You think he did it?"

"I'm sorry?"

"Instead of the butler."

Martina laughed and shook her head. "You are something of a sleuth yourself." She placed her palms on the desk and pushed herself up.

Mary-Shane took the hint and rose also. "Well, it's been a pleasure." They shook hands. "I'm glad Evvie Stork is in good hands." She didn't dare, suddenly, ask to see Evvie. Not yet. That would have to wait a bit.

Martina straightened some papers unnecessarily and looked embarrassed. "I wanted to meet you because I wondered who you were that you could cause such a commotion."

Mary-Shane said: "I'll bet Miss Polly has a picture of me and throws darts at it."

Martina laughed. "Hardly. She does not confide much at all, but I have a feeling she sort of admires you. But be careful. She is a powerful, arbitrary woman, and right now she is grieving."

"About Wallace."

"And Gilbert," Martina said. "Her son and her grandson."

Mary-Shane realized—Gilbert, wherever he was hiding, was as good as in prison, or on death row. And it was the end of the Burtongale lineage. "The poor woman."

Martina's thoughts were elsewhere; she had the oddest little smile. "Maybe we could have lunch sometime, Mary-Shane."

A possible new friend? "I'd like that," Mary-Shane said. A little alarm was stirring, ready to go off though. Now what was that?

At Roger's house, she found Vic's car in the driveway and noticed an unmarked car with government plates at the curb. Two silhouettes sat in the government car. Vic was just coming out. "Oh, Mary-Shane. Good timing. See that car up the street? That's two detectives who are going to be keeping razor eyes on you. I told

Roger all the rules. You let them know every time you leave the house. You keep the place locked up tight. You call those guys"(he handed her a business card with a phone number inked on it)"on their car phone and they'll be in there in no time flat. Got that?"

That evening, Mary-Shane was brushing her teeth in the first floor bathroom when somebody knocked. Elisa? Brush and foam in teeth, Mary-Shane opened the door. Kippy. "Wha-?" she asked and bubbles blew out of her mouth.

"Mom." Low voice.

"Ywhea." She brushed, spat, ran water.

"Are you going to marry him?"

She rinsed her mouth, then the brush. "Kippy, it's too early to tell."

"If you do, can I have my own room? Rudy snores. He farts too, and the whole room smells."

She toweled her face, glad to be enjoying a lilac smell. "Darling, if that day comes, you'll have your own room. I promise."

"Meanwhile," Kippy asked, "are we going back home soon?"

She frowned. "Don't you like it here anymore?"

"I do. But it's just not home, you know?"

She knelt down and shook his pajama lapels. "You getting along all right with Rudy?"

"He's got a great computer, and we're working on stuff."

Memories of shareware flitted into her mind. "No more funny stuff, got it?"

"No Mom." Low voice. "Okay, well, goodnight."

"We'll be back in our place soon, I promise."

"Not before I get to know Rudy's computer, okay?"

During the night, after making love with Roger and after they both fell exhaustedly asleep, she had a nightmare. She was somewhere under, under... what? water? ground? A dark face stared at her; a jackal? with antlers or something? Wiz stood someplace on a far ledge, reaching out to her, mouthing words Mary-Shane could not understand. She would point up, then down, then hold out her hand. There were other faces and bodies, too. A lot of strangers crowded around her. Was this an elevator? Across the void were the ones she longed to talk to: Wiz, Harleigh Hale, Johnathan Smith, Frank MacLemore (he was doing the same thing Wiz was, pointing, waving, holding out something). Then too, there was an airplane. It lay near the ship. No, it was part of the ship. There was a light on inside and when she went near, someone waved to her. Someone she knew. Smiling. No, crying. Pointing. For the ship and the plane were all part of some kind of enormous gadget. A bomb. That was it. A bomb. She had a vision of red fires raging for months, for years, all around the earth.

She woke with a strangled cry and sat up. Rubbed her eyes and listened to the rain. Roger's steady breathing drove the toothache of fear away. Just a dream... She flopped down, pulled the cover up, and went back to sleep.

Chapter 56.

In the morning, all the noise three children and two dogs could make, they made. Mary-Shane felt kind of housy-happy peaceful presiding over breakfast. Kippy and Rudy argued over toothpaste, which Mary-Shane resolved. Elisa was mad at Mary-Shane for using Susan's old hair curler, which Roger resolved; Elisa shortly came with a contrite face and kissed Mary-Shane's cheek. And so it went. "Don't you think you ought to take a day off?" Mary-Shane suggested, rubbing his back while Roger cooked. She would like nothing better than to spend the day in bed with him.

The children watched. They all knew.

"I'd love to," Roger said, "but you have no idea of the work I've got sitting there. Especially now we've got lab results coming in on the dead animals."

Mary-Shane filled the plates of the children cafeteria style as they passed by. "What an organization you've built here," she said. In the back of her mind was the thought that soon the story she'd done yesterday would attract national attention and maybe she'd be on television. Not that she cared, except it might mean someone would take her seriously as a news person.

"'Yeah," he said over his shoulder, "I missed my calling. I should have studied restaurant management." Later, he looked wonderful in his dark suit and raincoat. He carried a briefcase and umbrella. And on the arm panel inside his luxurious Porsche lay a pair of leather gloves. She leaned in and sniffed the leather. "Oh, scrumptious."

He gave her his direct look. "I love to hear you laugh."

"What do you mean?"

He reached out and put his arm around her neck. He pulled her face close and whispered: "I mean you beaming and handing out pancakes, naked under that robe, and your laughter just tinkling in that old kitchen. Nobody has laughed like that in there for a long time."

She kissed his temple. "I'll tinkle in your kitchen as long as you'd like."

He roared off, nearly running over a trash can, and she laughed. He looked sheepish and she waved, doubling over. He peeled away grinning.

When she walked into the newspaper office, she knew immediately something was wrong. Jules's office had a peculiar empty look. Oh Jesus, she thought as she walked with leaden feet to her desk. There it was, a note: "See me. Mart Willow."

232

"Yes?" Her voice was a whisper, her knuckle cold and trembling on his door frame. He turned his red face toward her. "Sit down."

She sat down and waited, counting the pulse beats in her neck.

It took him a moment to finish what he was doing and speak.

She could barely hear him. And the world was aswim. "Coffee?" He pointed to the full service counter in the wall of his office. She shook her head. "Miss MacLemore, overall you've done a good job here, even if you have been late a lot and so on, I think Jules has discussed all that with you." He slid a sheet of paper before her. Her blurry eyes could only make out that it was a letter, but she couldn't read it. "Jules is no longer a member of the staff. He was asked to move to the editorial side directly under me and refused. So he was terminated." He paused to let that sink in. "As a consequence, we are making some other reassignments. You will no longer be working the police beat."

Mary-Shane had seen it coming, the minute she'd seen Jules's empty office. That kick had been headed her way for a long time. "I considered putting you back on the obit desk, but then our Ethiopian friend has that under complete control. So I must inform you, Miss MacLemore, that I am terminating you effective right now."

A cold surge of adrenalin shot through her. She was numb, and it felt as though her life were draining away through her legs.

"You will have two weeks' notice pay, plus two weeks' severance pay, plus whatever benefits the paper owes you. You can see the personnel people on your way out to arrange all that." He rose and extended a pink hand.

She rose on shaky legs, backed away. There were lots of things she wanted to say, but couldn't think of any just then. Floating out of his office like a dead log in water, she heard herself say: "I saw the first kick coming for years, but I completely missed the second one. Good work, Mr. Willow. Hope you become human some day."

She drove to the apartment in a daze. Roger had given her a house key, but she wanted to be alone. Someone had piled bags of blossoms on her doorstep. Oh Jesus now what? Someone else had begun sweeping the mess up and evidently left in disgust. Mother, no doubt. A broom, a dust pan, and a trash bag stood nearby. Pink/white rose petals made a tongue from the mouth of the bag to the cement.

She walked thrashing through the beautiful mess and unlocked the door. Inside, just under the door, she found a slip of paper. Someone had printed in ballpoint: Green Witches Will Help You, Don't Fear. She left the note on the coffee table, overwhelmed, and went into the bedroom. She left her good clothes on the bed, and lay down. Unable to nap or even think clearly, she dressed in jeans, crew socks, running shoes, t-shirt, and sweatshirt with hood. She felt as though someone had ripped a hole in her. She'd shot herself in the foot. She'd done this herself. She'd been warned, and she'd barged right ahead. Worse, she'd gotten

Jules canned. Now she was farther than ever from her goal of being a professional news reporter; and, in San Tomas, she was plain finished. Miss Polly and Mart Willow would see to that.

She sat by the sea in her Mustang, and felt low.

Her hands gripped the steering wheel as though she and Old Bessie were doing ninety, but they were just parked at the beach and going nowhere. Definitely going no place. How am I going to face Mother? Here I was employed and proud of myself (didn't know it even) and now I'm out on the street. How am I going to face Kippy? He depends on me for medical coverage, not to mention little things like food, shelter, etc. How am I going to... she lowered her face onto her knuckles... face Roger? Here at least I was working at something moderately intellectual like writing, even if it was obits, and now I don't even have that. She stepped out of the car, slammed the door shut, and walked toward the sea with her hands in her pockets.

Gulls screamed and she watched them fight over food. They reminded her of Mart Willow, the Mart Willows of the world, tearing each other to pieces over crumbs. A gray giant with horn shell beak was bruising a little white gull and it backed away with eyes hungry and feathers awry. She tossed a pebble at the gray gull and he backed away viciously screaming at her, threatening with his wings. "Right, Mart," she said.

It was cold at the rim of the world; a drab day like inside a glass marble on a rainy day. The sea crashed in, rugs and carpets of it unrolling. A few hardy surfers in black wetsuits braved the elements. Their heads and spread arms rode on the water. She could see now that the earth was truly round. As she stood on the damp sand, she almost had to look up to see the surfers. Fascinated, she stared at them, mounting wave after wave, while the noise of the sea and the gulls garbled into a single drone. The *Cold Thing* stirred. Sluggishly.

COME   HERE... it said in the back of her mind where there were no waves, only a standing pool...

COME   HERE... it repeated drowsily and she walked forward. *YOU   ARE BLESSED—LET   US   LOOK   AT   YOU...*

...And she stopped when she felt the cold water around her ankles. She looked down. Gulls cawed, wheeling, and the sea pounded but her head was clear again. She shrieked and jumped out. Her pants, her shoes, her socks were soaked. The icy seawater shocked the tenderness between her thighs and snapped her out of this suicidal reverie. She screamed mentally at the hidden eel: "I may be down right now but I'm getting right back up again. I'm in love and nothing is going to take that away from me!"

The eel backed away puzzled leaving her mind empty except for the memory of its presence that was like a throbbing wound needing to heal. She bought aspirin and coffee at a Marx and drove to the apartment. Again the waiting blossoms, growing soggier in a changing wind that brought stabbing rain drops.

Chapter 57.

Next day, still shell shocked, Mary-Shane drove the kids to school. They trooped into the marble garden of saints at St. Andrew's. Kids buzzed around each other like ions. She drove home to Roger's house. Home? Roger had been regretful, actually very supportive, a real sheep dog. Could her life really be changing gears like this? Hard to believe. Free of work-a-day, she gingerly tried to make a housewife of herself, maybe a super-Mom. She began to feel a little better, thinking about immersing herself in home life. She could swing by once a month at the apartments and collect the rents for Mother. If this got serious, they'd even have an extra apartment to rent. But whoa there, she thought, take it one day at a time. On impulse, she stopped at a supermarket. Scary business, the Mary in her said; what if he kicks me out? What if he turns out to be a secret pederast or something and I have to leave him? And now out of work? Take a chance, the time is ripe, the Mary-Shane in her said. Who dares wins.

She bought a pile of stuff, including fifty pounds of dry dog food and a case of wet dog food in cans. Pushing the cart around, she planned some meals for this (her?) new family.

Arriving home, she loved the gray sky, the chill air smelling of earth and weeds and water. These things reminded her of someplace faraway and good. Everything required learning. Opening the balky screen door, hassling with a pile of keys to get through the heavy wooden front door, backing the car down the long drive and around the back to the kitchen entrance. Keeping the dogs tied up (they were all mud and paws, barking happily to be played with) while she brought in the groceries. Then she had to learn the stove. And the washer and drier. And the air conditioner/heater. Everything in the house was old but solid. Everything worked well according to the engineering of forty years ago.

"Woofer and Tweeter, your dishes are big as kiddy pools," she told the dogs, remembering Kippy's wading pool when he was three. She stood bravely in the muddy yard while rain slatted down and tried to figure out how a 5'4" woman weighing 115 pounds could tilt a fifty pound bag of dry dog food into a twenty-foot wide dish without slipping a disk or slipping and landing face first in the mud. The latter of which happened. Finally she had the dog food rumbling into the dishes, and the dogs threw themselves happily slobbering over their dishes.

She took off her muddy clothes inside and wrapped Roger's bathrobe around herself. She waded through a week's worth of Chatfield laundry and eventually figured out the washer. A load of clothes in the drier (Roger!) had lain for days and now smelled like limburger cheese. Peeyoo! she held her nose. While the laundry rumbled and tumbled, she went into the kitchen and put everything she'd bought away. In the process, she sponged the shelves clean of thick miasmas of crud. They needed relining with fresh bright shelving paper, she decided.

She was on her hands and knees, with hair disheveled and cheeks streaked, the bathrobe spotted with soapy dirty water, when Roger tromped in at lunch time. "You still in your bathrobe?" he asked, looking at the clock.

She made a growling face and knotted her fists at him.

"You're playing dog," he guessed.

She stormed up and kicked his shin with her bare foot. "Bathrobe my elbow, I've been cleaning and and laundering and and..."

"Easy." He captured her kicking and dirty and carried her into the living room. "I saw all the grocery bags and the mops and soaps and buckets. Do you know there's soapy foam running down the driveway and out the gutter for a block and a half?" He mauled her neck with his lips. He started to pull open the bathrobe to kiss her caramels.

She stopped him. "Roger Chatfield, you take off your muddy shoes and leave them outside. Then you march up to bed and get some rest."

He hugged her. "You sound like a wife."

She held her bathrobe closed. "You need a wife, Roger. Your shelves are full of crud. The laundry is all mildewed and piled to the ceiling..." She pushed, and he went upstairs.

By the time she padded up the stairs, he was sound asleep. She crawled in beside him and fell asleep in his warmth, while the noon heat lingered slowly.

When they awoke a little later, the room was filled with a chromed light sliced by louver slats of shade. "What time is it?" she murmured.

"Two in the afternoon."

She noticed the drizzly light outside. "Oh my God. Gotta pick up the kids."

"You needed your sleep, darling."

"When you call me that I feel like melting."

"Did I say that? You make me melt, Roger."

"Mmmmmmmm...." They made long lazy love, rolling and sighing, nuzzling and kissing, and afterward they lay side by side listening to the rain. "I love you, Mary-Shane."

"I love you, Roger."

"There hasn't been anyone in my life like you, ever."

She murmured: "Susan was a beautiful woman."

"Yes she was. I loved her, and I still love her memory. But I loved her in a different way than you. She was a Burtongale; picture a younger Patricia. Same poise, reserve, clever conversation. You are, well, hotter. Wilder. More romantic. I want to keep you."

"I want to keep you, Roger."

"Mean it?"

"Honest." She kept a palm cupped between his legs, and they nearly fell asleep again.

But he had to go. He was charged with energy. Regretfully, she sat wrapped in a blanket while he donned cords and dark T-shirt around his tanned wiry body. Slipped heavy gold watch over hairy wrist. Arched back while pulling on heavy white socks over even toes. Stepped into running shoes. Buckled zoo belt. Sweater. Windbreaker. "You look like a woodsman," she said. "I could bite you."

"Oh I nearly forgot," he said. He pulled a sandwich baggie from his pants pocket.

"Yuck," she said. Several dead bugs were inside. She shivered. They were huge. "What are those Things?"

"Spiders," he said holding the baggie up to the quicksilver daylight.

"Ack." She saw husks, dried liquid, broken legs like wires, brown fur all jumbled together.

He sat on the edge of the bed. "Think. Andy the bear died the same time Johnathan Smith was ripped apart. Lilly the jaguar died the same night Wiz disappeared, and the ME later determined Wiz had been mauled by something like a big cat."

"You think the jaguar killed her?" Mary-Shane asked.

"There are a lot of loose ends yet, but something has to make sense in all of this."

"Wiz wound up outside the zoo, and the jaguar was dead in its enclosure."

"Precisely," he said. There was an ominous glint in his eyes. "What's the connection? Is it people? Science? or something supernatural? The whole situation is nuts, Mary-Shane. We have a dead gorilla. Most loving beast you could imagine. Suppose now you get the gorilla to kill someone..."

"But whom?" she asked.

"Whom are we missing?" he asked.

"Christopher Marlow. The head in the jar."

"Okay, maybe he got killed the same night Adolph got killed. But let's fast forward. Now it's a couple of nights ago, and our white rhino dies. Suppose again there's a dead human involved."

"Who this time?"

"One of our zoo security guards is missing, disappeared while on his clock rounds the same night the rhino died. The unarmed parking lot guard variety. Steady man, been with the zoo a million years, never any trouble. Missing a few days now."

"Does Vic Lara know all this?"

"Of course. We reported the guard missing."

"Was Lara surprised?"

"I don't know."

"I wonder if Lara is killing people."

"Anything is possible, Mary-Shane. Remember George Washington was killed by the spiders, but not a single spider was found?"

"You mean J.W. Washington." She recalled the whisk of his broom, the snap of his scoop.

"You knew him?" Roger asked in surprise.

"I met him briefly. I had an attack by the pagoda and he came to the rescue."

"The pagoda?" Roger frowned. "Hmmm, interesting. That's covered with White Stuff. Anyway, this morning I was thinking. It's the reverse of the gorilla situation. There we have a dead animal, the gorilla, but no human body. Here we have a dead human, but no dead spiders. Unless..."

She helped: "You went into the whatchamacallit..."

"The insectary," he said, "and I started combing through the cells one by one, table by table."

"Sounds creepy," she said.

"It was, sort of. I could never be an entomologist. I was alone in there and it was sort of dark because of the weather outside. Things kept popping and crackling, and I kept thinking a big tarantula would crawl up my back any second."

"Gawd-rrrr," she said making fists and shivering as the very thought of such a beastie climbed up her own spine instead, making her do a little dance to shake away the imaginary spider.

"I found these"(He waved the baggy, making broken legs dance.)"jammed behind some cardboard dividers as if they'd been trying to get out. Dried up, broken, dead as doornails."

"That would seem to confirm your hypothesis."

He looked at her. "Maybe. If we can find the bodies connected to the deaths of the rhino and the gorilla, we may have a case."

"We, Sherlock?"

"I, me, myself, Watson. You, by distant safe consultation."

"Thanks. I loathe spiders. All animals have their place but if I see a tarantula in the wild I just scream. If I scream, will you come and rescue me?"

"I will always rescue you, even when you don't need it."

"Don't underestimate how much a woman may need it."

"I'll be back to rescue you just as soon as I finish this piece of business at the zoo," he said.

"What's that?"

"There is a huge boulder down along one of the main drags. Not something you'd notice much, but one of the guards commented that there might have been an earthquake because he was sure the thing had shifted position about twenty feet."

"A huge boulder?"

"We're talking about fifty tons, Mary-Shane, at least. I went there and looked at it and I didn't tell anyone, you're the first person I've told, but his time clock was lying there—with the strap going partly under the boulder. And then I noticed a very faint smell; like a graveyard."

"Pooo." She held her nose.

"Yeah. If he's under there, then we've tied another pair of loose ends sort of halfway together. We've got guard and rhino. Then all we need is to find the rest of Christopher Marlowe and see if he's got gorilla marks on his neck or something."

She checked the clock. "I'll pick up the kids. Bye, Roger."

He came up behind and gave her a hug. "Bye darling," he said. "I haven't said that to anyone in years."

She turned and kissed him tenderly. "Take care of yourself, baby. I've never ever called anyone darling in my life. I don't want to lose you, darling, okay? Come back to me, please. Darling, darling, darling." She nipped his nose with her lips.

"I promise," he said and strode out with a jaunty, happy expression.

Chapter 58.

The sunken marble garden of St. Andrew's looked melancholy, drowned in rain as children trooped out and were whisked away leaving only a lonely echoing emptiness. Like my heart always was, she thought as the children clambered in, and realized how much it would hurt if she lost Roger now.

Dinner was over. The kids were in the den, chins in hands, elbows on their thick blanket, watching a Disney movie. Roger rolled in late. He looked wrung out. He took her in his arms and squeezed with an extra dimension of nervous energy. "I was right," he said. "We found the poor guy underneath. Had to bring in an industrial crane to lift the boulder. Johnny Gep, crushed flat—it was unbelievable. Some incredible force lifted that rock and turned it over. Fifty tons. Turned it like a pebble." She sat with him while he ate in the kitchen. "The rest of Wallace's body was found in the tanks under the Pagoda. Workers had hell digging through all that white stuff. He'd been mauled by birds. And there was a dead owl, not that it's proof of anything. Still, Vic Lara may have something about his alien theory."

Jules and Patricia stopped over on Friday evening. Mary-Shane welcomed them at the threshold, feeling a sense of family. The house had the smell of the Chatfields, a mix of dog and kid and laundry-once-a-week. But also of fireplace and dinner table and popcorn in the den. I never had any of that, the little girl inside said wistfully. Kippy, Elisa, and Rudy were playing Monopoly near the fireplace while cartoons spun unwatched.

Roger and Jules were sitting in the kitchen drinking serious booze. Jules looked shriveled and unshaven; she almost felt like giving him a bath, he looked so much like a muddy sheepdog. He seemed to be drinking lately. Woofer and Tweeter were barking and pawing for her attention. An older blonde woman, still tall and attractive though the hair color must be rinse, stood behind Jules. Roger introduced her: "Patricia Burtongale Loomis, Jules's wife." Jules was flushed and unshaven. He raised his glass, pushing aside Patricia's objecting hand. "I drink to the great Mart Willow," Jules said. "The son'f'bitch." Down went the whiskey, and Jules had a coughing spasm.

"You are making a scene," Patricia said primly.

"It's about time," Jules said. He drank a glass of water.

The kids were put to bed. Jules looked like a freight train had hit him, but he dropped sugar cubes in his coffee and stirred and seemed determined to hang in there. "You two belong together," Jules said. Patricia tried to sshh him, but he made a face and she backed off. "Patricia, you Burtongales are always so correct and reserved," he said, "but sometimes, honey, you just have to open your fly and let it all hang out. There, now don't look shocked, I'm just being figurative."

She crossed her arms. "You know damn well I don't agree with much my family says or does and that's why we never get invited to anything. I've been on your side for thirty-five years, so don't go giving me any lectures now, do you hear?"

"Aw, honey, I'm sorry." He hugged her sloppily and she patted his back. "I'm upset because once again the old barra-, I mean lady has stuck it to a couple of mortals and here we are. This poor little kid over here's got a crippled son" (Mary-Shane felt her cheeks flush)"and a mouthy mother and Christ all who knows what else to contend with, and it bothers me. Mary-Shane, I love you, do you hear? No, I don't mean like that for cryin' out loud. I mean like a daughter. My darling and I tried and tried, you know, bless her soul, but we just never had any children. Ain't that the pits? I'd be mighty proud to have a girl like you as a daughter. You're pretty, you've got spunk, you've got that fresh honest approach. Oh what a fool Willow is. What fools the Burtongales are. You'd make a great reporter. I'd'a let Perry take you out there and whup you around and slap you into shape and we could'a sent you to the big time and been proud'a ya. So what do we get instead? Coverups! Hush hush! I tried to blow the lid off, Roger, but I couldn't make it to first base past the old battle ax. Your mother, Patricia, pardon me. Mary-Shane, I just wanted you to know a few things. S'not fair."

Roger cleared his throat. "We're marry-ins, aren't we?"

"Where to begin?" Jules rubbed his hands together, took a deep breath, slapped his hands together. "When you marry into the Burtongale family, the rules of the game quickly become clear. Miss Polly runs the show. Everyone jumps when Miss Polly says jump. They ask how high on the way up. My dear, I'm going to ask you to forgive me for anything I say that may hurt your feelings."

Patricia blinked. She said in a clear (was there however a tremble?) voice: "It's all been said a thousand times between us so go ahead, there won't be any surprises."

"When I married into this family," Jules said, "I was a hot young journalism student just out of Columbia with everything going for me. That was when Kennedy was president and it seemed the sky had no limit. I worked on the New York Times for a year and met Patricia at a fancy dinner. One thing led to another and we came out here. At the time it seemed the best of all worlds—in love with a beautiful woman and her family just happens to own a newspaper! I became city editor ten years later, and by gosh, here I am twenty-some years later, still city editor but for a day or less."

Patricia patted his hand.

"I'm okay, honey. Actually in a way it's a relief. Now I clearly see the biggest mistake of my life, and that was staying in this town. You and I should have packed up years ago and gone who the hell cares where, even a hick town and I could be a hick reporter. Finally I'm free. Polly has nothing left to hold over me. And that's probably why I'm going to blab it all tonight. And yes, my love, there are some things I have NOT told you. The Burtongale line is coming to an end. The Burtongales were a good institution in their time. They were vigorous people. Tough, ruthless. They built this town out of nothing but some pine trees overlooking the ocean. That was over a hundred years ago. Now their blood is tired, and there aren't any strong ones left. Ever since people can remember, there's always been a Miss Polly and a Wallace Burtongale. There have been, to be exact, six Miss Pollys and five Wallaces. Isn't that odd though, a family pattern? A strong mother, a vigorous only son, and several beautiful daughters to rope in the best outside talent available. Sounds almost like some kind of genetic engineering. But the best engineering runs out. Goes flat. Goes bust. Just think for a moment. Patricia and I have no children. Janine and Mart have sons; no Miss Polly there. The late Wallace, who is sixty, and Margery, had only one son Gilbert. And guess what? Gilbert was a high school dropout, a druggie, and alcoholic with a history of arrests and violent behavior. There won't be another Wallace. End of the line. Why do you think Miss Polly is such a tyrant? She stays alive because she knows she is the last Burtongale matriarch. And her son Wallace was the last real Burtongale man—educated, powerful, intelligent, above vices like dope and booze. The two of them are holding the scene together. Do you know why Miss Polly brought in Mart Willow? Because this was the first generation in a hundred years when there wasn't a strong Burtongale man or woman to run the paper! Mart was a washout from a Midwestern rag where he angered everyone, but Miss Polly thought he was stronger than I and so she made him the master of the ship. Again, twenty years ago. I always figured he'd eventually move on up and out, but I've always been a terrible guesser. Mart has one quality. He kisses ass. No, he has two qualities. He would stab his own mother for a nickel. He had Miss Polly buffaloed and she worships the ground that pig walks on. And now to the sixty-four dollar question, Mary-Shane. Why does he hate you so much? The answer is simple." Jules looked a mixture of surprised that she didn't already know.

His eyes told her he seemed to realize that of course she couldn't have guessed, and she waited for the revelation.

"He hates you because you're good at what you do, which he isn't; because you have that inner poise and springiness that he doesn't; because you have integrity, which he can't afford to have; and because you smile too much and must be happy, which he's never been. Get it? He's a miserable sycophant, caught in a position he can't handle, and he defends himself by getting rid of people who might one day be a threat."

Mary-Shane laughed. "Me? One day?"

"Don't knock yourself. I could have been exec editor, and you could one day have become one of the first women city editors in this part of the state. That story you wrote, that got us fired, was first rate."

Rain splattered against the windows. The oak tree bumped its branch against the eaves. The roof rattled and pattered with water.

Patricia slapped her knees. "Well, it's late and I'm getting tired. You've said the truth."

"May I add deferently," Jules said, "the last flickering candle of Burtongale strength, integrity, and nobility shines here beside me." They'd all had just a tad too much to drink, just a tad. Glasses were put in the sink. Coats were gotten. Umbrellas were popped open. Mary-Shane gave Jules a peck on the cheek, and a long hug, as they left.

Chapter 59.

Two days later, a cold, damp winter wind of the sea stirred around San Tomas Peninsula. "They're gone," Rudy whispered in the leaded bay window pane. Kippy heard the purr of the departing Porsche. His Mom and this man were going off on a big Saturday night date and they were very happy. If Mom and Roger got married, then Rudy, Kippy, and Elisa would become brothers and sister. Kippy also knew what it probably meant. His mother would have more babies. In a way it was wonderful, because he'd never wanted to be an only child. Now it was becoming a reality, and scary. Elisa seemed pretty cool, but Rudy was such a brat; would he, Kippy, really want to live with these people forever?

"C'mon," Rudy bawled. "Let's go. We can catch Captain Colorado for a coupla hours."

Elisa glared after her brother. "You're going to have a brain hemorrhage with all those computer games!"

"I'll just go watch for a while," Kippy said, drawn to the computer game without really wanting to be, and not wanting to offend Elisa because he thought she was against the computer games. To his surprise, she followed him.

Rudy tore the nails out of the door, and left it banging wide open. What if they come back early for some reason, Kippy wondered. Mom would be displeased. His school work was getting sloppy and Sister would send nasty notes home, but he just couldn't seem to summon the concentration.

"Wow," Rudy said. "Look." Captain Colorado emerged from a welter of computer graphics and music. He vaguely resembled a younger version of that crabby, weird old Mr. Wallace Burtongale who had been Roger's boss at the zoo. "Hi kids, welcome to another evening of fun, danger, and excitement!" Kippy frowned. This was almost like when he and Jeremy had loaded in the bootleg game Jeremy had purchased from a street kid... Kippy began to sweat. There it was again, the feeling of being sucked in and unable to stop. He could see it too in the rapt eyes and glistening foreheads of Rudy and Elisa.

"This time, kids," Captain Colorado said, "let's go on a different kind of tour, deep, deep into the galaxy..." A portrait of space emerged on the screen. The light bulb above went out with a pop. Stars swirled in unbelievable glory. The three children gasped at the beauty. A galaxy swirled in the video monitor. Captain Colorado said: "Our ship is snagged on a reef, so to speak; snagged on a star, or more properly, on a world...a shoal in space..." The kids gasped again. A giant opal appeared against the black velvet display of the solar system with its single nubbin of starlight. "Our mission, Space Cadets, is to liberate the ship and its cargo from this shoal of space so the journey can continue. So let us go in..."

The surface drew closer. Kippy saw a white cloud ring around a blue Pacific atoll; summer vegetation in the wrinkled and twisty spine of the Andes; and then the east-southeastward looking gorilla skull that was the continent of Africa. *"...as our dear captain and his brave crew did so many eons ago. Let us try, somehow, to find our ship and its people, save our cargo of a million souls, and either settle here, or move on!"* The music flared in martial glory. Then the screen went blank.

"What was he talking about?" Rudy asked.

"I don't know," Kippy said, "are you sure this is a game we ought to be playing?"

"If you ask me," Elisa said, "we're getting into trouble."

The words unrolled in pica: Hey, are you guys in? —Jer.

Elisa sat down and pecked on the keyboard: Hi, Cadet. Yes, we're along for the ride. Are you Captain Colorado?

Answer: Are you kidding? I don't know who's doing this or how. I'm scared but I can't put it down. That you, Elisa?

Kippy frowned jealously.

Yes, this is Elisa. So where does the game take us next?

In answer, the screen flickered a couple of times. Then there was a clear color TV image of... "Fish," Rudy said curiously.

"Oh look at that one," Elisa said bending close as though peering into an aquarium.

Kippy looked closely and saw several bright yellow fish circling. "I've seen those before," he said. But where?

She gave him a questioning look. Her cheek was next to his, and he saw a flurry of shyness or embarrassment in her white eyes, a flush in her tan skin. "Where?" she said with a tremor and a challenge in her voice.

"At the Marine Aquarium in the zoo," Kippy said. "Those are some kind of fish that live off the coast here. But that's not a picture of the Marine Aquarium."

"Oh yeah? How do you know?" she sassed.

"Because there is a tangle of junk behind those fish, and the walls in the Marine Aquarium are bright blue and clean. That water's murky."

Elisa said sharply, wanking Kippy's ear (dumb girls!) so that he pulled quickly away and whispered: "Okay, Captain Colorado, Jeremy, or whoever you are, take it away! Like, make it happen!"

THANK YOU ... something whispered in their minds. *HAVE YOU COME TO RESCUE US?*

"Yes," Elisa said and Kippy wished she would shut up.

WE ARE HAPPY... IT HAS BEEN A LONG LONG TIME...

Rudy brayed: "Yeah, baby! Captain Colorado to the rescue!"

LET US REACH OUT AND PERCEIVE YOU...

Elisa screamed and held her ears. Rudy flew back, banging into Kippy. And Kippy blacked out, feeling as though cold water had been poured over him.

This was to be a special evening out, and Mary-Shane found Roger to be the most wonderful, romantic man she'd ever met. She was sure the kids were okay with Elisa in charge. First, Roger took her to the OmniMart Mall in the northern part of town. There, they strolled among plashing fountains and twittering birds. They looked at china ware, at silver dinner services, at furniture and lamps. The music was jazzy and stylish. Rich old band tunes poured out of furniture-radios like cream into coffee. He took her to Martelevich, which advertised on TV. that they were the store with the score. She peered through the sinuously winding and unwinding threads of light amid pearl and crystal in the display window. "Just think of the money..."

He whispered while nipping her earlobe: "Don't worry. Martina Strather volunteered some funds Miss Polly had set aside; so anything we buy goes on a Burtongale credit card. As a kind of apology, I guess, or who knows."

"So Miss Polly doesn't hate me?"

He shrugged. "I don't think it was ever a matter of hate. The only emotion, if there was any, was to protect her family. With you off the paper, now it's a matter of her grandchildren's happiness. She does care deeply about Rudy and Elisa."

"Doesn't she think I'd be bad for them?"

He shook his head. "I don't think so. Maybe she sees something special in you. I know I do."

In a back room, while Roger went for a stroll, an older lady with half-lenses, and two thin girls in shapeless dresses, fussed over her. The outfit they put together for her included an understated black mid-calf dress, white silk blouse engorged with lace and pearl, a black velvet bow tie, black toreador jacket, and weird looking black hat (a hockey puck, designed to ride raffishly over her forehead, falling out of balance, and therefore emphasizing the graceful penned line of her jaw and chin in counterbalance). Then, some initial measurements for a wedding dress... She twirled in the mirrors, glowing. Her lips sparkled. Her cheeks had a pink flush. Joy and light carouseled in her eyes, and she did remember how Mother had looked on the swing, being pushed by Kippy, but the memory did not alarm her. There was, well, just something magical going on. White Stuff kicked up, minute flakes settling just as quickly; everyone was used to it and ignored it by now.

Roger had gone down-mall and picked out a fresh suit for himself. While it was being tailored, he picked up colas and a tub of popcorn. They sat together and watched shoppers. She was happy to sit quietly beside him. Their bodies pressed together in unobtrusive places, adding always that oneness, that awareness of the precious other. If I should lose you now...

Something was still out there in the barrier reefs of her mind, a spark of the eternal and uncaring, under a mosquito swarm of stars; and what value human life in that grand and icy scale? ...But she pushed all such thoughts aside and slipped her arm through his. He wore a new dark-blue suit, powder blue shirt, and silk tie (stitches green and white, spare, upon a background royal blue); and stiff new walnut-colored wingtips which, he confessed, bit at the sides of his feet. As they stepped out of Martelevich, people turned to look. A makeover lady had been sent in from Farber's up the mall; in a half hour Mary-Shane looked utterly glamorous. She stared at herself in the mirror, turned this way and that, touched her cheeks, hung a glossy lip in disbelief. Roger looked pleased. Colantoni's for dinner: In the dim reddish glow, waiters in linen uniforms moved slowly. The busboys wore all white; the waiters wore white Eisenhower jackets with black trousers and shoes; the captains wore all black; the maitre d' wore black tails. All buttons were brass, polished to a golden hue.

Outside, beyond the plate windows, dusk fell like an ominous music. The sky was a gorgeous swirl of confetti. Night fell, and on the sea channel the distant lights of San Tomas Peninsula glittered. Ships, their masts crusted with lights, swept silently past.

A band kicked in: Jazz piano (soft, rippling); snare drums; thumping bass; doodling clarinet. Mary-Shane floated through it all like a lazy trout pushed by a drowsy summer afternoon stream. They joked and held hands over crab and shrimp salad in lemon dill in a bed of lettuce and parsley on a silver plate. They ate fresh lobster boiled on the spot to crumbly white consistency and dipped in mushroom garlic butter. Speckled potatoes, a noodle and egg twirl with caviar, and fresh fruit cup complemented the lobster. Desert was ice cream, chocomint cookie, and champagne.

Roger excused himself briefly and returned wearing his old but very presentable brown loafers. Giddy with champagne, they made their way upstairs to the dance floor. Lines of light pulsed in the blond hardwood floor. Mary-Shane rested her forehead on Roger's shoulder and they swayed to a slow rock tune. They threw each other around to the merry waves of swing. They marched back and forth and broke up laughing because neither really knew how to tango. There was no music, but her mind happily filled it in: *Rrrrrummm, rrrrrummmm*, they went dancing giddily, first one way, then the other... *Rrrrummmmm, rrrrrummmmm;* in one direction they put their cheeks together and stared into space... *Rrrrrummmm, rrrruummmmmm*, in the other direction; she threw herself on her back in his arms while he stared into her eyes...

Afterwards they went for a long walk down a deserted beach. The lights of San Tomas glittered innocently across the bay.

On the way back she told him: "This has been the happiest evening of my life."

His eyes told her he was scared but happy.

Arriving home, they tripped laughing and then shishing through the doorway. As Mary-Shane kicked off her shoes, she noticed: "Hey, look at all this White Stuff." There were big flakes like goose feathers drifting around the room.

"Ah," he said dismissingly, "I'll vacuum in the morning."

Mary-Shane stole down the hall and checked the boys. Rudy had a piece of White Stuff stuck in his hair. She brushed it aside with the wry observation that if there were White Stuff or Purple Stuff or Any Kind of Stuff near, Rudy would wind up with some in his quills. She kissed his forehead and noticed he seemed hot.

Then she checked on Kippy. He snored as though he'd been chopping wood all day, and lay sprawled. She pushed his legs—two cinnamon sticks, one slightly thicker than the other, one knee full-sized and the other always struggling to keep up in growth—together and pulled the cover over him. Kissing him, she noticed his hair was damp and he was hot. She felt his forehead and frowned. Were these kids brewing something?

Elisa always slept cool. Hardly moved. Her mahogany hair lay as if someone had arranged it. Her big puppy hands lay by her cheeks, fingers lightly curled. Yes, she too snored with open mouth and felt warm. What was going on here?

By the time Mary-Shane got to bed, Roger was snoring loudly.

"Party animal," she said and kissed his left nipple. Then she turned over and went to sleep.

In the morning, the kids seemed okay and Mary-Shane took them to school.

On the way home she stopped to see Jules and Patricia. Jules looked deathly pale, still stretched on the sofa. "He's been under a lot of pressure," Patricia said. "He's been drinking more."

"He drinks a lot, huh?"

After a pause, she said: "I'm afraid we both do. Drink more than we should. But he's been slugging it down."

"Is that one of the reasons you've decided to move?"

"He told you that?" She sounded as though another layer of Burtongale pretense had been painfully torn off of her like a bandage from a sore.

"Yes. And I don't blame you."

"Thank you," Patricia breathed. Mary-Shane felt there was a pathetic quality about her like someone asking permission to be human.

Mary-Shane relished her brief role as wife and mother of three. Kippy got his own room after Roger and Mary-Shane cleaned out a mess of dusty bric-a-brac in a room where Wallace Burtongale II had romped as a toddler in the 1890's.

She was having more dreams than she'd ever had before. Was it Roger's cooking? All this juicy sex they were having? The dreams were not pleasant, but they left no nightmare ketones, no strangled cries that Roger could comment on, but then he was a heavy sleeper. Always, in the dreams, she seemed to be walking along a corridor. Sometimes it was a narrow corridor and there were incredible beasts behind the closed doors. Sometimes she even glimpsed them: ants big as cows; giant mollusks floating in brine with only their antennae and the tips of their shells showing; many-legged horses fluttering by underwater on Pegasus wings; they would notice her, sometimes, but they never made a move toward her. Other times, it was not a corridor but a walkway in a great open space like a scaffold around the fiftieth floor of some huge building. Usually it either looked like the surrounding air was thick with gray fog, or else it looked as though they were underwater, for huge fish swam by.

(*Wiz's face seemed to stare at her through a lot of water*).

Sometimes it seemed there was an airplane lying nearby, at times with all the lights in the cabin lit, at other times dark as a tomb.

Once, it was none of the above, but like floating on your back in the pool at night with all the lights off, and with thousands of fireflies overhead. Only these fireflies did not wink out; they were stars, and that was the cosmic sea, the dim ember of her sleep-mind was sure. She awoke from this one with a slight cry. She lay listening to the soft rain, and Roger's snores, and wondered why she had the lingering feeling that something terrible was about to happen.

Chapter 60.

A tuna boat set out from the north coast on a slightly choppy sea.

The sixty-foot gray boat strained under full power toward the open waters.

The morning sun glinted on its port holes and deck hatches.

Without warning, the sea around the ship began to roil. Puppets of foam reared up. The foam seemed to replicate itself, growing larger, bobbing to the surface. The crew scrambled to their posts, pointing, yelling, wondering if they had run aground or fouled a sub.

Like an iceberg, a giant fist of White Stuff rose out of the sea, closed around the boat, and pulled her down.

Within moments, nothing was left but the empty sea, choppy in places from the desert wind, with odd flecks of white, like melting foamed plastic, floating...

Chapter 61.

In the morning, after dropping the kids off at school, Mary-Shane decided to stop by her apartment and pick up her bathrobe and a few things, pack a proper suitcase and move in with Roger.

Something was not quite right, she saw as she drove down her street. The street was the same, but somehow looked different, as if she'd been away for a long time. Then she realized what it was. She wasn't quite the same person she'd been before this relationship with Roger Chatfield. So she might as well have been away for years. She imagined the apartment would probably seem small and tawdry after she'd started getting used to the big house. But it was still her true home. Mustn't forget that. Mustn't let go too much, not set myself up to get hurt, in case he...

Something else was wrong. What? Water dripped from the green tree crowns. Here and there, old folks doddered along with their canes. There: White stuff along the telephone wires. She stared up at the wires. It looked like snow; no, shaving cream; no, maybe...

Pulling up at the curb of her mother's apartment building, she saw some of the stuff lying on the little grassy patch on the sidewalk. What was this stuff anyway? She touched it hesitantly. Plastic? It was dry and neutral. She picked a piece up and smelled it. Faint plastic smell. Foamed plastic! That was it. Foamed plastic. Maybe some kids had played a joke on someone. She looked up worried. The white stuff ran ominously to the roof beams of the apartments. She got her key out as she pushed through the gate...

...And slowed down. Her door, which was locked, had a rim of white stuff all around, sealing all the cracks and openings. Same with the windows.

She had trouble with the lock. Finally she pushed the door open and gasped. The inside of her precious home had been trashed. Books, papers, notebooks lay open. Tables, chairs, lamps were overturned. A lamp was broken. Trashcans had been emptied on the floor. Cabinets stood open.

White Stuff oozed out of the electrical outlets, out of faucets, even the cable TV outlet, and hardened into foamed plastic. White Stuff ran along the walls and ceilings wherever electrical wiring was buried; she could tell, because it ran perpendicular and crossed over outlets. And then: Under the sink, the modem which she had stashed after Kippy's wolf misadventure: It was totally encased in White Stuff. Afraid to touch it, she looked closely and saw that shiny new wire ran through the White Stuff. Ran... She stumbled along in her running shoes... ran into her bedroom, made a trail like something dug by a gopher, and swirled itself around the telephone there. The TV, the radio, the toaster in the kitchen, all the appliances looked as though someone had gutted them. She tried to work the

252

telephone answering machine, but the wiring inside the buttons had been leached out.

The picture tube hung out of the TV and seemed to be following her like a big eye. White Stuff creaked like foamed plastic as the screen turned and faced her.

She backed away ready to scream.

A face appeared on the screen, black and white like an old movie, and snowy as though it were coming in over rabbit ears. It took her a moment longer to recognize who it was. *"Hello, Mary-Shane,"* Wiz said and her glasses slid down her nose. Her voice came fuzzy through the White Stuff as through a torn speaker.

"No," Mary-Shane said.

"Yes, Mary-Shane. Where is the ship?"

"It can't be you," Mary-Shane said.

"The ship, Mary-Shane. Where?"

"There is no ship."

"There is one last line of defense," Wiz said.

Mary-Shane felt her entire body shivering. "I have your glasses in my car. And I stood in the morgue and looked at your bones. You are dead."

Wiz's face changed. The picture faded. Mary-Shane screamed.

Her first call was to St. Andrew's, but the receptionist said the students were all in class. The news was breaking on the radio as Mary-Shane drove through town, and she was furious that she couldn't be on the city desk. She pitied Jules, fired just before the story of his lifetime. Why had her apartment been trashed? No matter, I am losing my marbles finally, seeing a dead person on a broken TV tube.

Confused faces peered from doors and windows as White Stuff dangled from their trees and telephone poles. Mary-Shane heard distant sirens. She passed a group of people clustered around a spot on a corner sidewalk, possibly where someone had fallen into a coma. The governor was expected to declare an emergency in San Tomas County at any minute. What the White Stuff was, nobody knew. End of the world? A ravaged environment gone mad?

Mary-Shane ran up the stairs to Dr. Stanislaus's clinic and yanked on the door. Locked. She peered in through the glass panes. The dark corridors were choked with White Stuff.

Mary-Shane stopped on Mulberry Street. She left the car running, went in to see Mother. Found Mother in the kitchen stirring coffee. "Hello, Mary-Shane darling."

"Hi Mother." She noted her mother's transfigured look. There were flecks of White Stuff in Mother's cobwebby hair, and Mary-Shane picked them out. "What has happened to you?" She suppressed a sob. "To all of us?"

"I have been having the most wonderful conversation with your father, Mary-Shane. He keeps asking about you."

Mary-Shane shook Mother's shoulders. "He's been dead for almost twenty years! Stop it!" Hot coffee spilled on Mother's arm.

"You mustn't be so excited, Mary-Shane. Always excited. It wears one out." She didn't seem to notice the steaming coffee.

Mary-Shane dabbed furiously. "Sorry, Mother, PLEASE. There is something going the fuck on all over town. Don't fall apart on me, I just can't stand another weight on top of all the rest!"

"Here, here," Mother said and pulled her close. Mother stroked Mary-Shane's hair as Mary-Shane fell to her knees and rested her head against Mother's frail body. Mother's fingers ruffled Mary-Shane's thick curls. "I know you don't understand but I'll tell Daddy hello for—"

"STOP IT!!" Mary-Shane balled her fists against her temples and screamed and popped up like a cork. She ran to the phone and dialed Roger's number at work. While the phone rang, she felt a quake, heard a low rumbling noise, felt the house swaying. She watched as Mother gripped the table with both hands trying to steady it. Crash crash crash went precious crystal bowls and china vases and ceramic figurines hitting the floor and breaking. "Roger," she shouted when he answered, "do you have any idea what's going on?"

The phone line was fuzzy. She heard him shouting: "Hello! We just had an earthquake. I don't know what's going on, and all the animals are shaken up. There's White Stuff all over the place. You can't get near the Pagoda."

"Roger, I'm going to pick the kids up. I'm at my mother's and something is wrong with her."

"Bring her along," he yelled. "Meet you at school."

Mother smiled broadly. A piece of plaster sat on one shoulder, big enough to be noticed by a sane person. She had her head cocked and was nodding, as though someone were speaking with her.

The streets were jammed with ambulances, fire engines, and police cars coming and going. Every telephone company truck, every power company, cable television, water company vehicle was parked along the curb somewhere. Manholes lay open, their heavy steel covers dragged aside while crews in orange jerseys and white hard hats tried to puzzle out and fix the damage. White Stuff gummed everything up.

Sister Sincere stood like a traffic cop on the front sidewalk. The children were lined up by classes. The littlest ones huddled in rows of two, holding hands and looking scared. Teachers formed a skirmish line.

Rudy, Elisa, and Kippy were already breaking from their classes because Roger had managed to get there before Mary-Shane.

Kippy pecked a kiss on her forehead. "Hi Mom."

"Hi, sweetie. Glad to see you. Looks like we're all safe."

"Hi Dad, Hi Mary-Shane," Rudy blared. "The earthquake threw all the books off their shelves."

"Nobody was hurt," Elisa said.

The power was out. Roger's house was dark and cold. He brought in loads of firewood from the yard. The dogs barked and jumped. "Poor guys," Mary-Shane said. "The quake must have spooked them." She picked cottony wisps of White Stuff from their fur. "What IS this stuff?"

Mother's eyes were bright. "It's insulation, dear. They're blowing the ceiling. It's going to be real warm during the winter and nice and cool during the summers, you'll see."

Mary-Shane sat down and put an arm around her mother's shoulder. "Mommy," she said (first time in yea how many decades she'd called Mother that), "Mommy, look at me. They blew the ceiling twenty years ago. Remember? Daddy was home from work to make sure they did everything right."

Mother clutched Mary-Shane with a hand like a cold claw. "We will see your father really soon."

The power was still out when darkness fell. That was when the kids stopped having fun. Things started getting creepy. It was the first touch of desperation.

Fire crackled powerfully in the huge hearth. Mary-Shane cooked some soup on the fire. There was some stale bread to warm up. Nobody was very hungry. Roger had found batteries and the radio now dominated their attentions:

"...new reports of a tidal wave traveling up the coast. Out at sea, the eighty-foot boat "Fishy Tails" with thirteen people on board sent out a brief and choppy distress signal earlier today, then fell silent. Search planes went out from Blue Harbor, but Coast Guard officials say the boat has not been located. Local marina officials say the ship was skippered by a seasoned fisherman. Unofficial sources have told KSTC Radio News that they believe the boat has disappeared at sea in connection with the mysterious White Stuff that has been raining in San Tomas. KSTC's Angela Moorehead has more:

"Chuck, I've been speaking with University of California at San Tomas meteorologist Vernon LeGrier. He says that the flaky or fluffy white material we've been seeing most closely resembles volcanic ash in that it gets into everything, but he says there is really no close comparison. The White Stuff, as everyone is calling it, resembles the stuff of which insects build their cocoons, but seems more likely to be a derivative of common silica, which comprises most forms of soil, sand, and rocks. In fact, most the earth's mantle is composed of silica. It may actually be coming up out of the earth itself like some kind of 'toothpaste.' Several witnesses claim to have seen it extruding from sewer pipes, underground electrical conduits, and the like."

"Thanks, Angela. The Mayor persuaded the Governor this afternoon to declare San Tomas a disaster area and ask for federal assistance. Between the earthquake, which was a moderate 5.5 on the Richter scale, and this White Stuff blowing around, and people still keeling over on the streets, nobody knows what is going on, but everyone is convinced that something big is happening. The Governor today appealed for calm and promised to keep order, prevent looting, and get things back to normal..."

Chapter 62.

Mary-Shane drifted into the kitchen and took a cola (lukewarm, yuk) from the refrigerator. Sipping, she stepped out into the front driveway and looked up at the stars. It was a hot, dry night and there were lots of stars. She saw lots of airplanes and helicopters overhead. She remembered the Air Force in XVI East, and hoped they would solve the mystery soon.

The phone rang, and she stepped into the kitchen to answer.

"Hello, pretty little lady."

Her imaginary hackles rose. "Who is this?"

"Remember me? Ha ha ha. The Moonboy, is who. I want to speak with you very, very serious."

"Go on."

"Is this the clothing lady from the woods by the zoo?"

"Yes. How did you get my number?"

"You got a son named Kippy?"

A chill ran through her. "Yes."

"His name and number was in the baby clothes you gave to Mabel Stork for Evvie. Den de lady who answer say to call here."

"There has been nobody at my apartment."

"A lady wid a funny voice. Wiz, she say."

"Oh God."

"Dass what I say. I need help and I am afraid to go to the hard man, Mr. Victor. He come in here and beat up my soldiers."

"What could I possibly do for you?"

"I been losin' de good troops, Ma'am Old Friend. Like fust it was Christopher Marlowe, gone widdout a trace. And now Mabel Stork done disappeared. We all afraid down in de woods, Ma'am, in dis snow."

"What about the Santeria?"

"What? Oh, dat garbage. That was some passin' through Indios from Belize. They long gone. We too busy staying alive to dabble in dat. Besides, I-and-I a God-fearing JahJah man and the rest is good Christians. But dem people—"

It was hard to understand him, given his accent and the traffic noise and sirens. "What people?"

"The straight people, Ma'am O Buddy Mine. The ones, you know, wid the long black cars and the fancy schools. They been here on this spit of land longer than you and I and Santeria."

"Please, Moonboy, I have things to do."

"I be to the point den. Sometimes they come down here, the straight people soldiers, and they hunt for us like wild beasts. They was here again th' other night."

"Why do they hunt homeless people?"

"For the one they worship. The Bad One."

Baby Stevie flashed through her mind. "What can I do to help you? Yes, I would like to nail those bastards too."

"Then you believe me. Good. I want you to come with your buddy the Hard Man. Come to the Old San Tomas Cemetery behind the Basilica. The straight people, they worship Satan, they be there. I got the skinny from my troops, Old Friend. You come. Bring down Babylon wrath. Bring the hard man wit his guns and flashlights. Make it rain, Lady. Please."

"Give me your number. I'll call you back."

First she lay down on the living room couch and thought about it. The agonizing memory of the dead baby in her arms came back. Yes, she wanted to help. More than anything else (aside from having Kippy safe) she wanted to get her hands on the woman in the car who had brought the baby back and wanted another, live one. She wanted that woman and her worm of a husband ("we don't want any trouble") by the neck with her bare hands.

Mary-Shane leafed through the phone book. Jules? Perry? Whom could she find on such short notice? She thought better of calling Jules, because she was afraid more for him than for herself, about getting him into more trouble than she already had. Perry she dismissed; busy with poor Matilda. She called Vic. He answered on his car phone. "Didn't expect to hear from you so soon."

Cut the crap, she thought. "Vic, you need to know something. I've had a tip that the Satanists are going to meet in the cemetery by the basilica tonight for a black mass."

"Thanks, but I've had the same info. Know what I'm doing? I'm on South 15th Street where all the jewelry stores are and guess what, I'm the only cop available to guard the whole street. They've got broken shop windows and sprung doors, and if any of that stuff gets ripped, I get ripped. They ship me a new asshole from Marx. So I'm sorry, but I'm not interested right now."

"They might kill another baby. We've got to stop them."

He yelled: "No! We are stretched thin. I got two guys sitting on your doorstep and I want you to stay in that house with the doors locked."

"Can your two cops go with me?"

"No. You even suggest that and I'll pull them off there."

He hung up. She called Perry at home, got a tired voice. "Huh?"

"Perry! It's me."

"Mary-Shane. Hey, I'm glad to hear your voice."

"How's it going?"

"Oh, still the same. Matilda is still in a coma. They're turning her twice a day and I wash her down to prevent bedsores. Keeps me pretty busy. Gotta exercise her arms, legs, and hands so they won't curl up."

"Perry, have you got access to Herald equipment?"

"Yeah, sure. But—"

"I know, I was fired and it's all under lock and key. Listen, I need you and I need an infrared camera. Can you come up with something?"

"I dunno, Mary-Shane. Awful short notice." He yawned. "There is an infrared service available to the photo lab for different night shoots. It would mean renting, though. It would show up on the Burtongales' tab."

She told him the reason for her request, and he sounded astonished. "So," she said, "you could say it was for a good cause based on an anonymous tip. If we can't shoot 'em with guns, we'll shoot 'em on film. Proof, you know; if it isn't violating their civil rights."

"Where and when do I meet you?"

"Thanks, Perry!" She told him the arrangement and hung up. Next she called Moonboy. "Vic can't come, but I'm bringing a friend from the newspaper."

"Hallelujah, Ma'am. By the church then. Look to the door."

She called Father Lawrence. "Mary-Shane, how nice..."

"Father, I've had a tip there's going to be a black mass in the cemetery behind the basilica tonight. I've called the cops and they're too busy to mess with religious stuff tonight. I don't know if you guys can get worked up about it, seeing as how there's all this other weird stuff going on."

"Mary-Shane, dear, I'll try to get hold of the Bishop. We've all been busy at the hospitals. Whatever you do, I beg you, stay home and lock your doors. We have been trying to nail those people for a hundred years—"

"A hundred years!"

"—Yes, it's a secret but I'm telling you so you stay out of there. They are the worst murderers."

"Who are they, Father? Seal of the Confessional?"

He laughed dryly. "They don't do Confession. Some are prominent people from San Tomas and others are from all over. They network, they are underground, they are very clever. Don't go near them."

"Thanks." She let the receiver drop. No sense getting the old guy any more upset than he already seemed. She tried one more person. "Hello? This is Mary-Shane MacLemore."

"Oh yes," Martina Strather said. "How are you? I'm surprised the phones are working. Are the lights out where you are?"

"Yes, yes. Martina, I just wanted to let you know. There's going to be a black mass at the cemetery by the basilica. Remember, I told you I'm worried about the children in the Jungle?"

"You want me to go?"

"If you want."

"Give me an hour to make a few calls. I'll call you."

Mary-Shane found Roger sawing wood in the back yard. She hugged him. "I have to ask you a favor." He turned the saw off; its grinding wound down. He wiped sweat and sawdust from his forehead. She told him of her plan. "Honey, you're crazy. You could get killed."

"Perry is big. Moonboy knows how to handle himself."

"Mary-Shane, Mary-Shane," Roger said sitting down hard.

"Roger, You need to stay here with the kids." She saw that she would get nowhere with him. "Roger, I love you very much. I promised I would always be honest with you; otherwise I would have just gone out the back window or something. I may be able to catch the woman I told you about. The Baby? Stevie?"

"I want you alive and well."

She took his hands. "You have taken risks; remember your stories about the desert?"

"Yes, but I was single and had no children."

"I'm going to go do this."

"You want to be famous?" he asked bitterly. "A big story?"

"No," she whispered, "I just want to be with you and have you be proud of me."

He hugged her. His eyes looked wet and she realized he had lost his wife and did not want to lose Mary-Shane.

She squeezed. "I'm a big girl, Roger. I'll be back."

Chapter 63.

Martina never did call back.

Mary-Shane got into her Mustang and pulled up alongside the detective car. The two men inside looked alarmed. "I'm going to the store for a few minutes," she said.

One flicked a cigarette butt away. "Lady, we're here to watch you and your kid. You're supposed to stay—"

"I know, and I'm truly sorry, but I don't have time to explain. You guys forget about me, okay? Keep an eye on that house because the son of a bitch may come after my son." She left them sitting open-mouthed and peeled off in a stench of tire rubber.

The Basilica of St. Mary Consoler floated, shaped like a bread loaf, above the black tree crowns. In the parking lot Perry shut the engine off, opened the window slightly and listened. No choir tonight, Mary-Shane thought. Stained glass windows looked iron in the moonlight.

"Where's Moonboy?" Mary-Shane whispered, more to the wind than to Perry.

"Doesn't anybody guard this place at night?" he asked.

"I dunno. Look, the church door is open."

Perry grasped Mary-Shane's elbow, and she was glad. No choir. The only music was the low drag of desert-born wind around the gargoyles and through the sweeping eucalyptus trees. The moon looked down in shock and surprise.

"I'm gonna pee my pants," Perry said.

"Come on, let's get that scoop." She towed him along. "What's that?" Something lay on the threshold, deliberately placed there, she was sure: a toy telescope, a child's plaything. As she bent over and reached for the telescope, a bit of White Stuff somersaulted slowly by, brushed by moonlight.

The door swung open the rest of the way with a faint creak.

"Come on," Mary-Shane said. She took a step into the darkness. She was not going to be afraid. There was too much at stake here—her career, her future and therefore Kippy's; and the lives of people who must be saved from these dark minions.

"Okay," Perry said holding her back. "This is the point of no return. You're still game?"

"I'm game."

Perry shrugged and went in first.

She clung close to him, holding handfuls of his jacket. The absence of Moonboy touched strings of fear inside her; but maybe he was just hiding in the church—that seemed logical.

The interior of the basilica was quiet as a sunken ship. For a moment, with the small side door open, wind strayed across the pews. Perry pulled the door shut. Mary-Shane was afraid to clear her throat. The organ pipes gleamed high up at one end, the tabernacle door at the other. The only light on inside was a small red sanctuary lamp, little more than a pinprick. The air smelled of incense, burnt beeswax, and floor polish. Something went creak and Mary-Shane jumped against Perry's back. Just something wooden, settling in the night, she thought. A rational explanation for everything.

"Up there," Perry said softly, pointing to the clocktower. His voice rippled away like a pebble dropped in water.

Mary-Shane and Perry tiptoed toward the back of the basilica. Thump, something went right by Mary-Shane.

"Oh good God," Mary-Shane wailed.

"Only a cat," Perry said said. A gray mouser perched on a collection box. His eyes were like smoldering pennies. His gaze followed them.

Perry gripped Mary-Shane's hand tightly, and she was glad. She could deal with something she could see, could grab in her hands, could upside with a shovel; but the unseen, lurking unnerved her. Except the *Cold Thing*. For that she was waiting with open fingernails.

A doll face smiled sweetly in the shadows. Fingers curled around Mary-Shane's arm. The fingers were Perry's and the face was that of the Virgin, holding Jesus in one arm, the other hand raised blessing. Perry had nail heads of sweat on his forehead.

They went up a narrow winding stair case that seemed to thunder woodenly, even though they tiptoed. Any minute, Mary-Shane thought, a hundred policemen will come and arrest us. And maybe it would be a relief.

Up, up into a growing draft of fresh air. Was it the sea or the wind she heard? A wash of full moonlight grew brighter with each step. They were in the bell tower, 60ish feet above ground. Two large bells, one the size of a chair, the other the size of a table, hung in the room. A carillon rack with smaller bells was embedded in the east wall. The room was otherwise unadorned. Plaster had fallen off and lay untouched. Circuit breakers and other unknowables of plumbing, heating, and electricity were sunk into the plain wood beams.

They walked across the wooden floor to the north wall and peered out of the window.

"Jesus," Mary-Shane said.

"I can't believe it," Perry said.

Mary-Shane remembered the cheap telescope, a child's toy bought at a supermarket, that she'd been clutching. It had spaceships and Saturn's on its sides.

Magnification was 10X. She looked through it and saw figures moving in the graveyard.

"I believe," Perry whispered, "it's what they call in the trade a Black Mass."

Mary-Shane stared hard. She made out figures moving in a circle, holding hands. They looked like...soldiers?

"Survivalists," Perry said. "They believe the end of the world is at hand." He imitated Moonboy: "Armageddon for Babylon, and maybe they right, who knows? Jah and Satan their final fight. And these boys not Jah's."

Mary-Shane saw dark clothing with flower wreaths, and now that Perry had mentioned it, she caught the glimmer of rifles and highly polished combat boots. Banks of flickering candles draped the tombstones like a moss of light. She made out reddish light flickering in black shells or pots. Something... a dog or cat ...lay inertly ...now a figure moved in from the circle. A flashing... what? ...a knife. A brief, strangled cry rose up out of the willow trees. Mary-Shane handed the scope to Perry. "They just butchered a dog or cat." She picked up the camera and began shooting, hoping the people below would not see her. The camera picked up infrared emanations, which were invisible to the human eye. No flash was required. Perry took over and filmed nervously. Even the whirring of the camera was scary; she wondered if the right gust of wind could carry it the two hundred feet to Satanist ears. She tried to make out individual faces, but in the dim light could not recognize anyone. The infrared camera would capture details the police could decipher later. She watched in horrid fascination as the ceremony wound through its paces, much of it broadly decipherable as a mockery of the Mass. The acoustics of the sunken cemetery were such that sound clung within its walls as though afraid to sail up into the free air. As Mary-Shane's eyes became used to the gloom, she was able to make out scattered bits of detail. "Perry," she whispered, "they are about..."(she counted)"twenty, some armed." The Satanists were standing in a circle before a tall figure wearing a dark cloak. The tall figure had his arms outspread. He wore some sort of... Her head reeled. She had seen this in a dream somewhere... Some sort of a dark furry mask... A jackal head? Did its eyes glow red, or was that her imagination? Her mouth was dry, and she shook like a leaf... The men were bent over, raising something... A wooden something... A large cross, bottom up... A smell of smoke reached her... Pitch... Were they going to burn a cross?

Mary-Shane stared through the toy scope, then lowered it. "Perry," she started to say, through chattering teeth, "I'm losing my cool. Maybe we'd better..."

"Mary-Shane, we've got to call the police. This is out of our league."

"Okay," she whispered, too scared to disagree.

They tiptoed back down the steps. Oh God, Mary-Shane thought, they'll hear us rumbling on the steps. They'll come and slice us up.

Once again they were in the silent basilica. The sanctuary lamp burned like a red eye. The air was thick and stale. A cloud had shifted and the moon bore down like an operating room light. The stained glass flowed with life. Saints looked down with alarmed eyes. Fingers were raised in blessing, or warning. Leaded lips seemed to be parting, ready to speak. They all had faces shaped like lemons, like the moon, almost like aliens. Was it possible? St. Peter offered a key and seemed to be mumbling...

Mary-Shane froze, afraid to step outside. "What if they see us? Won't they have lookouts?"

"We'd be dead by now if they had. But let's not tarry."

Mary-Shane peered outside and took a shuddering breath of fresh air. Suddenly, it was a huge task just to get back to their car.

From the cemetery below, stray crosswinds brought a snatch of voice, a murmur of song, or was it the wind in the leaves?

"My God," Mary-Shane whispered, "are they getting closer?"

Perry frowned. "What's that?" He pointed to a dully glowing object in the corner, on top of the organ. They walked over on the whispering floor and let their eyes adjust to the deeper darkness.

Mary-Shane felt the final residue of her self-control slipping away. She had a glimpse of the object and started to wail. It was a jar, and in it, a dark shadow among dark shadows, was the head of Moonboy. She recognized his eye, which stared at her, wide open.

"Huh?" Perry said, and bent over to stare at the jar more closely.

At that moment, an ax descended on Perry's head with a sickening crack of bone. Blood spattered all over her.

Mary-Shane tried to reach out to help him, but dark figures popped out of the shadows all around and she fell backwards with a strangled cry. She lay stunned on the hard floor while they set upon her, hard men with cork-blackened faces, commando caps, and pointing guns. She caught a last glimpse of Perry's stark, dead face, eyes wide open. Blood ran from his mouth, and more blood was spattered over his forehead which lay on the keyboard pressing down. Making organ music: A deep, shuddering chord drifting between minors and augmenteds... dimly, Mary-Shane heard the thunder in the organ pipes and remembered the night Vic Lara had almost left her in the bottom of the Jungle...

No time to let her mind wander now...

...This, she figured, was the hour of her death, and she was too dazed from shock and being roughly handled to reflect much. So this was how it went, she thought, this fast, when you died. The men held hands over her mouth, grasped her arms, pinned her, all in one efficient body of motion. She struggled, kicked, and a fist landed in her gut, knocking the wind out of her. Dazed, she felt herself being lifted. Carried down into the cemetery like a piece of driftwood.

The smell of pitch, the stink of smoke, were markedly noticeable now. She felt her hair dragging on the ground. Her frame of vision passed something burning: a dog's head on fire, like a Hallow E'en pumpkin with a candle inside, burning in the hollow of its tongueless mouth. Its eye sockets were hollow and glowing.

The jackal face grinned down at her. *AT LAST,* it said into her mind without seeming to actually speak words, *WE ARE TOGETHER, BLESSED ONE...*

"No!" she screamed through the rough fingers mauling her face.

WE WILL BE UNITED FOREVER.

She started to scream, but a hard oily rag was tied around her head, painfully tearing into the corners of her mouth and pushing her tongue back in her mouth so she gagged. Roughly she was tied to the cross, head up. Oh God, she thought, they are going to burn me alive.

The jackal-mask (Gilbert? she wondered) stepped close and embraced her. His breath was foul upon her. His eyes had a deep red glow—was it a reflection of fire, or a fire within? *COME INTO THE SHIP...*

Why are you doing this? she wondered. She heard other voices: "Hey man, enough is enough." "Just burn the bitch and let's get outta here." "You're crazy, man." "Gilbert, what are you going?" "You can't be serious?"

I AM DEAD SERIOUS.

"Hey look," someone said, "company."

"It's Them," said another.

On the horizon, a pair of headlights crept in and winked out. She stared with longing at some hope, any hope, of salvation. A long black car had pulled up and three men got out. They wore black hats, black suits, black scarves against the raveling wind.

"Cops?" someone asked. Mary-Shane detected fear and uncertainty among Gilbert's followers.

LET THEM COME CLOSER, the jackal-head thought to her, sneering.

One man threw down his gun. "I'm outta here." His footsteps crashed away. Another followed. Gilbert's remaining followers closed ranks. She spotted a few conservatively dressed civilians among them; churchgoers, one would have thought; wormy men wearing gloves and hats; owlish women in tight coats, blue-rinse permanents, glittering pearly glasses; a tall bald man in gray suit, who might have passed the collection basket on Sundays; several hard-faced women in long drab coats, furry hats, and thick glasses ("why make such a big deal out of it?") and several mousy looking men with sloping shoulders and servile heads ("we don't want any trouble") and these worst of humans were all shuffling quickly away now. To their dark glossy cars, to their country estates maybe...

The Gilbert jackal's red eyes glowed crazily as it watched the three men approach. *I WANT TO KNOW WHO THREATENS THE SHIP...*

As the three men approached, Mary-Shane made out their Roman collars now, a tiny wink of white against the otherwise black clothing. She recognized poor old Father Lawrence from St. Cosmas. The other two must have been borrowed from another parish. They looked like three windblown shadows in the dim light. They reminded her of gunslingers by their steady pace and three-abreast marching order, each holding up a communion wafer with one hand and cupping the free hand underneath the other. These three guys—she couldn't decide if they were gloriously brave or ludicrously nuts—were crossing this bleak wilderness to confront the blackest evil in the universe. A crazy image popped into her mind. Spaghetti westerns. Or was it seven samurai? On they walked, gunslingers of the spirit world. The wind blew their coats up. Their stoles fluttered in the wind. Father Lawrence stumbled once, slightly, but got right back in step. The wafers shone like pebbles in a straight line.

"Let those stupid motherfuckers come in here," Gilbert said in a voice that sounded as if strained through cloth, "we'll give them a show."

As the priests walked across the stark playing field between Jungle and basilica, White Stuff blew between their feet.

THIS WILL BE ENTERTAINING said the Gilbert jackal, caressing her breasts.

The ground shook. Earthquake, Mary-Shane thought dully as her body was rattled, tied to the hard wooden cross. Several more of Gilbert's followers deserted, dropping their weapons and running with thudding combat boots.

Father Lawrence was down. The other two priests kept walking, like two toys in The Nutcracker Suite, holding the hosts instead of wooden guns. Tombstones in the cemetery rocked. The ground rolled in waves and White Stuff blew up. All three priests were down now. Father Lawrence had gotten on his knees but had fallen feebly. Father No.2 was on his knees probing in the grass with his fingertips—for the fallen host, Mary-Shane thought.

The Gilbert Thing's eyes glared. She felt its hot breath on her, reeking of garbage: *WATCH ME...* It snatched up a burning pitch pot and ran toward the priests.

Father Lawrence lay limply. Several yards ahead, the other two priests were on their hands and knees, drunkenly wobbling as the ground shook yet once more. The new temblor rattled Mary-Shane's body against the wooden cross, jarring her further. She tasted her own blood.

Then: She heard a faint keening, like a cat meowing.

Chapter 64.

The Gilbert Thing danced around the fallen priests, kicking them, stomping their precious cargo into the ground, laughing ferociously. She heard their screams as the monstrum poured boiling pitch on them. It was alone now. Its human companions had fled.

A long black car sailed into view.

Going about 90, Mary-Shane thought.

A red light twirled on its roof.

Its front grill flashed blue, white, blue, white...

Its siren keened like a knife being sharpened on a whetstone. The car turned from Canoga, missing the driveway into the ball field, and thudded across the sidewalk. From there the car skidded slightly on the grass, on the White Stuff, then corrected itself and kept flying.

The Gilbert Thing raised a large, swiney-hairy hand with vicious claws. From the center of the hand, a bluish ray of light flashed. A ball of light impacted the police car, putting out a headlight. Still the car came. The Gilbert Thing roared with rage and shot bolt after bolt of light. Then it turned

"Oh Jesus Help Me" Mary-Shane whimpered

aimed its palm

"Oh Jesus Please"

and fired a ball of cold blue light past her face. The shot nicked the wood so that splinters stuck in her cheek. Gilbert picked up the pot of burning pitch, and ran toward her.

"Oh My God My God..."

The madness and rage in his eyes were clearly visible through the jackal mask; or was it a mask? For the first time, she thought Gilbert was really in there. Until now, she'd thought of this creature as being a genuine demon. Now it seemed more like Gilbert in a disguise, which was more likely in the first place, only in her panic since the moment of Perry's death, she'd been to hysterical to think clearly. Gilbert (or was it really Gilbert? she wasn't sure) raised the burning pitch high to throw it over her. Tongues of spilled fire bannered over Gilbert's shoulder and he (it) screamed in pain.

The police car skidded to a halt in a fan of White Stuff. Its door flew open and out stepped Vic Lara, rifle in hand.

Mary-Shane managed to loosen her gag, and screamed: "Vic! Help."

The Gilbert thing drew near. *TOGETHER MY LOVE, WE WILL PERISH BUT LIVE ETERNALLY...*

Vic knelt to aim.

Mary-Shane held in a scream.

Red eyes glowed hungrily, teeth bared in a grin. Mary-Shane felt the *Cold Thing*, stirring under its rock, unperturbed, in the back of her mind.

Vic shot, and echoes slammed between the basilica and the hills somewhere in the Jungle as the M-16 rock 'n rolled on automatic.

The Gilbert Thing's jackal head exploded as a round entered its skull. Holes tore through the body, and it began to fall, jerked this way and that, and flaming pitch fell backwards on it, enveloped it. It rolled on the ground, arms upraised as claws that wilted in the heat...

Vic, holding the smoking M-16, hopped over the cemetery wall with flying coattail. A shot rang out. One of the Satanists, kneeling behind a grave stone, had aimed at Vic and missed. Vic fired on the run, and the man never had a second chance.

There were some seconds of silence during which Mary-Shane, bloodied and dizzy, coughed at the smoke rising from Gilbert.

At that moment, she realized that the *Cold Thing* had lived inside Gilbert also. Gilbert was dead, but the *Cold Thing* lived on. In her. In how many other persons? Gilbert was gone, discarded, and so would she be when her usefulness ended, but the *Cold Thing* prospered, intent on accomplishing its mission—to do what?

Vic erupted from the blackness among the tombstones spraying fans of flaming tracer bullets. Mary-Shane saw a shadow fly away, a gun slip from a hand.

I LOVE YOU, a last thought emanated from Gilbert as his innermost candle went out—not the Jackal Thing, but Gilbert the real person, slimy, perverted, but also pitiful. For the first time, despite all the evil Gilbert had stood for, she pitied him.

A wailing caravan of marked police cars hove into view on Canoga. The lead car slowed. When its driver saw Lara's car, he speeded up again, turned, and the other cars followed. A dozen sirens piped. Red white and blue flashes illumined the night sky like fireworks. High beam headlights rolled forward in a wave. Vic cut Mary-Shane loose, and she collapsed in his arms. "Oh God, Vic, they killed Perry."

He held her tightly as she cried. " I told you to stay home."

The ball field swarmed with uniforms. Abruptly, a stillness descended. The organ music stopped. They had found Perry.

Mary-Shane did an assessment of herself. Bloody cheek, aching bones, cuts and bruises, a couple of burn marks from spattered pitch.

Ambulances rolled in. A policeman sprayed Gilbert's charred and melted corpse with a fire extinguisher. EMT's in white jackets checked the dead priests. Policemen with dogs and shotguns poured into the cemetery. Flashlight beams, and the thicker beams of police spotlights, played among the trees and tombstones. Mary-Shane thought of having lost Perry and cried out loud. "I never should have come here. I got Perry killed."

"You bet you never should have," bellowed a powerful voice. Bishop Mulcahy, dressed in a long silk bathrobe, stood with arms akimbo. He had a large cigar in his mouth, and his steel rimmed glasses glinted sternly. "You were warned to leave this in competent hands. I warned Lawrence too, and he warned you!"

"Oh shut up," Mary-Shane said wiping her eyes. "These priests were doing what your church trained them to do. I made a mistake I'll always regret, but at least I did something."

Bishop Mulcahy's mouth fell open.

"For a hundred years," she said, "you have sat in your house by the church and done nothing but smoke cigars and fart to yourself."

"Quiet," Vic said, giving her arm a tug. "He's doing the best he can. We all are."

Mulcahy whisked his cigar out of his mouth and cleared his throat. "Young Lady," he said, "Rumph!" Red white and blue lights danced in his glasses.

"Don't Young Lady me," she said.

"Young Lady, er, rum." He stared, jammed his cigar back into his mouth, and stalked off trailing a scarf of expensive smoke.

A car rolled in, and Martina Strather got out. She walked up to Vic, put her arms around him, and kissed him. Mary-Shane stared at them. Martina helped Mary-Shane up. "Vic and I recently fell in love."

Nothing surprised Mary-Shane anymore. I should have realized, she thought.

Vic said: "Mary-Shane called me. Ten minutes later Martina called me. Then Father called me. Finally the bishop called me. Then Martina called back and said she thought you were all going to be out here. You people don't know how dangerous these Satan-buddies really are. So I said, fuck these jewels, I can't be sittin' here drinking cold coffee and eating stale donuts while you guys are all getting killed. I put in an emergency call to the central switchboard and headed out here."

Mary-Shane put her hands over her face to wipe away the tears. "Thanks."

Vic produced a flashlight and waved its beam over the crumpled body by the cross. "Finally," he said, "I nailed that son of a bitch. Mary-Shane, I'm so sorry it cost us Perry to cream this piece of dog shit. I've been after him for a long, long time."

Mary-Shane looked down at Gilbert Burtongale. His lidless eyes, his contorted (screaming?smiling?) mouth were open in death. EMT's had backed their ambulance close. Vic told them: "Double-bag this one for me, okay you guys? He's extra stinky garbage."

"Vic," Mary-Shane said, looking at Gilbert's destroyed but once again human features, "I thought for a while there he was wearing some kind of mask." Even as she spoke, she knew it wasn't true. It had been the *Cold Thing*. For the first time, she'd gotten a clear look at it, and now she tried not to remember that it lived in her brain as it had in Gilbert's.

Vic's flashlight beam poked about. "You must have been mistaken," he said, "there's no mask anywhere around. That's just Gilbert."

Chapter 65.

Mary-Shane rode to the hospital in Vic's car. Martina Strather sat in the back seat with a comforting hand on Mary-Shane's shoulder. From the ER they called Roger. It was hard to keep from blubbering. "You don't move an inch from those kids. They're going to slap a few bandages on me and I'll take a cab home."

She sat on a gurney, sniffling, when Martina came in with haunted eyes. "Are you ready to go home?"

"Yes."

Martina took off her own coat and held it. Mary-Shane, shivering, accepted. "Matilda Stein passed away an hour ago. The nurse said she was in the room, changing a bedpan, when Matilda suddenly sort of cried out, sat up with her eyes wide open, and then fell backward. She was dead by the time the nurse dropped the bedpan and got to her side. Matilda died just minutes after Perry did."

Mary-Shane remembered her dreams of the ship, of the long corridors, that seemed to beckon to her also. "Almost," she said dreamily, feeling Martina's hand gently on her back leading her outside where Vic waited, "as though he came to get her, isn't it? Like he had to go somewhere, and wanted her to come with him."

Part II

This Shoal of Space

Chapter 66.

The following morning, Roger took the kids to school. Mary-Shane had bruised ribs, scratches, burn marks, a black eye, and a sprained wrist. She also had a big wound in her soul. She packed Mother's belongings in the trunk of the Mustang and drove her to Mulberry Street. The house looked like an old lady who had just been through a lot. Its doors and windows hung open and fresh air and sunlight flooded it from all directions.

Still the White Stuff blew up, blizzards of it. Old people complained of respiratory problems; doctors warned of health hazards to the lungs and eyes. The earth itself seemed queasy, always a tremor away from the next temblor. The city still wailed with sirens. Here and there, a smoke pillar rose from yet another fire.

Mary-Shane drove by her place, but didn't have the heart to go in. She hoped the home owner's insurance would cover the massive damage (White Stuff bulging from every nook). She frowned. Put her foot on the brake pedal. Noticed the van parked near her house.

She left her car running, got out, and strode to the van. Someone had painted over the windows, so she could not see inside. She tried the doors. Locked. Walking past on the way to her car, she yanked on the rear door handle—and, to her surprise, it opened.

She almost lost her balance as momentum carried her with the door. Inside was a maze of electronic gear. A pretty young Air Force blonde in fatigues and radio headset was busy twiddling knobs. A sergeant with gray hair and lots of wavy chevrons made an angry face. Touching the large gun on his belt, he snarled and pulled the door shut, slamming it in her face.

Roger waited in his driveway. "Mary-Shane, one more death." She removed her sunglasses, checked her shiner in the visor mirror, and squinted at him. "Miss Polly," Roger said.

"I don't care right now."

"Martina wants us there before the estate goes into probate."

Mary-Shane relented. Roger shifted the car through its gears on the winding road to the mansion. The ocean looked innocent below, little waves like lace doilies for afternoon tea. "I hate this town," she said.

"If the kids get something out of the estate, we can leave San Tomas."

"We?" she asked.

He looked startled. "Should I make that maybe?"

The words, you big handsome moose, the words!

"Mary-Shane, I know it's early, but I was wondering if you would consider becoming engaged to marry me." She slid her sunglasses down and stared at him over the lenses, darkly. Roger looked as though he wanted to stop the car and run away. "Of course," she said feigning a shrug. It took his face a minute to change from stark rejection to joy. "You would?" He stopped in the middle of the street and they threw their arms around each other. Cars honked, flowing around them.

Martina Strather stood before a small crowd in the sitting room of the Burtongale mansion overlooking San Tomas Peninsula from high atop a hill. Besides Roger and Mary-Shane, various Burtongale siblings and spouses were in the room, maybe fifteen people. She recognized Jules, Patricia, Mart Willow, and one or two others. Martina said: "I found her this morning. She had gone into Wallace's baby room and evidently just... went to sleep. With Gilbert and Wallace gone, she just didn't feel she had anything left to live for."

There was a brief statement by Walt Kargis, attorney and longtime confidant of Miss Polly. He was in his 80's, a slim man, white-haired, with pained eyes. He had a smooth voice like warm water running through long pipes. "A great loss to all of us. I have asked you here, not for the reading of the will, which will come later, and you are all remembered in it, but—" He paused and wiped a tear away. "—Miss Polly and I had a chat just last week, almost in premonition I would now say." Kargis put on his reading glasses and unfolded a piece of paper. "She wanted me to expedite certain matters. For one thing, if you don't already know, Mart Willow is terminated at the newspaper effective this hour." He looked up. Mary-Shane and Jules exchanged looks of amazement. It was quiet in the room. Mart Willow was turning from red to purple. "Further, Jules Loomis is appointed Executive Editor of the Herald, replacing Miss Polly in that position." Jules rolled his gaze upward. Patricia covered her mouth with her hands and gasped. The attorney sat down.

Martina Strather stepped forth again, clasping her hands over her long flat belly. "Miss Polly seemed depressed the last few days, and we tried to cheer her up, but I think she knew her time was coming. First" (she pointed to a stack of faded leather-bound journals on a side table) "Mr. Loomis is asked to examine the secret diaries of her ancestor, Wallace Burtongale, who traveled in Africa during the mid 1800's." (Jules nodded his acceptance) "Second and last, Miss MacLemore, she asks you to handle this." Martina handed a box to Mary-Shane. Inside was the African statuette Johnathan Smith had died for. "Miss Polly requests this be returned to the Rev. Smith's Museum of Satan back east when you are done with it."

Jules had stuffed his pipe, lit it, and was now puffing contentedly. "And I'm making you police reporter."

"I guess I'm glad," she told Roger, clutching her box and hurrying along with him to the car. "It'll never be the same without Perry though."

Roger drove along the twisting roads, down toward the sea. She lifted the statue (it was light) and looked underneath. It was hollow. "Look, Roger, there are little wisps of that White Stuff in there." She frowned. "It's almost as though the White Stuff were coming right out of the wood." She looked again. "There was something else in here."

Roger downshifted. "I've got a contact as UC San Tomas who would just love to look at that thing."

She clutched the statuette tightly. "Let's get the story!"

Roger and Mary-Shane drove to the UC San Tomas campus. She carried the statuette in its box. Dr. Vernon LeGrier was a middle-aged black man. His head and beard were peppered, giving him a mellow and distinguished appearance. LeGrier had an easy smile that poked out like the sun after a storm, given his usual scowl and the armor of his personality that had withstood stupidity and prejudice through a long and distinguished career. He examined the wooden object. Peering through a magnifying glass, he reached for a dental pick.

"What do you think?" Mary-Shane could not help asking in the lab which was silent except for a drip in the sink and the clicking of a defective fluorescent light. No bubbling test tubes, no blinking comedy computers, no weird assistants.

LeGrier shook their hands. "What we have here is a real curiosity."

"Oh?" Roger and Mary-Shane both said and leaned forward for an nth look, but she at least could not see anything more than before.

"Yes. First, the statue appears to have been hollowed out a long time ago, how long I won't know until we do some more tests. There are minute traces of some sort of plaster inside, which leads me to believe that the statuette was filled in.

"Second, there are traces...you can see them under the light here" (he held it under a fluoro, and Mary-Shane leaned real close) "...of some other material. Looks like old, badly forged, crumbly iron. But among them are traces of a quite complex ferrous molecule that could only have been made under technologically advanced conditions." He pointed with a shaky dental tip, and there appeared to be dark crumbs in the knife marks made by whoever had hollowed this thing out.

On whiteboard nearby were hastily written diagrams and chemical formulas where he must have scrawled the results of his research.

"There is one other thing," LeGrier said.

Mary-Shane and Roger waited.

"It's something that may having a bearing on this but I'd appreciate your keeping quiet for now. When we've had a chance to study it more, the word will come out soon anyway. It's—those earthquakes. They're not earthquakes. They're—well, we don't know what they are. It's just—they have the same seismic signature as tiny little nuclear explosions. It's nonsense, of course, but the resemblance is uncanny, similar to the way nuclear nations do regular testing to make sure their technology is working."

Mary-Shane, Roger, and Jules had lunch at the zoo deli. The zoo was almost deserted. The pyramid of White Stuff in the middle, cordoned off with yellow police tape, loomed menacingly on the nearby horizon. Roger said: "Things are nutso at the zoo. A lot of the employees are calling in sick but I know some are just scared. Especially with that heart attack rumor going around."

"You're going to get a lot of rumors at a time like this," Jules said. "I've been reading those old diaries. Mary-Shane, I'm now really sorry I told you to squelch your story earlier."

"Thanks." She made a mental note to return that book to Father Lawrence, then remembered he was gone.

"That old guy Wallace I went to Africa, brought back a bunch of stuff, and went nuts. His diaries, which I don't think anyone has seen in a hundred years are full of references to pain in his soul, pain in his head, things talking in his head. Whatever the demon is or was, it promised the Burtongales great fortune, but the price was steep. Their sanity. Wallace I finally couldn't stand it. He dumped his African statues out at sea."

"Including the sphinx that talked in his mind," Mary-Shane said.

"Right. But it was too late," Jules said. "Whatever pact he had made with the Devil, it stuck."

Roger said: "Then we have the earthquakes, as though something is trying to get out of the ground. And the White Stuff—totally unexplained."

"There was," Mary-Shane said, "something else bugging me. I think I remember something. The thing in the back of the truck, that got Charlie and Frank and Attila killed. It was a statue stolen from a museum in Chicago. Gilbert called it a core. That's a computer term, isn't it?"

Jules said: "You got me."

Roger nodded. "Core. That's an old term for main memory. It was made of iron rings looped in a lattice. Vern said there had been iron in the statuette. The sphinx might have had some iron in it. So then..."

"There would be a third iron kind of outer space thing floating around somewhere in San Tomas," Mary-Shane said.

"Yeah, like maybe right there," Jules said pointing at the pyramid of White Stuff, which was by now over a hundred feet tall and twice as wide at the base.

Mary-Shane shuddered. "A spaceship approaches earth long ago. Why do spaceships come to earth? In the movies, it's usually to colonize, take us over. The spaceship blows up. Its brain somehow survives, though in pieces that try to find each other. What better tool than a wealthy explorer who will stop at nothing?"

"Maybe there were more pieces," Jules said, "but so far we know of only three. One is the sphinx that got dumped at sea. Two is the rain god, the hollow wooden statue of which we have, but the core of which is lost somewhere here in San Tomas. The third is the Ivory Coast statue that Frank and Attila and Gilbert stole. Something is under all that White Stuff at the Pagoda, one of the statues, and I'm willing to bet it's another piece of the core."

Mary-Shane felt some relief. "I'm not crazy—there is a very real presence in the pit of my mind, somewhere, but I'm not the only person. This—this force, this ship, sends suggestions that seem very real. Like Wiz talking to me from a dead TV tube. Or the dreams Kippy and I have been having, of something in the sea. Or me seeing my dad. They are all metaphors, somehow, created by a ship that's trying to repair itself. The problem is—will the ship destroy San Tomas, maybe half of California, before it realizes there's no hope? Will any of us get it out of our minds before we really go out of our minds?" The men stared at her dumbly. She ventured: "Maybe the only way to win this one is for someone to go down into the sea, into the ship, and tell them the truth."

Jules had a dark look. He shook his head. "I dunno, Mary-Shane. They, whoever they are, the aliens, may not want to know the truth. They may destroy us all—and what do they have to lose?"

Roger and Mary-Shane went to his office, locked the door, and made love on the floor, under the filtered green light that poured through the high windows. The world was in chaos, and having sex seemed the most urgent thing to do. It was evolution at work, she was sure.

Then she drove to the paper. Jules called her into his office. He had been reading old books and now he rubbed his eyes. Tomes were spread before him; leather and canvas bound books that, as blanks alone, would be worth hundreds of dollars apiece today. She approached them with awe, touching with her fingertips. Crisp (stick and nib?) ink text filled the pages in straight, wire-mesh penmanship.

"Mary-Shane, I want you to start a daily column on this situation. Go as many pages as you need. Quote anyone, call anyone, do anything to fill the column with the kind of crisis information you'll need. Everything you do is by-line. Oh, and by the way, your salary is doubled."

"Thanks," she said, dazzled by the honor, dazed by the turnaround in her fortunes.

He winked. "You get my old office until I can hire a new Managing Editor. I'm going to throw Mart Willow's crap out the window, have his office fumigated, and then move in there myself."

"Good for you," she told him. "Mind if I borrow a couple of those giant books?"

"Be my guest."

Lugging a pile of mildewy tomes, she struggled to her old desk in the obit section. A group of reporters followed her.

"Nice to see you again," Spike said.

"It's good to be back. Ooff." She dropped the books on her desk and dust rose. She looked around. "I didn't expect to see the place again." They crowded into the obit area. Spike reached under his desk and pulled out a big candy box. "We all got together and bought some chocolates to say thanks you. We are all sooo glad to be rid of that man." They all clapped.

"Those are very large books," Spike said when they were alone. As Spike packed up for the day, and the afternoon faded into a golden silence, she read:

"...no longer trusting to the sound sense of my faculties, indeed filled with fear as to what might otherwise befall our zoo, our family, and our town, I resolved to undo both the progress and the mistakes that had been the outgrowth of my third African journey. Thus, with a heavy heart, I ordered the Chinese workers brought in. Our magnificent sphinx, brought to California via the Indian Ocean at great expense, was to be sunk deep in the Pacific near San Tomas. The voice in the back of my mind, however, continues to torment me. I fear it is too late. How long will I (and God forbid, my descendants?) have to suffer the schemes of this thing...?"

As she read, her heart pounded. Yes, her mind cried with a life of its own, that's what I've been feeling at the back of my head. It was more powerful than ever, so powerful that it hurt.

...COME CLOSER...

Feeling the *Cold Thing* she burst into tears and slammed the book shut. Even with Gilbert dead, nothing had changed. Somehow, she must get the *Cold Thing* out of her life, even if she had to pry it out of her brain with a Swiss Army Knife.

Chapter 67.

"Are you guys sick?" Mary-Shane asked over breakfast. Elisa shook her head. Kippy shook his head. Rudy shook his head. Heads hung. "This is a first," Roger said as he joined them with his own plate. "Usually they wolf down everything in sight."

"I think we're all getting the flu," Elisa said dejectedly. Her glance flickered toward Kippy, who glanced up briefly, and What secret were they sharing? Something was going on.

"Do you feel that you need to stay in bed?" Roger asked. "This on a Saturday morning?"

"The boys could lie in the living room and watch cartoons," Elisa said.

"And you?" Roger asked.

"I have a very important project to do on my computer," Elisa said with gleaming eyes. Mary-Shane felt a tingle up and down her back. Computer?

The kids ended up going out on the rear lawn to wash the dogs. She checked out Roger's computer system but found nothing wrong. "What are you doing?" he asked, carrying a coffee mug and the paper.

"Nothing," she said, joining him in the living room. She turned on the expensive German clock radio just softly enough that she could barely hear it. The sound had that comforting, calm sound of a baseball game in a far room on a lazy summer day. KCST anchor Chuck Elder was just reading the ten a.m. news: "...Seismologists at UCST have counted over a hundred small aftershocks after the temblors that have rocked San Tomas and indeed this part of California in the past few days. City inspectors are combing public buildings for cracks, but no significant threats have been unveiled, thanks to California's history of strong quake-proofing laws. Coast Guard officials have confirmed that there is a huge iceberg off the coast of San Tomas, only this ice berg is not made of ice, it's made of, you guessed it, White Stuff. Coast Guard and Marine Fishery boats are on their way to the area. Reports say that a solid block of White Stuff is floating or anchored in the water, rising as high as fifty feet in some spots; the depth of the phenomenon is not known yet. An unmanned camera-bearing submarine called the Underwater Photo Reconnaissance Submersible Robot, or U-Pho, is being airlifted from Scripps Laboratories in San Diego. U-Pho, you may remember, has filmed such sea wrecks as the Titanic, the Lusitania, and a lost Russian space capsule. Scientists at UC San Tomas's Burtongale Biology Laboratories have announced some preliminary conclusions about the mysterious White Stuff that has been plaguing this seaside resort for over a week now. Professor Vernon LeGrier, speaking with KCST's Angela Moorehead, had this to say: '...um, the so-called White Stuff appears to be a rather simple set of compounds. It has a light, papery quality, but it's fire resistant. It's got a crystalline composition in parts, which leads us to believe that it is actually manufactured somehow like common sand and then blown or stretched or threaded by some unknown process into this papery glassy plastic. It's not foamed plastic either. The most surprising thing is that it's not uniform. In some parts of town it contains large amounts of cellulose, which is the stuff of which tree trunks and plants are made. In other places there is hardly a trace of cellulose. It appears to me that someone, something, some force buried in the earth or hidden in the sea is manufacturing this stuff in different places and just simply using whatever materials are at hand..."

Mary-Shane nuzzled comfortably, back against Roger's strong, warm body, and fell fast asleep. She dreamt an innocent childhood dream about Daddy. How she had loved him! How she would run down the garden path to the gate when he was getting out of his car after a long business trip! What a beautiful dream.

Then dogs licked her face, kids jumped on the bed, disrupting her dream. Roger chased them all out, and Mary-Shane fell into a deep much-needed dreamless sleep.

The Herald came out in the morning with a huge black border on the first page. The headline, in thick black letters, cried out: HEIRESS DEEDS MANSE TO NUNS. The accompanying story was written by Jules. Smaller headlines on the page read:

POLICE WRAP MURDER SERIES. Mary-Shane had written this one, using a lengthy interview with Vic Lara. She kept it straight, mentioning Satanism but glossing over the last moments with Gilbert; who would believe it? She left off with Vic's shooting of Gilbert, and Vic's theory that Gilbert had been responsible for a lot of the killings around San Tomas.

BISHOP MUM ON EXORCISMS. Jules had written this one. Bishop Mulcahy said he might make a statement after a 'reasonable period of sober reflection and prayer' and after consulting with the Vatican.

FEDS VOW CONTINUED QUAKE AID, SNOW PROBE. This one, written by Mary-Shane, had quotes from Dr. Stanislaus as well as Drs. Black and White. Vernon LeGrier had promised an interview.

POLLY BURTONGALE, 88, HEIRESS, TOWN BENEFACTOR. This was Spike's piece, with a jump to the obit page after a few opening grafs at lower right of the first page.

Jules declared from his office door: "This paper is out of the dock and running on the open sea for the first time ever."

Privately, when Mary-Shane showed him her first two pages, which he liked, he told her: "I've already had two calls from major newspaper chains that might be interested in buying the Herald. I had to beg off, of course, saying Martina Strather was appointed executrix and we'll have to see how the whole thing shakes out of Probate. If ever, given all that the Burtongales own."

About mid-morning, ten twenty to be exact, Mary-Shane had a call from St. Andrew's. Sister Sincere's voice was low and direct. "Miss MacLemore, I don't want to scare you now, and I think everything will be okay, but I must tell you that Kippy took a fall just now."

"Oh?" She sat bolt upright. "How is he?"

"He is going to be taken to hospital. His leg may be broken."

"No."

"Miss MacLemore?"

"I'll be right there," she said dropping the phone.

Chapter 68.

When Mary-Shane drove up to the school and saw the cream and red ambulance, she felt like crying, only fear dried up her eyes and made her heart pound. She found Kippy being loaded onto a kind of chair-stretcher. His face was white as paper. He gritted his teeth in pain and stared horrified down at his leg, which was dressed in white splints and bandages. His knuckles were white as he gripped the stainless steel bars.

Mary-Shane remembered to control her tears just long enough to get on her knees and cradled his head. His eyes were wide with pain. He held himself stiffly, sucking tortured breaths. "Oh Mommy," he said, "it hurts."

"It's okay," she said, "we're going to the hospital and get it fixed." She felt her heart breaking.

"Am I going to be all right?" he asked, turning scared eyes toward her. She squeezed his upper arm, feeling the new muscles there. "You'll be fine," she said.

Sister St. Cyr said: "He was playing basketball with the boys and they say he twisted the wrong way and went down. They heard the bone snap. Sort of a popping noise." Mary-Shane stood numbly by the ambulance, trying to sob but paralyzed. Her chest heaved, only to fight a huge weight that was descending on her. Sister Sincere reached out and grabbed Mary-Shane's lapel and shook roughly. "Let's get in, Mary-Shane, the boy needs to get to hospital." Mary-Shane let herself be half pulled, half pushed into the cold steel jaws of the ambulance just as the paramedic physician assistant bent close with a hypo of morphine. In a corner, Sister St. Cyr sat with eyes closed praying silently. Her pasty white fingers were kneaded like dough around hard black rosary beads.

Chapter 69.

Dr. Isaac Boutros, Kippy's doctor of old, showed up quickly at the E.R. He'd been on rounds right there in the hospital and he could only stay a minute. His eyes reflected worry and kindness as he pumped her hands gently. "You'll see, Mary-Shane. Everything will turn out okay. You must hope and pray. I am ordering all the necessary tests now and I will return to see you later."

Mary-Shane did pray. Sister St.Cyr left around noon, promising Father Drinnan would mention Kippy during Dispensations at his evening Mass at state prison. He would ask the prisoners to pray for Kippy also. She pressed the black rosary into Mary-Shane's hand before she left.

Mary-Shane held Kippy's hand under the white tents in the emergency room. He felt warm to her. She called a nurse, and Kippy's temperature proved to be 101. God let it be flu. Please...

"I'm not real scared just now," Kippy told her.

"I'm not either," she lied. "Maybe just a little. Not a lot, though."

"Me neither," he said. "Not a whole lot. Just a little."

Before the bone could be set, Kippy had to go through X-Ray. There, in a semidark of quiet procedure and dull, careful routine, plates slammed through the huge machines as exposures were taken. Next, blood tests. Kippy went through all the needle sticks with a stoic face. Partly, she thought, it was because he was already doped up. She remembered the cancer years, and felt strangely detached. This wasn't the little five year old who'd suffered through that. And this wasn't his young mother caroming from cushion to cushion of life. Those two had triumphed. They had walked out of this fucking place hand in hand and chins up. This was a whole new ball game. This was a ten year old, and his worried thirtyish mother. Only the Doctor was the same (Boutros, Egyptian, Coptic, best bone man between LA and San Francisco, a Burtongale catch. Thanks, Miss Polly).

Then came the specialists. They nodded, they conferred, they pointed to X-rays, they made gestures, they walked away and came back. They sipped coffee and nodded some more. They generally avoided looking in Mary-Shane's direction; perhaps (oh I'm kidding myself) they don't know I'm sitting here around the corner in a cold draft wishing it was all a joke and we could go home now.

Kippy was in the cast room. He'd had his leg set and now the cast man was wrapping the fiberglass into place.

Dr. Boutros came and sat next to her. "Mary-Shane, there is a tumor in his right tibia. That's the thin little hard bone you feel below your knee to your ankle."

She remembered every bone. "Is he going to die?" she asked.

"We have to take the leg off."

283

"He loves to play basketball," she said. She felt dull and saggy.

"Mary-Shane," he whisked in his little accent, and she studied the crisp white hairs around his gold eyeglass frames, the caring brown eyes behind thick lenses, the soft cocoa skin furrowed with a thousand horrors and worries, "we have won the fight once before, together, and we are going to win it again now. Got that?"

She nodded.

"He will play again. You should go get something to eat," he said. "It's six o'clock." What? How could that be? But he was right. The hospital corridors glowed snow-blind with too many fluorescent lights. Evening shift people trundled about in surgical gowns. She went to the cafeteria and forced herself to eat half a burger and some fries, not tasting anything. A middle aged man with a cigarette in one hand and a similar burger in the other hand was wolfing away; why not him? she asked, why not that guy? Why my Kippy and not some other kid? Why any kid? Why, God? We pray and pray and what do we get? She sniffled.

"Mary-Shane." She turned. Roger, Elisa, and Rudy walked in. Roger sent the kids to get trays and order in the line (which was virtually empty because dinner was over but the cafeteria wasn't closed yet). He squeezed her hands. "I'm sorry."

"We beat it once," she said. "Why is it back?" He started to say something. She bawled. He slid around and sat beside her. He held her close and rocked her. Elisa and Rudy sat quietly.

"Let's all go up to see him," Roger suggested.

The charge nurse dictated hospital rules: Two visitors per patient at a time in the rooms, or five in the guest room. So they sat together with a huge Mexican-American family. Kippy, Rudy, and Elisa put their heads together for a serious powwow that made Mary-Shane curious. "What are you gabbing about?" she prodded them.

"Just, um, about our rooms," Elisa said. "We want Kippy to get home soon." Mary-Shane sensed something awry. But she checked Kippy's reaction, and he nodded as Elisa spoke.

"Well it's nice to know you're wanted at a time like this," Mary-Shane heard herself blather. Roger held her hand, and she thought, last time I didn't have that either.

She sent Roger and the kids home about seven. Kippy had some pain and she got the nurse to give him codeine, which put him right out. He was in the pediatric section, so it was okay for her to spend the night. An LVN brought a cot, which was placed right next to Kippy's bed for her. She lay down to rest, planning to get up, shower, comb her hair, maybe drive home and pick up some clothes, but she fell hard asleep.

She had horrid dreams about dead people. Father Lawrence, wearing his long black soutane, stood someplace under water on a metal beam. He waved his arms and his face flexed in driven expressions. His eyes looked desperate. The metal beam on which he stood was torn off at one end, melted like a bar of sealing wax thrust into fire. Wiz stood darkly shaking her head. Like, no, don't something, but what? Grave men in bright garments woven of gray light, like angels neither good nor bad, or maybe both, were carrying a stretcher deep into a wall, through a doorway without exit, and when she looked closely, it was Kippy on the stretcher. Somewhere nearby was an airplane with all its lights on—but fish swam in and out of the cockpit windows.

A hand shook her. It was the nurse. She had a tray of food for Kippy, in case he wanted to eat. She rose groggily, shaking her head. Kippy was still lying on one side. Mary-Shane bent over him anxiously. He was still breathing. She pulled the cover up to his chin. The nurse said: "Doctor Boutros is on the floor. He asked to see you in the corridor."

Mary-Shane found him in a nook between a palm and a picture, reading over some procedure sheets. When he saw her, he put the papers away and looked grave. "Mary-Shane, we were calling you at home this morning. I'm afraid I have more bad news. The lab found some suspicious white blood cells. I had the radiologist go back and check the x-rays again. I am indefinitely postponing the amputation. We think there may be more tumors."

"NO..." She sagged against the wall.

"I'm sorry," he said. "I think we have to be very tough just now. We will do more tests, and right now it's not conclusive. But there is a sixty per cent chance that there is a small tumor in the other leg, and also one on the hip right near the kidney. And what that means is that there may be the beginnings of metastasis. We have to know right away."

"Is he going to die?" she asked.

"That is in God's hands," he said. "He is a very, very sick boy."

Mary-Shane called her mother.

"Oh hi," came the drawling, dawdly voice.

"Mother," Mary-Shane cried, "Kippy's cancer is back."

"I think you should take him to the doctor then," Mother replied.

"Are you drunk?"

"I'm knitting," Mother said. "Would you like to join me?"

Mary-Shane hung up and called Roger.

"Oh my God," he said. "I'll do whatever I can." His words and his tone of voice, however well-intentioned, had a cold finality that enraged her. "He's not dead yet, and I'm not going to let him die!" she screamed and slammed the phone down. Then she ran outside to get some air, pushing aside startled nurses and staring patients.

Chapter 70.

Mary-Shane quit her job at the newspaper. A specialist flown in by the Burtongale Estate discovered yet another tumor, this one in Kippy's brain. Metastasis had set in. He had less than six months to live, Dr. Boutros said. I will die with him, Mary-Shane thought to herself.

She took Kippy home toward the end of the week. It was a sunny day, filled with bird song and flowers. Kippy seemed in good spirits. "I'll be playing basketball again before you know it," he told her. He patted her knee. "Don't worry, I'll get through this one okay just like last time."

That evening, after dinner, they all sat and watched Disney movies in the den. Mary-Shane had the illusion that she'd had a bad dream and now was reality. They were a family; how could Kippy die now that he finally had a family? She went in the bathroom and cried quietly for a while so nobody would know.

Later, as Kippy was going to bed, she sat by him. It was as if they were alone in the big house, with the wind blowing gently outside, and pine boughs rubbing against the house saying how wonderful it was to be alive.

"Mom," he said, hands folded on chest, eyes glittering into a ceiling of thoughts, "I'm not sure I can take it again. The chemo, I mean."

"Kippy," she said and pressed a hand over his. She knew what he meant. He'd already received massive doses of poisons designed to kill the tumors, at the expense of sickening his healthy body too. It was okay now, but in a few days he would be immobile, glued to the floor, gasping, vomiting glassy fire. She remembered it all from before. "Kippy, darling, you HAVE to! I'm going to be with you every second, do you hear? I'm going to suffer with you, and we're going to make it together. You've got to! You have a family now."

<hr />

"I'm sorry I yelled at you," Mary-Shane told Roger as he held her. They lay, dressed in pajamas, on the bed.

"I understand," he said. His tone told her more: he would stand by her. But would it be enough? Would all the hopes and prayers be enough?

Jules and Patricia visited next day. So did Martina. So did Sister St.Cyr. Some kids from school came, including the boys who had been playing basketball with him; they brought a basketball and signed their names to it. Several girls came with their parents and wrote hearts and valentine messages on Kippy's cast. Kippy preened in all the attention, but tired easily and had to go to bed.

Roger swapped Elisa's bedroom on the first floor for Kippy's on the second, so that Kippy would have easier access to the kitchen.

Vic Lara and Martina Strather stopped by. "We're working hard to adopt Evvie," she said. "Oh, didn't Vic tell you? We're engaged to be married next year."

"That's great," Mary-Shane and Roger said.

Vic said: "Mary-Shane, I'm sorry your son is so sick."

Mary-Shane said: "I wish you had left me to die when Gilbert..." Immediately she realized that then Kippy would have died alone, and she covered her face and cried.

Chapter 71.

Mary-Shane became increasingly isolated in the house. Roger went to work, and since the zoo was barely a block away, he could come back every two or three hours and check on her, hold her, look in on Kippy, spend a few fatherly minutes with him. Even to get groceries, she would send Roger in the evening. The house, the town, the world, her life seemed to be shutting around her like a dark fist closing. What was there now? Roger and his children, sure, but what could anything mean to her if she lost Kippy?

When he was asleep she wandered around the house. She clutched a torn and dowdy housecoat around her with cold hands. She had not washed her hair in days and it resembled a bird's nest fallen and crumbling around her face. Sometimes her face glistened wetly and she would run a wrist absently over it, leaving faint grime. Only when Kippy awoke did she hurry to the bathroom, afraid he would scold her, and she would rinse her face with a hot, wet towel. When she looked in the mirror she saw that she was getting thin. Her eye sockets looked huge. There were pale, listless creases in her cheeks and her face reminded her of old St. Cosmas, where rainwater ran like tear drops down the faces of age-blackened statuary.

Kippy was afraid at night. He would cry for her, and she would run from Roger's bed to Kippy's. Even Mary-Shane worried (and she could see the worry in Roger's eyes) about Rudy and Elisa. She was beginning to think that perhaps she ought to move with Kippy back to the apartments, perhaps one that hadn't been trashed with White Stuff, into an environment in which he would feel more familiar.

And the White Stuff continued its reign of terror. At times, water or power, or both, would be disrupted. For a while, the whole town might have no power. Then, water might erupt from closed faucets, blowing out old gaskets, and then settle with a dire gurgling, an animal having gorged.

Or, the ground might shake. Lights would flicker on and off. Cars ran into fire hydrants. More people collapsed in the infamous San Tomas Coma. Traffic lights swung back and forth like Chinese lanterns, red, amber, green.

Darkness was falling.
Kippy was asleep.
Rudy and Elisa were due home from school.

Mary-Shane watched bits and flotsams of White Stuff trafficking through the halls and rooms. She shuffled to the broom closet, got the vacuum cleaner out, and began to vacuum. What was on the floor went into the sucking mouth. What was in the air seemed to stay teasingly out of reach. Angrily, she tore the brush off and, using just the hose, staggered around trying to catch the damn stuff. She lugged the heavy, wheeled motor/container with one hand and tried to aim the hose with the other. She stumbled several times, lunging for a big flake while being jerked back by the weight of the motor. She reconnected the power cord (it flickered down twice, as if trying to prevent her) and vengefully kept after the debris. She followed the trail around a corner and it thickened. She stopped and rubbed a dirty cheek. What?

This was that dark corridor toward the end of the house where nobody seemed to ever go. There were a few closet doors and she pulled them open one by one. Dust made her cough. There were old boxes, old bags, fire hazard, debris she'd clean out once they were married. She laughed a crazy honk. Married? Dead, more like it. Nothing was going right anymore. Hadn't she always known it was meant to be like this?

Feverish images entertained her mind: Take Kippy and jump off the Morgan Freeway Bridge. Go swimming in the ocean and slowly sink...

What? The door at the far end. White Stuff seemed to be oozing out from under the door. She leaned close to peer inside, but the keyhole was overflowing with White Stuff.

As she leaned close to the door, however, a cold breeze flowed over her face like a greedy hand. How could this be? She started back as though someone or something had touched her. She touched her cheek and then looked at her fingers.

A fleck of White Stuff dissolved on her finger tip.

It smelled of the sea, of fish, of brine. She rattled the door handle. Locked. No, nailed. Panting, grunting with effort, she pulled out the four large, rusty nails someone had clumsily banged in on either side. She pushed against the door. It resisted. With her body she slammed it, yelling.

W W W H H H O O O S S S S S S H H H H H... went a big cloud of White Stuff, and she screamed because it came up around her like a gray body with arms, with grasping hands, with reaching fingers... For an instant, in the middle of that agitated whirling cloud, she saw the *Cold Thing*, not an eel but a jackal face with five antlers. It grinned, its teeth the color of yellowed ivory. It had three red eyes that stared at her with greedy interest. An instant later, the illusion was gone.

White Stuff closed around her. Suffocating her. She turned and ran. Stumbled, fell. White Stuff clogged her mouth and nostrils. She clawed it out. Held the rag hem of her housecoat over her face and staggered forward. Behind her, the door slammed shut. White Stuff collapsed in a knee-deep pile. Coughing, sputtering, sobbing, she used a corner of the hem to wipe her lips. She brushed the crust from her nostrils. She dabbed one eye, then the other.

Rudy and Elisa stood staring at her. She started. Their faces had a waxy sheen.

"What are you doing?" she demanded.

They kept staring at her.

She was on her side, still sprawled. Quickly she gathered herself to her knees. "You know something about this, don't you?" she shrilled. "You know something about this White Stuff, admit it!"

Rudy and Elisa, just in from school, still in uniform, carrying their book bags, turned and walked away.

"You little sneaks!" she shrilled after them. She shuffled through the White Stuff and yelled up the banister: "You little sneaks! Come down here! I want to know what you..." but her voice trailed off and she sat on the foot of the stairs. Her hands dangled between her knees and her head lolled. She reached up and grasped her dirty, scraggly hair. She wanted to scream, but she had already done that and her throat hurt. She wanted to cry, but she'd done that and there were no tears left.

"Mom!" Kippy called. "Mom!" His voice groped through the stark corridors. Oh my God, she thought, can't let him see me looking like this. She dashed into the bathroom on the first floor and washed her face. Combed her hair.

"Mo-o o o m m m!" he bellowed. She pushed open the door to Elisa's former room and went inside.

"Darling..." she started to say.

Kippy sat up. Rudy and Elisa, still in school uniform, sat on the bed with him. They all made big eyes at her. "Mom," Kippy said, "I think we need to tell you something."

Chapter 72.

Roger waited in his office as darkness fell. He opened the middle drawer of his desk and took out the large Kraft package and set it on his knees. The phone rang and he picked up the receiver. "This is Roger Chatfield."

"Roger, this is Dean Mollinger of City University, New York. I am returning your call."

"Glad to hear from you, Maud."

"It's been a long time, Roger. How's life?"

"Oh..." He wrestled with the package, and out spilled his resume. "...It's had its ups and downs."

"Mostly ups, I hope."

"How about you?"

"Ups and downs." Long ago, they had been lovers. She was a beautiful woman and they'd kept in touch, maybe a Christmas card, a phone call every five years. "I called a friend at Vermont College in Kaukasin, Vermont. You always wanted to go there."

"Yes." Years ago he'd spent weekends there with Maud. Chill autumn nights; crisp stars; gloomy trees with fire in their leaves; hearth fire flickering in leaded windows at Kaukasin...

"They are interested, Roger. Send your resume right away."

"Wonderful. My family and I need a new start. I've been meaning to make this move for a long time, and then—recently, some events—well, maybe I'll tell you about it one day."

"I heard about San Tomas. It must be dreadful out there."

"Dreadful? Yes, that's probably the word. I want the position if they offer anywhere near the right money."

"I think they'll come in low but within your range. I think you can jack them up five grand no problem." After the call, Roger stood, stretched, and sighed. He dialed home. Mary-Shane answered. He said: "Hi, Honey. I think I'm going to be a little late. I think I found something..."

"I'll fix supper for the kids," she answered. There was a dullness to her voice.

"I'll see you in a while," he said and hung up.

As darkness fell, as the green filtering sunlight from the roof gave way to creeping night, and the electric lights went on, Roger reflected upon the state of his life. He did not care to stay on at the zoo. He felt betrayed by the Burtongales; by Wallace; by Polly; maybe even by Susan, snatched away in the prime of her beauty. Susan ... he began to shake, remembering their love for each other. She always wanted to have another child. Always loved to put on magic shows for the children at school. Loved children.

But I have my two kids, he thought, I must not forget that. I am in love with Mary-Shane, but where is that going? Her mother is insane, and now she is breaking up. Poor Kippy. I must think of Elisa and Rudy. If it is just a matter of Kippy being sick, then we can manage. But if Mary-Shane can't take the pressure and if she is going the way of her mother, then maybe we'd better step back and give this thing a long look. Tears welled up in his eyes.

What am I going to do? The only time I ever felt like this was when I buried Susan. Roger Chatfield got on his knees and started to cry. All the years of tears were in there, and he hunched on the floor, holding his face, sobbing like a child. He did so for a long time.

Chapter 73.

"We have something to tell you," Elisa told Mary-Shane with a meaningful glance toward Kippy.

Kippy took a deep breath. "Mom, we got into the computer games again."

Mary-Shane sat down. "I don't believe this—"

"We didn't mean to," Rudy said.

"Shut up," Elisa told him. "I was doing my homework on the computer, and Jeremy kept pinging me with electronic mail messages. That's how it got started."

"I knew you'd be mad," Kippy said.

Mary-Shane picked up the phone and dialed Anne's number. The phone endlessly burred, but nobody answered. A faint tremor made the walls crackle, and the line went dead. Mary-Shane let the phone slip from her hand and held her aching forehead. She felt overwhelmed. The hand shook, making her fingers spasm silently against her eyebrow, as if scratching or pointing. "Why?" Mary-Shane asked.

The children looked down. "Because," Kippy said, "it's Captain Colorado."

"That's make believe!" Mary-Shane yelled.

"Please don't be mad," Kippy said. "I think it's the only way I can save my legs. I think only Captain Colorado can save me."

"Stop that!" she yelled. "Stop it, Kippy. There is something out there in the sea, and it's evil. It's killing people right and left. It's eating our minds and turning us into vegetables like your grandmother. Doctor Boutros is going to do everything he needs to..."

But Kippy turned over on his side, facing away from her, and pulled the blanket up to his face.

"Honey..." she started to say, then anger got the best of her. She stormed out into the hall, taking a chair with her. She propped the chair against that door. The draft from the other side was cold and smelled oceanic. Bits of White Stuff fluffed up like idly warning fingers. Mary-Shane puffed and groaned, sliding a heavy dresser into place against the door. Why in the hell couldn't Roger get home and help her? The hell with him. She pressed the four nails back into place. Then she piled chairs, a desk, the dresser, books, magazines into place until she had formed a solid wall five feet tall. That would block them. For good measure, she went into the kitchen to get a hammer and more nails from the odds 'n ends drawer.

Elisa stepped forth from the shadows. "Mary-Shane?"

Mary-Shane knelt down and opened her arms to her.

Elisa came closer, but not enough to be held. "Mary-Shane, we love you but we are very worried." Elisa's words rained like nails and tacks on Mary-Shane's wounded ears. "We think you should wash yourself and go out more. Buy some new clothes. We're ashamed because you look terrible."

Mary-Shane rose. "You horrid little brat!" She slammed Elisa with the palm of her hand, leaving a red palm print on her cheek, and Elisa flew off in silent shock.

Mary-Shane sniffled, rubbing her forefinger on her cheek. She went to the living room and dialed Dr. Stanislaus's number. The receptionist patched her right through. "What is it?" he asked. Back to no name.

"I think I have lost my mind," she said.

"Very well," he said. "Next Tuesday, same time?"

"...no time," she said, letting the receiver rattle into the switch hook.

Chapter 74.

Roger decided it was time to stop feeling sorry for himself. He washed his face in the bathroom and went back to work. Working late meant to avoid going home. As deeply and passionately as he loved Mary-Shane, he must put the well-being of Rudy and Elisa first.

The phone rang after dark; Vern LeGrier, the meteorologist at UCST. "Roger, interesting news. We analyzed the iron residue in the statuette. It's not iron really, but a very ingenious alloy. The metallurgy people think it's a light-weight ferrous molecule that has somehow been bonded with some complex ceramics. Apply a current, and this thing lays out a long, low magnetic field that you could detect several buildings away, even on low amperage. We are talking here probably artifact beyond any technology we have right now. It has a crystalline structure AND it's a near superconductor!"

"Vern, not my field."

"Roger, every phone line out of here is buzzing right now with chemistry and physics experts calling their buddies at other universities. This may not be the perfect superconductor, but this is one that works. If we can duplicate it, we can have an energy efficient world, better computers..."

"Vern, that sounds very nice."

"Roger, Roger, this particular structure is so perfect it could not have been manufactured on this earth..."

"Back to the alien spaceship, Vern? I thought that's out."

"We are talking pure space manufactured, zero-g, zero-atmosphere crystal here. They're still cranking it through the electron microscopes, going deeper into the structure. You're an animal man, right?"

"I've been told that."

"I was watching a flight of birds recently," LeGrier said. "They were flying along in the familiar V-formation. I looked closer and saw that they seemed to drift into a vaguely wave-shaped formation. I wondered to myself: Could these birds be setting up the carrier wave, a very low frequency brain wave, by forming the tight V like an aerial, maintaining it by brain waves? Does our mystery material somehow tie together human brain waves? Wait! One more thing. These little pieces we've been looking at are picking up scads of White Stuff. Know what? I think the iron compound manufactures it."

"But how?" Roger asked.

"Hell if I know. Or why. I thought you might be interested in helping me think. Want to meet me? I have an idea."

Roger thought of Mary-Shane, of the kids, that he should be with them. "Sure," he said wearily, "why not?" Part of him longed desperately to be with her, to

295

charge in like a white knight and make everything better. The other part of him could hardly face her anymore. Still, he loved her, and the pain tore him up inside. He must think of his own children before anything else, and yet Kippy was such a loveable kid—

"Earth calling Roger, Earth calling Roger."

"Huh?"

"You still here, buddy?"

"I'm sorry. Got a lot on my mind."

Vernon LeGrier owned a VW bug and drove with a quick, sure hand. "I understand. Let's find some more of that dark metallic stuff and then we'll get you home."

"I'm game," Roger said.

"I think I know where to look."

"Okay," Roger said, his mind on things at home. He wanted to get Elisa and Rudy out of here. He was just putting off going home and asking Mary-Shane to move out.

"Under the theory that the White Stuff proliferates near this crumbly magnetic material," Vern said, "we have to find any more mountains of White Stuff. There is a mountain of White Stuff around the Pagoda, and we've found two objects inside, the statue Frank and Attila stole from the museum years ago, and the statuette the theologian brought with him. There was another piece stolen from the same museum, and Vic Lara thinks it's somewhere in San Tomas. There's a hill of White Stuff up the grade eastward." As he drove, he rambled: "Imagine, a comet comes in. Hits the atmosphere. Its core blows up. Chunks streak away as meteorites and explode further down..."

"No," Roger said, "number one, comets are not artificial. Number two, explosions would destroy your crumbly material."

"Right," Vern said. "Okay, let's revise it. A space ship comes in, crashes in the sea out there, and all this White Stuff comes up." He corrected himself. "The Air Force would have seen anything coming in, so this would have happened years ago. There are no Indian legends, so we can say ages ago..."

"Too much guesswork," Roger remonstrated.

"A spaceship," Vern said, "is coming to earth. Why? who knows. To collect seashells. It explodes. Parts rain down. A nut here, a bolt there, a melted circuit board..." He stopped and scratched his head. "That doesn't make sense somehow."

As Vern took the VW east on Canoga, White Stuff roiled on the streets. There were almost no cars out, except an occasional police car or ambulance headed to some small disaster. And lots of fire engines. "My God," Vern said as they started uphill on the outskirts of town, "look back there."

Roger looked back, and saw a city in flames. At least seven huge pillars of black smoke were rising from scattered locations. People were dropping in their kitchens, in their reading chairs, in their beds. They were dropping lit matches, smoldering pipes, burning cigarettes which in turn caused fires. "Looks kind of like the end of the world," Roger said.

For the next twenty minutes the car chugged up State 495. "Hey hey hey," Vern said, slowing abruptly. "What have we here?" He halted. A mountain of White Stuff reared up. A charred sign stuck out of the White Stuff, askew: "Harleigh Hale, Bookstore/B&W Arts." They got out in the chilly mountain air looking at this mountain of White Stuff that looked like a kid's theme park someone might have dreamed up. All it needed were garish signs and lights. But there were only the stars above.

The mountain of White Stuff was about thirty feet high and made a wavy, irregular cone maybe forty feet in diameter. Bushes, a pear tree, part of a picket fence, an old tire, newspapers, a black book with a gold embossed title ("Satan And You"), even the stiff legs of a dead jackrabbit stuck out. Roger tested the White Stuff with his foot. It felt vaguely spongy. He tried the pick. The axe went in and out easily, though the material was a little sticky. Within an hour they had cut their way straight through the mountain without encountering anything noteworthy. Their feet crunched on the debris of Harleigh Hale's former habitat, the abode of Winky, as Mary-Shane had related to Roger. They sat on a tree stump in the starlight next to the mountain and inhaled the night air.

"Gives you an appetite," Roger said. His cheeks burned pink. Vern went to his car and brought back a paper bag. "I forgot to eat today. My wife will kill me if she sees it, so let's do lunch."

"Mmm," Roger said. Two ham sandwiches, an apple, a kid box of chocolate chip cookies, a box of apple juice. It all went down well. Vern even let Roger have the apple. "Maybe this was a waste of time," Vern said afterwards, as they walked around their mountain.

"Wait a minute," Roger said. Something drew him. Something warm mysterious exciting. His midsection felt that youthful flush of anticipation. He felt his sex swelling as though he were an adolescent, aroused for no discernible reason. He laughed. Vern looked worried. "Roger. Roger? Roger!"

"Hang on," Roger said. He felt drunk. "What did you put in that apple juice anyway?"

"Come back here," Vern said.

Roger walked into the tunnel of White Stuff. This had to be some kind of kid's story, he thought, a play land. He looked at his hands and they had a faint glow. He got on his knees in the middle of the tunnel. Vern shouted something. Ignoring Vern, Roger leaned close and probed with his fingers. The dry stuff crumbled as his fingertips crushed it. Like snow without the wet or cold.

Already, in the tunnel, new crystalline stalactites were building up...

He crushed them, forcing his hands in, until he encountered something mushy. And hard. He worked frantically. His heart pounded, ready to jump up his neck. He had to had to had to had to...

What he pulled out was a crushed cage. He frowned. The wire came apart in his hands and he pulled it away from the base. A big cage. A big bird. Of course. Winky. He brushed White Stuff away with his elbow. Inside the cage were Winky's things. His glass drinking bowl. A plastic dish filled with a mixture of fat, mue, and birdseed. A rotten apple; at the zoo, Roger knew, Winky was very fond of apples. "Vern!" he called, lifting the flimsy paper bottom out. "Vern!"

Vern's feet thrashed in the White Stuff as he came running.

Roger felt his skull singing full of electric, no, magnetic, no, telepathic energy as he lifted the paper bottom away. There, under a replaceable bottom meant to keep the cage clean, was a black cylinder about a foot long and of the same diameter as a flashlight.

"Jesus," Vern said, reaching out.

Roger dropped the cage and raised the cylinder up. Foam rose from its sides. "It's the missing core from the statuette."

"Look at that," Vern was saying.

Roger felt his heart patter into his jaw. As he pitched forward face down, he thought oh no I'm dying and then his face flopped into a pillow of White Stuff.

Is this heaven or hell?

Roger was underwater.

Crazy.

No really.

He had no trouble breathing.

He couldn't see, but did not panic. Instead, he pushed through the wall of mue and there, there, why that was the pagoda in the zoo. Everything was dark. Bubbles rose in a few places. A light shone from the pagoda door. A tall, slender figure waited there. He ran toward her. It was Susan, very shapely in her black magician's tuxedo and top hat.

She opened her arms to him. Her eyes glittered as she spun in a ballerina dance of joy. Her face... He spun with her until his lap filled with seed. How cool she felt. How bright she looked. But it was she. It all came back to him; the tossed hair; the wink; the serious smile full of love.

Oh how I love you! he thought

"I love you too, darling. Come, I have wonderful things to share with you." She turned and walked into the light, into the pagoda, and he followed gladly.

Chapter 75.

Woofer and Tweeter barked and bounced against the door.

"Someone feed those fucking animals!" Mary-Shane yelled into the darkness as depression numbed her beyond pain.. Fuck them. Let the dogs die. She went upstairs and crawled into bed. She lay for a long time curled in a fetal position unable to think of anything but White Stuff whirling around her. She longed to take Kippy in her arms so they could die together, be free of the cancer and the White Stuff, free of everything that was tearing the world apart, go down into the sea and die together, but she was too tired. What did it matter anyway? Soon the world would be a hell of raging fires as the ship invoked its last line of defense; or what the sphinx thought was its next line of action after sitting on the ocean floor for nearly a century building the largest nuclear bomb in history. Mary-Shane didn't care. Her mind was on smaller tragedies, and they seemed more important to her. She was afraid to go see Kippy because perhaps he too had turned against her, even though he was dying, and if so, there was nothing left. Nothing.

Sometime during the night, the phone rang. Blindly she reached out, grappled it off its hook, across the sheets without moving anything more than her arm, and to her ear. "Miss MacLemore?" It was Vernon LeGrier and he sounded dismal.

"Yes," she said dully.

"I'm afraid I have really bad news for you. I was with Roger and I guess it's my fault. I got him to go with me to look for some... clues... I'm afraid he fell into that same coma right before my eyes. I'm at the hospital with him now. I'm waiting for the doctor and..." She let the phone slide away. It retracted on its spiral cord and fell on the floor. LeGrier's voice sounded like that of a person in one of those movies where people shrink to flea size: "Hello?... Hello?" Then the line cut off, replaced by a loud beeping. She shoved a pillow over the edge and it landed on the phone and she could barely hear its bleating noises anymore.

A crash woke her. She sat up. Where was Roger? Then she remembered that he was dead. Or in a coma and lost forever anyway.

Someone screamed—a familiar voice—Kippy?

She staggered out of bed, adjusting her nightgown strap with one hand and sipping from a glass of stale water with the other. Down the stairs and to that awful hallway.

She saw the rays of light pouring ragged and anemic, like a wound bled white, before she even rounded the corner, and she knew that dreadful door was open again.

"Kippy!" she screamed.

All three children lay lifeless on the floor. Rudy lay with mouth open, hand on chest. Dead? Elisa lay sprawled in her nightgown with White Stuff fluffing on her.

Kippy lay on his side and his shriveled legs looked stick-like. "My baby!" she screamed and fell on her knees. Crawled toward him. And as she did so, darkness enveloped her. She choked, falling face down, sinking into... death? or the dreaded coma?

She pushed herself up on hands and elbows. Her own face lay dead between her hands. Her eyes were closed and her face was expressionless—not a peacefulness, but a blankness. She rose up and looked down at her body. It's this coma, she thought. Oh God it got us all! She saw, past their sprawled forms, the shades of three children walking away through the forbidden room. No time to try and figure this out—some form of spirit walking or astral projection? She was dimly aware of the *Cold Thing*, watching her.

"Kippy! Elisa! Rudy!" she cried. But the children did not hear her. Or did not want to. Kippy was wrapped in a sheet sitting in a wheelchair. His face looked pale and exhausted, his body shriveled. He leaned like an old man (Mr. Vecci) slumped over one arm rail, face to one side, and Mary-Shane thought he might fall out. Elisa pushed the wheelchair into a sweltering light. Rudy clung to Elisa's nightgown. All three children looked mesmerized.

"I blocked that up!" she screamed. But the forbidden door stood wide open, and a fan of light emanated. She felt a cold breeze and smelled a tang of the sea— faintly briny, fishy.

"No!" she screamed and chased after Elisa. It was a long, long path. Impossibly long for this house. She kept running—nobody would take her Kippy away, nobody!

Elisa's hair fluffed lightly in the wind. Mary-Shane's feet splashed in water and she looked down, surprised. The floor had turned to beach sand. Chilly water lined with threads of foam washed in. The tide was turning. Salt water stung a cut on her foot—this was not just a dream! The kids were already far away. Mary-Shane fell down. Cold water soaked her gown and iced her thighs. "Kippy," she cried from the bottom of her soul, "I don't want you to go!" Sobbing, she staggered to her feet and walked further into the sea. The kids had not looked back. "Take me with you!" she yelled, but the wind snatched her words away.

She was walking through the basilica, only the floor was sea water. Like a sinking ship, the basilica was tilted forward. Saints with quizzical faces held out things to her: A key, a lily, a book, a candle, a coin, a baby... Their faces glowed and their haloes seemed like space helmets. No human had ever been so buttercup yellow... Mary-Shane slogged on toward the altar, just as the ground moved, and now she was underwater...

It was night. The world was underwater. There! The kids were visible. Kippy looked shriveled in his wrapping sheet. Rudy helped push the wheelchair. Elisa's eyes glittered for an instant; had she looked back?

They were... where? The zoo. They were in the zoo, moving toward... The pagoda. Where J.W. Washington had interrupted her *Dark Feeling. Whisk whisk, snap snap,* she remembered. Gone. Dead. The pagoda portal was open. Rudy and Elisa, dripping wet (weren't they cold?) pushed the wheelchair inside. "Wait! Please wait! I'll go with you! Don't go in there alone!"

But they did not look back. Elisa's back was the last thing she saw of them before the light swallowed them. As she fled toward the pagoda, Mary-Shane saw the sun-decoration smiling. The mossy round concrete-relief happy-face of a smiling sun that had floated toward her mind before J.W.'s interruption. Now, it detached from the wall and floated to meet her. *WELCOME,* it thought to her. The little rays wiggled like octopus arms.

She ignored it and ran toward the door. The sunlet flew at her and disappeared into her. She stumbled over the step and entered the blinding light.

The machinery in the pagoda thumped on and on and she heard the *Cold Thing* again, the same voice that had tried to lure her into her pool, into the sea, to her death, into Gilbert's arms: *COME, THIS IS THE WAY...*

Wiz stepped up to meet her. "Hello, Mary-Shane." Wiz looked light blue and was bright. They were somewhere in the sea, deep down. It reminded Mary-Shane of promotional movies she'd seen about tropical diving and fishing places that had exotic names and impossibly blue water. Colorful shiny fish moving in precise unison waved first one way, then another like a flag fluttering in wind. Reefs were dimly visible in the faint light.

Mary-Shane saw an airplane on the sandy sea bed. Its windows were dark; no, one light glowed by one of the passenger seats. She could guess who was sitting there, bringing her chocolate or a toy from some sales convention.

Looking farther, she also saw a structure here underwater. As in a huge hangar, girders floated up to unguessable heights. Crossbeams extended out of eyesight. Long corridors, endless dotted ceiling lights, stretched in all directions until they curved out of sight. Lights everywhere shed small cotton balls of light. The airplane she'd seen in dreams—it was there, crusted in algae, and dimly glowing inside. The airplane actually sat on a swelling bulge, she now saw, and she was pretty sure that swelling bulge was the nuclear detonator that sat on some underwater vent capable of uncorking the hellish energies of the earth's molten outer core. Here and there on the ocean floor were tiny little volcanoes, like African ant hills, and syrupy licorice smoke poured from these vents.

There were figures all around. Standing on the girders. Walking in the hallways. Floating in midair or was it midwater?

Wiz reached out her hand and Mary-Shane felt its coolness. Wiz's face was bright was though there were a sky-blue light in her skull. "You weren't supposed to come."

"Kippy!" Mary-Shane cried. "My little baby. He's in here somewhere."

"You have a lot to learn about the ship," Wiz said.

Mary-Shane ran forward. "Where is my Kippy?" She saw him then. He was still in the wheelchair. Slumped and lifeless. A door of light had opened before him. "Kippy!" she cried, and the water did not distort her voice. It sounded as though she were in a dry hallway. Rudy and Elisa stood back. Four male shapes stepped out of the door. Churning fire threw blankets of light. The four men took the wheelchair. Kippy looked like a husk about to be thrown on a hay fire.

Mary-Shane ran forward. "No!" Wiz cried out behind her. She ran anyway. The men : Harleigh Hale, Charlie Best (battered skull repaired), and two... she did not have time to recognize them before the door closed and men and wheelchair were gone. Mary-Shane ran up and threw herself against the door. But there was no door. It was a solid wall. "Where did they take him?" she cried but Rudy and Elisa were walking away.

"Come back here!" she screamed running after them. She reached for Elisa, but her hands could not make solid contact. Wiz had a concerned face: "In here, we do what the Captain says."

Mary-Shane sniffled. "Cap- Captain Colorado?"

Wiz nodded. She told Mary-Shane: "You must conform or a bad thing will happen to you." Mary-Shane shook Wiz's shoulder and it felt like a slab of bacon from the fridge. "Wiz, you never used to talk like that."

Wiz said: "This is the ship."

"Where are we?" Mary-Shane demanded.

"This ship is from far away in the universe. Full of life forms to colonize the earth. Don't anger Captain Colorado."

Mary-Shane felt dizzy. "Why are we underwater? Why are fish swimming around in here?" A twinge of amusement shifted Wiz's lips and cheeks for the first time into a sardonic parody of humor. "Fish? Water? You Warm Dulls are all imagining things."

"Warm Dulls? What are you talking about?"

"There are three kinds of captives on this ship. First, there are the animals that are locked up and we don't get to see them. Then there are the two types of captives from earth: The Warm Dulls, like you, who don't learn much, and the Cold Brights, like me, who serve the ship. Look around." Mary-Shane did, and saw that some of the figures standing around were lit with a bright light, like blue-white computer screen glow, and others were rather dull looking like (she looked at her hands) herself. She turned to Wiz, panic gripping her heart: "Wiz, they aren't going to make Kippy a Cold Bright, are they?" She had this intuition: That

Warm Dulls were the coma people, who had bodies to go back to, and the Cold Brights were the souls of the dead, trapped in this purgatory.

Wiz's expression was veiled. Mary-Shane reached out frantically. "When will we know?" But hands grasped her from behind.

"You have other things to do," Wiz said. Mary-Shane recoiled in revulsion as Cold Bright hands and bodies propelled her toward a door. It felt repulsively like being touched by floating refrigerated pickles, and she screamed.

Somehow, in this crazy half invisible structure, they were going up a ramp. A round oven door beckoned at the end of the ramp. Reddish-yellow fire flicked out. The tongues of sun-thrown flame melted in the water and floated upward. "No!" she screamed but they threw her in.

Elmer's Family Diner. Mary-Shane Lull, in shiny black shoes, white socks, and frilly pink dress, skipped among the legs of grownups and joined her parents at the eating booth. She crawled up into the booth next to Daddy, who sat opposite Mommy. Daddy, big and jolly, was always laughing. His eyes were warm and dark. Mommy was always a little sharp and jealous when Mary-Shane showed preference for Daddy. Auntie Lisbet once told Mommy it was only because Daddy was away on sales trips so much, not to make a big deal about it, but Mommy's eyes looked hurt and resentful anyway.

"Did everything come out all right?" Daddy could be so gross, but always so funny and so loving. She stood up in the booth and hugged him, smelling his aftershave and his scalp through thinning black hair. "I love you," she whispered.

"Mary-Shane," Mommy said, "sit down, you'll make the seat dirty with your shoes." Daddy hugged her and said "Aw never mind, her little feet won't do any harm. You're Daddy's little girl, aren't you?"

"Yes," she said, resting her cheek against his neck. Her arms were scissored over his shoulders. "Daddy..."

"What, little princess?"

"Promise you will never leave me."

"Me? Leave you?"

"I don't want you to go."

Mommy looked concerned. "What is she babbling about?"

"Doris, don't be so hard. She's just a little girl." Daddy cooed at her. "Daddy will never leave you, sweetheart."

Mommy seethed. "You're away for weeks at a time. I clean her and dress her and everything, and you come home for a weekend and spoil her rotten."

"Aw Doris..."

Mary-Shane burst out in tears. "You're not just here for the weekend, are you? You're going to stay now, aren't you?"

His lips went tut tut. "Well, darling, you know I have to go out and work hard. Tell you what. Next year I'll be manager. Then I can work from home; I'll never have to go away again."

"That would be wonderful," Mommy said showing a flood of relief and joy. "Yes!" Mary-Shane cried happily. "But can't you just stay with us from right now on?" He tapped a deck of cards on the table. His hands were thick and pink. "Just one or two more trips, Mary-Shane darling. I'll tell you what. Before I go, we'll plant a nice garden together and whenever you think of us together, you go out and water it, okay?"

"That would be really neat," Mary-Shane said.

Suddenly she was alone in the dark house. Mother was sobbing somewhere, awful sounds like wood being ripped, one cut at a time, with a saw. Auntie Lisbet floated close: "Mary-Shane, I'm afraid something terrible has happened. Your daddy won't be coming home today. You see, his plane fell in the ocean and he is now an angel in heaven."

"No!"

"...But he will be watching out for you all the time, every day of your life..."

"No!"

"...And one day, when you go to heaven, you will be together again with him..."

"No!"

"Honey," Daddy said back in the diner, "you have such a sad little face." He reached over, picked up a tear from her cheek, and put it on the tip of his tongue. "Mmm," he said, "could use a little bit more salt."

"Wayne, stop it," Mother said.

The waitress put platters of hamburgers (still sizzling) down on the white and blue checked cloth; fries, a big basket full, and a bottle of ketchup; and a green and white bill with pencil scrawls, that right away began soaking up grease. A fly circled around and landed by the edge of a ketchup blob that was still red in the middle but had dried up and hardened to a dark brownish color around the edges, and around that was a larger wet-stain just faintly red. She studied this little cameo as if she were a scientist and it were a complex interaction between life and death, between the moon and the tides, at the very core of the universe. "Honey," Daddy interrupted her, "I love you more than anyone has ever loved anyone."

"Oh good, Daddy." She turned away from the ketchup; she wiped her face and clung to him.

"Mary-Shane, let Daddy eat."

"Do you really, Daddy?"

"Yes, I do. Sweetheart, not a minute goes by, in some sales meeting in Chicago or Denver or someplace, when I'm sitting in a room full of strangers, that I don't think of having you and Mommy next to me like we are all right now."

"Will you take me with you when you go, Daddy?"

He laughed. "Sweetheart, you will go when your plane comes. My plane leaves tonight, but I promise I'll wait for you."

"Oh, Daddy." She glowed inside.

He said: "We will be together forever."

"And Kippy too?" she asked.

"Who?" Mommy said.

"Kippy," Daddy said, "her son. Just wait and see, Doris. Kippy will be a fine boy."

"I guess you're right," Mother said stirring her coffee with a worn look. "One more child to look after. One more child."

Wayne grasped Doris's wrist. "Darling, I love you so much. I'm sorry I didn't quite make it. The damn plane got something caught in its fuel intake and dropped like a lead balloon."

"I understand, Wayne. We understand, don't we, Mary-Shane?"

They all linked hands. "Yes," Mary-Shane said. "We understand."

"Good," Daddy said, standing up. He lifted Mary-Shane out of his way and put her on the seat. "I gotta go now." He did a little jig, pulling his baggy trousers up. He searched in his pockets until his eyebrows rose brightly and then he put a five dollar bill on the table. He kissed Doris.

"Daddy," Mary-Shane cried out. Daddy hugged her against his big warm chest. "Darling, this is how it will be, forever and ever, once you get off your plane. Until then, I don't want you to cry and I don't want you to miss me and I don't want you to give Mommy a hard time, because soon we'll be together again."

Mary-Shane cried and cried and cried until there were no more tears. Daddy held her the whole time. Then he dabbed her cheeks with a napkin. She began to feel a warm glow inside. Daddy unbuttoned her shirt one button. He reached inside with two fingers that barely fit. For a second, there was a twinge, almost but not quite a pain, as though he had tweezed something off the edge of her heart. Then she felt wonderful. "There!" Daddy said. Dazed at how good she felt, she looked down and saw a little white pebble the size of a pin head between Daddy's fingers. "There," he said, "you had quite a stone on your heart." Then he was gone (Cold Bright). The waitress towered beside the table, apron and notepad against checks. "Is everything all right?"

Mary-Shane beamed up at her. "Ooohhh yes."

Like a cork shot from the champagne bottle, like a leaf swirling in a river, like a bubble released underwater, Mary-Shane floated upward through the magnificent interior of the ship. She felt light and airy and wonderful. She floated to a long dark corridor. Wiz reached out her hand. "Hello, Mary-Shane." Wiz was a Cold

Bright, and Mary-Shane knew there was no way back for her. "I will take you to the heart of the ship," Wiz said.

They walked down a long corridor that twisted occasionally. It was like walking in a museum. On the left and right, spaced ten or more feet apart, were dioramas: Mabel Stork and Moonboy looked up from a moonlight dinner of canned sardines and dry bread near the basilica. Harleigh Hale and Charlie Best paused in the act of dusting books. Harleigh stood on a small ladder. Charlie was polishing some boxes. Harleigh waved. "Promise me one thing," he hollered. "Take good care of Winky for me, okay?"

Drums pounded and whistles shrilled as witch doctors with white paint on dark skin danced around while the famous man with the white smile raised his index and fore fingers in apostolic blessing. (Wiz nudged her. "That's Lome, Togo, 1984).

Another diorama appeared: On a truck, in a bleak snowy forest in the mountains, lay a black slab of stone hazily representing an African devil god of some sort. Mary-Shane gasped: Frank sat right next to her, alive, driving; the body of Charlie Best might still be warm on the state highway behind them.

More dioramas flashed by. They were walking rapidly into the past. Touareg, Blue People, rode by on camels along the caravan route from the Atlas Mountains in Morocco, through the edge of the Sahel, to Timbuktoo on the plains of Mali, and on to the Sudanese Nile. A Portuguese ship sailed by in search of a better spice route to India. Africa languished in its long sleep. Roman soldiers marched by, escorting a caravan of wild animals for the arena. Egyptian priests paraded slowly into the temple of this god in stone, bringing incense and sacrifices.

Faster and faster the dioramas flew by, blurry and unintelligible. Each was the captured essence of a truth or a moment in time where a piece of the ship's brain had been.

"How could a ship have a brain?" Mary-Shane asked.

"You might call it a computer," Wiz said.

Mary-Shane felt blithe; couldn't remember why she'd come to this sunken ship.

"We are lying comatose somewhere, that's how I figure it," Wiz said. "We Cold Brights are the smartest here, and we're very proud of it."

"Do you see any fish, Wizzie?"

Wiz laughed. "Fish? No. Why?"

"Just wondering. Never mind." Poor thing; didn't seem to know she was dead. They came to a door and the dioramas stopped fleeting past. The last diorama was of dinosaurs fighting. They had to walk through it some thirty feet to a door marked in strange red letters (a stencil from another galaxy?). Inside the diorama was a rank smell. "Don't be afraid," Wiz said. "Nothing here can hurt us. It's the ship's way of telling you its story. I have been here many times."

It was night in a primitive jungle with huge ferns and tall trees with tiny crowns. Something plashed in a pond on her right; snorted; and she jumped. Ahead, in the brilliant starlight and moonlight, an armored tank moved in camouflage; no not a tank but a lizard splashed with orange, black, and white polygons, with a mask-face and terrible teeth.

"Were dinosaurs brought by the ship?" Mary-Shane asked.

Wiz shook her head. "This ship carries totally alien life. A whole spectrum from crawlers and swimmers through runners and fliers. They all have either three of everything (eyes, ears, arms, and so on) or five. Just as we have two of everything and the animals have four."

"Spiders have eight."

Wiz shrugged. "Yes, but the point is it's 99% an even number. Always. With this kind, it's always an odd number."

Before Mary-Shane had time to reflect how unearthly such a thing must be, the door slid open and they entered.

"This is the command room," Wiz said. "This is where they run the ship." She ushered Mary-Shane (fish swimming around unnoticed by any but Mary-Shane) into a crowded kidney shaped cabin. The walls bulged with shapes she took to be control equipment.

WELCOME, thought a face in the wall. It was an old, tortured, but quite human looking face with a mouth, a nose, and otherwise your basic two of everything.

"Captain Colorado," Mary-Shane guessed.

The face laughed uncomfortably. It appeared to be pressed into too small an area, and had limited wiggling and twitching room. "Bright young lady. Too bad you're not wanted here."

"Why am I not wanted?"

Captain Colorado rolled his eyes up as though she were dumb. "You're blest, silly girl."

"Who are you really?"

He gave her a hurt look. His eyes glittered near tears. "I'm Wallace Burtongale the First, Lady. Couldn't you guess?"

She shook her head. "Not at first. But now I see the resemblance."

"We're all finished, aren't we?"

Before Mary-Shane could answer, another spot nearby blurred, and Miss Polly's face appeared. "Hush now, old grandpa ancestor. We will soon be free."

"You must be one of my descendants," the 19th Century Burtongale said to Miss Polly. "Yes, I recognize your mind. We have touched before, although you would not have understood."

"It's okay," Miss Polly told Mary-Shane, "don't you worry about a thing, my dear. Say hello to Martina and Jules and Roger and of course to my darlings Janine and Margery and Patricia. These Cold Brights keep saying they're getting out of here, but frankly I think we're in for a hell of a long ride."

"That's right," Wallace said. "We are going back to the stars. This is not a place for us to disgorge our cargo."

STOP THAT, another voice thought.

As Mary-Shane watched, the wriggling sun detached itself from a far wall where it had been hidden. It was the same sun she'd seen in the wall at the Pagoda, but it was not smiling now as it flew close to Wallace, stopped in mid air, and hissed at him.

Miss Polly's frightened face winked out of existence. Mary-Shane wondered if the Burtongales were to be trapped in that nightmare wall forever.

But Wallace laughed. "You can't hurt me, sun. We've been cooped up in here for over a hundred years, and you don't scare me anymore." As if to reinforce Wallace, five other Wallace faces opened up in the wall. Mary-Shane recognized the Wallace she'd personally met. And even Gilbert was there! They all barked and yelled in a melee at the sun. "Sons!" Wallace the First yelled. "Go away. I'll handle this." The other faces disappeared, leaving the wall blank except for the Wallace I cameo.

A voice Mary-Shane had not yet heard, but which she somehow recognized, burbled up: "You must not say things that are negative." A hoary looking old eel-head slithered its long mottled neck out from underneath the machinery, and Mary-Shane could not tell if it was of the ship or of the sea, but she felt a chill of fright because it was the *Cold Thing* that had nearly lured her to her death in the pool and later in the waves. At last, it was no longer in her head. The eel seemed near hysteria. Shocked, she stared at the *Cold Thing*. "We cannot seem to repair the ship, no matter how we try. You must not make jokes, Wallace."

A third voice spoke up, and Mary-Shane recognized it for the distortion that it was: "Waak, you oughta give it a rest, Wallace, you gotta big mouth, ya hear?" It was an underwater Winky, complete with colorful feathers and beak. But this was not the real Winky; this guy had two intact wings.

Flashes of insight, of understanding, began to come over Mary-Shane. She felt the ship trying to help her comprehend its world. The ship was trying to put itself together. What ship? she thought—why, of course the ship that had been damaged by an impact with a stray asteroid one hundred million years ago. Pieces of the core brain had ended up various places, trying to reach each other in vain, and had extended feelers to nearby objects, especially living things. The sphinx dumped into the sea, containing the largest core segment, had combined the aspects of an underwater eel, a sunken ship, and a downed airplane. The chunk in the water under the Pagoda had adopted the sunlet, which happened to be an ornament on the outer wall of the 19th Century structure in the zoo. There must have been a chunk in Winky's cage, hidden there by Charlie Best, and for which Attila and Frank had killed Charlie at Gilbert's bidding—yes! So much of the picture was coming together now for her, for the ship, for the entire world which had almost evolved in an entirely different direction.

"Teresa Wiz Kcickiwicz," Wallace I said, "come close. You too, Mary-Shane Lull-MacLemore."

The sunlet and the eel hovered watchfully. The parrot cocked his head.

Wallace I said: "Tell me if my guess is correct. The ship is unrepairable."

Stop it stop it stop it... the eel, the sunlet, and the parrot shrilled mentally.

Mary-Shane said: "I think you're right, Wallace. What do you think, Wiz?"

Wiz shook her head slowly.

The apparitions looked at Mary-Shane expectantly. Wallace waited brightly for her to support his theory. The sunlet smiled warmly, hoping Mary-Shane would refute Wallace. "If you want my opinion," Mary-Shane said, feeling like Alice in Wonderland, "there is no ship."

BABBLEBABBLEBABBLEBABBLE said all the faces in the wall, appearing simultaneously and trying to knock each other aside.

SILENCE, said the eel, and it was clear he was in charge here. Not a sound as he extended his bloated blue-gray body mottled with splotchy growths. It was, Mary-Shane thought, like watching a fire hose unwind underwater.

A flight of golden guppies or something flashed past. All the guppies turned at once like a sail being tacked and darted away through the walls. Nobody but Mary-Shane seemed to notice.

The eel spoke: "I cannot seem to get the ship repaired. I cannot seem to feel any of the cargo in their storage bays. Is there a chance the ship was destroyed on impact with the atmosphere? If so, the crew would be very sad. On the other hand then perhaps that explains why we have been unable to reach the crew all this long time. They could all be dead as well."

"Who and what exactly are you?" Mary-Shane asked.

Wiz nudged her sharply, but the eel answered: "We are the brain of the ship, Mary-Shane Lull-MacLemore. We are the program that feeds the animals, guides the ship, disciplines the cargo, kills intruders, yes, kills some of the animals if need be to show the others, but we can heal them as well."

"You can?" she asked, not quite remembering why this was important.

"Yes. Do you hurt?" the eel asked.

"No," she said.

"Her son does," Wiz interjected.

"Oh?" the eel asked. "We have not killed him, have we?"

"I don't know," Wiz said. "Not up to the time he entered the ship, at least you hadn't."

"Then you must go quickly and find him," the eel said. "Go, Mary-Shane Lull-MacLemore, you are not wanted here. You are blest and must return to your pen."

"My pen?" Mary-Shane laughed and raised both hands to her mouth. She pictured a cow mooing in its barn, and laughed.

"Hurry," Wiz said taking her arm. "You must obey."

"Meanwhile," the eel said, "we will make a last desperate attempt to contact the crew who are our masters. They created us and only they can decide whether there is a ship or not."

"There is no ship," Mary-Shane said. "You must understand that. You must stop all this. You must return all these people to their bodies and leave us alone."

There was no answer. The sea quaked lightly. Bubbles rose. Fishes darted for cover. Mary-Shane looked back briefly before the door slammed shut. The eel, the sunlet, the parrot, and several Wallaces were watching her leave.

As she left the control room, Mary-Shane heard another voice. It was the *Cold Thing*, which was another metaphor or avatar for the Pilot. It said to someone she could not see: "There is the other thing we can do. The last communication we had from the outer ship was that a space object was about to strike us. Maybe it has not struck yet. Maybe we can set off the final line of defenses. I will make that decision now."

Two dinosaurs tangled in their diorama. Mary-Shane and Wiz ran. The dioramas flashed by quicker and quicker. Then slowed as Wiz and Mary-Shane returned to their starting point in mid-ship. "Here is where I leave you," Wiz said.

Mary-Shane said, knowing it was hopeless: "Wizzie, don't go."

"We all have to go," Wiz said. "Don't worry. This will be over soon. Then we will go back to our bodies and I'll buy you lunch at Vogelmann's like I promised." Seeing her look, Wiz made a brave grin and said: "Don't worry, I saw what is in your mind, but I don't believe it."

Mary-Shane watched helplessly as Wiz receded and grew smaller, still with that gap-toothed smile, and disappeared into a micron. Or into nothing? As she looked about, Cold Brights were popping out of existence like bulbs going out. Warm Dulls milled about babbling, holding each other. They reminded Mary-Shane of pictures she'd seen of medieval mental patients.

"Mary-Shane!"

She turned and who was it but Father Lawrence. "Oh Lord am I glad to see you," she said leaned into his embrace. But the skin under his clothing felt hard and cold like refrigerated meat, and she screamed. He was Cold Bright. He said: "Hurry! We must save the world!"

"What do you mean, Father?"

"This avatar of the Pilot—if it feels the ship is threatened, it has the power to create a nuclear explosion that would put the Earth into a deep winter for a thousand years and kill all life on it. The technology was originally intended to help their ships defend themselves against stray space objects. We've got to reason with the Pilot. Destroying the Burtongales and half of San Tomas is nothing compared to what it can do now that so much of it is back together."

She ran alongside him as he walked in long strides, surprising for an old man. Then again, he was Cold Bright. "How are you feeling, Father?" she asked carefully.

"Mary-Shane, little dear," he said. He still wore the black suit and stola in which he had died near the Basilica that night; and carried his breviary. "I know I will not be going back. Poor Wiz, she can't accept it. Can't blame her, you know, so young and full of life. But I'm old and I've been waiting for God to take me for a long time. I can't wait to be reunited with Our Savior."

"Then there is a God?" she marveled.

"Oh yes. He is in here." Father Lawrence pointed to his heart.

"And Satan?" she asked.

He smiled. Pointed to his temple. "That's all up here." He motioned with his breviary. "Come, we have a lot to do."

She followed him along a wide corridor. Dull Warms waited on either side. It seemed people here were largely frozen in place unless interaction was needed. "You will be very happy," Father Lawrence said striding ahead.

In a great hall under hushed lights (a travel terminal? lots of people hurrying; lots of voices bubbling under the high roof) four men and a boy stepped out of the crowd. "Kippy!" she cried suddenly remembering.

He grinned and stretched his arms out.

"My Kippy!" She ran toward him.

"Mom!" his child voice piped, just this side of adolescent crackle. He was Dull Warm, and they embraced. Now she recognized the other two men, who had come with Harleigh Hale and Charlie (head intact) Best: Frank MacLemore, and Harold G. "Attila" Wilkins. All four men were Cold Bright. Frank still had that tough flavor, but he was Cold Bright and subdued. "Hello, Mary-Shane. I guess maybe you're surprised."

"No, Frank, not anymore."

He gestured. "This is my boy, huh?"

She nodded.

"He's a fine boy. We hugged each other..."

"...Yeah, we did," Kippy agreed.

"...And I told him I was a damn fool to miss out on him. But one day we'll all be together." He took a deep breath and sighed. "Can't tell you how many times I've said to Mr. Best here how sorry I am about what happened."

Charlie Best brightly waved a cold hand. "Aw hang it up, Frank. You're a good poker partner now that we're all together."

"Yeah," Frank said. "We'll wait till dawn comes and blows the cigar smoke away." His eyes met Mary-Shane's and she knew; Frank knew that he wasn't going anywhere but away once the party was over. "It gets boring after a while," he told her softly. "Take care."

"Dad," Kippy breathed anxiously.

Frank took his hand. "You hear me now, boy. You be good and do your homework and stay out of trouble, unlike your old dad here. I love you very much and do you know what?"

Kippy sadly shook his head.

Frank raised his hand and in its palm appeared a shiny chrome bicycle, six inches high, but modeled in perfect detail. "See this here bike? When you come back to see me, this here bike's gonna be waiting for you, life-sized. Hear?"

Kippy's eyes lit up.

"You got lots to do, boy, so you run along with your Momma. Say thanks to these fine gentlemen here for fixing your legs."

Kippy waved over his shoulder: "Thanks."

Charlie Best, Harleigh Hale, and Attila smiled and waved. Frank blew a kiss, something Mary-Shane had only see him do when he was drunk.

The ground shook again. "Hurry," Father Lawrence said.

Kippy ran on ahead. Mary-Shane yelled: "He wasn't kidding. You can really run. Oh Kippy we're going to have so much fun!"

"Yeah," he yelled, "I'm going get a bike. I'm going to play basketball and football and volleyball. I'm going to race Rudy and win. I'm going to do handstands and somersaults. I'm going to bounce around on the bed until... whooppeee!"

The ground quaked.

"Hurry," Father Lawrence said. He wasn't a bit out of breath. His legs were long and his stride tired Mary-Shane.

"Can't we slow down?" she asked.

"No time. More things to do."

The room might have been a cocktail lounge in a fancy hotel. Maybe even in the corner of a ballroom. But nobody stood behind the amber bar; nobody to pull down a tinkling glass, slap in some ice, and pour a crackling ounce of Grand Marnier. And the furniture was all draped with heavy robes the color of fresh red lipstick. Romantic music throbbed like thick cream. The lights were dim and reddish, a sweet pinkish red like watermelon or depression glass, not a violent red like Crank's. Mary-Shane burst in, not knowing...

...That Roger was dancing with someone. At first, Mary-Shane saw only Roger's broad back, clad in a tuxedo. Then Mary-Shane saw the Other Woman. She was dressed up as a magician, in a kind of feminized tuxedo with bulges in the starched shirt front, where breasts must be; a delicate waist; and a fullness in the trouser legs where a woman's hips and thighs would be. She wore a black top hat. Her blonde hair ruffled in the underwater current.

Mary-Shane stopped. Her heart was pounding in her neck.

The Other Woman had her arms around Roger's back (her hands were blue) and she and Roger had their eyes closed. The music swelled around them, and they clung to each other in a promise of foreverness. Then the Other Woman looked over Roger's shoulder. Mary-Shane recognized a Cold Bright.

Roger clung to her, but Susan pulled away.

Mary-Shane stood frozen.

Susan tap-danced over, waving her black wand. She threw the wand up (*drum roll*) and it exploded in falling kerchiefs (*applause*). She removed her top hat. (another drum roll) She waggled her fingers, and white birds flew out. (*applause*) The birds flew away melting into the ceiling. Susan threw the hat away melting into the wall.

Susan took Mary-Shane in her arms and propelled her into a dance. Susan was surprisingly strong. Mary-Shane stumbled, but Susan held her upright. Her grip was firm but gentle. Around and around they twirled. Mary-Shane grew dreamy and put her cheek on Susan's shoulder, not minding the cold. Susan pressed her abdomen against Mary-Shane's. Their venues mounds collided, and Mary-Shane felt a gob of drool on her lower lip, as if she were heavily drugged.

The dance slowed.

Susan had Mary-Shane bent over backwards. Susan leaned forward as if to kiss her. Mary-Shane felt warm inside and watched Susan's mouth draw near. Susan's bright blue mouth opened and Mary-Shane dreamily thought she was going to kiss her. Susan's lips distended and for a moment as her cheeks grew round, Mary-Shane thought Susan was going to throw up. Instead, an alabaster size triple-A egg popped from Susan's mouth. (*applause*) Susan reached up with one hand and grasped the egg. (*drum roll*) She jammed the egg between Mary-Shane's legs, pushing it way up into her. For a minute she did something there, then pulled away (*applause*). Mary-Shane gasped, bending over double. She felt numb and had this ache in her gut where the egg had been thrust.

Susan twirled away on tap-dancing feet, around Roger, who tried to catch her, then away toward the wall. Her last act was this: She stopped in mid-twirl and motioned for Roger to go over to Mary-Shane. (*flourishes—ta-daaa!—applause*) Roger clapped politely. Susan curtseyed, then vanished through the wall.

The music caught a new beat. Roger cried out: "Mary-Shane! My God, I thought you were losing your mind." He clattered across the hard shiny dance floor.

Mary-Shane looked down at herself. She had somehow become dressed in a white wedding gown that reached to the tips of her white calfskin pumps. She also wore elbow length white gloves; she saw as she smoothed the gown over her flat belly and appealing figure. Her boobs gleamed up at her like two vanilla ice-cream scoops, caramel nipples barely peeking, and she giggled.

"Hey," he said, impressed, "come on, let's cha cha." He took her in his arms.

The cold went away. At opportune moments during the cha-cha, she clung to him for warmth. Not, after all, a Cold Bright; whew! "Dance me around, Roger

Dodger!" The old sauce was back. Peals of laughter rained from her mouth. They did the Monster Mash, making faces at one another and dangling their arms.

Then, the music changed; a spicy, dark tango heavily laden with sexual innuendo: *RRUmmm, RRumm,* they went, back and forth. *RRUmmm, RRumm* They marched along. *RRUmmm, RRumm...* He stopped, and she twirled in his arms, landing with her face looking up into his. *RRUmmm, RRumm...*

Then they marched the other way. They stopped, slammed together, stared faces-together at the far wall. *RRUmm, RRUmm...*

"Were you going to leave me?" she asked.

"Yes," he said.

"Everything is going to be better now," she said.

"Yes," he said. "I was a fool. Will you still marry me?"

"Yes." They kissed, and Mary-Shane felt woozy from the tips of her toes to the outside diameters of her curls.

"Hurry!" Father Lawrence said from the doorway. Rudy and Elisa peered around the door. "Hey Mom," Kippy yelled, "quit mugging with old Roger and get your ass in gear. This place is gonna blow!"

"That's mostly in movies," Father Lawrence said without much sternness in his voice. Mary-Shane and Roger linked hands and ran after Father Lawrence. She noticed that now, her wedding gown was gone and she wore a sweater, jeans, and loafers. Kippy joined his hand with Mary-Shane's and ran quite well, as though he'd been doing it for months.

BEFORE YOU GO... thought the eel.

The 'ground' sank beneath them, almost toppling Father Lawrence, who had to do a quick jig to stay upright. As if on an elevator, they sank through layer after layer of girders and lights and staring faces.

...Sank down to the true ocean floor. This was a mulmy plain broken here and there by a protruding rock. Here and there, a black vent steamed. Deep sea bottom scavengers patrolled like slow planes. A ray suddenly flapped, sending up dust. Then the ground (ship ground, not sea ground) they were standing on began to move magic-carpet fashion. It slid silently over rocks and over dropped objects (a bottle, a can, a boot, a fishing pole, a seat, a toilet ring, a child's shoe, a sunken rowboat, a bone...)...

Oh, now look at that, Mary-Shane thought. A sunken wooden boat. Crusted with algae and growth. A haven for schools of silver fish like pen knives. This thing, whatever it was, must love living things; must suck them out of the sea, off the land, bring them close to itself.

NO, a voice thought, *NOT QUITE.*

Ahead, as the magic carpet slowed, were lights. Real lights, poking down through the iceberg remnants of White Stuff. A submersible, U-Pho, shaped like a hot dog pinned in a hamburger bun, strung with lights, hung at an angle. The Navy was getting close.

Sitting on the ocean bottom not far from the plane was an object so encrusted that it was hard to make out, but Mary-Shane vaguely recognized a cat face and she suspected it was the sphinx Wallace I had dumped here over 100 years ago. U-Pho's light cone was directed on the sphinx's crusty form.

"Go on, quickly," Father Lawrence urged. "We will wait for you." He put his arms over Kippy, Rudy, and Elisa's shoulders.

Mary-Shane and Roger stepped off (just a change in textures, a vague shading from dark green to muddy green) and were inside...what?

DEEP SPACE, the eel said somewhere.

Mary-Shane and Roger were in the command room again where she'd been with Wiz. Roger looked around and shook his head with awe. The walls were straight and there were no Wallaces or Pollys in them. Just a lot of white walls and boxes and square and round shapes like in a futuristic kitchen. No, not a kitchen— the controls of a starship. The ceiling was glass. Or whatever passed for glass millions of years ago someplace far away in the galaxy. Bright crystal stars studded a black background. No twinkling here. No atmosphere outside. No ocean either.

Mary-Shane realized: This was the universe, seen from the avatar Pilot's perspective. The avatar thought there was still a ship; hence this entire almost supernatural effort that had created chaos in San Tomas.

"This is the central command core of the ship, you are right," someone said, a face in the reflections within reflections in glass walls. It shifted constantly. She recognized a five-antlered jackal face like that in her dreams. It was something thin, or maybe half in another dimension. As it moved, it became invisible each time it turned its head. Then the face would turn again, and it looked like that demon again. Was she finally face to face with the creature that had reached out into her mind and stayed there, guided by her dying father's last thoughts so many years ago?

"Are you the Pilot?"

No.

She sniffled, realizing that Daddy had thought of her as the plane hydroplaned across the surface, slowed down, and sank intact, drowning the passengers and crew. Daddy had loved her. The hole in her heart filled up with his love, and so much pain went away.

"Who are you?" Mary-Shane asked the enigmatic figure that would not or could not fully reveal itself.

I am nobody. I am a shadow. I am a holographic image living inside the ship's brain.

"But the ship's brain is in pieces."

I am a piece of logic embedded in the core brain, and my time to be invoked has finally come.

"You are a thing like the eel or the sunlet?"

No.

"You are the jackal devil?"

No. You mean the analog Pilot. Now gone.

The *Cold Thing*—gone? "How do you mean?"

The Pilot consulted me before making a decision. The logic is irreversible, made eons ago by our masters. The Pilot no longer Is, and I am in charge now.

"Then what are you?"

I am the logic of my makers. I am who they were. I am the final Am.

The ground trembled. "Don't destroy our world," Mary-Shane asked, "please." Somehow, she didn't think it would. It would have a darker purpose.

There is not a lot of time, it said. *I am your glimpse of the race who created this ship. We sent ships like this in all directions of the universe. Our goal was to colonize any world we could, destroying the life forms there, and putting in their place our own. Your world was such a world when we approached. Now, we cannot get away and I do not know why.*

Mary-Shane said: "Your ship blew up. Everything was destroyed, every living thing on board including your creator and your cargo."

That is a valid logical domain, the holo said.

"A few pieces of your computer scattered all over Africa. Some of them finally were brought together and have enough electromagnetic power to simulate a ship. But there is no ship."

All observed facts support your lemma, the holo said. *It is clear we cannot accomplish our mission here. I am the final piece of logic, and now I must invoke myself.*

"Why the people in comas? Why the killings in the zoo?" Roger asked.

The ship was trying to check its cargo. It reached the nearest sentient biomes.

"Why the string of heart attacks?" Mary-Shane asked (remembering how the *Dark Feeling* had made her own poor heart beat itself virtually senseless during the attacks).

We needed samples. We were constantly sampling the creatures on the ship.

"But we're not on the ship," Mary-Shane said. She was ignored.

"Why all the people dropping into comas?" Roger repeated.

The eel-metaphor has been sampling. Trying to establish which of the cargo were still alive and reachable.

"You restored my son's legs and cured him of cancer. Can you leave us a cure for cancer?" Mary-Shane demanded. If they had cured Kippy, then surely...?

Hurry, the holo said, ignoring her; she wasn't even sure it had understood her request. *You and the other living ones will be released to your sleeping bodies. It is time to terminate the ship.*

"Please don't destroy our world," Mary-Shane asked. Roger stood by, horrified.

We do not destroy without a purpose, said the Final Program. *We will leave you, in case another of our ships finds your world.*

"And the Cold Brights?" Mary-Shane asked with relief and curiosity and concern.

The holo shrugged, if a being vaguely reminiscent of an ant's front end could shrug. *...Their souls will go to another Authority...*

The ground shook, and Roger and Mary-Shane held onto each other.

The vision of the interior of the space ship was gone forever. Father Lawrence receded. The kids ran across the ocean bottom, without stirring up slime, and clung to Roger and Mary-Shane. They five looked up and watched Cold Brights wink out one by one: Johnathan Smith. Father Lawrence (waving or blessing or both). Harleigh Hale, Charley Best, Frank MacLemore, Attila.

Moonboy, Mabel, Christopher Marlowe. Perry, Matilda. Wiz...

"Oh, look," Rudy blared.

In a glowing cave-like area, like the infirmary at the zoo, were animal Cold Brights: Adolph the Gorilla, sitting in a corner holding his head depressed, so sad; Lilly the Jaguar, curled into a ball and Mary-Shane imagined Lilly's nose looked dry; Andy the Bear; Buster the Rhino, a gray shadow against the wall; where the spiders and other things were, Mary-Shane could only wonder. One by one, they winked out.

The Dull Warms gathered on the ocean bottom as the ship's lights winked out one by one. An old man with brown teeth the color of peanuts was upset, asking everyone where his little granddaughter was.

"Look," Kippy shouted. Chains descended toward the crusted sphinx. Dowels of light from the submersible were guiding steel clamps into place. Someone, the Coast Guard, Mary-Shane supposed, U-Pho, was about to raise that old sphinx...

But as she thought this, it went poof.

It quietly imploded.

It winked out of existence, disappearing from U-Pho's grappling hooks, falling down in a shower of stardust that briefly twinkled and then darkened out of existence.

Mary-Shane awoke with a start. Her limbs felt numb and stiff. "Where am I?"

Jules Loomis hovered over her. "You're back. My God. I thought we'd lost all of you. Roger is babbling in the other room. You're in the hospital safe and sound, all of you."

She reached up. "Kippy?"

Jules's expression was unreadable, and she began to panic. Had it all been a dream? Jules shook his head, touched with a great wonder. He said: "I just saw him and Rudy and Elisa. They were laughing and trying to see who could walk the fastest without running. And I think Kippy was winning, only they all fell down in a pile and were laughing so loud the guard came and yelled at them. Kippy's legs seems completely fixed, Mary-Shane."

Mary-Shane lay back. "Thank God."

Vern LeGrier interrupted in a booming voice: "I am SO glad you guys are all back in one piece. The White Stuff is disappearing, blowing away all over town. People all over town are waking up unharmed from their comas. This whole episode appears to be over."

Mary-Shane sat up with an effort. "Good. I guess I'll go see Chatfield next door and ask if he wants to tango."

Jules looked baffled.

"An in joke," she said.

Epilog

— i —

Five years later in a New York City skyscraper, Jules knocked on a door.

"Come in, come in," said the publisher, who had arranged the meeting.

"Thanks," Jules said and entered. He put his briefcase on the floor. Then he peeled off his raincoat and placed it, along with the umbrella, on a chair. He sat in the other chair.

The publisher, a tiny man named Origaki, wore a black mod suit with baggy pants, tight jacket, white shirt, and black bolo. His thick glasses glittered. "Coffee?"

Jules loosened his collar. "No thanks. My wife and I stopped at Times Square and had coffee." He had put on weight. His hair had turned white. And he had given up the pipe at Patricia's urging.

Origaki said: "I believe I'll have a cup. I hope you aren't unhappy with the rain here in Manhattan." As he poured fragrant coffee, he turned his face toward the skyline. Sky scrapers loomed in roiling mist. "So," Origaki said. He pointed to a brown package on the corner of his vast desk. "We meet the author of San Tomas Visited."

"That's me," Jules said, leaning forward and tapping his fingertips together. He tried not to betray his anxiety.

Origaki sat back, totally in charge, and his glasses glinted. "Tell me, what makes you write such an illuminating account of those events five years ago? Is it the money?"

Jules shook his head. "Not at all. When I announced last year that I would be retiring this past summer, the family got together and decided to liquidate our interest in the San Tomas Herald. We are all very comfortable, I assure you."

"Good," Origaki said. "Got tired of the business?"

"Sure," Jules said. "After thirty years, I had gone as far as I would ever go. Executive Editor of a decent size morning paper. And the truth is, after those events five years ago, nothing anywhere near as interesting ever happened again."

Origaki laughed. "I can appreciate that. You have tried, what, every other publisher in New York?"

"Word gets around.".

Origaki nodded, a shade more somber. "I don't mind being last, Mr. Loomis. I make no secret that we go for glitz and flash. Our sales are monumental. The secret of our success is that we are timely, Mr. Loomis. Therefore I will unfortunately also have to decline your book."

Jules sat back, feeling defeated and yet for some strange reason relieved.

Origaki said: "If you had come to me five years ago..."

"...I was very busy then," Jules said. "I only wrote the book this year. That is, Mary-Shane and I had started it, but events took over and somehow we never did finish it together."

Origaki smiled sadly. "There were a spate of books, some of them good, others quite ridiculous. After a year or two, the excitement died down. After all, there was no proof of anything. Divers found no girders in the sea. No trace of a ship.

"The broken remains of the old sphinx were there, true, but its guts were made of very ordinary crumbly stone with veins of carbon and iron. You can dig it out of the ground in West Virginia by the truckload.

"Then there is the scientific monograph published by Drs. Stanislaus, Black, and White, stating that in their opinion the mental effects witnessed in San Tomas were a memorable but hardly extraterrestrial manifestation of mass hysteria.

"You yourself say, in your own book, that Chief of Police Victor Lara has steadfastly refused to offer an opinion other than four-letter expletives telling the reporter to leave his office or said reporter will exit via a window.

"Then there is the Vatican. They refuse comment. Bishop Mulcahy has been installed as Archbishop of San Francisco; he claims it was all a lot of malarkey. He says there was no genuine Satanism involved in the phenomenon, only the misguided deeds of twisted souls; and he says the Church has seen effects like this before: mass hysteria again.

"The various government agencies involved are of course not allowed to comment, though we know the Air Force closed its secret dossier four years ago."

Jules interjected: "What about the evidence of nuclear radiation?" Since Mary-Shane and the others had only been spirit walking, so to speak, they could not have been affected by the leaking drums in the airplane. There had been no drums of such waste listed in the plane in which Wayne Lull had died, and yet U-Pho had found dozens of such drums in the plane.

Origaki shrugged without a break in his smile. "Who knows? They fell off a Navy barge, perhaps, rolled into the plane, what does it matter?" He sat down with his coffee. "Finally, there are the reporter and the assistant zoo curator, both of whom were extensively quoted in various publications and have had nothing new to say. They insist they were in a ship, et cetera. We have heard all this before and I'm afraid it's nothing new. There isn't even a trace of this remarkable white shaving cream or whatever to be found anywhere in San Tomas; people have tried."

Jules stopped himself from leaving just then. "You can take a potting spade," he said, "go anywhere in San Tomas, and in five minutes have yourself handfuls of White Stuff in the shape of wire. It's all over in the soil!"

"Yes, of course," Origaki said. "Dr. LeGrier, who incidentally favors the view that there were really aliens and a ship, has stated that much of the wire could be traced back to the World War II government contracting firm of Herrera Y Hijos, which made millions of feet of wire during the war. So that proves nothing."

"I know all that," Jules said. "That is why I concentrated on the human angle. On Mary-Shane's mother, who never fully regained her sanity, and died shortly after from a brain aneurysm. Did you read that? And Evvie Stork. Vic and Martina Lara, who took in Perry and Matilda Stein's kids, also adopted Evvie but she kept running away. Did you read that, huh? How Evvie ran away got into drugs and after numerous rehabs finally hung herself in a police station with a sock she pulled off a guy in the drunk tank? That Evvie and Doris Lull lie buried next to Miss Polly in the Burtongale mortuary? Did you read that? Do your readers care?"

Origaki squinted regretfully. "It's old hat, Mr. Loomis. As you know, Mr. Martin Willow covered all the family stuff in his rather"(Mr. Origaki's tongue visibly slithered across his lower lip at the thought)"searing intimate family memoir."

Jules slapped himself on the knees and rose. Mart Willow, now managing editor of National Business Weekly in Chicago, always managed to strike home one more kick. "You seem to have covered everything."

Origaki smiled and lit a cigarette. A ball of smoke rolled away. "I'm sorry, but I hope you understand."

Jules took his package. "I understand. I was a reporter and an editor for many years. I probably wouldn't print this either."

Origaki rang a buzzer and strode to the door. "I want to thank you for bringing this to my attention." He offered a hand.

Jules shook it. "Well, thank you too. For your time. At least you gave it some thought. You are well informed."

Patricia was waiting for him in the marbled, slushy lobby that smelled of coats and shoes. Voices echoed all around as he homed in on her concerned, loving face. Her eyes read his disappointment and were ready to offer solace. Her mouth had a bittersweet smile, ready to pour forth words that would warm him like a hot drink. She slid her arm through his. She pressed her still firm, still curvy body against him. "Oh honey, did he say no?"

Jules nodded. "I'm going to do us all a favor," he said. In passing, he dumped the manuscript into a trashcan.

"Darling!" she protested.

They walked out into the rain, and he opened his umbrella for her. "It's over," he said.

— ii —

In Vermont, the rental car knifed through slushy snow. Patricia's cheeks glowed as stark, leafless trees flowed by. She had the letter of invitation on her lap. The return address, written in Mary-Shane's neat, if crabbed penmanship, read "Roger and Mary Chatfield, 94 Hollow Log Lane, Kaukasin, Vt." Mary-Shane had stuffed in a pencil-drawn map on children's loose-leaf.

Jules puckered his lips and made a kissing sound. Patricia slid her arm through his. Winter had struck Vermont that very afternoon. Burlington had been packed with skiers as they drove through. The sky looked puffy and gray; the temperature bobbed up slightly, and the air smelled of more coming snow. Radio station WKAU stated that more of The White Stuff was about to come down.

"The White Stuff," Jules chuckled. "Remember that?"

She shivered. "I try not to."

Jules laughed. "Imagine. I was upset nobody would publish my book. Just think how close earth came to being colonized by aliens sixty-five million years ago."

"Or blown up just five years ago," she interjected.

He was still thinking of the spaceship, millions of years ago. "There would have been no you, no me, if the three-eyes, the five-foots had won the race of evolution."

She patted his leg. "Well they lost, so there."

"By a hair," he said. "By a hair. Imagine. They made it all the way across who knows how many light years of space, all the way into our atmosphere, and then something went wrong. Maybe they were coming in a few hundred klicks too fast. Or at the wrong angle. Or they met up with a chunk of space rock...BOOM, finished! And the earth turned out to be the planet it is today, even with Mart Willow and his kind on it."

She sat up straight and put her arm over his shoulder. "Forget that creep. Look, there's Elisa." It was four p.m. and already the last wan sunlight was being leached away. The sky leaned swollenly against a big stone house on a hill. Smoke dribbled from the chimney. Lights were on inside, golden and homey. Sleds, skis, and a toboggan leaned against the house. A child stood alone in the middle of the lawn, holding a snowball.

"That can't be Elisa," Jules said. "She's too young."

Patricia squealed. "That's her. That's Julia."

"No," Jules said meaning yes as he pulled the car up beside a pile of freezing slush. Just then, the house door burst open. Two dogs exploded onto the lawn. People stepped out of the house, and Jules counted them off one by one. He and Patricia hadn't seen the Chatfields in four years, so this was a shock. Kippy, 15, ran out on long slim legs. Rudy, 14 and chunky, almost chubby, puffed out the door after Kippy. The two boys tossed a football between them. Then a tall, attractive woman stepped out, with long dark hair, white knit sweater, and dark corduroys.

"Mary-Shane?" Patricia asked.

"Put your glasses on," Jules said. "That's Elisa. Holy cow, she's eighteen and going to the University of Vermont."

Elisa stepped protectively behind her little sister, who would be just five now, Jules thought. Looked a lot like Susan and Roger, Jules thought, beautiful dark skin and big dark eyes. Elisa made the girl drop her snowball, and in the brief tussle that followed, the girl's hood fell back exposing thick curls. But she was also Mary-Shane's daughter. No wonder the aliens had said she was 'blest;' they would not harm captive animals that were with young, for it was the ship's mission to encourage the breeding of life as the ship streaked among the stars. And Mary-Shane had been very much with young when she spirit walked to the ship; with Julia, to be specific.

Elisa took little Julia by the hand. Jules and Patricia got out. "Brr," Patricia said, holding her scarf around her neck. Elisa spoke in a mature voice: "This is our little sister Julia, named after you, Uncle Jules. Say hello, Julia. Say hello."

Jules squatted and Julia (who had probably been primed for this all day) ran over. She hugged him. She kissed him on each cheek. "Hello, Uncle Jules. Hello, Aunt Patricia. So nice to see you. Won't you come up to the house?" She was too cute, Jules thought, adoring her.

Elisa kissed Jules and Patricia. They followed Julia up to the house. "Daddy said he'll be a little late. He has some papers to grade, and a few students to meet."

"How is your dad?" Jules asked.

"Fine," Elisa said. "He's a full professor now." As they approached the house, the door swung open. There stood Mary-Shane, looking more beautiful than Jules had ever seen her look before. She looked a little more mature, but her face was still of that model-quality beauty. Her lips still had that saucy fun squiggle. Her figure, though on the short side, was ripe and shapely as ever without being either too much or too little. On Mary-Shane's arm was the latest addition: Roger Jr., held lovingly.

Kippy and Rudy crowded in behind Jules and Patricia as the knot of family forced its way through the door. "Smells wonderful," Jules said, sniffing. The interior was all heavy wood and dark brick and smelled of bread, coffee, and pasta. He looked at the computer, the stacked books, the kid pictures. He noted the one-winged parrot, grumpy in his disturbed sleep. He saw the scattered pencils and erasers, the unmistakable withered plant on a corner desk, and said: "Looks like you're finally The Author."

Mary-Shane made a wry face. "Well, it's not the crime beat, but I've had enough of that to last me a lifetime. I'm education and arts stringer for the Kaukasin Voice (isn't that a SCREAM?) and I've been steadily publishing articles in child care magazines."

Patricia took Roger Jr. on her arm and cooed: "This one here is another Rudy." They all laughed happily, crowding inside.

"Let's keep in the warmth," Mary-Shane said. Julia (ruffle!) stepped to the door. Oh how she resembled her parents, thought Jules, watching his goddaughter, with (drum roll!) Mary-Shane's curly hair and Roger's ruddy skin and Susan's steady eyes (flourish!). Nice touch, Jules thought, remembering the story of the egg in the space ship, and Julia's birth eight months later—(ta-daaaa!)—the baby of Roger and Susan and Mary-Shane:

...A little touch of Susan's magic (a last wish, a gesture of love), the Pilot's final goodbye... (applause!)

— iii —

As Julia stood on tiptoes to grasp the door handle, she took one last look outside before her bedtime. With big serious dark eyes she peered at the landscape for a long minute.

Snow fell among fragrant pine trees. The sky was dark blue like stained glass, and full of stars. The snow was like a beach, and the stars were like an ocean. Out there it was very cold.

Inside it was warm and cozy.

Julia closed the door.

John Argo has lived and traveled extensively in North America and Europe, and is fluent in several languages. He holds degrees in English and Computer Information Systems. A firm believer that bliss is found in small things, his many delights include gardening, Classics, climbing through ancient ruins, and finding his e-books in airport kiosks. When not drunk with Celtic melancholy or singing hard rock songs in the shower or walking among the bikinis of Solana Beach, he writes science fiction and suspense novels. Like most of us, he loves a good movie, the sound of rain and the smell of woodsmoke in the still of an April night, and the company of his intriguing wife. Like most of us, he laments that life is too short, the wind is very sweet, and a train passes far away. His website is http://www.johnargo.com/.

Genre titles by John Argo include *Neon Blue* (suspense), *Pioneers* (SF), and *Lantern Road: 8 by Argo* (SF anthology).

More John Argo writings may be found at http://www.thehauntedvillage.com/ and http://www.neonbluefiction.com/.

Printed in the United States
6167